Also by Jenna Hartley

<u>Love in LA Series</u>
Inevitable
Unexpected
Irresistible
Undeniable
Unpredictable
Irreplaceable

<u>Alondra Valley Series</u>
Feels Like Love
Love Like No Other
A Love Like That

<u>Tempt Series</u>
Temptation
Reputation

For the most current list of Jenna's titles, please visit her website www.authorjennahartley.com.

Or scan the QR code on the following page to be taken to her author page on Amazon.com

SCAN ME

Irreplaceable

jenna hartley

ISBN: 9798386499198

Editing: Lisa A. Hollett
Cover: © 2022 Indie Sage Designs

For Kristen.

You're the Alexis to my Lauren. The Harper to my Juliana. The... Well, you get it.

You've shown me the meaning of true friendship, and it is your love and support that has inspired the incredible female friendships in my stories.

Thank you for holding my hand. For always being there and listening, whether it's about my stories or life.

NOTE TO READERS

Dear Reader,

Harper's story contains situations some of you may find distressing. If you've struggled with infertility or had a traumatic birthing experience, sections of this book may be difficult to read. I did my best to handle these topics with care, in the hopes that others would feel more comfortable sharing their own experiences.

So much of infertility, pregnancy, and motherhood is shrouded in secrecy or stigma, and I don't think that's good for any of us. My partner and I were fortunate that we didn't struggle with infertility, but my labor and delivery (and recovery) were rather harrowing.

I think a big part of the reason I struggled so much with writing Harper's story was because I was fighting it. I didn't want my own experience to color yours as a reader. It's been five years since I gave birth to my daughter, and I knew I had a lot of unresolved trauma related to her birth, but I think I underestimated how much it was impacting me.

Writing this book finally helped me move past some of that, and my wish is that it will help you too. Whether it helps you heal or inspires you with hope, or even just gives you an escape, I hope you can feel the love and attention that I brought to this story. That I strive to bring to all of my stories.

With much love and hugs,
    Jenna

Content Warnings

This story contains explicit sexual content, profanity, and topics that may be sensitive to some readers.

For more detailed information, visit the QR code below.

Playlist

"When I'm With You" by Kaskade, Colette
"La Vibrazioni di una donna," by Nek
"Love Like That" by Kaskade, Dani Poppitt
"Moon" by Kayne West
"Home" by Vicetone
"Hate You + Love You" (Feat. AJ Mitchell) by Cheat Codes
"Craving" by ARTY, Audien, Ellee Duke
"Worlds Collide--Edison Cole Remix" by NERVO,
Edison Cole
"River" by Bishop Briggs
"Lean on Me" by Cheat Codes, Tinashe
"I maschi" by Gianna Nannini
"Feels Like Love" (Feat. MIYA MIYA) by Syn Cole,
MIYA MIYA
"Safe With Me" by Gryffin, Audrey Mika
"Skin" by Sabrina Carpenter
"Over It" by Audien
"Un'Estate Italiana (Notti Magiche)" by Gianna Nannini,
Edoardo Bennato
"Talking to the Moon" by Bruno Mars
"I Wanna Know" by RL Grime, Daya
"Nightlight" by ILLENIUM, Annika Wells
"A Te" by Jovanotti
"Inside Out" (Feat. Griff) by Zedd, Griff
"Ninna nanna ninna oh" by Coccole Sonore

"Ti sposerò perchè" by Eros Ramazzotti
"Anywhere With You" by Afrojack, Lucas & Steve, DubVision

You can find this playlist and more at
https://www.authorjennahartley.com/playlists

CHAPTER ONE

Harper

"Why don't you get dressed, and then we'll talk?"

I nodded, staring at the ceiling tiles as I heard the snap of latex gloves, the trash open and close, then the door to the examining room. I blinked a few times, telling myself to move but struggling all the same. The paper rustled beneath me when I shifted, the sound echoing in the empty room.

Empty.

Vacant.

Just like my womb.

As with the two times before, the procedure hadn't worked. I wasn't actually pregnant, despite a positive test a few weeks earlier.

I'd been poked and prodded enough to have bruises dotting my arms. But other than my battered heart and a huge deficit in my savings account, I had nothing to show for all my efforts. *What a waste of time and money.*

With a heavy sigh, I pulled on my clothes and checked my hair in the mirror. Getting pregnant was supposed to be fun, joyful. Yet all I did was stress and despair. Were my eggs mature? Was the sperm clean? Of good quality? Was the syringe close enough to my cervix?

I tugged at the corners of my eyes, not wanting to cry—again. When I'd started this journey, I'd been so optimistic. So naïve. And while I still wanted to be a mom, I wondered if this was the universe's way of telling me it simply wasn't in the cards.

Still, I couldn't help but imagine what it would be like to be pregnant. My hands hovered over my stomach, and I tried to envision it full with a child. Tried to picture what my child would look like.

Would they have straight brown hair like me? Would they have my green eyes and Cupid's-bow lips? Or would they resemble their father—a man I'd never even met? A number in a database. Someone I'd selected during a drunken night with my girlfriends, chosen for his desirable traits—handsome, intelligent, a volunteer.

There was a knock at the door, and I shook my head to clear it. It didn't really matter now. None of it mattered.

"Come in," I called.

"Hey." The nurse, Sylvia, peeked her head inside, the silver strands of her hair glinting beneath the fluorescent lights. "You ready?"

"As ready as I'll ever be," I sighed, dreading what came next.

She gave me a warm smile, and I followed her down the hall to Dr. Fulton's office. I kept my eyes down, trying to ignore a woman I passed, her large belly everything I wanted. Avoiding the walls where smiling babies and happy families were on display.

I was thirty-seven, single, and childless. So, yeah, I was neither happy nor smiling because my life was so far off course from where I'd hoped to be by this age.

When I entered Dr. Fulton's office, she glanced up at me

from her computer and smiled. It was the type of smile that held pity, regret. The type that said to brace yourself.

"Harper. Come in."

Her brown hair was tucked in a tidy bun, her legs crossed neatly, white lab coat pristine. I took the seat across from her, feeling as if I were going to my execution.

"Try not to get too discouraged," she said once Sylvia had closed the door behind her. "The intrauterine insemination didn't work, but it's not all that uncommon." She gave me a kind smile, her white teeth flashing brilliantly against her dark skin. "There are other options. This is just the beginning."

And that was the problem. It already felt like this had been going on forever, and it was "just the beginning." I nodded woodenly. When I'd started this journey, I'd opted for IUI because it was less expensive, less invasive, than other options. Now, after three failed attempts, three rounds of blood work, ultrasounds, and being pumped full of a stranger's sperm by my doctor, I was…exhausted. Overwhelmed. Ready to throw in the towel.

I let out a deep sigh. Maybe it was time to accept that I just wasn't meant to be a mom.

"Our next option," Dr. Fulton continued without missing a beat, "is in vitro fertilization. It's expensive and more invasive, but the success rates are higher."

"How much higher?" I asked, not entirely sure whether I was referring to the cost or the chance of success.

I needed hard data. At my age, it felt as if I were in a race against time. I'd spent the last year preparing for this procedure—gathering the courage, picking the sperm donor, then making sure my hectic work schedule allowed me to have all the necessary appointments.

"Around forty percent, and I'd have to refer you to a specialist."

"Forty?" I scoffed, nearly choking on the word. "That's not great."

"No." She folded her hands on her desk. "And depending on your insurance, it could cost upward of $12,000 per cycle."

"Twelve..." I swallowed. "Thousand?"

Shit. I'd known it was expensive, but was I willing to shell out $12,000, or possibly upward to $40,000 for multiple rounds, even knowing I might never get pregnant?

I shook my head. "That's a lot of money for something with such a low success rate."

"It is. And it can be very emotionally draining, as you've seen with the IUI. If you're considering it, I'd recommend talking with someone who specializes in counseling IVF patients."

I pinched the bridge of my nose and closed my eyes briefly. Why was this so complicated?

"Look," Dr. Fulton said. "There's no need to decide anything today. Go home, take some time to think about it. If you decide that's the path you want to pursue, I'm here."

I thanked her and nodded, going through the motions as I checked out and left the building. I headed for my car, feeling numb as I turned the key in the ignition. In a daze as I drove home. By the time I pulled up to my place, I wasn't even sure how I'd gotten there. I couldn't recall a single part of the drive. I unlocked the door and stepped inside to switch on the light.

"Surprise!" Juliana, Alexis, and Lauren popped out from behind the kitchen wall.

I stumbled backward, my heart racing. *Holy...* My three best friends were all smiling, and I was completely caught off guard. "What's this?"

"Well..." Juliana bit her lip, her blue eyes sparkling with joy. "I know it's early still, but we're so excited for you!"

It was then I noticed the pink and blue banner with "Congratulations" written across it in a bold font. My chest tightened, stretching like a balloon about to pop, and then I burst into tears.

"Hey," Alexis cooed, wrapping her arm around me. "Hey, what's wrong?"

"I'm not having a baby," I said, though the words were garbled. "I'm not pregnant."

"Aww, honey," Lauren said as they all gathered around me, closing in protectively.

They ushered me over to the sofa, but none of them spoke. It was nice, just knowing they were there for me. I might not have a partner to face the world with, but these three women were my best friends, and we'd been through so much together.

They were the only people I'd told about the IUI. None of my family or coworkers knew, and after today's news, I was glad. I'd dreaded my family's questions about the father, but I knew my friends would never judge me. In fact, they'd been the ones to encourage me to finally go for it.

Alexis handed me a tissue, her caramel gaze reflecting compassion. "Do you want to talk about it?"

I shook my head, dabbing at the corners of my eyes. "No."

"It's okay," she said, rubbing circles on my back. "Whatever you need, we're here for you. Okay?"

I blew my nose, and the atmosphere of the room seemed so subdued compared to the frustration and rage swirling within me. "Thank you."

We sat in silence a moment longer—my friends giving me space to process—before I finally said, "It was a chemical pregnancy."

Alexis nodded knowingly. Of the four of us, she was the only one who had kids. "I'm sorry."

"What does that mean?" Juliana asked, brushing her blond strands away from her face. "A chemical pregnancy."

"It's a very early miscarriage. It's not uncommon," Alexis said. "Though that doesn't make it easier. I, um—" She let out a deep breath. "I had one a few months ago myself."

I grabbed her hand and squeezed, wondering why she hadn't said anything. But then I realized—it was because of me. She hadn't wanted to hurt my feelings by talking about a pregnancy when she knew how badly I wanted a baby myself.

"Are you and Preston trying for a third?" Lauren asked, running a hand through her waves.

Alexis lifted a shoulder. "We're not *not* trying."

Lauren laughed and shook her head. "Mm-hmm. I thought you said after Blair you were done having kids?"

I sniffled, and Alexis squeezed my hand. "I'm sorry, Harper. This isn't about me—or at least, it shouldn't be."

"No," I said. "I'm happy for you, truly. I'm just... Am I a terrible person if I admit that I'm the tiniest bit envious?"

Okay, perhaps tiny was an understatement.

"No," Alexis said, her tone filled with compassion. "You're human."

"Why does this have to be so hard?" I asked aloud, not expecting anyone to answer.

"I know this is going to sound cheesy, but maybe it happened for a reason." Juliana smiled gently. "Maybe you aren't meant to get pregnant at this time or in this way."

"You're right." I stood, anger mixing with my sadness. I couldn't stand it. "It does sound cheesy." My eyes burned as I fought back more tears. "Maybe I'm not meant to get pregnant at all!"

I stalked toward my bedroom, nearly slamming the door behind me. I couldn't stomach the fact that I'd been pregnant and then I wasn't. I'd seen the two lines on the pregnancy test, and then the doctor told me there was nothing there. How could there be nothing there? They'd shot enough sperm at my cervix that something should've stuck. Right?

Ugh. I collapsed on my bed, the tears hitting the comforter before I did. I couldn't do this. I screamed into my pillow, letting it all out. I couldn't put myself through month after month of expensive and painful treatments, only to have it end in more disappointment.

After a while, I heard the door open and then felt the mattress dip beside me. I caught a whiff of jasmine—Juliana. "I'm sorry, Harper. I didn't mean to be insensitive."

"I know." I sobbed, unable to hold back anymore. And I did. Because of all of us, Juliana probably understood the most. She'd been engaged and lost her fiancé. I'd just lost the wisp of a baby who'd never existed. But it was more than that —I was losing hope.

"I'm sorry I snapped." I pushed off the bed so I was sitting next to her. "I'm just…" I let out a deep sigh that spoke of my despair. "I'm so disappointed. And not sure where to go from here."

"Well—" she wrapped an arm around my shoulder "—you have options. And no matter what you decide, I'm here for you. We all are."

I nodded. "I know." I used the back of my sleeve to wipe my eyes. "I do. And I appreciate it."

"You know you're like a sister to me." She pulled me in for a hug. "You were there for me in Thailand. And you were the only one who didn't think I was crazy for clinging to the notion that Ryan might still be alive."

I blew my nose as Alexis peeked her head around the corner to my room. "Hey. Everything okay?"

Lauren stood behind her, and I felt their concerned gazes. It was nice to have their support, even if it was a bit suffocating at the moment.

"It's fine. I'm fine."

"Mm-hmm." Lauren crossed her arms over her chest. "You know better than to bullshit us, Harper."

I rolled my eyes and stood. "It's probably for the best. Morning sickness would be a bitch with the work schedule I have coming up."

I was flying to Scotland tomorrow, where filming would take place on a rom-com. I'd be there a few weeks before setting off for Bali to scout locations for another script from the studio—a futuristic, dystopian thriller. And a million other things besides.

While Alexis and Lauren talked, I went to grab my laptop from the living room. Juliana followed me, glancing over her shoulder before addressing me. "Are you sure this is a good idea?"

I lifted a shoulder. "I'm fine. Besides, those treatments aren't going to pay for themselves."

"Harper," Juliana chided.

I let out a deep sigh. "Yeah. Okay. I'm fine physically. Emotionally—I'm a bit of a mess."

"Which is completely understandable."

"I just don't get it." I tugged on my hair. "We did everything right."

She gave me a gentle smile and placed her hand on my shoulder. "I know. And sometimes things don't turn out like we expected."

"Yeah," I scoffed. "Sometimes they suck."

She blew out a breath. "Or...sometimes they turn out better than you could've imagined. Give it some time."

I shrugged out of her touch, busying myself with packing. "I'm not like you. Any of you," I said when Lauren and Alexis joined us.

Juliana furrowed her brow. "What are you talking about?"

"I've never really been in a serious relationship. Never

had someone propose to me. I've never been in love," I admitted. _____ of it, but—" I shook my head. I'd admitted more than I'd intended to, but my emotions were going haywire.

"But…?" Lauren nudged me.

"I don't know." I stared at the floor. "My job isn't wholly to blame. I have the worst taste in men."

Lauren laughed. "You certainly have a type."

"I can't help it," I sighed. "I'm like a bad-boy magnet."

If only I could make myself fall in love with Crew Dixon. He was the owner of the Hollywood Heatwaves and one of the sweetest guys I'd ever known. Humble. Down-to-earth. Just a good man. We'd spent a lot of time together the past six months, thanks to the fact that his dear friend, Harrison, was married to my best friend. And while we'd gone out a few times, there'd been little spark and no chemistry.

It just seemed like there was a disconnect. Like I was trying to force my heart to get on board with my head because he was a good guy, we had mutual friends, and he wanted to get married and have children.

"Girl." Lauren hummed. "You need to find a bad boy who's a good man."

"Right." I rolled my eyes. "I think it would be easier to find a unicorn."

"If anyone gets that, I do," Lauren said. "But have you ever stopped to think about why you gravitate toward the bad boys?"

"Because they're hot," I said, as if it were obvious.

She nodded. "I don't disagree. But I think if you dig deep, you'll realize there's more to it. As much as you say you want a family, you're afraid of commitment. You're afraid of something."

I scowled.

"Is it?" She crossed her arms over her chest, and we stared each other down.

I glanced away. "Whatever."

Before she'd started dating Hunter, Lauren had always been jaded, cynical, and opposed to relationships. Now she was the love guru? Psh. Right.

Alexis and Juliana nodded their agreement, their expressions grave. Deep down, I feared they were right. I *was* running. I'd been running my whole life.

"I'm exhausted." My shoulders sagged. "I've given up on love. I just want a baby, and I don't understand what went wrong. I'm so sick of not knowing."

Juliana nodded. "Sometimes not knowing is worse than knowing. The unknown sucks."

She pulled me in for a hug, somehow understanding what I needed without me admitting it. As we stood there, tears bleeding into the expensive silk of her shirt, questions raced through my mind. Was something wrong with me? Would I ever find love? Would I ever be a mom?

"You're going to be okay," Lauren said. When I didn't answer, she said, "I mean it, Harper. Whether you have to adopt or do IVF or whatever, you are going to be a mom someday. I know it."

"I wish I shared your confidence." I backed away, cringing as I saw the wet spot on Juliana's shirt.

"Here," Juliana said, holding her hand up to my arm. "As my mom always used to tell me—I'm giving you a shot of confidence." She pointed at the muscle and pretended to depress a syringe.

I laughed, preferring her medicine to any of the medical

interventions I'd received the past few months. "Thanks. I needed that."

She smiled. "Maybe this trip will be a good thing. A chance to take your mind off the IUI and IVF and whatever other acronyms you want to throw in there."

"Maybe," I said, though I didn't believe it.

"You never know what will happen." Lauren shot me a mischievous grin.

I appreciated their encouragement, but I wasn't sure anything could possibly change my situation that drastically and quickly. The IUI had failed. I hadn't applied for adoption —a process that was also time-consuming and emotional. And my prospects of finding a man, a partner, were slim.

Still, I wanted to believe things could change. I wanted to believe that miracles did happen. Even if at the moment all I really felt like doing was giving up.

CHAPTER TWO

Harper

The leather of my sandals hugged my feet as I meandered down the dusty dirt road. It had been almost a month since my chemical pregnancy, and I'd been busy with work. Immersed in my job, exploring a new country, it was easy to forget about my life back home. It was easy to ignore the pain, the disappointment.

After a day of meeting with local officials to discuss logistics for filming, I'd stopped by the hotel and grabbed my camera before heading into town. This area of Bali had enough amenities to satisfy the production team and A-list actors, but it was also perfect for the futuristic, dystopian thriller the production studio envisioned. And the locals had been eager to work with us, which made my job that much easier.

The longer I walked, the more my cares faded away. There was something to be said for the ability to go wherever you wanted, whenever you wanted. As much as I desired a child, I knew I'd miss this freedom. The spontaneity. I loved exploring new places, meeting new people, trying new foods. And while I didn't want to think that becoming a mom meant giving all that up, I understood there would be sacrifices.

I lifted my camera, framing a shot of the coconut seller before depressing the button. I was never without my camera, but lately, I'd been gravitating back to it more and more. And not just as a tool for work. There was something magical about filtering your view of the world and translating it from a three-dimensional reality to a two-dimensional image, capturing that moment in time. A moment that would never be repeated and could never be duplicated— much like a human life.

Two children skipped down the street, squealing with glee. I lowered my camera and watched them, my good mood dissipating. As great as my life was, I was lonely. I'd seen much of the world, and I wanted to set down roots.

Deep in the recesses of my heart, I clung to that dream. I'd always imagined that falling in love, being a mother, would be my biggest adventure. But life didn't always turn out like you expected. And at this rate, I worried it would never happen.

First, I'd given up on the idea of being in a committed relationship, opting instead for a sperm donor. And now… *now* I wasn't sure I had it in me to endure in vitro fertilization or struggle through an arduous adoption process. I just didn't think I could open myself up for even more disappointment.

The clouds shifted, the sun peeking through to highlight the market as I approached. I was officially off duty. And not just for the evening. For the next week, I planned to relax on the beach, explore the rice fields, and do whatever I wanted. Alexis had suggested I take a vacation, and I knew she was right. I needed a break. I needed to take a step back, slow down, and regroup.

I twisted the bracelet on my wrist and smiled down at the

reminder of Juliana. She'd given the leather-and-silver bracelet to me for my birthday years ago, and I loved both the simplicity of the design and the symbolism. It was similar to an *unalome* and reminded me that the path of life wasn't always straight, perfect, or even headed in the "right" direction. Perhaps something I needed to remember now more than ever.

I let out an exhale and scanned the market, debating where to head first. A man across the street caught my attention—his stern expression at odds with the lively atmosphere. His olive skin glistened in the sun, dark brows slanted low over dark eyes, arms covered in dark ink. I traced some of the designs with my eyes, momentarily distracted as I used the zoom feature on my camera to home in on him. Some of the script appeared to be in Italian; all of it was incredibly beautiful and intricate.

I continued to peer at him through my lens, admiring the corded muscles of his arms, the strength evident beneath his linen shirt. And then there was his face—hard, unrelenting, and incredibly handsome.

His brown eyes surveyed the surroundings, and his dark brown hair was tousled like he'd been running his fingers through it nonstop. He was breathtaking in his intensity, and there was something about him that made it difficult to look away. I snapped a few shots, changing the angle and settings a few times before a little boy approached.

I watched their interaction, surprised when the man's expression softened. He laughed when the boy pointed to his biceps and flexed his muscles, the man's face transforming into something almost too beautiful to behold. My camera would never do it justice, but I tried all the same, snapping a few more shots of the unlikely duo. Despite the man's stony exterior, he was a natural with the little boy. He inspected the boy's arm then followed him down the street.

I wandered through the market, stopping to look at some of the booths. Even though I wasn't sure I'd ever have a child at this point, I couldn't resist purchasing a children's book. It was tradition after all. For years, I'd been collecting children's books from all over the world. I always wrote the date and place where I acquired them on the inside page, adding them to my library as if they'd one day be needed.

I took my time, stopping to purchase some fun earrings for Juliana before I reached an open field. I was surprised to find the man from the market playing soccer with a bunch of local kids. I smiled and watched the way they interacted.

I lifted my camera, taking a few shots. Zooming in as he ran across the field with grace and speed. He was a natural, and the kids clearly adored him.

When he scored a goal, they all jumped on top of him. He was smiling and so were they. So was I, for that matter. Their clothes were getting muddy, stained with grass, but they didn't care. They were having so much fun.

I snapped a few more, the stunning scenery and the gorgeous man making me want to linger. There was something about the man that kept pulling me back to him. At least until my stomach grumbled, reminding me that I hadn't eaten since breakfast. I put my camera back in my bag and headed to one of the nearby restaurants. While I ate and pored over a guidebook, a new text came in from Juliana. My day was winding down, but back in LA, hers was just beginning. Despite the time difference—first in Scotland and now in Bali—she'd been texting me almost daily for the past few weeks, and I knew she was worried about me. She didn't ask how I was doing, didn't mention the pregnancy, but I knew she'd always listen if I needed to talk.

Juliana: Enjoy your vacation!

I sent her an image from my phone, one I'd taken at the hotel earlier. It had a beautiful view.

Juliana: Makes me long for Laucala.

I smiled, knowing how much she'd enjoyed her honeymoon there. I'd had fun helping Harrison plan it. The pictures Juliana had shown me were jaw-dropping, but I knew it was the alone time with Harrison she treasured even more. And despite my sadness over my own situation, I was so, so happy for Juliana.

After finishing my meal, I decided to explore a little more. It was darker now, but there were still a few people milling about along the main thoroughfare. The weather was so pleasant, I decided to walk toward my hotel instead of taking a tuk-tuk. As I was crossing the street to check out a food vendor, I heard the crunch of the gravel beneath tires before I saw a flash of headlights. The car had taken the corner quickly, barely giving me time to react.

I shrieked and leaped out of the way of the car, my heart racing. I grunted, landing on the ground with a thud.

A cloud of dust swallowed me, and I sat there stunned. They'd almost run over me. If I hadn't jumped out of the way, they would've.

I started coughing, trying to fan away the dirt. I blinked a few times, grit making my eyes feel as if they'd been rubbed with sandpaper. *What the hell?*

The car was stopped ahead, the brake lights glowing in the night. I tried to stand but winced when a sharp pain shot through my ankle. *Shit.*

The back door to the car opened, and a man climbed out. I stared at his shoes, scanning up his muscular legs, up that chiseled torso and tattooed arms until I met his face. And the sight of the man from the market had me swallowing hard.

Up close, he was so…intimidating. So imposing. So handsome. The way he stalked toward me made my stomach tighten and a frisson of excitement race down my spine.

"Stai bene?"

I blinked a few times. Had I hit my head too? I was pretty sure I was in Bali, but it sounded like he was speaking Italian. He certainly looked Italian with his olive skin and intense brown eyes. And he'd asked if I was okay in a voice that flowed over me like velvet.

"Are you okay?" he asked, repeating himself in English.

"Sto bene," I answered, my brain still struggling to catch up. I'd spent years studying Italian, and using it felt like muscle memory. I tried to stand again but couldn't. Apparently, I wasn't as fine as I claimed to be.

"Pensi che sia rotto?" The Italian man crouched to the ground, his brows creased in concern. A moment later, the driver joined us, twisting his hands together.

"Saya minta maaf. So sorry," the driver said, switching between Balinese and English. I didn't speak much Balinese —just enough to get around.

"I'll handle it, Kadek," the Italian barked in a burst of anger.

Kadek ducked his head and took a few steps back, almost cowering. The Italian closed his eyes briefly and took a deep breath, his shoulders relaxing. When the Italian turned to me, his brown eyes were filled with concern.

"Rotto?" the Italian asked again, his hands hovering above my leg. Those hands. Those…*fingers*. My god. I shook my head. The man *was* a god.

I didn't think it was *rotto,* or broken, but it was definitely sprained. Putting weight on it wasn't a good idea. So much for my vacation, I sighed. How was I even going to get back to my hotel?

"Vieni con me."

What? I jerked my head back. "Um, no." I frowned. "I don't know you." There was no way I was going with this man. In his car. To god knows where. I didn't care how hot he was.

"Ah...English," he said, the words lilting as he spoke English with his Italian accent. "American, no?"

I nodded, noticing that people had started to gather, gawking at us. I could hear their hushed whispers, and I pushed off the ground, determined to stand. I wobbled but then nearly fell, the Italian catching me before I hit the ground.

He lifted me into his arms as if I weighed nothing, and without realizing it, my head instinctively went to the crook of his neck. I inhaled out of surprise and, damn, he smelled good. His arms tightened around me almost protectively, and I felt surprisingly safe as he carried me over to the car. He gently placed me in the back seat so my feet were resting on the road.

What the... He'd just picked me up. And I'd let him!

"Calm down," he said, perhaps sensing my frantic thoughts. "I'm not going to hurt you."

I wasn't so sure about that. The Italian seemed like a man who had the power to wreck me. Definitely a bad boy with those tattoos and his dark, hungry gaze.

He knelt to the ground, appraising my ankle with surprising tenderness.

"Are you a doctor?" I asked, the concern evident in his features.

He shook his head, his hand light on my skin. "No, but I think we should take you to one. Your ankle is already starting to swell."

My ankle was sprained at best, and I didn't have to call my dad—a small-town general practitioner—to know what to do. Elevate it, ice it, and reduce the inflammation.

"I'm fine. Really. I'll just head back to my hotel. My father is a doctor, and…"

"Here?" he asked.

"No." I shook my head. "No. Um, back in the States." I smoothed my hand over the buttery leather, surprised by such luxury. Air conditioning. Tinted windows. My eyes widened as I took it all in.

"Relax," he said. "Please. I'll take good care of you." He flashed me a wicked smile, and I had no doubt that he knew how to take very good care of a woman's body. "Promise."

When I hesitated, he said, "You can trust me."

I didn't even know this man's name.

Even so, I found myself intrigued by the Italian. I'd seen his kindness in the market earlier. The way he'd interacted with the locals. And it was clear he felt compelled to make this right. To ensure that I was okay. Still…what did I even know about him?

He liked playing soccer. He was Italian. Friendly with the locals and great with kids. He had money, from the looks of it. He was hot.

It wasn't enough. "I need to go back to my hotel. My boss is waiting for me," I lied. I was officially on vacation. My boss didn't care where I was. My friends knew I was in Bali, but that was it.

"Why don't you call him, then?" the Italian asked, sliding into the back seat. "Tell him I am taking care of you."

"Yeah, but who *are* you?" I asked, not bothering to correct him that my boss was a woman.

He glanced away then back at me, his brown eyes beguiling. The way he spoke in his rich, heavily accented voice captivating. "Enzo. And you, *uccellina?*"

I frowned. *What did it mean?* I racked my brain for another similar word in Italian but came up short. "Harper."

"Harper." He rolled the word around his mouth, and the

way he said it was so sensual I thought I might combust. Especially with the heated way he was looking at me.

Get it together, Harper!

"Thank you for the offer—" I moved to leave "—but I'm sure it's just a sprain."

"Even so," he said, placing his hand on my arm. "I would feel better if you would allow me to have a doctor examine it. It's the least I can do."

I sensed that this man—Enzo—was used to getting his way. And at the moment, his insistence was to my benefit. So, I fumbled in my bag for my phone.

I huffed. "Okay. I'll send my boss a text." I leaned away so I could share my location with Juliana.

Juliana: Hey. You okay?

Going home with a man.

I didn't want to worry her. It wasn't like there was much she could do at the moment. But I wanted some kind of insurance policy. For now, this was as good as it was going to get.

Juliana: Be safe. Have some fun!

"All good?" Enzo asked as he slid closer to me and closed the door. He asked Kadek to continue on.

I nodded, returning my phone to my bag.

He leaned in, enveloping me with his scent. He smelled like bergamot, like all my fantasies rolled into one, and if I closed my eyes, I'd swear I was lazing in a Sicilian orchard at noon. My chest rose and fell, but I didn't hear warning bells blaring in my head. If anything, my body was giving me the green light.

Though, really…could I trust my body when it came to

men? This one seemed no different from any of the others. A bad boy who was controlling. *Hot.*

Not hot. I shook my head. I needed to break this cycle if I wanted to find love, a family.

Too late for that.

"Where are you taking me?" I glanced around, trying to pinpoint any landmarks. We were headed in the opposite direction of town. The opposite direction of the hospital.

"Back to my house. I have a doctor on call."

Wait. What?

"I, uh—" It was getting darker as we headed toward the coast. My ankle throbbed, my chest tightening the farther we drove. *Why* did he have a doctor on call?

He finished typing something on his phone and placed his hand over mine. "You're safe, *uccellina*."

"What does *uccell*—" I paused, trying to remember the pronunciation.

"*Uccellina,*" he repeated the word he'd used earlier.

"Yeah. That." I furrowed my brows, trying to commit it to memory. But then a bump jostled me in the back seat, and the movement made my ankle hurt even worse. *Shit.* I sucked in a breath and attempted to ignore the pain. "What does it mean?"

"I thought you were fluent in Italian," he taunted, a smile playing at his gorgeous lips.

I shook my head, pleased by the compliment, even if it was teasing in nature. "I studied Italian all through college, even spent a semester abroad. But I'm not fluent, and I'm out of practice."

"I see." He grinned. "Well, I'd be happy to help you practice my native tongue. All you have to do is come with me."

"I–I—" I stuttered, wondering if he'd intended for it to sound as seductive as it had. Because it certainly conjured up a range of images, me riding him while he commanded me to do just that. It had been way too long since I'd had sex. "I kind of already am since you kidnapped me," I ground out, mad at myself for being so easily seduced by his looks.

"Kidnapped?" He scoffed, though he seemed amused as he settled back into the seat. As if the idea of *him* kidnapping *me* was insane. "All you Americans…you think every Italian you meet is a member of the mafia."

I rolled my eyes. "I do not."

Though when Kadek pulled off the road and onto a gated drive, I was beginning to wonder. Not so much about the kidnapping, but the mafia ties. The closer we got to the house, the more questions I had. It was huge. And gorgeous —much like the man sitting beside me. The front of the home was surrounded by palm trees, and it was three stories tall.

I was still looking at the exterior with its dramatic uplighting when Enzo asked, "Do you think you can walk?"

I was in a foreign land. In the middle of nowhere. With a man I didn't know. But it was going to be okay.

At least that's what I kept telling myself.

I nodded, but when I attempted to stand, a pain so intense shot through me and I yelped. I nearly fell to the ground before he caught me. He scooped me up, cradling me to his chest.

Holy shit.

His muscles. His brown eyes this close. Perhaps I should've been scared, but at the moment, this man and his luxurious house were way too distracting.

A woman in a white shirt and black slacks—another member of the staff, no doubt—came out to greet us. Her hair was slicked back in a bun, and she dipped her head almost as if bowing to royalty. "Mr. Bianchi."

I consoled myself with the fact that there were numerous staff. Which meant witnesses. But…if he truly was mafia, then they'd be made men. They'd know how to hide the bodies and clean up any evidence.

Just stop, Harper. This is not a movie. And Enzo is not part of the mafia.

"Could you please get us some ice?" Enzo asked. "My friend has been injured."

Friend. Ha!

Even so, he'd gone to great lengths to make sure I was okay. And this house… *Damn.* I read the sign just beside the door, "Mizuki House."

"It means beautiful moon or water moon," Enzo said as the front door swung open.

The door itself pivoted in the center, allowing people to pass down either side of the massive wood plank. It was a work of art with its linear carvings. Enzo's footsteps echoed on the tile floor—white tile with white walls, verdant green vines growing down the sides. I was still trying to take it all in when he stepped in farther to reveal a long bar that ran the length of the room, a huge living area with luxurious furnishings.

I could easily imagine my friends' reactions. Lauren would flip out at the interior design. Alexis would appraise the house as if to list it. Juliana would be planning the perfect party for the space, and here I was, being carried like an invalid.

I blinked a few times as a pool came into view. This house was over the top. The pool seemed to stretch to the edge of the cliff, and…was that the ocean?

Who the hell is Enzo Bianchi?

CHAPTER THREE

Enzo

Harper glanced around the living room, her mouth agape. I could imagine putting that mouth to good use, but at the moment, I was more concerned with her ankle.

"This is…" Her eyes widened, and I tried not to laugh as I carried her across the tile floor.

"You like it?" I asked, her reaction both surprising and refreshing. As was my body's response to her. She felt so good in my arms, and my skin tingled where we touched.

"Are you kidding? It's incredible. This is yours?"

I smirked, reluctantly placing her on one of the plush couches overlooking the pool before taking a seat nearby. The water glowed from beneath the surface, large clear floats bobbing like giant bubbles. I wanted to give her the best view. Not that Mizuki House had a bad view. Whether you were on the ground floor or gazing out from one of the many decks, the scenery was phenomenal.

"For a little while longer, yes."

I'd been in Bali for several weeks, extending my stay again and again. Part of it was my desire to avoid my problems—

the press—back home. But a bigger part was the sense of peace I felt here.

No one knew me. I was able to wander around without fear of someone photographing my every move, stopping me for an autograph. I hadn't felt this sort of freedom since before I'd signed on with Milan FC all those years ago. And I wanted to enjoy it for as long as possible.

One of my favorite things was hanging out with the local kids. They were so pure and fun. Experiencing their joy for the sport was contagious. And it was a reminder of why I loved the game. I'd lost sight of that lately—I'd been trying to suppress too much pain. And it had been sucking even more out of me than I'd realized.

I wasn't eager to return to Italy or my problems there. An ex that was still struggling with our breakup. The press that was eager to see me stumble. A team that doubted my abilities to play at the level I had been. At the level expected of me.

Apart from a few text exchanges with my agent, Val, and a few calls from my mother, I'd been left blissfully alone. I had nowhere to be, no obligations. And I hadn't realized how utterly exhausted I was until I'd come here. Until I'd just stopped.

I was still working out daily, but I was also getting more massages. Taking walks on the beach. Enjoying the scenery. My assistant, Nico, had knocked it out of the park with this property.

Koming approached and handed a bag of ice to Harper before addressing me. "The doctor will be here soon. May I get you anything else?" she asked in a hushed tone.

"Thank you, Koming." I turned to Harper. "Would you like a drink? Something to eat, perhaps?"

"We can make anything you like," Koming said to Harper almost eagerly. "Anything at all."

"Could I have a glass of water, please?"

What was it about this woman? She'd captivated me from the moment I'd discovered her sitting on the ground, dust coating her skin. Her green eyes had peered up at me, full of strength. And I'd seen even more of that determination and stubbornness from her in the car. It was sexy.

Koming nodded. "Of course. It would be my pleasure."

"Thank you, Koming," Harper said.

"And you, sir?" Koming addressed me.

I shook my head. "I'm fine. Thank you."

The waves crashed against the cliffs, and I draped my arm over the back of the sofa. "So, Harper, what are you doing in Bali?"

"I'm a film location scout." She ran a hand through her hair. It was a beautiful shade of chestnut and fell in waves that caressed her shoulders.

I nodded, though I couldn't stop staring. I'd never felt such a strong pull to a woman, and I wanted to know why. "What does that entail?"

"Lots of travel. Negotiation. Research. Photography." She seemed to light up when she talked about her work, especially the photography.

"Photography?" I asked as Koming delivered Harper's drink, then disappeared again.

Harper smiled but then winced as she bent forward to adjust the ice on her ankle, her movements graceful like a ballerina. She had the body of a dancer—long and lean, with a flat stomach and small breasts. Her forest-green linen shorts showed off her olive skin, her tank top dipping low on her chest. Her nipples pebbled against the fabric. I wondered what it would be like to touch them, lick them.

She arched an eyebrow, and I knew I'd been caught checking her out. "Yes. I'm the production team's eyes and ears, so I tend to take a lot of photos to give them an immersive experience."

She explained some more, and I nodded, intrigued by her job, by her. She was passionate and smart. Determined. "And that's what you were doing tonight?"

She removed a bottle of pain relievers from her bag and popped some into her mouth. The way her throat worked around them had my imagination racing into overdrive. My hand cupping the back of her head as I thrust in her mouth. Her lips...

"No." She laughed, the sound bringing me back to the present.

"What's so funny?" I asked, shifting in an attempt to hide my arousal.

"I'm actually on vacation. Well, as of this evening, I was. So much for that now." Her lips twisted, and she leaned forward to adjust the ice pack.

I frowned. This was my fault. I'd lost track of time playing soccer. And then I'd been impatient and pushed Kadek to drive faster. If I hadn't...

"I'm sorry," I said.

"It's not your fault."

That was debatable. Even so, I asked, "So what did you have planned for your *vacanza?*"

"Visit some local temples. Lounge by the pool. Take some yoga. Get a massage or three." She leaned back, running her hand through her hair. "I suppose I can still do that, at least."

"Is that a typical vacation for you?" I asked, trying to push aside visions of her lying naked on a massage table.

Harper grinned. "I'm not sure I have a typical vacation. I'm often on the go for work, and I like to see as much of a place as I can while I'm there."

I understood that, which was why taking time off was

even more important. These past few weeks had shown me that. I wasn't sure the last time I'd let myself stop. Be.

"Downtime is important, as is rest."

"Is that what you're doing here?" she asked.

I rolled my lower lip between my teeth. "For the most part."

Did she not know who I was? Could I really be that lucky?

Harper arched an inquisitive eyebrow, biting her lip as she seemed to assess me, then the house. Before she could press further, Koming appeared with the doctor at her side. She introduced him, translating for us. While he examined Harper's ankle, I studied her. The curve of her lips, the delicateness of her features.

Eventually, he announced that her ankle was sprained, as she'd predicted. He advised her to rest, ice, and elevate it. It was a relatively low-grade sprain, and with luck, it would be mostly healed before she returned home in a week.

Unfortunately, he hadn't brought any crutches with him. He recommended picking them up at the pharmacy in town tomorrow since it was already closed for the night. We thanked the doctor, and then he and Koming left.

Harper crossed her arms over her chest, drawing my attention there despite her smug expression. "I told you it was a sprain."

"And I told you that you needed to stay off it."

She glared at me. I glared back. The air crackled with electricity.

"Now that you're satisfied," she said, interrupting our silent stare-off. "I'd like to return to my hotel."

"Oh, I am far from satisfied," I rasped, feeling off-kilter. What was it about this woman that made me act so recklessly?

And I was being reckless. If this got out… If she discovered who I really was…

"You're right. It's getting late, and I'm sure you're tired." I called for Koming and asked her to have the car brought out front.

We talked on the way back to town—of Harper's friends, her vacation, Italy. I didn't offer any specific details about myself, and she didn't ask. I still couldn't believe I'd told her my name was Enzo. I'd never gone by that name, and I would've hated being called it by anyone but her. But hearing the name Enzo from her lips was like a drug…like freedom.

When Kadek pulled up to the hotel's front entrance, I hesitated. Was I going to do this? Risk exposure?

Did any of that matter, considering the position I'd put Harper in? There was no way Harper could get inside on her own. And while I could've asked Kadek to take her, it seemed wrong somehow. I rubbed my chest, knowing my tattoo was just beneath my hand. A reminder. And I knew what needed to be done.

With a heavy sigh, I pulled on a baseball cap, careful to keep it low on my face. I helped Harper out of the car and wrapped my arm around her waist to steady her. My body hummed pleasantly from the contact, distracting me from the reality of what I was doing.

She winced, and I wanted to pick her up and cradle her to my chest, but I had a feeling if I tried to carry her through the hotel, she'd throw a fit. And the last thing I wanted was attention.

I only hoped I could make it out of the hotel without being recognized. Without being asked for a picture or an autograph.

"Where's your room?" I asked, gritting my teeth.

I ducked my head in an attempt to remain unseen. This was going to take ten times longer than if I just picked her up. But I knew what it was like to be injured, and I was trying to respect her dignity.

"Third floor. Room 304."

I nodded, and we hobbled in the direction of the elevators, though I took most of her weight. It was an even farther walk than I'd expected, and every step only made me feel worse. Harper was having a difficult enough time getting to her room, even if I knew she was trying to hide it. I could see the way she babied her ankle and winced any time it hit the ground. And what was she going to do once she got to her room—just sit around when she'd had all these amazing things planned?

When we finally arrived, she plopped down on the bed. The hotel was nice, though not as luxurious as my vacation home. And I did have all those extra rooms going unused—five, in fact.

My impatience had caused her injury. And I'd ruined her plans.

And then I'd snapped at Kadek, when it wasn't his fault. I'd since apologized for it, but I'd hated seeing the scared look in his eye.

For not the first time, I considered inviting Harper to stay with me. She'd have staff to help her. *I* could help her.

Was I insane? If Val knew I was even thinking about this, she'd kill me.

And yet, the idea was tempting. This woman was tempting. I didn't know why I felt so responsible for Harper—aside from the obvious—but I did. She seemed like the type of woman Papà would've approved of.

"I'd walk you to the door, but…" She gestured to her ankle then shrugged.

I shook my head, running a hand over my chin. I couldn't just leave her here. Not like this. It didn't feel right. And frankly, I didn't want to.

"Change of plans," I said.

She furrowed her brow. "Huh?"

"You're staying with me for the next week."

She laughed so hard, she fell back on the bed, giving me an even better idea of what she'd look like naked. Sprawled out on my sheets. Writhing as I made her come with the name only she called me on her lips. Beautiful. Absolutely beautiful.

She propped herself up on her elbows, her green eyes narrowed at me. "You can't be serious."

I nodded, though I continued to question my sanity. "I am."

"Enzo," she sighed, sitting up. "I can't."

"Why not?"

She shook her head. "Because I don't know you."

"Can you honestly tell me that you want to stay here—alone? Stuck in your hotel room for the next week?"

She lifted a shoulder. "I planned to get some crutches. It'll be fine."

It might be fine, but it was far from ideal. And for some reason, I wasn't ready to say goodbye. Something kept pulling me back to Harper. Based on the way she was looking at me—the way she'd looked at me most of the evening—she felt it too.

I sank down on the bed next to her. She seemed surprised but didn't protest.

Maybe all the massages and sea air were going to my head. Maybe it was the extended vacation or the freedom from the paparazzi. I had no idea, but I'd never felt so relaxed. So free to be myself. It was easy to forget who I was back home, forget the pain, and just allow myself to be me.

"My hotel is already paid for," she said.

I lifted my shoulder. "So?"

It was clear she wanted to come with me, yet she wasn't allowing herself to. It made no sense.

"If I'm staying with you, I'd want to pay my fair share."

I shook my head. "No. Absolutely not."

"Enzo," she chided.

I stood, tired of this conversation. She was exasperating. *"Vieni."*

"You can't just snap your fingers and expect me to come with you. Especially not when you still haven't told me what *uccellina* means. Or anything about yourself."

"I just don't understand why you deny yourself what you want."

She sighed. "Ugh. Do you have to be so…*Italian?*"

"Well, yes." I chuckled, enjoying the way she scanned my body. "I've never been told that's a bad thing."

"It's not. And your offer *is* tempting."

"But?"

"It's too much."

I shook my head, unwilling to relent. "It's not enough," I said, kneeling before her. "Please. I feel awful that I ruined your vacation and caused you to become injured. Let me make it up to you."

She wavered, and I sensed she was close to relenting. If nothing else, I had to admire her steadfastness and resilience.

"What's the point of vacation," I said, "if not to indulge?"

She let out a deep sigh. "Enzo…"

"Or…" I lay down on the bed next to her, making myself at home as I crossed my feet at the ankles. "I could stay here if that would make you more comfortable."

She huffed. "You're insufferable."

I held my hand up to my ear. "Hmm. I'm not sure I understand that word. It must not translate to Italian. *Hai detto indimenticabile?*"

She laughed, slapping at my chest. "Insufferable not *unfor-*

gettable."

"Yes, but perhaps I am both." I grinned.

"That remains to be seen. Though you are persistent."

"So, you'll come."

She leaned closer, tantalizing me with the prospect of kissing her. "What does *uccellina* mean?"

I smiled. "Little bird."

"And what should I call you?" she mused.

"*Leone. Pantera...*" I listed some of the strongest, most fearsome animals I could think of.

"*Tardigrade.*"

I jerked my head back. "What is that? A large, *fierce* snake?"

She laughed, delight dancing in her eyes like the devil. She typed something into her phone then held it out to me. I stared at the image on the screen. Squishy. Ugly.

"This—" I pointed "—this is what I remind you of?" *Che brutto.* "Like a pig covered in moss."

She laughed so hard she snorted, which only made me smile. All I saw was how beautiful she was. "*Bellissima.*"

Harper didn't fall under my usual type, apart from the fact that she was beautiful. But it was more than her outward appearance; she intrigued me. I wasn't used to women turning me down. And they definitely didn't huff and roll their eyes at me like this one currently was.

She dipped her head, cheeks flushing with color. "I can't fight you anymore."

"Good." I smirked when she met my gaze.

We stared at each other a moment, something unspoken —a current—passing between us. Before she could change her mind, I called down to the front desk to request a bellhop. "I promise you won't regret it."

"I'm not so sure about that," she muttered.

Neither was I.

CHAPTER FOUR

Harper

"Why do you have such a big house anyway?" I asked from my perch on the guest bed.

The staff had delivered my luggage and unpacked it, leaving Enzo to help me to my room. It was getting ridiculous, really. The way he insisted on carrying me. Not that I minded being cradled to his chest, his scent infiltrating my nose. For such an imposing man, he was surprisingly gentle.

This house, though…Mizuki House…it was truly ridiculous. Even in the short time I'd been here, the staff had been incredible. And the house itself—the guest bedroom alone was larger than my apartment back in LA. And it was one of six. *Six* beautiful, luxurious bedrooms with pristine bedding and, I assumed, ocean views. It was too dark now to see anything beyond the pool. But my room had a private balcony with a little wading pool at the ledge.

Insane! It seemed like something from one of the movies I worked on, not a place I'd actually get to stay. *Me!* Stay here.

I admired a batik painting on the wall across the room. The design was vibrant and intricate. And the more I saw of the place, the more in awe I was. I couldn't even imagine the cost of something like this. Yes, Bali was relatively inexpensive to visit. But still, this was a six-bedroom villa overlooking the ocean with staff, with…

"My friend Val was supposed to come with me," Enzo said, interrupting my mental calculations. "But she had to stay home."

I nodded, considering, trying to push down the flare of jealousy that sparked in my blood. Was Val more than a friend? And why did I care?

I told myself it was because I was about to spend the week at this man's house and he was a stranger. But I knew it was more than that. I was attracted to Enzo. Okay, more than attracted. How could I not be? He was a freaking god.

Dark hair. Big brown eyes. Full lips.

Then there was his body, which was like a work of art. Hard angles and smooth planes. A masterpiece. I wondered what he did for a living. Where he lived. I had so many questions.

"Friend?" I asked, my mind coming back to that word.

"Yes. Just a friend," he said with a smug grin.

"Yet you'd bring her with you on vacation?"

"You told me you enjoy traveling with your girlfriends. Juliana, Alex—"

"Alexis." I nodded, thinking back on our conversation on the drive over. "And Lauren."

"Same for me with Val." He lifted a shoulder. "She's like a sister."

He crossed his arms and leaned against the wall. Strong. Tall. Lean. Graceful.

When I met Enzo's gaze, he was scanning me. His eyes hooded. Lips parted as if in anticipation. He felt it too—this *pull.*

"Besides, I just got out of a relationship. I'm not looking for anything serious," he said.

Wasn't that the story of my life? The hottest men were either taken or players. If I had to guess, Enzo was a player. A man that gorgeous had to have women falling all over him.

I wasn't looking for anything serious either. Or anything at all, really. Though the idea of sex with this man was undeniably tempting. Even so… I didn't know him.

It was one thing to stay at his home. In the past, I'd met up with other travelers and shared lodgings, meals, whatever. Though, I typically paid my fair share. But it was another thing entirely to sleep with a stranger. A man I'd only met earlier today when his driver had nearly run me off the road.

"Were you together a long time?" I asked.

He rubbed a hand over his chin, the scruff rustling against his palm. "Too long, yes. I should've ended it sooner."

"Why didn't you?" I kept waiting for him to tell me he was done. To stop answering my questions. But to my surprise, he didn't. He kept talking. He seemed to want to talk, even if his answers were a bit cryptic.

"It was easier than the alternative."

I smoothed my hand over the duvet cover. "Which was?"

"Disappointing my mamma."

I grinned. "Aw. You're a mama's boy."

He pushed off the wall and stepped closer, pressing his palm to the mattress. His face inches from mine. "I can assure you, I am *all* man."

I rolled my eyes, though I couldn't ignore the way my skin prickled from his words. His proximity. He was right. He was so undeniably masculine and virile that sexuality oozed from his pores.

I could practically hear Lauren's voice in my head, egging me on. Urging me to seize what the sex gods were offering and just sleep with Enzo. But then I yawned, effectively ruining the moment.

"You are tired. I will let you rest." He turned for the door.

As exhausted as I was, I wanted to soak in the large tub, or at the very least, take a shower. Wash the dirt from my skin. There was no way I'd climb into the pristine sheets in my current state. I stood and winced the moment I placed any weight on my foot.

"What are you doing?" The command in his voice was evident, the power. So much so, I shivered.

"Going to take a bath. Brush my teeth." I didn't want him to watch me hobble toward the bathroom.

"No. No. No." He crossed the room in a few strides.

"Enzo." I placed my hands on my hips, trying to project strength despite my current state. I hoped my ankle would heal quickly because I hated being stuck in one place. I hated having to rely on someone. "I'm fine. You can't do everything for me."

"Col cavolo!"

To hell with that!

I wanted to laugh, but he was so serious. His brows furrowed, forming a crease between them. His expression stern and unrelenting.

"Though, perhaps you are right. I will confirm that the staff will have crutches and ice for you in the morning."

"Thank you," I said, surprised by how quickly he'd relented. "Are you going somewhere?"

"I have…business."

"But how will I shower all by myself?" I teased, wanting to ask him more about this mysterious "business" he had.

His slow, mischievous grin made my core tighten in anticipation. Then he spoke, his voice deeper. "I would be happy to assist you."

"I'll be fine on my own." My tone was breezy, nothing like the fire I felt from his gaze.

"That may be true. But it would be much more fun together."

"Maybe."

"Definitely." He stepped closer.

My own body was thrumming with need. He tucked my hair behind my ear, tracing my jawline before trailing his thumb over my lower lip. I opened ever so slightly—an invitation. And he pushed his digit inside, entranced by my mouth.

"*Uccellina*, I'm used to getting what I want," he rasped. "And right now, I want you."

We stared at each other as if transfixed, and then he trailed his thumb down my chin. Lower still, until he was tugging gently against the center of my tank top, tracing down my sternum.

I sucked in a jagged breath, my nipples hardening to tight points beneath my shirt. And then I glanced away, straightening. "I can't."

"You have a…boyfriend?" he asked in a harsh tone. "Husband?"

"No." I shook my head, crossing my arms over my chest. "I have standards. *Rules*."

"What kinds of rules?"

"I don't sleep with someone I just met," I said. Then added under my breath, "No matter how badly I might want to."

He put some space between us, heading for the door. "I shouldn't have pushed you. I won't let it happen again."

Disappointment swirled within me, and I headed for the bathroom before I could change my mind. I wasn't ready to jump into bed with him. My body was. Oh, was she begging me to do just that.

In the past, I'd always had a firm three-date rule, even

with the bad boys. *Especially* with the bad boys. Though, if there was a man worth breaking it for, it was Enzo.

I smiled to myself as I sat on the edge of the tub, waiting for the water in the shower to get warm. Lauren had been right—you never knew what might happen. I had a feeling this next week was going to be interesting.

THE FOLLOWING MORNING, I WOKE TO A GENTLE KNOCK AT the door. Koming peeked her head in, and I made sure I was decent before sitting up against the headboard.

"I brought you crutches, Ms. Harper." She set them next to the wall closest to the bed. "A brace and fresh ice."

"Thank you." I smiled and slipped on the brace before placing the ice on my ankle. I hadn't taken any painkillers since before going to bed, and it was stiff.

"We also brought breakfast." Another man entered, carrying a large tray of food. I had to close my jaw at the sight. The presentation was incredible, showing an eye for detail.

"Wow." I surveyed the food or, rather, the feast. In addition to the meal, there was coffee, fresh orange juice, and water. I was definitely glad I'd agreed to come stay at Mizuki House. "This looks delicious. Thank you so much."

"May I open the balcony doors for you?" she asked. "It's lovely out."

I nodded, taking a bite of the granola. Mm. That was good. Crunchy and salty with a hint of sweetness. I took another and nearly groaned. *Really* good. "Yes, please."

"Would you like anything else?"

I shook my head, not sure what else I could possibly

want. They seemed to have thought of everything and then some. "No. Thank you. This is wonderful."

"If you'd like something else, please don't hesitate to ask. You can press one on the phone on the nightstand," she said as she backed out of the room.

As soon as they were gone, I pulled out my phone and took pictures of my meal. I couldn't help myself. It was just *so* sumptuous. The sheer curtains billowed in the breeze, the sound of the ocean crashing against the shore.

I exchanged a few texts with Juliana while eating breakfast, and I knew she was checking in since I'd told her I was going home with a man. I assured her I was okay and promised to tell her more later. Then I quickly scanned my inbox, but nothing urgent popped out at me. I needed to upload my photos and work on my report for the studio at some point, but they weren't expecting those for a few weeks. Besides, I was on vacation. It could wait.

Instead, I grabbed my e-reader and picked up where I'd left off in the latest Meghan Hart novel. She lived near my hometown of Fall River, but I hadn't read her books until I was stuck in Germany on a layover from hell. Ever since then, I'd been hooked.

For Christmas, my mom had bought me several signed print copies. You could only get them from Bibliolater—a charming bookstore in neighboring Alondra. It was funny to think that many, many years ago, I'd babysat the owner's son, Liam.

I smiled, thinking of home. Of the stories Meghan Hart wove. I knew they were fiction, but they filled me with hope. Hope that maybe one day I'd be like her characters and find my own happily ever after. Even if that seemed like more of a stretch than ever. Still…two days ago, I never would've imagined I'd be here. In this insane house with an insanely hot man.

I shook my head and immersed myself in the pages as I nibbled some fruit. I was gripped by the story of a parkour athlete who was injured and the physical therapist he was slowly falling in love with. She was about to help him into the shower when I was startled by the sound of raised voices. Or just…Enzo's voice.

I blinked a few times, disoriented. His tone was terse, and I recoiled from the anger I could hear pulsating off him. I couldn't make out the specific words he said, but they were soon followed by a loud splash.

I hobbled over to the balcony to peer down at the pool below.

"Cazzo!" he shouted, then dove in.

My eyes went wide when I realized that he'd thrown his phone into the pool. The next thing I knew, he was climbing out of the water slowly, running his hand through his hair. He looked intense. His body perfection.

I swallowed hard as water raced down his chest and disappeared into a tight navy Speedo that clung to his skin. It left nothing to the imagination. The curve of his dick was visible, and I was totally gawking.

Then he turned and walked to the back of the property, disappearing behind a wall. Where had he gone? What was he doing? And who had he been talking to that had pissed him off so badly?

I'd been so distracted that I'd completely overlooked the view. And what a view it was. The backyard was comprised of outdoor decks, the pool, a long stretch of grass that led to the ocean. I'd guessed as much last night, but seeing it today…just *wow*.

I stood there a moment, careful to keep my weight off my injured ankle before returning inside to wash my face and get dressed. I had no idea what the day held, but I found myself both nervous and excited about the possibilities, despite my injury. I'd just finished brushing my teeth when there was a knock at the bedroom door.

I dabbed my face with the towel and hobbled to the bedroom before calling, "Yes?"

The door opened, and Enzo stepped inside wearing a white terry cloth robe that looked as fluffy as a cloud. His hair was still wet, his feet bare. His face seemed relaxed, nothing like I'd expect after the scene I'd witnessed earlier.

"*Buongiorno, uccellina.*"

"*Buongiorno.*" I smiled.

We stared at each other a minute, and I couldn't tear my eyes away from his. The brown was a rich color, like the most decadent chocolate. Yet it was something in their depths that held me captive—an unspoken pain I could understand and relate to, even if I didn't know the cause of it. I briefly wondered if his rage was a manifestation of that pain.

"How is your ankle?" he asked.

I lifted a shoulder. "It's...okay. Koming brought me a brace earlier, and that helped some."

"I've arranged something for us. Something else that might help."

"You have?"

He nodded. "But it's downstairs. Would you like to come?"

"What is it?" I asked, my curiosity getting the better of me. He might have a temper, but I didn't get the impression he'd hurt me. He'd never been anything but gentle with me.

"You'll see." He stepped closer, and I let out a little squeak of surprise when he scooped me into his arms. He was warm, and he smelled of delicious bergamot.

"I have crutches now, you know? You don't have to carry me everywhere," I teased as he padded down the stairs and then out to the backyard.

"Maybe I want to."

"Where are you taking me?" I asked, noting that he was following the same path he'd taken earlier. Out to the building at the back of the property.

We passed by a gorgeous outdoor shower. Then through a hallway to emerge by another, smaller pool. This one covered in mosaic tiles that glinted in the sun. Ivy draped over the side of the walls, only adding to the feel of the luxurious secret garden. Enzo carried me through another door.

The space smelled of vanilla, and gong music played through unseen speakers in the background. I blinked a few times, my eyes trying to adjust to the darker room after the bright sun. Two massage tables were set up, with two women waiting. Watching us with warm smiles.

I grinned. "A massage?"

Enzo nodded and set me on one of the tables. He held my gaze as he continued to touch me, and electricity sparked between us. I had no idea how I was going to relax when he made me feel like this.

"Your massage therapist is well versed in injuries and aware of your ankle. She will avoid massaging below your calf where you're injured."

"Wow." I nodded, impressed by his thoroughness and thoughtfulness. "Thank you."

He dipped his head then he left me to change.

I was facedown on the table when Enzo and the women returned. My massage therapist had a firm and confident touch, with just the right amount of pressure. The more she worked my muscles, the more I relaxed. By the time she'd finished, I'd forgotten all about my ankle. And pretty much anything else since I'd melted into the table.

"Are you okay?" Enzo asked long after they'd left. At least, I thought it had been a while. I still hadn't moved.

"I think I've died and gone to heaven," I muttered, facedown.

He chuckled, and when I heard rustling, I lifted my head. He pushed off the table, his back to me as the sheet fell from his hips. My mouth went dry as I scanned his naked form. The tight, lifted globes of his ass. The tattoos marking the skin of his back.

"*Uccellina?*"

I quickly dropped my head, realizing he'd asked me something. "What was that?"

"I asked if you needed help changing."

When I finally dared look up again, his body was covered by the robe. I sat up on the table, gathering the sheet about me. When I met his eyes, his stare was intense, trapping me in his molten gaze. The air swirled with possibility, with desire and longing. We stared at each other a moment, the tension stretching between us like a rubber band on the verge of snapping.

He took a few steps back, testing the breaking point. Despite the distance, our bodies remained connected, tethered by some invisible link. As much as I tried to deny it, one look had me desperate for him. And judging from his clenched jaw and tightened fists, he felt it too. He was fighting it too. Fighting and failing.

It felt as if I was standing at crossroads. I could tell him I could manage and do it myself. Or I could have a little fun. This was vacation after all. And it had been *so* long since I'd had sex. Too long. I'd been so focused on work and getting pregnant that I hadn't had time for much else.

Screw the three-date rule. It wasn't like it had served me well in the past. And it definitely wasn't now.

I let the sheet fall to my waist, the material opening to reveal more of my legs. I was naked, and Enzo eyed me hungrily. When he stepped between my thighs, I knew he was going to kiss me. I also knew I wasn't going to stop him. But I didn't realize how it would feel when he wound his fist in my hair, his lips crashing against mine, bruising, punishing, claiming.

Enzo kissed like a man possessed, and I was dizzy, delirious, lost. I'd never been kissed like this.

My body was on fire, and I wanted to burn. I didn't fear the flames; I wanted to become them. I wanted to be reborn as something new. He'd called me *uccellina*, little bird—but in this moment, I felt more like a phoenix.

He kissed down my neck, grazing my shoulder with his teeth. He skimmed his lips over my nipples, and I nearly combusted. He smoothed a hand up my thigh, edging closer to my center. To where I really wanted him. Everything about his touch radiated strength and control.

Outside, the waves crashed against the shore, and I could feel the tide surge within me, seeking release.

"*Ancora*," I groaned when he nipped my skin. It wasn't gentle, but I didn't want gentle. I wanted more.

"You like that?" he asked, his tone conveying surprise.

I nodded, biting back a grin. His dark smile made me shiver in anticipation as he dove back in, scraping his teeth along my shoulder.

I reached inside his robe, eager to explore, to feel him without anything between us. I was greeted by velvet skin wrapped around his hard length. And the most decadent moan I'd ever heard.

"*Uccellina*," he growled, gripping the back of my neck and forcing me to meet his gaze. His eyes were hooded, voice gruff. "*Che cosa mi stai facendo?*"

"What am I doing…?" I trailed off, my brain too distracted to attempt translating. To me, it sounded beautiful, lyrical. It was almost as if his words were weaving a spell around me, luring me in.

"Lie down." His quiet command had me doing just that.

Everything about Enzo was so masculine, so powerful. And I imagined if he'd told me to come, I would've orgasmed from his words alone.

He grabbed my wrists, lifting them above my head. He hesitated briefly, his eyes focused on my bracelet before he said, "Now, don't move. Not unless I tell you to."

I nodded, so very eager I feared it verged on desperate. The pressure built, lust overriding my better sense.

He skimmed his fingers down my arms, over my sides, before dragging them along my legs. I gripped the edge of the massage table, and he appraised me as if I were there solely for his pleasure. Both our smiles vanished, and I wanted to rub my thighs together, but I knew better. His command had me rooted to the spot, eagerly awaiting what would happen next.

His dark hair was shiny, and I ached to run my fingers through it as he explored my clit with his fingers then delved inside me.

"*Sei magnifica.* You feel your pussy, sucking my fingers in, holding me tight?" he rasped. "Imagine how good my dick will feel."

His shoulders were strong, and I interlaced my fingers, squeezing my hands together to avoid the temptation to map his body as he took full control of mine. I leaned my head back. I was ready, my body poised to climax even as I wanted to draw this moment out as long as possible.

I'd felt so broken the past few months that this experience was incredibly empowering. Or maybe it was the way he looked at me. Because even though he was the one controlling my movements, guiding my body, I was the one who'd brought him to his knees. As he leaned forward, licking my clit, lapping up my juices, he appeared like a supplicant at an altar.

"*Deliziosa,*" he muttered then resumed his ministrations until my legs were shaking, and the pleasure built and built and built until it finally burst. Waves of ecstasy crashing over me.

I cried out and reached for him, needing to hold on to something before I floated away.

When he met my eyes from between my thighs, his lips were slick with my desire. "On your knees." Then he softened. "As long as you think it won't hurt your ankle."

I shook my head. "I'll be fine."

When I did as he said, the sting of his palm against my ass made me freeze. The shock of it had me momentarily stunned, but as he rubbed the spot with his hand, I was struck by a sudden revelation. I liked it.

"Mm." I could hear the smile in his voice, and it was as if he'd known this about me before I'd ever considered it.

I'd never had a man treat me so roughly, and I liked it. The way he fisted my hair. The tightness of his grip on my hip. The bruising way he kissed me. I liked that he wasn't afraid I might shatter at the slightest touch.

He grabbed my hips, pulling me back to his mouth. "Oh! *Oh.*"

The moment his tongue hit my sensitive flesh, my knees nearly buckled. But he continued to feast on me, relentless in his pursuit of my orgasm. He licked and sucked my clit, fingering me until I was on the brink of coming again.

I wondered how he could extract so much pleasure from me. I'd never experienced a high quite like this, and I didn't know how much longer I could hold out. But I trusted that if I did, he'd make it worth the wait.

I was panting, close to begging, when he growled against my clit, "Come for me."

His gruff voice traveled through me, detonating the explosion I'd been so desperately holding at bay. And what an explosion it was—such a sudden rush of sensations and colors that I was delirious. But he didn't stop, not until I was limp and barely able to hold myself up.

It was only as I was coming back down to earth that I heard him say, *"Buono." Good.*

Dear lord, that was more than good. That was… I didn't even have words for how incredible he'd made me feel. When my friends had talked about sex in the past, I'd always listened with a bit of skepticism at their life-changing orgasms. But Enzo had converted me; I was officially a believer.

"Girati." He gave my ass a gentle smack, announcing his intent that I turn over.

I smiled, amused that he'd been reduced to one-word commands. Pleased that he'd resorted to his native tongue. Hearing him speak Italian was sexy as hell. And I would do whatever he wanted if he continued looking at me the way he was right now.

"On your back." He clenched his fists as if to keep from touching me. "Legs spread."

I did exactly as he asked, feeling myself grow wetter as he stared at me while palming himself, the robe hanging off his shoulders. Watching him was erotic, the way his hand slid up and down, his grip tight, eyes hooded.

He was a sight to behold—utterly perfect. Those deep creases at the waist, a trail of dark hair that led to the most impressive hard-on I'd ever seen. Impressive and beautifully unique. I'd never been with a guy who wasn't circumcised— the foreskin still covering the head.

He crawled on top of me, running his nose along mine before tracing my jawline, moving down my neck, my breasts. Compared to his earlier touch, this was gentle yet still incredibly sensual. I closed my eyes, sighing as he circled my nipple.

But when he clamped down, hard, my eyes popped open in surprise. But mingled with it was delight, especially when he flattened his tongue over the skin. My body was at war, trying to process the pain then the pleasure. A pain so exquisite it was pleasure.

"You like that?" he asked, and I nodded. He seemed pleased. And then he nipped at the other one, soon soothing it with his tongue. "Do you want more?"

I nodded again.

"I'm going to need to hear that from your lips."

I swallowed, not entirely sure what I was getting myself into. But I sure as hell wanted to find out. "I want more."

"What do you want, Harper? Tell me."

"I want…" I swallowed, trying to determine what I wanted most and first. But the words came out unbidden. "*Ti voglio*. Take me." I released my plea to the air. *I want you. Take me.*

CHAPTER FIVE

Enzo

Take me.

Harper stared up at me with such fire and trust, and I needed to be inside her. Needed to feel her pussy gripping my cock. Needed to lose myself in her before I completely unraveled.

I wasn't sure what had changed for her since last night, but whatever the cause, I was grateful. Because an arduous workout, a walk along the beach, and a massage hadn't been enough to quench my thirst for Harper. If anything, I wanted her even more now. And I *would* have her.

Her body beckoned me closer, even as I'd pushed her harder and further than any woman before. She seemed to like it. To crave it as much as I did. It was almost too good to be true.

I scrambled for a condom I'd stashed in my robe earlier. I'd found a strip of them in my toiletry bag, promo from some event I'd attended. I was glad I'd had the foresight to grab one.

I quickly slid it down my length, goose bumps coating my skin as I watched her writhe before me. She was so fucking sexy. In the back of my mind, I knew this was a terrible idea, but I shoved away those thoughts.

I was so eager to be inside her, I buried myself to the hilt in one powerful thrust. And then I stilled. Fuck, she was so tight, so warm.

"*Perfetta,*" I sighed.

"Enzo." The name was whispered on a sigh—pleasure mingling with exasperation as I kissed my way down her neck, filling her, stretching her. I was still getting used to being called Enzo, but I liked hearing it from her lips.

Unable to hold back anymore, I started thrusting, driving into her as I bent forward to suck her rosy nipples into my mouth. I could feel the pressure building, but it wasn't enough. I needed more, deeper, harder. I slid my arms beneath her back, pulling her closer. *Needing* her closer. Our skin was slick from the massage oil, and she quickly slid into position.

"Oh!" Her eyes widened, the new angle bringing us closer, burying me deeper still. It felt amazing. "Oh yes."

I smashed my mouth to hers as I guided her up and down on my cock. She raked her nails across my skin, and I leaned my head back, relishing the feeling. Like lightning. She felt so good, so fucking good. And I was going to come soon if I didn't slow down.

Instead, I nipped her breast, knowing how much she'd liked the bite of pain earlier. I liked it too, and it was such a relief not to hold back. Not to have to rein it in like I had in the past. To let go and enjoy, to lose myself in her and this moment.

Harper's pussy clenched in response, gripping me like a vise as I flattened my tongue over her nipple. Her ass filled my hands, and I spread her cheeks wide, allowing my cock to go even deeper.

She smoothed her hands over my chest, and they seemed

so small in comparison. Everything about her was small next to me. I liked it. Liked this feeling of dominating her so completely, of taking what I wanted and giving us both what we needed.

I squeezed my eyes shut briefly, my body taking over. "Fuck, you feel good."

"So do you," she panted, clutching me as if I was her salvation. "So, *so* good."

I tangled my fingers in her hair, burying my nose in her neck to breathe in her almond scent. She tasted amazing, and she felt even better—her smooth skin brushing against my hard planes. Her soft breasts crushed between us.

I held on tight, pumping harder as any remaining control was extinguished. I wasn't sure how much longer I could hold out. I was holding on by a thread when she came hard and fast, and it was a beautiful sight to behold.

"*Sì. Yes*," I grunted, fisting her hair, the silk flowing over my skin like a waterfall.

Her walls clenched, and I finally let go, exploding inside her. With a few more pumps, I was spent, and she fell back on the massage table, my body draped over hers. We remained there a moment, catching our breaths.

"I'll be right back." I ducked into the bathroom. I disposed of the condom then grabbed a warm washcloth for her. "Spread."

She lowered her knees, flashing me that pretty pink pussy once more. She was gorgeous. And I wanted to lick her, so I did.

"Oh god." She moaned, throwing an arm over her face. "I don't know how much more I can handle." Though, it was clear she loved it. "Is it possible to die from pleasure?"

"It seems like an experiment worth trying." I adopted a serious tone.

She giggled and nodded, her cheeks filled with color. It

was the most gorgeous shade, like the sunsets over my *nonno's* vineyard. Everything about this woman made me think of home. But not the avarice or vanity or drama, only the best parts—the warmth, the beauty, the love.

"Do you want to find out?" I arched an eyebrow, tending to her with the washcloth. I was game if she was.

"It wouldn't be a bad way to go," she mused with a sleepy smile.

I sensed she was tired, and I could certainly do with some rest before round two. We were quiet a moment, both catching our breath.

"Thank you," she sighed, turning to look at me with a glazed smile.

I chuckled, a pleasant hum spreading its way through my limbs. "Do you always thank someone after having sex?"

She screwed up her features. "Um, no, actually. I think that was a first." She covered her face with her hands. "And that was…embarrassing."

"It was—" I pulled her hands away from her face, kissing her cheeks before straightening "—my pleasure." I smirked. "Thank *you*. I didn't hurt you, did I?"

She shook her head. "My ankle is fine, though I'm sure other places will ache later." She pulled her lower lip into her mouth, tantalizing me with that simple move.

I picked her up and carried her to the bathroom, where we showered—Harper sitting on the built-in seat while I stood—and then I wrapped her up in one of the bamboo robes. I swept her into my arms and carried her back upstairs, depositing her on the bed. A gentle breeze made the curtains billow, and she flopped back against the mattress with a satisfied smile.

I joined her and then used the phone on the nightstand to call down to the kitchen for some sustenance. While we waited for the food, I asked her about her bracelet. It was similar to a symbol my dad would often draw to remind me that progress wasn't always linear. And that everything I did took me closer to my goals, even if it didn't always feel like it. But surely…she couldn't have known that about me. No one knew that except Val.

We ate in bed, and I wasn't sure I'd ever done anything so hedonistic. It wasn't the food that made me feel that way; it was the company. The sense that we had all the time in the world, with nowhere to be and nothing to do.

A while later, Harper smoothed her hand over my back, her fingers tracing the patterns of my tattoos. I felt more relaxed than I had in a long time. She'd hesitate any time she came to one of my small scars but then quickly resumed her exploration. I lost track of time, of any cares I had until she said, "Tell me about your tattoos?"

She was quiet, the sound of the waves crashing in the distance the only noise. I opened my eyes and let out a deep breath. "What about them?"

"Well, I can read some of them." She ran her nail over my shoulder and down my bicep, the sensation both electrifying and soothing. "But I want to know why you got them. What they mean to you."

I rolled onto my back, giving her a better look. The sheet shifted, revealing her breasts. I trailed a finger over her shoulder, circling one nipple then another. Her skin was so beautiful, so pure compared to mine, which was covered in ink. I marveled at the differences.

"They're so fascinating."

I laughed, pulling her into my arms as I peppered her with kisses. "I think you're pretty fascinating."

She softened into my embrace, fitting perfectly. Everything about this—about her—seemed right. Which also seemed crazy. Even so, there was a connection I couldn't deny.

"Some are for my family." I released her and indicated to a few tattoos.

"Who's Sofia?" Her tone was hesitant, gentle, yet questioning.

"My mamma." I swallowed. Most people knew everything about my life, down to the brand of underwear I wore. Or at least they thought they did. It was almost *strange* to have to share about myself.

Harper slid her hand over my heart, her palm warm on my skin. "That's right. You're a mama's boy, aren't you?"

I chuckled and tucked my arm behind my head. "We're close, yes. Especially since my papà died."

"I'm sorry. Losing a loved one is never easy."

I nodded, swallowing back my emotion. "My father always pushed me to do better, be better. Without him," I sighed, "I wouldn't be the man I am today."

I could tell she had a million questions ready to burst from her lips. So, I said, "He's the one who encouraged me to become fluent in English. He's the reason I have this tattoo." I indicated to my chest. "To remind me of what I stand for."

She propped herself up on her elbow, studying my chest as she swirled her finger around the design there. "And what do you stand for, Enzo?"

My voice was low when I spoke. "*Quando finisce la partita il re ed il pedone finiscono nella stessa scatola.*"

She furrowed her brow, and I wanted to kiss away her confusion. "When you finish the game...the king and the pawn end up in the same box?"

"We all meet the same end."

"That's...true." I tried to read her expression and failed.

"In the end, money, power...none of it means anything," I explained. "The only thing that matters is how you treat people."

"Mm. Well, you've definitely treated me *very* well."

I chuckled, tracing her dips and curves with my finger. I'd never done something like this. With other women—at least early on in my career—it had been a quick fuck in the bathroom. A blow job beneath the table.

Even in the four years Giada and I were together, we'd had nothing close to the intimacy I felt with Harper. Intimacy was a luxury I'd never been able to afford, despite the millions in my bank account.

I settled over Harper, peering into her green eyes. They were so honest, so open, I wanted to drown in them and be reborn. I wanted to be the man she saw me as—one who was worthy of her time and attention.

My length nudged against her, and she sucked in a breath. "Enzo."

I angled my hips, wanting to be closer. "Yes, *uccellina?*"

"Is this…" Her eyes darkened, lips parting. "Is it always like this for you—the sex, I mean?"

I shook my head, pressing my lips to the pulse on her neck. "No." I rocked into her, as if to prove my point.

She closed her eyes on a groan, my cock sliding between her legs. She felt so good. So fucking good. And even though we'd had sex not that long ago, I needed her again. I wanted her again, so I told her.

"*Ti voglio ancora,*" I whispered into her hair, knowing how much she liked hearing me speak Italian.

"*Ti prego,*" she sighed. "Please, Enzo. I want you too." She dug her heels into my back as if spurring me on. She wanted me just as desperately as I wanted her.

Unlike the first round, I took my time, easing into her inch by inch. Her walls clenched around me, and I wanted to stay there forever.

"So, you have a brother who's in construction." I leaned back in my chair, the ocean breeze wafting over the cliff as crickets chirped nearby. "What's the rest of your family like?"

The candlelight flickered off Harper's face, her hair in loose waves that made her look even more relaxed. We'd just finished dinner, and as usual, the staff had gone above and beyond. I felt like a king.

I'd divulged more than enough and certainly more than I'd intended. I wanted to blame it on the wine, but I knew it was this woman. Something about her made me trust her, made me want to let down my guard. I could tell she was curious about me, but she was respectful enough not to pry.

"I'm from a small town in Northern California. My parents were high school sweethearts. My mom is a landscape architect, and my dad practices medicine. My brothers —" she rolled her eyes, though she was grinning the entire time "—are a mess."

I laughed. "Your family sounds lovely."

She was lovely. She'd come down to dinner wearing a patterned dress that flowed about her thighs, the neckline dipping low on her bronzed skin. Her feet were bare apart from the wrap around her ankle.

"They are," she said with a wistful smile. She toyed with her earring, the gold sparkling in the candlelight. "My dad loves to cook. Whenever I'm home, we have these huge Sunday dinners."

I smiled, wishing my dad were still alive. He'd been sorely missed both at family dinners and my games. He'd always been my biggest supporter. He'd pushed me, challenged me, both on and off the field.

"Do you visit often?"

"Whenever I can. It can be difficult with my hectic work schedule, but I'm supposed to visit later this summer for Dad's sixtieth birthday. What about you? What part of Italy are you from?"

I watched her a moment while she ate. Telling her where I was from didn't seem like such a big deal, considering how many million people lived there. "Milan."

"Will you return after your…business is concluded?"

"*Sì.*" Though I wasn't looking forward to it. The longer I was away, the less interested I was in returning. There were decisions that had to be made. Decisions I'd been avoiding.

"You don't sound too pleased about it."

I lifted a shoulder and sipped my drink so I wouldn't have to answer. "My life back home is fast-paced. Complicated."

She nodded. "I can understand that. Though, *Italy*," she sighed. Her smile was wistful as she peered out over the ocean. "Have you ever had fresh-squeezed orange juice from one of those funny machines?"

I laughed. "Does it taste any different from other freshly squeezed orange juice?"

"Maybe. I don't know. It's just more fun. It's all part of the experience." She grinned.

We talked for a while, of nothing and everything. The conversation flowed as easily as the wine. And it was the nicest evening I'd had in a while. Harper was well-traveled, intelligent, and kind. And it didn't matter what the topic was, she always had something interesting to contribute to the conversation.

"Thank you again for dinner," she said as the staff removed our empty plates. Then to no one in particular, she added, "That was orgasmically delicious."

I shook my head with a laugh. "'Orgasmically delicious?' What does that even mean?"

She grinned, her hair swaying about her shoulders. "You know, when a meal is so good it just...*ugh*." She clutched her stomach. "It hits all the right flavor notes, and it feels like an orgasm in your mouth."

"An orgasm in your mouth..." I rasped, my blood rushing straight to my cock as I repeated her words.

"Yep." Her cheeks took on the same hue as the wine.

"Mm." My lips tilted into a smile, the taste of her orgasm still fresh on my mind.

We'd spent most of the day in bed, only taking a break after lunch for a movie. The house had an amazing theater room, and I'd been happy to let her choose the film. Listening to her explain what went into the filming and the locations had been fascinating. And as someone who was often standing in front of the camera, I felt an even greater appreciation for what went into a photo shoot.

"Do you enjoy cooking?" she asked.

"My life doesn't leave much time for cooking. But I do love my *nonna's pasticcio*. It's—" I brought my fingertips to my lips and kissed them. "*Perfetta*."

"I'd love to have that recipe."

I chuckled. "I'm sure you would, but my *nonna* would kill me if I shared it."

She smiled sweetly and batted her eyes at me. "I'll do whatever you want."

"*Whatever* I want, huh?"

The image of her bent over the couch as I thrust inside her came to mind. As did the vision of me filling her mouth with my cock, her swallowing down my come. Talk about an orgasm in your mouth.

I shook my head and refilled my glass from the bottle of wine on the table before doing the same for Harper. "It's a family secret. The only people I'm allowed to share the recipe with are my wife or children. Though that will never happen."

"*Ever?*" She stared at me as if I were speaking a foreign language, though I was pretty sure I'd answered in English.

"Let's just say, I consider it highly unlikely."

That silenced her. An awkward tension settled over us, and I felt the need to say something. "What about you? I suppose you want it all—husband, white picket fence, two kids—a boy and a girl."

She lifted a shoulder but wouldn't meet my gaze. Finally, after a shaky breath, she said, "Well, yeah. I want to find love, a partner. I want—" she swallowed "—*wanted*, a big family."

I wanted to ask more, but before I could press her on it, she asked, "Do you know what's for dessert?" with a hopeful note to her voice, clearly desperate for a change of subject.

Considering how many times she'd let me off the hook about my life, I figured I owed it to her. So, I chuckled, hoping to lighten the mood as well. For someone so small, she had a big appetite. "I can't believe you're still hungry."

"I'm not. But there's always room for dessert. Oh…" She smiled as Koming approached the table with a tray of treats. "That looks so freaking delicious."

Koming went to place one before me, but I declined with a thank you. Harper eagerly accepted the affogato, and I delighted in her excitement.

"Thank you." She smiled then glanced over at me after Koming had left. "None for you?"

I shook my head. "I don't do sugar."

"Like…*ever?*" She sounded horrified.

I chuckled. "No."

"I mean, it explains why you look so good. But damn. I love sugar way too much to ever give it up." She attacked the dessert with her spoon. "And I *love* affogato."

What was not to love? I wondered, though I was

thinking more of the woman than the dessert. In less than forty-eight hours, she had thoroughly charmed me. Val might kill me for what I'd done, but in that moment, I knew I'd do it all again to have this time with Harper. Her presence calmed me, grounded me, in a way nothing else had in years.

"Have you done much exploring since you've been here?" she asked between bites.

I shook my head. It was embarrassing to admit, but my life was so hectic and privacy so rare, that I'd mostly relaxed at the house. Well, apart from a few excursions to town, which had always ended with me playing soccer with the kids.

Her question was a good reminder of what this was—a vacation fling. Nothing more. Even though it felt like more.

"Have you tried much of the local cuisine?" she asked.

"Why would I when I have a five-star chef on-site?"

"True." She tilted her head. "But it's fun to explore the local culture and food."

"What would you suggest?"

"Oh boy." Her eyes sparkled like they had when she'd talked about photography. "Where to start? Well, the market has some great finds. This dress and my earrings came from there."

I nodded, taking my time to appraise her. "What else?"

"Snake fruit. Have you tried it?" I must have made a face because she said, "Yeah. Weird name, right?"

"Yes. What's it like?"

"It looks like a snakeskin, which peels off like a lychee. Inside, it has a similar taste and texture to an apple."

That didn't sound so terrible.

"Maybe when my ankle is healed, we can go into town and find some."

I chuckled, her enthusiasm infectious. Was it the wine, or

was she always like this? I was coming to think it was just who she was.

As my *nonna* had always told me—you could tell what kind of heart someone had from their eyes. Harper's were filled with light. There was sadness, sure, but also a sense of wonder and delight.

After dinner, I handed her the crutches, and we walked to the edge of the pool. She set her crutches aside and relaxed into the lounge chair overlooking the ocean.

She turned to look at me, evaluating me. "I'm really enjoying our time together. Thank you. I know we didn't meet under the best of circumstances, but you're a good man."

I leaned closer to her, lured into her orbit. Even so, I felt the need to warn her. "I'm not who you think I am. And I find that people are typically only 'nice' when they think they have something to gain from it."

"Wow." She blinked a few times. "That makes me sad, Enzo."

I lifted a shoulder. "It's the way of the world."

"Is that why you invited me to stay here?" One of her crutches started to fall, and she leaned forward, giving me a clear view down her dress. She wasn't wearing a bra, and my cock jerked to attention. "What are you hoping to gain?"

Your silence.

Your forgiveness.

But for some reason, her opinion mattered to me more than anyone else's had in a long while.

CHAPTER SIX

Harper

"I have a surprise for you," Enzo said after I'd hobbled down the stairs to join him.

We'd spent the morning in bed together, but Enzo had been gone all afternoon—to where, I didn't know. In his absence, the staff had taken excellent care of me, and I'd enjoyed a gentle swim in the pool, some reading, and another movie.

"You do?" I smiled, unable to hold back my enthusiasm. I'd stopped offering to pay because I knew it only made him angry. I'd stopped fighting this thing between us too, whatever it was. I might as well enjoy it while it lasted.

"Mm-hmm." He grinned and gave me a kiss on the cheek. "And I hope you're hungry."

"Ooh, a surprise that involves food. I'm liking this more and more." I smiled as he pulled back, gesturing for me to lead the way to the kitchen.

A couple stood at the counter wearing matching shirts and aprons, their hair tidy beneath their black wraps.

"Good evening," the woman said, and they both smiled.

"Hello." I turned to Enzo, my excitement growing. "Ooh. Is this a cooking class?"

He nodded. I was so eager, I nearly jumped up and down before remembering my ankle. I smiled and took a seat at the kitchen counter so I could introduce myself to the chefs. Enzo joined me, his hand on my thigh. And after a brief lesson about Balinese cuisine and the ingredients, we set to work.

We sipped on Bintang beer and learned about the first dish. Every so often, Enzo would lean over to make a comment or kiss me, and each time, the warmth I felt toward him grew. The desire. As much as I was enjoying the class, I was looking forward to being alone with him even more.

After a while, we moved outside, where the chefs had prepared a fire. They demonstrated how to make banana leaf parcels and then placed them over the heat to cook. While we waited, Enzo joined me on the lounge chair, opening his legs and pulling me back against his chest.

The ocean crashed against the shore, and the smells wafting from the fire were intoxicating. We'd transitioned from beer to *arak*, another local beverage, though with a higher alcohol content. I'd tasted it before but hadn't remembered enjoying the licorice flavor this much. I couldn't remember enjoying anything this much in a long time.

I still couldn't believe Enzo had arranged something so special for me. I wasn't sure anyone—apart from my girlfriends—had ever taken the time to create an experience that I would want. Something unique and enriching. Something completely delicious.

I turned back to look at him over my shoulder and couldn't resist kissing his lips. They tasted of licorice and something sinful, and I smiled. "Thank you."

"My pleasure." He brushed my hair away from my face and kissed me deeply. Finally drawing back but only to capture my gaze. Something passed between us—an energy or intensity I didn't know how to describe, but he seemed to feel it too.

"Uccellina..."

"Dinner is served," one of the chefs said, pulling us out of the moment.

I smiled and dipped my head, while Enzo stood to help me up. We thanked the chefs, and then they left us to enjoy the meal.

I stared at the platter, taking one bite of an item before moving to the next. Enzo chuckled from beside me. "Maybe I should call you *colibrì* instead of *uccellina.*"

I tilted my head, the sunset lighting his skin in a way that made it appear golden. God, how I wished I had my camera right then. I could use my phone, of course, but I didn't want to ruin the moment, so I took a mental snapshot instead, filing it away for later.

"Colibrì?" I asked.

"Hummingbird. You're always flitting from one thing to the next." He sipped his *arak.*

I laughed, knowing it was true. "My family always jokes that I'm a serial hobbyist."

He furrowed his brow, and I would've laughed at his expression were he not so devastatingly handsome.

"I'm forever trying—and quitting—" I rolled my eyes "— new hobbies."

"Like what?" he asked.

I took a bite of the grilled fish, and it melted on my tongue. So, *so* good.

"What *haven't* I tried? Paddleboarding. CrossFit. Krav Maga. Barre. Yoga. Pole dancing…"

"Pole dancing?" Enzo coughed a few times. "Like a…how do you say…" He paused, searching for the correct word before saying, "Stripper?"

"Yes." I laughed, knowing it was a common reaction. "It's my latest obsession, but I do it solely for exercise. And I'm usually fully clothed. Well, as clothed as you can be in booty shorts and a crop top."

He swallowed hard, desire snaking its way between us. "How did you get into that?"

"One of my friends had a bachelorette party at a pole studio. I can't even tell you how difficult it is," I continued on. "Considering my other hobbies, I figured it would be a piece of cake." I shook my head, still remembering the frustration, the burn of my first few classes several years ago. "But it's an incredible rush, especially when you master something like the Ayesha."

And it was unbelievably empowering. It didn't matter what size you were, you could rock the pole. Pole dancing was one of the best things I'd ever done, helping me love and accept my body more than anything ever had.

"What's the Ayesha?" His shoulder brushed against mine as he leaned past me to serve himself some more curry.

"It's like you're doing the splits, upside down, on a pole. Here—" I pulled out my phone and navigated to a video of it.

"*Porca vacca.*" He stared at the screen, his mouth agape. "Is that you?" When I nodded, my cheeks heated, and he swiped a hand down his face.

"Yeah." I shook my head, sliding my phone back into my pocket. "It takes a lot of balance. And a lot of practice. But when you get it perfect, it's beautiful. Sorry." I shook my head, waving a hand through the air. "I'm rambling."

"I like listening to you talk," he said, stopping me in my tracks. I turned to peer at him, sincerity ringing through his words. He tucked a strand of hair behind my ear, his eyes darting between my own and my lips. "*Vola con le proprie ali.*"

"She flies…"

"She flies with her own wings," he said.

I blinked a few times, stunned by the compliment. We'd only known each other a few days, but Enzo understood me in a way no other man had. He'd planned activities he knew I'd love. When we shared meals, I knew he intentionally requested more dishes so I could sample to my heart's content. And in bed, he seemed to understand what I craved without my asking.

This vacation—this man—were exactly what I'd needed. And I didn't want it to end.

He refilled our glasses with *arak,* and the longer we sat there, watching the sun set and the moon rise, the more my inhibitions fell away. I didn't care that the staff might see us. I didn't care about anything but enjoying this moment. In a few days, we'd both be headed home, and I wasn't sure I'd ever see him again.

I wanted to. God, how I wanted this to be more than just a vacation fling. But I knew it was impossible. Enzo lived in Milan—it was one of the few things I knew about him. I was from LA. And the reason this worked so well was because we were living in a bubble. This wasn't reality. Hell, any time I tried to find out more about him, he clammed up. But it didn't matter because I was having fun. And I fully intended to keep having fun as long as I could.

"What about you?" I asked.

"What about me?"

"What are your hobbies?"

In all the time we'd spent together, he'd told me about his friend Val and his parents, but nothing about himself. Not really. He'd never told me about his job. He'd rarely offered any personal information. And I often hesitated to ask, seeing the way it put him on edge.

Was he a spy? Part of the mafia? A fugitive?

He was too hot to be a politician.

I wanted to laugh at my outlandish theories, but he was

quite skilled at being evasive, almost annoyingly so. Still, I felt like I knew him. Or at least, I wanted to believe I did.

He wiped his mouth with his napkin before setting it down. "My…job doesn't leave much time for hobbies. Like yours, it involves a lot of travel."

"But surely you have some downtime," I said, knowing that if I pushed too hard, he'd shut down. Or worse, the mood of the evening would be ruined.

He lifted a shoulder. "It's very rare. That's why vacation is so important to me."

"What would you do if you had time for a hobby?" I asked, sensing that was a question he might actually answer.

He seemed to consider it, leaning back in his chair and running a hand through his hair. When he still said nothing, I started throwing out options. "I know—pole dancing."

He shook his head with a laugh. "No. Though I am very impressed."

"Knitting."

He laughed again. "No. Definitely not. That's a *nonna* hobby."

"That's sexist."

"It's realistic. She tried teaching me as a boy, and I *hated* it."

I was the one laughing now. "Cooking?"

He shrugged. "Seems more like a chore, though I do enjoy it from time to time."

"Maybe we should narrow it down more. Would you rather do something creative or athletic?"

"Both."

I frowned. "Both?"

"Mm-hmm." He seemed to be enjoying this game.

"Okay. Leatherworking?"

He laughed. "How obscure."

I lifted a shoulder. "Italy is known for its leather craftmanship."

"True, but then you could argue that I should try glassblowing."

"Oh. I have." I perked up, straightening in my chair. "It's actually really hard."

He took another bite of the curry. "Of course you have. You've tried everything."

"Not everything," I said. There were still many things I wanted to try and hadn't.

"Okay. So if you didn't pole dance and travel for work and whatever else, what would you do?"

"What wouldn't I?" I asked, excitement filling me at the possibilities. "I'd love to learn about locksmithing. I'd like to try archery. BMX biking."

"You are a true philomath."

"Philomath," I repeated the word.

"A lover of learning."

"Look at you and your fancy words," I teased.

"I'm not just a pretty face, you know." He smirked.

"Oh, I know." I scanned his body greedily.

Even though we'd had more sex in the past few days than I'd had in the past few years, I still wanted more. I also wanted more information. I was curious by nature, and his persistent attempts to evade my questions weren't helping. We'd slept together. I was staying with him. And Enzo's lack of willingness to share much if anything only inflamed my desire to know more about him.

I reached for a banana leaf packet, and I knocked over the curry with my elbow, spilling it across my lap. *Ugh.* I squeezed my eyes shut. *Just great.*

"Uh-oh," Enzo teased as I dabbed at my dress. "Looks like someone's had a little too much *arak.*"

"Says the man who keeps refilling my glass." I glared at

him. "How the heck do you expect me to get back upstairs on my crutches?"

He chuckled darkly. "I don't."

"Enzo." I tossed a ball of rice at him. "You can't carry me everywhere."

He stared down at his shirt as if affronted. "And you can't throw food at me."

"Why not?" I grinned and balled up another bit of rice. He narrowed his eyes at me, daring me. And then I launched it at him.

"All right. That's it." He tossed down his napkin then picked me up, throwing me over his shoulder.

"Hey!" I was upside down, but I had a great view of his magnificent ass. "Put me down!"

Grass turned to tile, and I knew where we were even without glancing up—the outdoor shower. He set me on the bench beside it before switching on the water. This was insane. I was going to take an outdoor shower under a full moon with the hottest man I'd ever seen.

The breeze coming off the ocean was balmy and warm, and I giggled at the idea that I'd somehow manifested this week. Or maybe Lauren had. She was the one who'd said, "You never know what will happen." *Unbelievable.*

"What's so funny?" Enzo asked, stripping out of his shirt.

My mouth went dry, and I stopped laughing. *Nothing.* Absolutely nothing was funny about how sexy this man was. He was exactly what I hadn't known I'd needed. And I knew that even long after this week had ended, I'd relive the memories of my time in Bali with Enzo.

"I just—" I tried to stand but faltered—the alcohol and my injured ankle making me unstable. I sank down on the bench once more. "This week...you. I *really* needed it."

The shower dusted us with a light mist of water, and I just wanted to stay here a little longer. Make it last.

"So did I." He cupped my cheek, and he opened his mouth as if to say something but kissed me instead. It was gentle and lingering, the type of kiss that spoke of an impending goodbye. We still had a few days left, but I knew we both felt it—that sense that this was ending. Reality creeping in on us.

He helped me stand, stripping me out of my dress before setting me back down on the bench, this time beneath the spray of the water. He grinned when he realized I'd been naked beneath my dress, and I smiled when he stripped out of his shorts to reveal his naked form as well. I supposed we'd both known it would all end up on the floor anyway.

He stepped closer, and I couldn't take my eyes off him. I took him in my hand, and he seemed hypersensitive to my touch, or maybe that was just my imagination. I kissed the tip, exploring, and his eyes rolled back on a groan. It made me feel powerful, sexy, that I could unravel this strong man so easily. Especially when other men I'd been with had complained that my hands—or worse, my mouth—were too small. Enzo didn't seem to mind my size. In fact, he seemed to prefer it, judging from the nickname he'd given me.

"*Oh dio. Oh dio. Sì,*" he hissed when I licked him again, this time from root to tip.

I took my time, exploring him, lavishing him with attention. I'd never put so much effort into giving a man pleasure, and I felt like a goddess. At least until he pulled out of my mouth abruptly and with a loud pop.

I blinked up at him, wiping the corners of my lips. "Did I do something wrong?"

"No, *uccellina.*" His tone was gentle, even though his muscles were clenched. "But I don't want to come in your mouth. Not tonight. I need to be inside you."

He produced a condom from his shorts and slid it on. I bit back a groan at the sight of him, and he picked me up and spun us around so he was sitting on the bench. I was on his lap, guiding him to my entrance. "Yes, Enzo."

There was so much I wanted to say, and yet, I didn't want to ruin what little time we had left together. I needed to accept this for what it was.

I wrapped my arms around his neck and leaned back so I could see. He rubbed his erection along my opening, coating himself with my juices.

"Get inside me," I panted, watching where our bodies aligned.

"You want me?" he asked, and I nodded just barely, not wanting him to lift his forehead from mine. "Take what you want."

Where had the domineering man gone? Replaced by this softer version of Enzo. I liked both sides of him. Liked that he was willing to let me take the lead sometimes, but also assume control.

I wrapped my legs around his back, arms around his neck, and I pulled him closer. Right where I wanted him. Warm water cascaded down my skin, Enzo's hands mapping my curves. And we kissed beneath the full moon, our bodies and hearts connected as we cried out to the stars.

CHAPTER SEVEN

Enzo

The sun warmed my skin, waves lapping in the distance. Harper was dozing beside me, her e-reader resting on the chair next to her. She looked so peaceful, and I took a moment to study her. The curve of her back as it dipped to meet her ass. The smooth, tanned skin that tempted me to run my fingers over her thighs. To part them with my hands and take what I so desperately wanted again and again and again.

I'd never felt so relaxed as I did now, resting beside the ocean with Harper. Perhaps it was the daily massages or the beautiful woman at my side, but it had been years since I'd felt so at peace. And while a big part of that unease stemmed from the loss of my dad, I was beginning to wonder if breaking up with Giada had something to do with this shift.

The past six months, there'd been an unspoken tension growing between Giada and me. As if neither of us felt fully satisfied but were unwilling to do anything about it. She'd clearly wanted more than I was able to give—marriage, children. And I'd always wanted more in the bedroom. More sex.

More control. Just…*more*. But it had been too much for her, and I'd stopped asking long ago.

Harper seemed to have no problem with what I wanted. And every time I pushed, she gave just as good. She was still the same determined, headstrong woman I'd discovered in the dirt lane, but she also knew when to submit. To surrender control. It was fucking sexy.

My phone vibrated with a call, and I tried to ignore it. I didn't feel like answering. I was on vacation. Well, apart from the photo shoot anyway. But that was done, and now I could unwind. I'd done some research for my foundation, Success through Soccer. I hoped to use the sport of soccer to connect with disadvantaged youth and provide them with structure and confidence. In addition to recruiting promising talent, it would give me a chance to leave a more lasting legacy. Something beyond the trophies and awards.

But right now, all I wanted to do was relax. I certainly felt relaxed after the latest round of sex with Harper, but it still wasn't enough to quench my thirst for her.

If anything, every time I had her only made me want her even more. It defied logic.

I wasn't sure I believed in soul mates or even love, but I certainly believed in destiny and signs. Harper had been put in my life for a reason, and maybe it was just for our paths to cross for this brief moment in time. But I wanted to think there was more to it. I wanted to think there was more to us.

But if I wanted something more than just this week, I'd have to tell her who I really was. And part of me liked that she didn't know. Liked that I could be free to be myself, not put on a persona the world expected. A small part of me worried how she'd react if I told her the truth.

When my phone buzzed, I sighed. I was tempted to ignore it again, but when I looked at the screen, I saw several missed calls and texts from Val. I answered it hastily, not wanting to disturb Harper. I walked to the edge of the yard, the waves crashing below.

"Lorenzo," Val said, and her tone immediately put me on edge. "You can't keep ignoring my calls. You have no idea what's been going on here."

I frowned. "What is it? What's wrong?" I braced myself for news. I knew Val wouldn't have called so many times in a row unless something big had happened.

"Aurelio asked for a meeting."

I jerked my head back. Despite how many years I'd been on the team, I'd rarely met with the team owner, Aurelio de Luca. The idea made my stomach clench with dread. Aurelio was a busy man, and he didn't often take time out of his schedule to meet with players.

I glanced back at Harper, but she was still resting peacefully. Even so, I was careful to keep my voice low. "Did he say what it was about?"

"No, but I can guess. Haven't you been online at all?"

I shook my head before remembering she couldn't see me. "No." And I hadn't missed it. The scrutiny. The opinions.

"Nico didn't tell you?"

"No. He knows not to disturb me on vacation unless it's an emergency."

She let out a deep sigh, and I squeezed my eyes shut, my earlier calm vanishing. I was afraid to know if this qualified as an emergency, so instead, I asked, "Should I come home early?"

"Aurelio's out of the country for another week, maybe two. No point in cutting your trip short. For now, just...keep a low profile."

"Right."

I glanced at Harper over my shoulder but didn't dare mention the tempting American to Val. Who was I kidding, thinking this thing with Harper could continue beyond this week? There was no way I wanted to drag her into the chaos that was my life.

"THE DOCTOR SAYS MY ANKLE IS HEALING NICELY, AND I CAN start walking more," Harper said, sipping some orange juice.

We had two full days left together, and it was a relief that the doctor was pleased with her progress. I had plans for us tomorrow—a surprise I hadn't told her about. And despite the fact that we'd taken it relatively easy, I'd hoped all the sex hadn't put too much of a strain on her ankle. Fortunately, that didn't seem to be the case.

"*Bene*," I said, turning my attention to her. "Just be careful not to push yourself too much, at least at first."

"You sound like you have experience." She bit off a piece of bacon.

Harper was curious by nature, but I was impressed with her restraint. Whether she knew who I was or not—and I was convinced she didn't—she never pushed too far. She always respected my invisible need for boundaries, despite how open she was.

Funny how some of my favorite qualities in her were the ones most lacking in myself. That said, she didn't live the type of life I did back home in Milan. And that was what made this time—and her—so precious to me.

"I've had a few injuries, sprained ankle among them."

She nodded but said nothing more.

"So I know you had a few items on your vacation wish list before your injury. I hope you haven't been too disappointed about how everything has turned out."

She laughed. "Oh, I have not been disappointed *at all* by

this vacation." Though I knew she was really speaking about me.

"We've gotten massages." I ticked off one finger, listing the items from her vacation goals. "Lounged by the pool."

She sighed, and I assumed that she, like me, was thinking about last night, when I'd taken her *in* the pool. My dick started to harden, and I had to glance away from her before I dragged her back to bed once more.

"Since you've been cleared for more walking, would you feel up to visiting some local temples tomorrow?"

"I'd love that." She took a bite of her croissant, and it made me smile. I'd noticed she was in the habit of sampling everything on the plate. She was so eager, so excited about everything. "We could even go today, if you want."

"Ah." I leaned in and kissed her cheek. "We could, but I have other plans for us."

"Mm." She leaned into me, and I relished her touch. The feel of her in my arms. Time was slipping through my fingers, and soon, this week would be nothing more than a memory. "What kinds of plans?"

I could hear the smile in her voice, and in that moment, I saw forever. The two of us sitting outside just like we were, watching the sun set. Kissing beneath a starlit sky. Making love beneath the moon. I saw it all.

But it wasn't reality.

I was living in a fantasy, and I should enjoy it while it lasted.

She stood from her chair and straddled me. When she ran her fingers through my hair, I closed my eyes. My hands were on her hips. The scent of almonds and salty ocean air forever linked in my mind with Harper.

"Plans." I forced out the word, my mouth going dry as she started to grind against me.

"Do they involve the two of us," she whispered in my ear. It felt like she was everywhere. "Naked. In bed?"

I hovered over the vein in her neck, her pulse racing beneath my lips. I had the overwhelming urge to mark her skin, to brand her as mine. I'd never had this feeling with other women, this need to claim. But Harper seemed to bring out both the best and worst in me. She drove me to my basest desires, while making me want to strive to be a better man.

"Yes, but…" I swallowed hard. "Later. We have to leave soon."

"Are you sure?" She was just as insatiable as me. Last night, I'd woken to her mouth wrapped around my cock, the moon shining through the curtains.

"Don't tempt me," I chided. "I have a surprise for you, but it requires us being on time."

She kissed my cheek then stood, and I felt my body sag in her absence. If that was my reaction now, when she was still here, how would I handle saying goodbye?

"Okay. I'll brush my teeth and finish getting ready."

I nodded. "Good. The car leaves in twenty."

We took in the sights along the way, bypassing the town until we arrived at the family compound where we'd be taking the art class. Harper wasn't using the crutches, but she was supposed to limit the amount of walking she did. It was a big part of the reason I'd selected today's activity. She'd be able to sit, and I had a feeling it was something she'd love.

We followed one of the staff into the darkened room, and Harper immediately gasped.

"Oh, this is amazing." She spun around slowly, taking in the colorful cloths decorated by hand. "I love batik painting."

A man came over to greet us and introduced himself before giving us a brief history of batik painting. I'd seen the colorful designs around town and at Mizuki House, but I hadn't realized the amount of work that went into creating them.

Once he finished, he led Harper and me to a table where numerous designs were laid out. He explained some of the symbolism behind them as we traced our selected designs onto the fabric with pencil and then practiced outlining with wax.

"Wow, this is…harder than I expected," Harper said, her tongue poking out from her mouth. She was focused on canting—using the pen-like object to apply the wax to the design. And I was so focused on her, I didn't notice the wax seep through the material until it was burning my skin.

"*Merda*." I pulled back, nearly dropping the cloth.

"Are you okay?" Harper asked, leaning closer to check on me.

"I'm fine," I grumbled.

"Boy am I glad the assistants are canting the real design." She laughed. "Judging from the practice, mine would've been a hot mess."

"My fingers would've been a hot mess," I joked.

"Now *that* would be a shame." She gave me a meaningful look, filled with promise for later.

Harper smiled and chatted with our teacher as she selected her border stamp, asking insightful questions about the process. The next step was the actual painting, and we sat next to each other once more.

"I get the feeling you want something from me," she said as she concentrated on her design. "Considering how nice you're being."

I knew she was teasing, so I played along and leaned in to say, "Oh, there's definitely something I want from you."

"Enjoying yourselves?" the teacher asked.

"Oh yes." Harper nodded, her excitement clear. "I've always wanted to try this!"

"You want to try everything," I teased, trying not to laugh at the cheeriness of her voice.

"True, but this is… Thank you. It's amazing."

The teacher smiled at us, and I smiled at Harper. "My pleasure."

It was one of the cheapest—and most fun—dates I'd ever been on. And yet, I would've spent anything to bring her this much joy.

"These colors are amazing," Harper said, patiently painting her fabric. "I can't believe they're all made from flowers, vegetables, and minerals."

"Yes. I thought you'd like that. It's what distinguishes this batik painting studio from many others."

She nodded. "I do. The entire day has been incredible. Thank you. No one has ever done something so thoughtful for me."

She leaned over to give me a kiss, and I didn't even worry about the fact that someone could see it and photograph us. Here in Bali, I had a level of privacy and anonymity that I hadn't felt in years. I would be as sad to leave that as I was Harper.

"It's my pleasure," I said. "I'm happy to do it."

"Even so." She returned her attention to the batik. "You're spoiling me well beyond what we agreed to."

I shook my head, wishing she'd drop it. "I like spoiling you," I finally said, surprising myself.

She said nothing more, and we continued painting in silence.

"You seem contemplative today," she finally said, dipping her brush in the blue paint. "You okay?"

I selected some of the orange. It was vibrant and reminded me of her personality. "I find myself dreading my return home."

She let out a sigh. "Do you know why I choose the mandala?"

"No." I shook my head and continued painting.

"For Hindus, it's a spiritual symbol that represents the idea that life is never-ending and everything is connected. It's about going with the flow of life. About letting go of resistance and moving forward."

"And that's what you think we should do—let go and move on?" I asked.

She kept her eyes trained on her design. "I think it's the only option we have."

We were both quiet as we finished the rest of class. The designs popped even more after they'd been dunked in a solution, and I knew how that felt. This week with Harper had been like that baptism, and I didn't think I could go back to the life I'd known before. But I wasn't sure I had another choice.

The fabrics were stretched out to dry, the colors even more vibrant and striking. Harper spoke about photography, comparing it to the process of developing film. And I fell a little more under her spell.

When the fabrics were finally dry, I folded mine carefully and went to hand it to Harper, only to realize she was doing the same. We smiled at each other, and it was a bittersweet moment. An acknowledgment of what was to come.

"I made this for you," she said. "To say thank you for this amazing vacation. The mandala can also be a symbol of joy and healing, and you've definitely given me that this week."

I nodded, accepting the fabric from her. "*Grazie, uccellina. Ne farò tesoro.*" *I will treasure it, like I will treasure this time I had with you.*

"This is for you," I said, handing her my batik. "I choose the birds-of-paradise to represent my nickname for you. But also because they are a symbol of paradise, freedom, and joy. All things you've given me this week."

She smiled and quickly wiped away a tear. "Thank you, Enzo. I've loved every minute of our time together."

"Even the accident?" I teased, wrapping my arm around her waist to support her as we made our way back to the car.

"Okay. Maybe not that, but everything else. And I can't be too upset, considering what came out of it."

I nodded. I knew exactly what she meant. I could never regret our time together, even if I hated to see it end. She'd given me the mandala for a reason, and I needed to accept the message. It would soon be time to move on.

CHAPTER EIGHT

Harper

I was lounging in the pool when Koming and another woman appeared, both holding a large tray of food. Enzo had been gone before I woke, and I vaguely remembered him kissing my temple before leaving. It felt more like a dream than real life. Every day spent with him did.

I knew this wasn't reality, but damn, it was nice. I couldn't have asked for a better vacation fling. Everything about it was extravagant, from the home to the man, and I told myself to enjoy it while it lasted. Which wouldn't be much longer.

Today was our last full day together, and I wasn't looking forward to the end. The goodbye. The batik class had given me a preview of what it would be like, and I still didn't know how I was going to do it. Walk away, knowing I'd never see him again.

He hadn't hinted at exchanging phone numbers. Emails. Nothing. Not even yesterday when he'd mentioned the fact that he was dreading returning home.

Koming and the other girl set the tray on the water at the

other end of the pool and pushed it toward me. As my breakfast floated out to me, Koming said, "From Mr. Bianchi." She grinned, clearly delighted by my reaction.

My phone rang just as I caught one end of the tray, and I grabbed my phone from the side of the pool. Lauren, Alexis, and Juliana came into view.

"Where the fuck are you, and why wasn't I invited?" Lauren asked.

I laughed, shading my eyes from the sun. "Check this out." I turned the camera around, giving them a 360-degree view. The ocean. The house. The pool. The floating breakfast.

"Holy shit," Alexis said. "That house! I want a tour."

I laughed as I returned the camera to me.

Juliana frowned. "I thought you were staying at a resort. That looks more like a vacation rental." She paused. "Wait… does that belong to the guy you met?"

"What guy?" Lauren and Alexis asked at the same time. "There's a guy?"

"Actually…" I leaned closer, eager to share. I rarely got to gush about my sex life, at least not in the past year or so, and I couldn't wait to shock them. "It's been amazing. I—" I glanced around and lowered my voice "—I'm having the best vacation fling *ever*."

"I need details," Lauren said. "Is he a local?"

I shook my head. "No. An Italian."

"Oh god," she moaned, and I nodded emphatically. "Italians are so *passionate*. Does he speak to you in Italian?"

I bit back a grin and nodded. Just thinking of Enzo's accent wrapping around me, his unruly hair between my legs as he pleasured me, had my thighs clenching. I wanted to close my eyes and replay the images until I was certain they were cemented in my mind—the scent of the ocean perfuming the air, his warm skin on mine. The quiet of the seaside villa. I wasn't sure I'd ever been happier or more at peace.

"God, I bet that's hella sexy," Lauren said, fanning herself. "I love when Hunter speaks in French."

"What's he like?" Alexis asked me.

"He's…" I swallowed, trying to determine how to describe Enzo.

"What she means is how's the sex," Juliana teased. "Don't hold out on us."

I glanced toward the house, some of my hair falling into my face. "It's… He's…" I was tongue-tied even just trying to describe it. I'd never been with someone like Enzo. Everyone else paled in comparison. He was intense and passionate, rough at times, yet gentle when he wanted to be.

"Uh-oh. She's got that dreamy dick look in her eyes," Lauren teased.

"Dreamy dick?" I rolled said eyes. "I do not."

"What's his name?"

"Enzo," I sighed. Just thinking about him brought a smile to my face.

We talked a while longer, and then I went upstairs to get ready for the day. Enzo was supposed to return around lunch, and I was looking forward to visiting some of the temples.

"You ready?" Enzo asked when I met him downstairs. He pulled me into him, his kiss a claiming. "You sure we shouldn't stay here?" he murmured against my lips.

Tempting as the idea was, I wanted to experience the temples. And this was our last day together in Bali.

"Yes. I'm sure." I grinned and slung my bag over my shoulder before realizing how light it felt. Too light. "Shoot. I forgot my camera."

"I'll grab it." He turned toward the stairs and took them two at a time.

"Thanks. It's probably on the bed or maybe on top of my bag."

I smiled at Koming when she passed. She returned my smile but dipped her head. I wondered if she'd heard us having sex last night. I wouldn't have been surprised if everyone in the vicinity had heard. It wasn't as if we'd been quiet. My cheeks were warm, but it was the memory of last night that set my body ablaze. Enzo's hands. His mouth. His cock. I swallowed then glanced toward the stairs. *Where is he?*

"Enzo?" I called. I gave it another minute, assuming maybe he'd stopped to use the bathroom. "Enzo?" I called again, heading toward the bedroom. What on earth was taking so long?

I turned the corner and found him standing over the bed, staring at my camera. His jaw was clenched, his entire body rigid.

"What the hell is this?" he ground out.

At first, I thought he was joking. But when I realized he wasn't, I frowned. "What is what? Why are you looking at my photos?"

"Why do you have so many photos of me on here? *Eh?*" He waved the camera around, and my stomach lurched. That camera had been an investment, and he was making me nervous with his cavalier movements.

And it wasn't just the camera that was worth something to me; the images were too. I'd been so distracted, I hadn't gotten to upload them yet. And I really couldn't afford to lose the photographs. It wasn't just the photos for the production studio, but a number of images I planned to sell to the stock photo websites to help rebuild my finances after all the failed IUIs. I still hadn't decided what I was going to do next on that front, but having more money in the bank was never a bad thing.

"Answer me," he practically roared, ejecting the SD card.

Enzo was a passionate man, but I wouldn't have ever guessed him to be so volatile. So unreasonable.

Though I supposed seeing him throw his phone into the pool that first day should've been a red flag.

"Wait. Stop." My eyes darted between the SD card and him, my mind trying to catch up. "What are you talking about?" *What* photos?

"At the market. Playing soccer." He glared at me and pocketed the SD card but still didn't return the camera. "Who do you really work for?"

I stared him down, unflinching. I didn't know what the hell had gotten into him, but he had no right to treat me this way. "I told you. I'm a film location scout for a production company."

"*Cazzate.*" Before I knew what was happening, he'd backed me up against the wall, his arms bracketing me in, my camera strap dangling down beside my face. We were both panting. Blood thumping through my ears. The sound of my heartbeat telling me I was alive, though he was livid and didn't believe a word I'd said. "*Rispondi.*"

"Answer you *what*?" I ground out.

His eyes glittered with rage. "Tell me why you have photos of me!"

What was the big deal? Why was he so upset? It was just a few photos. I could easily delete them. He was blowing this way out of proportion.

Unless... *No.* I pushed away my ridiculous theories about Enzo's life.

"I was photographing the market. You happened to be there."

"And the soccer field?" His nostrils flared, and my own anger threatened to bubble over.

"I took a picture of a street vendor too. And a woman

carrying a basket on her head. And a basket-weaving shop. So what?"

He inched closer, and my body went into fight-or-flight mode. My instincts urged me to use my self-defense training, but I didn't want to escalate the situation. This was all just a misunderstanding. And I needed that SD card.

"And I suppose you also *happened* to sprain your ankle."

I scoffed. Like I would go to all that trouble, especially knowing what would come of it. Because there was no going back after this. He'd crossed the line the moment he'd threatened me. The moment he'd accused me of...whatever this was. *Lying?*

"What the hell, asshole? Who do you think you are?"

He put his nose against mine, his breathing hard. "Don't lie to me, *cara*," he sneered. "You know exactly who I am."

Cara was the equivalent of calling me "dear" or "darling," but unlike when he'd call me *uccellina*, it wasn't sweet or playful. It was a jeer. I'd seen many sides of Enzo this past week. Sexy. Caring. Kind. Playful. Domineering. But never this...*this* anger.

I shook my head, my eyes stinging. "I don't think I know you at all." He was cold, cruel.

I needed out. I needed... I stepped beneath his arm and started throwing my things into my suitcase as fast as I could. With every item, I grew angrier and angrier. I'd been a fool. Thinking we'd shared something special. Something meaningful. What a joke.

What an asshole!

I scrambled to pack my bag while he watched. His gaze was shrewd, as if I was going to steal something. I'd never felt so cheap. So used. I was done. *This* was over.

I slung my bag over my shoulder and held out my hand. "I want my SD card. I will erase every single image of you. You can watch while I do it."

Though I knew the bigger challenge would be erasing the image of him from my mind. The imprint he'd made on my body. But I'd certainly try.

He pointed at the door. There was a steely edge to his voice, and I got the feeling he was riding a thin line, his temper barely leashed. "I can't believe I trusted you. Get the fuck out of my house."

I stood my ground. "Not without my camera and that SD card."

He crossed his arms over his chest, unmoving. Anger radiated off him with such intensity I feared it would burn my skin. Even so, I wasn't willing to give up.

"I'll say this in a language you'll understand," I seethed. "*Dammi la mia macchina fotografica.*"

"*Lo vuoi?*" I watched in horror as he reared back and tossed my camera out the window. It went sailing over the balcony and landed with a sickening crash. "*Vai a prenderlo.*"

You want it? Go get it.

I shook my head, disappointment coursing through me. All that hard work—poof!—gone. He'd stolen my SD card. Destroyed my camera. And he had the gall to treat me as if I was the one who'd done something wrong.

"Fuck you." I pushed past him and headed for the stairs. I was done. I'd known the bubble would pop at some point, but it had just burst spectacularly.

"You're all the same. Fucking vulture," he spat.

I stopped at the bottom of the stairs and turned to look back up at him one more time. So much beauty and so much anger wrapped into one mysterious package. I didn't care how hot he was or how amazing the sex was, Enzo was a dick.

I gnashed my teeth, tightening my grip on my bag. "And you're an asshole. Goodbye, Enzo."

WEEKS PASSED, AND I COULDN'T STOP THINKING ABOUT ENZO or "the asshole," as I'd come to refer to him in my head. He was everywhere, haunting me. It didn't matter whether I was meeting the girls for brunch in LA or talking with a client on-site in Croatia. Enzo was never very far from my mind. And I was mad—at him, at myself.

None of it made any sense. His freak-out or the things he'd accused me of. But my body didn't know that. It still craved his touch. His whispered words. His heated gazes.

I was better than that. Better than him.

I flopped down on my couch and switched on the TV. I had a million things to do, but I couldn't seem to find it in me to care. So, I lost myself in a show about dream weddings. I cried in every single episode, but the couples' stories were so beautiful, as were the weddings they created. And hearing the show's chef speak, his words ringing with his Italian accent, reminded me of Enzo, which only made me cry even more.

I covered my face with a throw pillow and screamed into it. Why was he still haunting me?

I told myself it was because of what we'd shared. It was intense and amazing. But it was overshadowed by how he'd treated me at the end. I didn't want to think about him anymore. I'd buried the batik he'd painted for me in the back of my closet. Why couldn't I bury my feelings for him?

Another month came and went. I hadn't gone on any dates, unless you counted a few events Crew had talked me into attending. I hadn't even thought about my fertility situation. Most days, it felt as if I was barely keeping my head above water. Something had to give.

With a heavy sigh, I shuffled up to Alexis's house. I was so tired, I'd almost skipped out on brunch. But I knew I couldn't. No matter what else was going on, the four of us had always made the effort to get together at least once a month.

"Harper." Alexis smiled when she opened the door. "Hey. Wow. Those look amazing." She took the box of donuts from me and offered a hug. "Come on in," she said, ushering me toward the kitchen.

I hugged Lauren before taking a seat on one of the barstools. "Bellini?" she asked as Juliana smiled, releasing the cork on a bottle of champagne with a loud "pop." I shook my head.

"You okay?" Juliana asked, concern creasing her brow. "You look…pale."

"I just—" I inhaled deeply and then held my breath, trying to suppress the nausea. "I haven't felt great since I returned from Croatia last week. I think I must have eaten something that didn't agree with me."

I couldn't even be tempted by the donuts from my favorite bakery. The entire car ride over, I'd felt sick to my stomach from the overly sweet smell.

"Hmm," Lauren chimed in. "I'd think anything you ate in Croatia would be out of your system by now."

I lifted a shoulder. I hadn't felt well for weeks. I was tired and nauseated, and I didn't seem to have the energy or desire to do much of anything. I'd been traveling nonstop, jet-setting across the world. And though I'd been doing this for years, the pace was beginning to wear on me. *Am I getting old?*

Alexis tilted her head, her gaze shrewd as she assessed me.

"What?" I snapped.

"Nothing." She smiled, and I could tell she was only trying

to be nice. It made me feel like even more of a bitch. I'd been short-tempered all week.

"I'm sorry." I hung my head. "The jet lag, stomach bug, or whatever… It's got me down."

"Are you about to get your period?" Juliana asked. "I know I'm always a little off when it's time for mine."

I paused, glass of water poised in midair. I did some quick mental calculations, slowly setting the glass back down. I should've had my period weeks ago. I'd been so preoccupied and busy, I hadn't even noticed.

I stared straight ahead. *How had I not noticed?*

"Ooh, girl," Lauren said, popping a strawberry into her mouth. "I know that face. You're late, huh?"

I bit my lip. "Yeah. I mean, maybe. But with all the fertility drugs and stuff I was taking, my cycle could just be out of whack."

"Have you slept with anyone lately?"

I rolled my bottom lip between my teeth and shook my head. "Not since…" I couldn't even bring myself to say his name. My girlfriends had assumed it had ended because it was a vacation fling, and I'd let them believe that because it was easier than the truth.

"But you and Enzo used condoms, right?"

"Yes. Of course."

"Every time?" Juliana asked.

I nodded, remembering how religious Enzo had been about using them.

"You had a lot of sex. Maybe one of the condoms broke?" Juliana asked.

I shook my head. "No. Not that I know of."

"You used to track your ovulation, right? You should see if you were ovulating when you were in Bali," Alexis said.

I pulled out my phone and skimmed through the calendar, stopping short. Yep. I definitely could've been ovulating.

Alexis leaned over, staring at the screen before brightening. "Oh my god. You could be pregnant."

I shook my head. Even though I wasn't on birth control, I didn't see how it was possible. "We used condoms. And even if we hadn't, I had three unsuccessful rounds of IUI. *Three.*"

"Yeah, but that'd be like Preston and me trying for three months. Even if I was ovulating, there's no guarantee I'd get pregnant."

I frowned. I'd never thought about it like that, but I didn't think it was the same. I'd been taking drugs to enhance my fertility. And my doctor had attempted the inseminations under the best possible circumstances. If I couldn't get pregnant in an ideal situation without condoms standing in the way, why would this be any different?

"Why don't you take a test? Just to see," Alexis added. "I have some upstairs."

I lifted a shoulder, considering it highly improbable. "Wouldn't I know if I were pregnant?"

Alexis and Lauren shared a knowing grin before Alexis said, "Not necessarily. When I was pregnant with Blair, I had no idea."

"Please," Juliana said to me. "Just to put our minds at ease."

"I don't see the point, but sure." I shrugged, too tired to fight it. "Why not?"

A few minutes later, I'd peed on a stick and washed my hands. I didn't wait for the results—what would be the point? Still, the minutes clicked by slowly until Juliana's gasp rang out from the bathroom.

"You're pregnant." When I said nothing, she came over and set the test on the coffee table before taking my hand in hers. "Harper, you're going to be a mom!"

I shook my head, still refusing to believe it. There might be two blue lines, but that didn't prove a damn thing.

"Were you exhausted last time?"

I frowned at the test where it sat on the coffee table, feeling their eyes on me. Juliana squeezed my hand as if to punctuate her statement before releasing me.

"Were you ever nauseated? Breasts tender?" Alexis asked.

I furrowed my brow. "No. But—" I turned away. "It doesn't mean anything."

I'd fallen for this before, gotten excited only to be devastated. And this time, it felt as if there was so much more at stake. This wasn't a random sperm donor I'd never met. I'd slept with someone. A man I couldn't stop thinking about, a man I now despised.

"I think you should make an appointment with your doctor," Alexis said.

"Why? It's probably just another chemical pregnancy," I said again, even though a twinge of doubt prickled my mind. *Could I actually be pregnant?*

Alexis was right. I had been nauseated, exhausted, moody. My breasts were tender, feeling as if my bra was squeezing them when it never had before. I had these crazy dreams that felt *so* real, and then I'd wake up confused and disoriented.

I was miserable, but I'd chalked it up to jet lag, work, sadness. And bloating. Whenever I traveled, I didn't eat as healthily as I liked, and sometimes, yeah, there was bloating. Now I wondered if what I'd thought was bloating was actually a baby growing inside me.

No. I shook away the thought. It was impossible. *Right?*

That night, I went home and opened a new browser window. I'd thought about doing this a million times, but I'd always talked myself out of it. With a deep sigh, I typed the name "Enzo Bianchi" into the search box and held my breath as I waited for the results to populate.

When they finally did after what felt like forever, I frowned. Page after page about a man in his seventies, the founder of a monastic community. *Okay.* Definitely not my Enzo.

I shook my head. He wasn't mine. He'd never been mine. But now that I might be carrying his child, I could no longer ignore the fact that I'd slept with him. And if I really was pregnant...well... I sagged. I'd cross that bridge when I got there.

I continued scrolling. The results on the second page were no closer. Nor the third.

What the hell? Did he lie about his name?

I would've tried Lorenzo or Vincenzo, but unlike Americans, Italians didn't shorten their names. Not for something like Enzo, which was a proper name itself. Even so, I figured it was worth a shot to search for Lorenzo or Vincenzo paired with the last name Bianchi. I tried both, feeling more hopeful, but neither yielded anything. And just like the night we met, I was left wondering, *who the hell is Enzo Bianchi?*

CHAPTER NINE

Harper

"Hey." Juliana was breathless as she sank down into the chair next to mine. "Sorry I'm late."

"No worries," I said, flipping the page of the magazine. I'd opted for the home design one over the parenting one. No use getting my hopes up. "Dr. Fulton's running a little behind."

She nodded, setting her tote next to her on the floor and pulling out a bottle of water.

"Busy day?" I asked.

She shook her head with a laugh. "Like you wouldn't believe. Ooh." She leaned forward, swiping a bridal magazine from the table. "Score! Your doctor has the good magazines. Good magazines but crappy schedule. I don't know how on earth you waited two weeks for this appointment."

I lifted a shoulder. "I didn't really have a choice. Dr. Fulton's pretty booked, and I don't have much leeway in my schedule at the moment either."

I'd been so swamped and exhausted, I hadn't even had time to do any digging on Enzo. That wasn't entirely true. I'd been scared to discover the truth, so I'd continued living in denial. Until Dr. Fulton confirmed the pregnancy—if she even did—there was no point wasting any more time on that man. Even in the name of research.

"Yeah, but girl, the suspense is killing me." She butted my shoulder with hers.

"I thought you *knew* I was pregnant." I repeated the motion to her.

"I do. I'm waiting for you to realize it's true." She seemed so convinced, but my mind kept going back to the condoms. I mean, what were the odds?

I rolled my eyes and flipped the page. "Mm-hmm. Okay."

"Have you thought about what you're going to do about Enzo?"

I shook my head, my stomach roiling. "No. No use thinking about it unless Dr. Fulton confirms the pregnancy."

And then, I had absolutely no clue. I didn't even know who Enzo really was or how to get in touch with him. Or if his first name even was Enzo. And if I'd had a way to contact him…I wasn't sure I wanted to. Not after the way he'd treated me.

Painful as it was, I'd replayed our argument dozens of times, searching for clues. Hints as to why he'd reacted the way he had. As to who he really was.

"Harper, are you okay?" Juliana's tone was gentle.

I nodded. "Yeah. Just anxious about this appointment."

Perhaps sensing I was desperate for a change of subject, she asked, "What about Crew? Are you still planning to go to the event with him this weekend?"

I nodded. "Yeah. He knows we're just friends." Though he'd been hinting at more lately. I'd just come from lunch with him, and he'd dropped me off at the hospital, buying my story that it was a routine appointment. He was such a nice guy, and I felt awful for lying to him.

"Want to go shopping for a new dress?"

I shook my head. "I'm just going to wear something I already have."

"You know what you need?"

Oh, there were so many things I needed. Where to start…

"Some pampering. Let's have a spa day before the event."

While that sounded tempting, I didn't have the time or the money for a spa day. I'd had to replace the camera Enzo had broken. Fortunately, I'd had just enough time to go back with my phone and retake all my photos of the film locations I'd scouted. It wasn't ideal, but luckily my boss had been understanding when I'd told her my camera was stolen.

Because of Enzo, I'd nearly lost my job at the studio in addition to all those stock photos. Even now, the reminder made me sick to my stomach.

I'd been slowly chipping away at the medical bills from the IUI, but I didn't want to spend recklessly, especially not if I was, in fact, pregnant. Despite Juliana's conviction, I still had my doubts. The absence of my period should've been enough to convince me, but I'd been disappointed too many times in the past to get my hopes up.

"My treat," Juliana added, continuing to type on her phone. "Alexis and Lauren say they're in. They'll meet us at the house later."

Before I could respond, Dr. Fulton's nurse, Sylvia, peeked her head out from the back. "Harper. You ready?"

I stood and Juliana followed me. "Hey." I smiled at Sylvia. "This is my best friend, Juliana."

"Welcome." Sylvia led us to an exam room.

I peed in a cup then talked through my symptoms with Sylvia before she left. She seemed cautiously optimistic, but I didn't want to read too much into it. The past few days, I'd been working long hours and sleeping any chance I got.

"Did I tell you what Marie asked for now?" Juliana asked

from her seat near the door. I knew she was trying to distract me by talking about her latest Bridezilla client. And while I appreciated it, I was too on edge to think straight.

I shifted on the exam table, the paper rustling beneath me. Before I could answer, there was a knock at the door. Dr. Fulton entered, Sylvia trailing behind her. It had been months since my last appointment, and we hadn't spoken in all that time.

"Hi, Harper. It's good to see you." Dr. Fulton washed her hands and then moved the sheet covering my stomach aside. "Let's see what we've got going on."

She squirted some gel on my belly and then gently pressed with the sonogram wand. An image appeared on the screen, a small blob indicating there was indeed a baby in my womb.

"Congratulations, Harper." Dr. Fulton flashed me a radiant smile. "You're pregnant."

The room spun, and I gripped the edge of the exam table to steady myself. Still, I wasn't ready to believe it. "Are you sure?"

She glanced at the screen then back at me with a wide smile. "You can see right here." She indicated on the screen and launched into some medical terminology that went in one ear and out the other. "Oh, I'm so happy for you." She wiped my stomach and covered it with my shirt. "It looks like you're about ten weeks along."

I sat up, swinging my legs over the edge of the table, and gaped at her. Ten weeks? If that was correct, my first trimester was almost over and I'd been completely oblivious. *More like, in denial.*

"This can't be..." I sucked in a jagged breath, spots dancing before my eyes. "This isn't..." I started again. "Possible. We used condoms. *Every* time."

Dr. Fulton's smile was sympathetic. "Condoms can be expired. Defective. They can tear."

Juliana placed her hand on my back, rubbing circles. But the movement only made me even more nauseated.

"I'm going to—" I stood, but it was too late. I emptied the contents of my stomach all over Dr. Fulton's gorgeous Manolo Blahnik heels. "Oh my god." I covered my mouth. "I'm so, *so* sorry."

"Now do you believe us?" Juliana asked.

I nodded, though deep down, I wondered why I hadn't realized I was pregnant. Wasn't that a mom thing—sensing your child? Alexis didn't seem to think so, but I wasn't sure what I believed. What did it say about me that I hadn't had a clue? That I was already a terrible mom, or that—yet again— I was getting my hopes up for nothing?

"Let me go get changed," Dr. Fulton said, seemingly undisturbed by the vomit covering her designer shoes. "And then we can discuss what's next. Sound good?"

I nodded, still afraid to uncover my mouth.

While she was gone, I rinsed my mouth in the sink but said nothing. Juliana sat quietly at my side, and when Dr. Fulton returned, we discussed how I was feeling. I only heard half of what she said about prenatal care and vitamins, my mind was still spinning. And then she asked if I wanted to hear the baby's heartbeat.

My own heart was pounding, the word "Yes" lodged in my throat. This was it—the moment of truth.

I couldn't speak. Even when Juliana squeezed my hand, all I could do was nod. Sylvia handed Dr. Fulton a Doppler after asking me to lie back. Dr. Fulton lifted my shirt and held the device to my stomach. And then…the most wondrous sound filled the room—like a wild horse racing across the desert.

I smiled through my tears as the realization hit me full force. "I'm going to be a mom."

Juliana squeezed my hand and flashed me a watery smile as Dr. Fulton moved the Doppler around my stomach. Her brow furrowed when the sound stopped.

"What's wrong?" I asked, my pulse racing.

When the galloping resumed, she smiled. My shoulders, every cell in my body, relaxed. The stress and exhaustion of the past few weeks faded into nothing but joy.

"Nothing. Everything sounds very good. Healthy."

"I-I…" I swallowed, the enormity of the situation crashing down on me. Oh. My. God. I was having a baby. *Enzo's* baby.

If Enzo was even his real name.

I frowned as Dr. Fulton switched off the Doppler and asked me to sit up.

"What's wrong?" Juliana asked.

I shook my head, blinking away tears. "Nothing," I lied. "I'm just trying to process it all."

Dr. Fulton smiled. "For now, just enjoy. We'll see you again next month. In the meantime, you'll want to start thinking about what genetic testing you might want to do, if any."

"Any recommendations?"

"I'll have Sylvia send you some information. But I suggest talking with the baby's father to see what his family medical history is. That knowledge can help you make a more informed decision when it comes to genetic testing."

It felt as if my head was going to explode. *Me.* I was going to be a mom. *Holy shit.* But even more than that, one thought overrode all others: who the hell was the father?

I mean, I knew who he was, obviously. But…I knew nothing about him at all. And this appointment had made my complete lack of knowledge about Enzo all the more apparent.

I was grateful Juliana had come because I spent the rest of the time in a daze. I barely heard anything as I checked out and scheduled my next appointment. And there was no way I could concentrate to drive.

"Come on," Juliana said, pulling me into her side.

I was pregnant. *Pregnant!*

I kept staring at the images from the sonogram, checking the details. It was my name. My date of birth. My…baby.

When we got to her house, I followed her inside. Harrison came out to greet us, giving me a hug before pulling Juliana into his arms. He murmured something in her ear, and I had to look away from the private moment. I was happy for Juliana—for all my friends—but watching them with their significant others only reminded me of the things I ached for—love, a partner, a family.

It made me realize that I didn't just want a baby. Now that I'd had a glimpse of what life could be with Enzo, I wanted it all. Or at least I had until he'd ruined it.

And while I'd planned to do this alone, now that it was actually happening, everything seemed so daunting. Hollywood maternity leave was a joke. In the film industry—both on the screen and behind the scenes—women lacked equality to an appalling degree.

Juliana's phone pinged, and Harrison released her so she could check it. "I'll be right back," Juliana called before disappearing down the hall.

"Can I get you something to drink?" Harrison asked.

"Sure." I took a seat on one of the barstools, realizing how rude my tone seemed. "I mean, a water would be great. Thank you."

He filled the glass and set it in front of me, resting on his elbows on the other side of the bar. I laughed, thinking how it felt as if he was a bartender. And then it hit me—I couldn't drink. For nine months. Or seven, now. *Whatever.*

"You okay there?" he asked, perhaps noticing the slightly hysterical note to my laughter.

"I, um…" I hesitated a moment but figured Juliana would tell him anyway. "I'm pregnant."

His smile was warm and reassuring. "I'm guessing it was a surprise, based on your demeanor. How do you feel about it?"

I sagged on the stool, grateful he hadn't immediately jumped to offering his congratulations or glossing over the situation. Harrison was intuitive, older, and wise. He also had an amazing daughter he doted on, as well as a son-in-law and grandchildren he adored.

"I'm still trying to decide. I've wanted a baby for so long. And I was prepared to go it alone, but this…" I shook my head, still trying to process everything. "I wasn't expecting this."

He nodded. "Welcome to parenthood, where nothing goes as expected."

I laughed. "Yeah?" But then tears pricked my eyes. This was *happening*. I was going to be a member of the club—*finally*.

"You're going to be a great mom," he said, placing his hand over mine. He met my eyes, and I knew he meant every word.

"Thanks," I said as he retracted his hand. "That means a lot. You did a good job with Olivia."

He chuckled, leaning back against the counter. "I'd love to take credit for that, but it's all her. She was always a good kid, and I'm proud of the woman she's become."

I nodded, taking a sip of my water. I hoped that one day I'd feel the same about my own child. I hoped I would be able to raise them well and that they'd want me to be part of their lives even when they were an adult.

"Hey." Juliana breezed back into the room. "Sorry about that."

I smiled. "No problem."

"I'm going to head out," Harrison said. "I'm meeting Crew, Reg, and some of the guys for dinner. We're supposed to talk about that fundraiser next month."

"That's tonight?" Juliana asked.

"Yeah, but we'll get together with the WAGs another time."

I tilted my head to the side. "WAGs?"

"Yeah." He chuckled. "Wives and girlfriends."

"I still think it should be wives and partners," Juliana said.

"Right." He chuckled. "Because I'm sure you'd *love* being referred to as a WAP."

I cringed, though it was funny. "The man has a point."

Juliana shook her head, then turned to Harrison. "You want to invite them here another time? We could do something out back."

"I'd love that." He gave her a peck. "Love you."

"Love you too." She smiled, her eyes never leaving him even as he walked away. It wasn't until the door to the garage closed that she returned her attention to me.

"Ah, to be a newlywed." I grinned, propping my chin in my hand.

"This look—" She pointed to her face in a circular motion. "This is how you looked any time you talked about Enzo."

My face fell. "Yeah. Before I realized what an asshole he was."

She tilted her head to the side. "Huh?"

I cringed. I hadn't meant to let that slip out, but luckily the doorbell rang, saving me. I rushed to answer it, assuming it would be Alexis and Lauren.

"Oh, Harper." Alexis wrapped me up in a hug. "I'm sure you have so many emotions right now, but being a mom is the best."

"Thanks."

"How are you feeling?"

"Like a hot-mess express."

She laughed, and Lauren gave me a hug. "Well, then it's a good thing we brought the spa to you."

"What?" My eyes darted toward the door, where several people were carrying in footbaths and massage tables and suitcases. "I feel disgusting."

"You won't by the time we're through. It's girls' night in," Lauren said.

The food arrived, and Lauren, Juliana, Alexis, and I ate while they finished setting up. Fortunately, we'd been too preoccupied for Juliana to press me about what I'd said earlier—about Enzo being an asshole.

"So, have you thought at all about how this will affect your travel schedule?" Alexis asked.

I choked on my food, coughing a little before taking a sip of water. "I haven't even… I haven't thought that far ahead. I'm still kind of reeling, to be honest."

I turned to Juliana, trying to remember any of the conversation. "What did Dr. Fulton say about it?" I racked my brain for answers, but none came.

"To email with any questions," Juliana said, and I appreciated her even more for going with me to the appointment.

"Please tell me you're going to find out if you're having a boy or girl," Lauren said.

I laughed. "Probably. I don't know."

"I get to plan your baby shower, right?" Juliana asked.

"Of course. I mean, that's still months away, though."

"Yes. But it's never too early to begin planning. You should start working on your guest list—coworkers, friends, family."

My eyes went wide as I was hit with a sudden realization. "Oh my god. I'm going to have to tell my parents."

Lauren smiled. "Girl, your parents are going to be so excited."

I appreciated Lauren's enthusiasm, but I had my doubts. "I'm not so sure about that. I doubt they'll be very pleased when they realize I got pregnant from a vacation fling, and the father wants nothing to do with me or his child."

My girlfriends frowned, then Juliana gave me a sympathetic smile. "You haven't even told Enzo. You can't possibly know how he'll react."

I'd been holding this knowledge in for weeks, and I couldn't take it anymore. "I don't know how to contact him," I blurted, finally admitting the horrible truth. "I don't even know if Enzo is his real name." I covered my face with my hands, shame coating my skin like the sunscreen I'd used in Bali.

"Wait." Lauren rubbed her forehead. "Back up."

So, I did. I told them everything. How Enzo and I had met. How it had ended. When I finished, it was so silent, you could've heard a pin drop. I braced myself for their reactions.

Finally, Juliana said, "Well, you were right. He *is* an asshole."

My friends weren't judging me as I'd feared. They were enraged on my behalf.

"An asshole who's now the father of my child. I mean, ignoring the fact that he deserves a right to know…"

"Whoa. Whoa." Lauren held up a hand. "Considering the way *he* treated you, he doesn't deserve anything from you apart from contempt."

I appreciated her anger, but still. "I'm pissed, but I have to think about my child. What am I going to tell them when they're older?" What was I going to tell my family? "God, this is such a mess." I shook my head, tears falling as the reality of my situation sank in.

I'd gotten my wish—I was pregnant. And while I wanted to enjoy it, all I could do was despair. My life was such a disaster.

CHAPTER TEN

Enzo

"Would you like a drink, sir?" a passing waiter stopped and asked.

I shook my head and thanked him, returning my attention to the hotel ballroom. The colors of Los Angeles's major league sports teams were splashed across the tables, and athletes and celebrities paraded around the room. I'd been invited to attend by the LA Leatherbacks—the soccer team that had offered a generous sum for me to transfer from Milan FC. A move I was still debating, though I wouldn't have much longer to decide.

The contract was for a little over a year. They wanted me to join them this season and finish out the next one. And then we'd have the option to renew.

What would Dad have thought?

Despite his insistence that I learn English, he'd always instilled pride in our Italian heritage. I'd only ever played for an Italian team. I'd even played for the Italian national team in several World Cups, but we hadn't won.

And that had always been a dream of ours—winning the World Cup. It was still a dream, though the window for accomplishing it was closing. I was thirty-eight, and this year's cup was probably the last chance I'd have.

I worried that transferring to the Leatherbacks would hurt my chances of being selected for the Italian national team. That said, the move to LA would give me more exposure. More field time. And considering the short-term nature of the contract and the fact that I was nearing retirement age, I felt honored that the Leatherbacks were so intent to have me join their team.

I just hoped Dad wouldn't see it as a failure.

I let out a sigh. I needed to focus on the event, not that I was doing a very good job of it at the moment. I was so distracted, I could barely remember my reasons for attending. Though that was nothing new. Ever since returning from Bali almost three months ago, my focus had been shit.

I glanced at my phone, unable to stop myself from checking Harper's Instagram feed. It was something I'd done regularly since returning from Bali, but especially the past few days upon arriving in LA. I was being courted by the LA Leatherbacks, but Harper was all I could think about. The more time that passed, the more I was convinced that she'd been telling the truth.

She'd posted some photos from our trip, though none of me. They were all of the scenery or the pool at Mizuki House, but nothing that would give away my identity. Since Bali, she'd shared a few pictures of a fishing town I couldn't place. Ocean views and terra-cotta roofs. And more recently, there had been a few photos of brunch food, some street art I assumed was in LA, but after that...nothing. Nothing for almost a month.

If Harper was going to post something about me, wouldn't she have done it by now?

I'd taken her SD card, but I'd been so irate, I hadn't considered the possibility of pictures on her phone until after she'd left. Nearly three months had passed, and she hadn't shared any, which meant she either wasn't planning to or she'd never had any in the first place. Either way, I was coming to realize I'd made a terrible mistake.

Desperate for more, I'd taken to scanning her entire feed. I'd done it so often, I'd practically memorized the images. Pictures of her smiling with those green eyes that had captivated me. Harper standing on a yacht with some friends. A white bikini showcasing that gorgeous body that made my mouth water.

I told myself I was doing it out of self-preservation, but my curiosity had turned into a sick obsession. I checked her feed almost daily, just as I was now.

I let out a deep sigh. I did *not* want to start the season like this. I needed to rid myself of distractions. That was why I'd gone to Bali in the first place—to clear my head and get away from it all.

And then I'd met Harper, and she'd given me a taste of freedom unlike any other. She'd acted like she had no idea who I was. Maybe she really didn't. I wanted to believe it was true—both in Bali and since. But then again, Giada had lied to me repeatedly, and I'd never suspected it.

"Lorenzo," a man's voice boomed. I slid my phone into my pocket and glanced up to find Knox Crawford, the owner of the LA Leatherbacks, approaching me with a smile on his face. "There are a few people I'd like you to meet."

"Of course." We shook hands, and I followed him over to where a small group had congregated.

"I'm glad you decided to take me up on my offer to check out the city and the team," he said before we joined the others. "The transfer window is closing soon. We'd be thrilled to have you join us. We're always looking to bring in new talent, especially of your caliber."

The final decision rested with me, but I was under an

immense amount of pressure to make the switch. After transferring to Milan FC a few years into my career, I'd spent the bulk of my time with them. I'd never considered transferring again, at least not until this opportunity had come along.

The negotiated transfer fee was sixteen million dollars, one of the highest sums in Major League Soccer. Considering my age and a chronic injury that had been flaring up since last season, I was lucky.

Fortunately, everyone was more focused on the potential transfer—and not just in Italy and LA. All over the world, people weighed in on whether I should make the switch, sometimes with very heated comments. I tried to ignore all the chatter, but it had been so loud lately it was nearly impossible.

"Thank you. I—" I froze.

A woman with chestnut hair stood out from the crowd, her bee-stung lips parted in a smile as she talked with a tall blonde in killer heels. I blinked a few times, positive I was dreaming. But there she stood, laughing.

Harper.

My attention was glued to her like the ball in a final game. This had to be a sign—her being here.

I scanned her body, drinking her in. She wore a flowy green dress that perfectly matched the color of her eyes. Those beguiling green eyes had been my downfall.

The dress was fitted through the chest before flaring over her hips. She looked radiant. And her tits were… My mouth went dry. Had they always been that full?

I shook my head, rubbing at the spot on my chest where it ached. It made me feel like a hypocrite. To have a tattoo about treating people with respect and yet doing the exact opposite. My dad would be ashamed of me.

And here was my chance to make amends. To apologize.

Perhaps sensing my attention, Harper looked up, our eyes meeting from across the room. It *was* her. She was here.

Why was she here?

This was an event to shine a spotlight on LA sports teams and all the good they did around the city. Members of the Hollywood Heatwaves football team were in attendance, as well as representatives from the LA Leatherbacks and the basketball and hockey teams.

For a moment, all my anger, all my doubts faded away, and time seemed to stand still. I was Enzo, and she was my *uccellina,* offering me the same solace I'd found with her in Bali. The type of peace I hadn't found before or since. Especially not since.

Her skin went pale, and I feared she'd faint. My feet moved of their own accord, each step bringing me closer to the woman who haunted my dreams and many of my waking moments too.

"Lorenzo?" Knox asked, halting my progress. He'd introduced me to a few people, but I hadn't heard a word they'd said.

Unable to stand there any longer, I made a hasty excuse and walked away. But when I looked back to where Harper had been only a minute before, she was gone. Vanished.

I glanced around, frantic to find her. I hastened my steps, seeing her back from across the room. But when I tapped on her shoulder, the woman who stared back at me wore a pair of unfamiliar blue eyes. Not the emerald gems I'd hoped to see.

I spun around and still nothing. Had I imagined her?

I shook my head. Okay. It was official; I was losing it.

I needed some air, so I headed out to the patio. But when I spied a woman in a green dress standing at the railing, I stilled. Either I was losing it or… *No.* I stared at her back, knowing it was her.

When I stepped closer, Harper's almond scent infiltrated my lungs, filling me with memories from Bali. I shook my head to clear it. As if I could somehow rid myself of the distraction she presented.

"*Uccellina.*" I placed my hand on her shoulder, and she jolted as if I'd electrocuted her.

"Oh my god. It *is* you." She turned, putting her back to the railing and the city beyond.

I stepped closer, eager for an excuse to touch her. I had so much to say. To apologize for. I'd been so wrong about her. "*Sì.* Are you okay?"

She shook her head and gripped the railing, swallowing hard as she did so. "I, um, I—" She took a deep breath. "I didn't expect to see you here. Or ever again, considering how things ended."

Did she really have no clue who I was?

Wow. I am an asshole.

"Harper," I said, softening my tone as I stepped closer. "I made a—"

My words were cut off when the door opened and several guests spilled onto the patio. Our privacy—or the illusion of it, at least—was gone.

I huffed, annoyed by the intrusion. "Have a drink with me. Let's go somewhere we can talk privately."

"About what? You made it very clear that we were done in Bali." She crossed her arms over her chest, which had the effect of pushing up her breasts. My attention was momentarily diverted there before I shook my head.

Sensing she wouldn't budge, I glanced around, afraid someone might overhear. "I just—" I huffed. "I want to apologize."

She said nothing, so I found myself continuing, despite my reservations. "I'm sorry." I held up my hands. "Truly. But you have to understand—"

She glared at me. "*Understand*? You had no right to do what you did. I offered to erase the photos of you. But you—" She shook her head, and it looked as if she might cry.

"I know. I *know*," I sighed, frustrated with the situation and myself. I'd let my temper get the best of me that morning, and I vowed not to let it happen again. "Let me make it up to you." I stepped closer and took her hands in mine. God, it felt so good to touch her after all this time. It felt as if my body had come alive again, and I wanted to do more than just apologize. "*Please.*"

She stepped out of my hold, putting space between us. It was as if we were doing a dance—one step forward, two steps back. "Why should I trust you? You yelled at me. You *threatened* me."

"I know. I was… I shouldn't have lost my temper. I'm sorry about the camera."

"It's not just about the camera. The SD card had all my photos for the studio as well as images I'd planned to sell to a stock photo website."

"Wait." Confusion and regret swirled through me, and I wondered if I'd misheard. "A stock photo website? Not the tabloids?"

She frowned. "Why would the tabloids want images of the market in Bali?" She paused, and I watched her dawning realization. "Oh. Of you? You thought I'd sell the images *of you* to the tabloids?" Her expression clouded. "I don't even know who you are, but I would never *ever* do that."

I pinched the bridge of my nose. *Cazzo.* I had gotten this all wrong. Despite how badly I'd treated Harper, she still hadn't sold me out to the tabloids. Literally. And it seemed as if she'd never intended to.

"I'll give the SD card back," I said.

She rolled her eyes. "I think it's a little late for that."

"No." I shook my head. "I *will*. I have it in the safe in my room upstairs."

"Really?" she scoffed, and I was relieved everyone else had gone back inside.

"Yes, really. And I'll replace your camera."

"It's fine. I don't need it anymore," she said, but it felt as if she'd told me she didn't need *me* anymore.

"*Uccellina, per favore.*" I reached out for her, covering her hand with mine. Couldn't she see I was trying?

"Don't call me that," she seethed, flicking away my hand. "Not after how you treated me. What happened to *quando finisce la partita il re ed il pedone finiscono nella stessa scatola?*"

I swallowed hard and dipped my chin. I hated the way she'd thrown my father's words—the words of my tattoo—back at me, though I deserved it. Hell, I'd thought the same myself. I hadn't treated her with respect like I should've. The respect she deserved.

But apparently, she wasn't done. "I can't believe that after everything…" She shook her head. "I mean, the things you accused me of…" The way she looked at me was a punch to the gut. "*You* were the one who lied. About your name. About who you were. *Everything* was a lie."

"Not everything." I invaded her space, trapping her against the railing. "The way you made me feel when we were together wasn't a lie. The batik—I chose that design because you made me feel joy and freedom like no one and nothing else."

The way she made me feel now wasn't a lie. I hadn't seen her in months, but our attraction was just as palpable and real as it had been in Bali. There was still so much unsaid between us. Surely she felt it too—the undeniable pull.

From behind me, a man's voice called, "Harper?"

Her eyes widened, and my attention snapped to him. We were about the same height, but we couldn't be more different in appearance. He was so very buttoned-up in his tuxedo, his broad shoulders and blond hair making me think he was an athlete. But he was so different from me. No tattoos. No scars.

I stepped back to give her some space, and he took that as an invitation to slip his arm around her waist. A surge of jealousy had me nearly growling at him to back off. *What the hell?*

I'd never experienced this type of possessiveness when I'd been with Giada.

Instead, I shoved my hands into my pockets and rocked on my heels, wondering if this was why Harper refused to have a drink with me. Was it because of him? Was she seeing someone—this *coglione*?

CHAPTER ELEVEN

Harper

Everything happened as if in slow motion. I was rooted to the spot, Crew pulling me close, while Enzo watched on. Enzo's fists were clenched, and I just wanted out of there.

"Hey." Crew hugged me to him. "I've been looking for you. You feeling okay?"

I hadn't told him about the baby, but I needed to. I was beginning to realize that he wanted more from our relationship than I could give. And he deserved to find someone who could give that to him.

I forced myself to answer. "Yeah." Though I was far from okay. I shifted between my feet, my eyes anywhere but on Enzo.

Talk about awkward.

Crew extended his hand to Enzo and said, "Crew Dixon, owner of the Hollywood Heatwaves."

Enzo shook his hand. "I'm—"

"Lorenzo Mancini." I could hear the smile in Crew's voice. "Your reputation precedes you."

Lorenzo Mancini?

Lorenzo Mancini. I repeated it again, though it sounded louder in my head this time.

Enzo was… My heartbeat sped up, my chest tightening.

Oh.

My.

God.

I'd heard Crew and Harrison talking about Lorenzo Mancini earlier—he was a talented soccer player who'd been offered the chance to transfer to the LA Leatherbacks. They'd mentioned a huge transfer fee. But never in my wildest dreams would I have imagined that *my* Enzo was *their* Lorenzo.

If only I paid more attention to sports.

I must have missed part of the conversation because I was surprised when Crew dropped a kiss on my head and said, "Don't go anywhere. I'll be right back."

What? No. No. No! Wait!

I moved to follow him, but Enzo grabbed my wrist. As soon as Crew was gone, Enzo asked, "Are you seeing him?"

"What?" I was breathless, eager to escape. I needed a moment to digest the news that my vacation fling, my baby daddy, was an international soccer superstar.

How could I not have put two and two together? I'd seen him play soccer, for crying out loud! I'd even searched for men with the name Lorenzo, though clearly Bianchi wasn't his last name. I'd suspected as much, but that hadn't helped me narrow my search.

All this time, my friends had known exactly who Enzo was. Well, they knew who Lorenzo Mancini was. But I'd never seen a picture of the sports legend. Even so, I felt like such an idiot.

"Are you—" He stepped closer, close enough that his breath grazed my skin. His words were laced with menace, and his bergamot scent wrapped around me. "Seeing. Him?"

I lifted my chin, anger coursing through me. "Since when do you care about me? I'm just a 'fucking vulture,' right?" I spat back his words from our last morning together.

Though, now I supposed I understood why he'd called me a vulture. He'd thought I was paparazzi. He'd thought I was going to sell my photographs of him. I could understand why he'd been so upset, but that didn't give him the right to treat me the way he had.

He gripped my chin. "Answer me, *uccellina.*"

He had no right...

I clenched my fists, anger warring with attraction. I didn't owe him anything.

"Let me go," I said through clenched teeth. "I'm warning you."

When he maintained his hold, refusing to back down, I kneed him in the balls. He cursed and released me, and I took the opportunity to escape. I was done. With this conversation. With him. I turned and walked away as quickly as I could.

I was getting too upset. It wasn't good for the baby.

"Harper, wait." His voice was garbled, his footsteps echoing against the slate tile.

I shook my head, doing my best to hold it together and not cry. Crew and Harrison appeared at the door. They took one look at me and frowned.

"What's wrong?" Crew asked, his voice filled with concern. His eyes searched me, and when I didn't answer, his attention darted to Enzo. "Did he do something, say something, to upset you?"

"Please," I pleaded. "I just need out." I pushed past them, intent on escape. I didn't want to talk. I didn't want to explain. I just needed— I glanced around and then ducked into the bathroom.

Before the pregnancy, I'd rarely cried. Now, I cried all the damn time. Sappy commercial on TV—crying. Lauren surprising me with my favorite meal for lunch at work—crying. Producer acting like a demanding asshole—crying. It didn't matter whether I was happy, sad, or even mad, I cried. And right now, I was freaking the fuck out.

I shut myself in one of the stalls, placing my hands on my thighs as I struggled to catch my breath. *Did that just happen?*

Enzo. *Lorenzo.* He was here.

"Harper?" Juliana's voice echoed off the tiled walls of the bathroom.

"Yeah?" I croaked.

"Are you okay? Harrison said you seemed upset."

I sniffled, wiping my tears with the ball of toilet paper in my hand. "Just a sec." I took a deep breath before opening the door to the stall. She watched me in the mirror as I washed my hands, taking my time to dry them as I attempted to collect myself. I'd totally lost it on him. Not that it was unde-served, but still…to knee him in the balls?

"What happened?"

"I ran into Enzo." *Enzo? Lorenzo?* I wasn't sure what to even call him apart from the asshole.

And *the asshole* was just as handsome as I remembered, perhaps even more so. My body had come to life, lighting up when he looked at me, was near me. He'd even apologized and seemed sincere. But then I remembered how he'd treated me. I remembered that he'd lied.

"What?" Juliana gasped. "He's here?"

I nodded, staring at the ceiling so I wouldn't cry again. I just needed to get through this and tell her. Then I wouldn't have to talk about it again.

"He's a soccer player. Lorenzo Mancini. Apparently, Harrison's a big fan." I lifted my hand to my mouth, as if trying to stop the tears I knew were inevitable despite my sarcasm.

Her eyes widened. "Holy…*shit.*"

His anger over the photos in Bali made more sense now. But I couldn't believe he thought so little of me. Despite how everything had ended, we'd shared something special. His apology made me think he agreed. At least until he'd ruined it by being a controlling asshole.

"And I yelled at him."

"You did?" Juliana released me, offered me a tissue before turning her back to the mirror and leaning against the sink. "Wow."

"Oh, it gets worse." I used the tissue to dab beneath my eyes.

"You told him about the baby?"

I shook my head. "No. I kneed him in the balls."

Her eyes went wide. "You didn't?" I could tell she was torn between shock and laughter.

Juliana's phone buzzed, and she pulled it from her purse before glancing at the screen. "How do you want to play this? Harrison says Lorenzo is begging to talk to you."

I sucked my lip into my mouth but shook my head. I needed time to get my head on straight before facing Enzo again. "I don't…" My chest tightened at the mere thought of having to confront him, and I placed a hand over my heart.

"Why don't I have Harrison get his number?"

I nodded, some of the tightness in my chest easing. "Yes. Good idea. Thanks." I couldn't see Enzo. Not right now. "I just want to get out of here."

And now that I had a way to get in contact with him, I didn't feel compelled to tell him about the baby. At least not right away. I needed time to regroup first.

"Of course." She typed something on her phone before saying, "Whatever you need." Her tone was light and breezy, much like I imagined her trying to calm an anxious bride on her wedding day. "We're here for you. 'Kay?"

"Do you think I'm a coward?" I asked as she pushed open the door to the women's restroom and peeked her head out.

"I think you're doing what you need to protect yourself and my niece."

I laughed. "What?"

"Well, you're totally having a girl, right?"

"It's too early to know."

"But you're still planning to find out, aren't you?" I knew she was trying to distract me, and for once, I was okay with it. I didn't want to talk to Enzo. Not now, and I wasn't sure when.

"Yes." I smoothed my hand over my stomach as I thought of the heart beating inside. "Though, I just want a healthy baby. I don't care, otherwise."

"That's good. I don't think Lauren can handle waiting again like we did with Alexis."

"Not another monochromatic, gender-neutral nursery," we said at the same time, laughing as we attempted to mimic her voice.

Lauren was a talented interior designer. She'd created a beautiful nursery for Alexis and Preston before they knew Blair was a girl. But I had to admit, the idea of a gender-neutral nursery didn't appeal to me. I wanted fun and color and… "Oh my god. What if he tries to fight me for custody?"

Fear clutched my chest.

Juliana steered me through the halls of the hotel, and I hoped she was paying attention to where we were going because I sure as hell wasn't. I was thinking about how my entire world had just shifted. I'd planned on doing this on my own. But in all my plans, I'd never anticipated this.

Enzo wasn't just *some* guy. He was rich—that much I'd surmised in Bali. Powerful. A celebrity.

I hung my head as we entered the parking garage, and she handed the ticket to the valet. "I barely have the money to raise a kid, let alone to fight an expensive legal battle to keep the child I've dreamed of. A child he doesn't even want."

Diapers were expensive, but so was college. And a custody battle against someone like Enzo…well. The valet pulled up, and Juliana and I climbed in. I felt a tight band around my chest, and it wasn't the seat belt.

"Wait." She paused before pulling out of the garage, frowning. "I thought you didn't tell him about the baby."

"I didn't."

But based on our conversations in Bali, I knew he never intended to get married or have kids. That was why our fling had worked so well. We were both willing to suspend reality —to forgo what we'd want out of a relationship—to be together temporarily.

Now, reality was crashing back into me like waves on the shore. I was still trying to pay off the fertility treatments. And while pride had kept me from accepting Enzo's offer to return the SD card, I was regretting it now. I could really use the income from the stock photos.

I needed to talk to Audrey. She was an attorney in Fall River, and as my friend, I knew she wouldn't mind the late call. I also trusted her discretion.

"Okay. First off, take a deep breath." Juliana placed her hand over mine, waiting until I'd inhaled slowly and let it out. "You have no idea how he's going to react."

Oh, I had a pretty good feeling he wouldn't be happy. I sighed, glancing out the window at the passing scenery. "God, this is such a mess. *I'm* such a mess."

All along, my plan had been to work as long as I could in my current job, while searching for other ones back home. Then, depending on the timing, I'd move home to the Alondra Valley. But Enzo's appearance certainly threw all of that into question.

"You're not a mess, and you *will* figure this out. You're a smart, capable woman. If you can find a way to make a beach look like the setting of a zombie apocalyptic rampage and convince the reclusive owner of a seventeenth-century castle to let you film in his home, you can totally rock this."

"Aww." I turned to glance at her. "Thanks, babe."

"Of course." She smiled and then returned her attention to the road. During the drive, Juliana distracted me with questions about the baby. It was nice to talk about the pregnancy openly since I hadn't told many people yet. Apart from my three best friends and their significant others, no one knew. Not my boss or coworkers, and certainly not my family.

"Are you going to tell your parents when you go home next weekend?" Juliana asked.

"Yep. That's the plan, anyway," I said as she exited the highway. "If I don't, I imagine Christmas would be extremely awkward." I could still hide the pregnancy for now, but by then, I'd be *way* too far along to keep it a secret. Not that I wanted to.

"I'm sure you don't want to talk about Enzo," she said, pulling onto her street. "But you'll have to face him at some point."

I scrunched up my face. "Do I, though?" I teased.

She laughed. "Pretty sure. You *are* having a child together."

"Yeah." I leaned my head back against the seat and watched the passing streetlights. "I know."

I still couldn't believe he was here. And man had he looked good. Even better than I'd remembered. His suit draped over his form as if it had been made for him, and considering the cut and the expensive fabric, I imagined it had been. His dark waves had me aching to touch them, and I was both pleased that he lived up to my memory of him and pissed that he somehow seemed even hotter still.

"The sooner, the better," Juliana said, interrupting my thoughts. "You don't want this hanging over you the rest of your pregnancy. Or at least, I don't want that for you. I want you to enjoy it."

"So do I," I whispered. "I've wanted this for *so* long."

"I know." She placed her hand over mine as she pulled into her driveway. "And you deserve to be happy."

I wanted to believe her, but I couldn't see how it was possible. Because every time something good happened to me, something else ruined it. And I didn't see why this would be any different.

CHAPTER TWELVE

Enzo

I paced the wall of windows in my suite like a caged animal. I certainly felt…trapped. Thought it had more to do with the fact that Harper had run off, and I couldn't chase after her. Not without the paparazzi following me. Thanks to the event and all the celebrities attending, those vultures had swarmed the exits of the hotel, and there was no way I wanted them sniffing around. Talk about a disaster.

I'd gone into this evening preoccupied with thoughts of the potential transfer. And now that seemed like the least of my concerns. I'd put off this conversation long enough, and a glance at the clock told me Val would likely be awake by now.

The phone rang twice before Val picked up. "Lorenzo? How was the event?"

"Fine. But I need to tell you something."

I could no longer ignore what had happened in Bali. And if anyone could handle a potential scandal, it was Val. This was her job, and I needed to trust her even if I knew she'd want to kill me.

She was quiet, likely sensing it was something she wouldn't like. "Okay."

"I met someone while I was in Bali."

"What does that have to do with LA?"

"She's from here, and things didn't end on the best of terms." Nor had tonight gone well. I adjusted myself, my balls still aching. Talk about a shit show.

Val's restless energy coursed through the phone. I could only imagine her expression. "Explain."

"I accused her of lying to me. Of taking pictures of me to sell later. But she acted like she didn't know who I was."

Val exploded. "Why the hell didn't you mention this before?"

"Because we were dealing with Giada's bullshit, and then news of the transfer went public, and I was mad at myself. And her—both of them," I clarified, dragging a hand through my hair. "Fuck. At the time, I felt like a fool for being so trusting."

"Tell me more about the pictures." Val's tone was razor-sharp. "Could they be damaging to your…reputation? Please tell me this isn't Giada 2.0."

"No. *No.*" I shook my head quickly. At least, I didn't think so. I hated that I even had to wonder, but that was the dark side of fame. People didn't care about me; they cared about what I could do for them. And they would twist the situation to their advantage.

"Do you have your laptop handy?" I asked. "I'm emailing the images to you now."

I scrolled through the images on the card until I got to the ones of me. I had to admit, Harper was talented. The way she framed the shots really drew the viewer in. And the colors and textures… They were all so vibrant and arresting. It was part of the reason I'd gotten sucked into looking at the photos on her camera in the first place.

When I closed my eyes, it was as if I'd been transported back there. I could still smell the scent of jasmine on the breeze that had blown through the house. I'd picked up the camera, excited about our adventure while also dreading our goodbye. In my haste, I'd pressed a button, and an image had popped up on the display screen. It had captivated me. I hadn't been able to resist peeking through the rest, seeing Harper's view of Bali. At least until…

"It's a good shot. *Really* good." Val seemed to be mulling something over. "And a few of you playing soccer with the locals. These would be perfect for the foundation."

"I know," I said, her question giving me an idea.

"Is that all?"

I wished that was all there was to it. "Well, that's it as far as the photos are concerned."

"What do you mean?"

I sighed. "I lost my temper when I found them. I stole her SD card and destroyed her camera." I gnashed my teeth, those memories fading as the image of our last day together reared its ugly head.

Val's silence was scarier than if she'd yelled. I almost wanted her to yell, but all I heard was a hushed "*Cazzo,*" from the other end of the line.

"Yeah. Shit." I rubbed the back of my neck. "I should probably tell you how Harper and I met…" I launched into a quick recap, my stomach filling with dread the longer I talked. The more I said, the worse it sounded.

"You should've called me *immediately,*" she said in a clipped tone. "What's her name?"

"Harper Allen," I said. "She's a film location scout for Rain Shadow Productions. But…" I rubbed the back of my neck. "I honestly don't think she knew who I was."

Val laughed and laughed, finally realizing I hadn't joined her. "How could she not? Your face is on billboards. Even if she isn't a soccer fan, there's no way she could miss you in those cologne ads."

I lifted a shoulder. Maybe Harper didn't read many magazines. Ads with my face were displayed in airports across the world, but I had a feeling Harper was used to buzzing right by that kind of thing. She was always so focused. And she spent so much time in airports, she probably tuned everything out so she could research her next hobby or whatever.

"Well…" I rubbed the back of my neck, knowing I was also to blame for this predicament. "I sort of told her my name was Enzo."

Val started laughing again, and the sound was beginning to grate on my nerves. "Enzo. Right."

"I'm serious," I said, even knowing how ridiculous it seemed. "To Harper, I'm—I *was*—Enzo Bianchi."

"Mm-hmm." Val's skepticism came through the phone loud and clear. "You lied about your name, your heritage. And then you risked your career…for what? A woman? Your father would be so disappointed."

Val's comment felt like a slap in the face, and I recoiled from her words. Val had been like a daughter to Papà. They'd both been equally invested in my career. And as much as I didn't want to admit it, her words rang true.

"That's it, right?" she asked. "*Please* tell me that's it."

I smiled darkly. *If only.*

"I saw her tonight, and it didn't go well."

"Oh, Lorenzo," she tsked. "Now is not the time to get distracted. Not when we're so close to achieving everything we've ever wanted. You're thirty-eight. Nearing the end of your career. You have one more shot at playing in the World Cup. *One.* And once you retire, you won't have the opportunities you do now."

I sighed. Val was right. I should've listened when she'd

warned me about Giada. She'd been a distraction. A beautiful one, just like Harper. But a distraction, nevertheless.

Playing soccer with the kids in Bali had reminded me of that. Success through Soccer was my life's work. The sport had given me so much. And while I'd donated to charities in the past, I had so much more to offer. But first, I had to keep the promise to my dad and go as far in the sport as I could. And that meant keeping my eye on the prize.

"I'm not distracted," I lied. "But…well, what am I going to do?"

"Nico and I will track Harper down and buy the rights. Have her sign an NDA or whatever."

I ran a hand down my face. Somehow I didn't think Harper would be pleased. "I guess."

"Lorenzo," she sighed. "Just don't get involved. *Please.* We'll sort this out. We always do."

When we finally ended the call, I still wasn't so sure.

Harper wouldn't even talk to me. I'd given my contact info to Harrison, but I had no way of knowing if he'd pass it along. Or if she'd even reach out to me. I briefly considered messaging her through Instagram, but that seemed…shady or something. And so I talked myself out of it.

I made a few calls then changed and climbed into bed. I stared at the ceiling for what felt like hours. It was late, and while I wanted to blame the lack of sleep on jet lag, I knew it was more than that. All along, I'd been concerned this situation with Harper would blow up in my face, but I'd never anticipated *this*.

Val was right about my dad, about all of it. I couldn't afford to lose focus now. I kicked off the sheets, tempted to go for a run, when my phone buzzed with an incoming text. I scrambled to check it, hoping it was from Harper while chastising myself.

Unknown number: This is Harper.

Thank fuck.

I programmed her number into my phone. Then I stared at the screen, typing out a response then erasing it. Doing the same again. Apologizing via text seemed inadequate. And as much as I disliked what Val had had to say about the situation, I knew better than to put anything in writing. I wanted to trust Harper, but I had enough sense to stop myself before I could make the situation worse.

Me: Can I call you?
Uccellina: It's late. I'm tired. Neither of us is in the right headspace to talk.

She was probably right about that, and I wanted to respect her boundaries. I'd fucked up big time, and I needed to tread carefully.

Uccellina: Are you free tomorrow?
Me: Yes.

I didn't care what was on my schedule; this was more important. *She* was more important. I just needed to apologize so I could move on. So I could stop thinking about her.

Uccellina: I can drop by in the morning if that works.

· · ·

I didn't know what was responsible for Harper's sudden change of heart, but I was grateful to have the opportunity to talk with her alone. I pushed away Val's warnings and gave Harper the details of where I was staying.

ME: HOW ARE YOU?

I stared at the phone for a long time, willing her to respond. But she never did.

I must have finally fallen asleep at some point because I awoke to the sound of a knock at the door. I frowned and draped my feet over the side of the bed, sunlight trying to break in at the edges of the blackout curtains. My phone told me it was after nine, but surely that wasn't right. I never slept this late, no matter what time zone I was in.

"Just a minute," I called, pulling on some sweat pants. I rubbed a hand over my face, feeling disoriented.

I peered through the peephole. Harper stood on the other side, clutching her purse as if it were a shield. I took a deep breath and pulled open the door, wishing I'd had more time to prepare.

"*Buongiorno.*"

I invited her inside but refrained from kissing her like I wanted to. She brushed past me, the hair on my arm standing on end. It was as if my body was reaching out for her, even when I wouldn't let it.

"*Buongiorno.*" She glanced around the space, her eyes anywhere but on me. I hated it.

"Have you eaten yet? Are you hungry?" I led her farther inside toward the couch.

She shook her head but said nothing.

"Can I get you some water? Something to drink?"

"Some water would be nice, thanks."

I went over to the wet bar, grateful for an excuse to move, to do something. I grabbed a bottle of water from the fridge and loosened the top before handing it to her.

"Thank you." She took a sip.

"Thank you for coming. How did you get up here, though?" The top floor had its own security guard, and the elevators required a room key.

"My friend Juliana plans weddings for some of the biggest celebrities in the world. It's her job to know how to access locations so that the couple can avoid the paparazzi."

I nodded. "She told you how to sneak in."

She lifted a shoulder, her pleased smile endearing. "More or less."

I nodded. "I, um—" I stood, smoothing my hands down my thighs. "I have something for you."

I went to the bedroom and returned with her SD card, a new camera, and a check. After I'd left the event last night, I'd ordered the camera over the phone and paid extra to have a courier drop it off within an hour. Harper swallowed hard and stared at the items but didn't move. It was as if she'd turned into a statue.

"Here," I said, holding out the camera for her. "For you." When she still didn't say anything, I peered down at it. "Do you not like it? Is it not a good model?"

She barked out a surprised laugh. "Are you kidding? It's *the best* model."

"Then why do you not accept it? Any of it?"

"Because…it feels like you're trying to buy me off. I mean, this camera had to cost at least $10,000."

"Buy you off?" I growled, stepping closer. "Harper, I bought this camera because I destroyed yours. I'm attempting to right a wrong."

She opened the case, blinked at it, then up at me.

Then back at the camera, holding it carefully as she removed it from the leather enclosure and studied the buttons, the lens. I couldn't tell what she was thinking. Did she hate it? The guy at the shop had assured me it was top-of-the-line, but now I was having second thoughts. Especially when she set it on the coffee table and gently pushed it away from herself before ignoring its existence.

"I know it won't replace the camera you had, but it's better," I said. "And here's your SD card." I pushed it and the check closer to her.

"And the check?" she scoffed. "If that's not hush money, I don't know what is."

"It's not—" I sighed. This was not going well. "I want to purchase the rights to the images you took of me. They're beautiful shots, and they'd be perfect for my foundation."

"Thank you, but you can have them. Well…" She pursed her lips. "You kind of already do."

I pinched the bridge of my nose, wishing I could go back in time. "If you won't let me pay you what they're worth, then I'll return them."

"Enzo! Would you forget about the pictures for a moment? We have bigger things to discuss."

I jerked my head back, surprised by her sudden outburst. "Okay. What is it?" I inched closer.

She smoothed her hands down her thighs, and I noticed they were shaking. She took a deep breath, then said, "I'm pregnant, and you're the father."

"*Scusami?*" Surely I hadn't heard her correctly. She nodded, but I shook my head, nearly stumbling backward. "*Non è possibile. Che cazzo?*"

"Yes fucking way," she blurted.

"Just…hold on. Wait a second." My chest was rising and falling, and I was doing my best to remain calm. To count slowly back from ten, but it wasn't easy. "We used condoms. *Every* time." Despite the temptation not to.

"I know," she sighed. "I mean, I didn't even think I could get pregnant." She peered up at me, her eyes pleading. "I had three failed IUIs—sorry, a type of artificial insemination—before we met."

I jerked my head back. "Wait." The room spun. "You *wanted* to get pregnant."

"You knew that!" she cried.

"Yeah. I mean—" I raked my fingers through my hair. This didn't… Nothing made sense. "In the hypothetical sense, I knew you wanted to get married, have children. But I didn't realize you were actively *trying* to get pregnant." My expression darkened, matching my mood as something sinister slithered over my skin. "Did you…plan this?"

She let out a deep breath and glanced toward the ceiling. "Yeah. I conveniently scheduled a trip where you just *happened* to be vacationing. And I totally schemed to spy on an Italian soccer player I'd never even heard of. Oh…*oh*." She held up a finger, her voice rising with every word. "Then I seduced you and poked little tiny holes in every condom we used so they'd fail."

Okay, well. When she put it like that, it did sound pretty ridiculous. But given my position, could she blame me for asking?

She shook her head and took a breath, something slamming down in her eyes as if she were shutting me out. Yeah, I guess she could blame me.

Fair enough. The condoms had been mine, and I'd always opened and put them on myself. If anything, I was to blame.

"You know what?" she asked. "You don't have to believe me that this baby is yours. And you don't have to be involved at all. In fact, maybe it's better if you aren't."

"Not *involved*?"

"Yes, asshole," she spat, fists clenched. "I'm not sure I want you around my child."

I gnashed my teeth, tempted to remind her that it was *our* child. But I didn't. I was still trying to process everything.

It wasn't every day I found out I was going to be a father.

A father—*me*.

Most of my life, I'd convinced myself I didn't want kids. Though I always loved connecting with young players, I just hadn't ever imagined myself as a dad. My life was devoted to the sport.

She held my gaze a moment and then removed a folder from her purse. "I didn't come here to argue. I came to talk about the baby. I've laid out a few options."

"What kinds of options?" I hedged as she placed a document on the table. At the top was a header for a law office in Fall River—Audrey Monroe. I frowned.

"Options for your involvement in his or her life going forward. As you can see here," she continued on, "I've had my attorney detail a few possibilities."

I jerked my head back. *Attorney. What the hell?* I struggled to reconcile my *uccellina* with this cold, no-nonsense woman.

"Option one. You don't wish to be involved. Your name will not be listed on the birth certificate, and no one will know you are the father."

Was she fucking serious?

Anger flooded me at the suggestion that I shirk responsibility. That I ignore my own flesh and blood. There was no way I was disowning my child.

"Option two." She licked her lips. Lips I'd kissed and worshipped. "We do a paternity test. After the results come back—"

I couldn't listen to any more. "Harper, stop." I grabbed her hands. "Just stop," I repeated when she continued to ignore me.

"Maybe it would be best if I leave this with you." She slid her hands from mine and stood without looking at me. "You can reach out to my attorney after you've had some time to think it over."

Fuck that.

She hurried toward the door, but I was faster, my long strides eating up the carpet in no time.

"Harper." I gripped her wrist, pulling her so her back was to my front.

My arm rested atop her stomach and between her breasts, and I was suddenly keenly aware of our position. Of the way she nestled in my arms, the tension vibrating between us. Of her breasts rising and falling and the smell of her skin as I placed my lips beside her ear. Of the shiver that ran down her spine.

"Let me go," she pleaded.

"Why? What are you going to do?" I teased. "Knee me in the balls again?" Though I knew it was a definite possibility.

She dropped her chin to her chest. "*Yeah…* Sorry about that. I panicked, and my Krav Maga training kicked in."

I chuckled, thinking back on our time together in Bali. "Another former hobby, as I recall."

"Enzo," she sighed. She sounded so tired, so…broken. And it nearly destroyed me.

I turned her so she was facing me. I cupped her cheeks, peering into her gorgeous eyes. "Please." My voice was full of anguish. "I just… This is a lot to take in. I'm sorry. I don't believe any of the terrible things I said."

"A small part of you must believe they're true. Otherwise, you wouldn't have said them." Her tone was gentle, but pain reflected back at me in her eyes.

I frowned, hating myself for how I'd reacted. For the way I'd made her feel.

"Regardless of what you do or don't believe—" she waved

a hand through the air "—I'm willing to do this on my own. I don't expect anything from you."

My hands tightened into fists, my knuckles turning white. "You don't expect anything of me?"

"*From* you," she said, as if that was much better. She might as well have said she didn't expect anything of me. And I honestly wondered if she didn't.

"I know this is a lot to take in." Her shoulders relaxed. "And I know you don't want children."

"I—"

She shook her head as if to silence me.

"Just...don't rush into any decisions. You're still in shock. I get it. I've had months to adjust to the idea, and it still took me weeks to even believe it was true."

"Because of the failed...procedures?" I led her over to the couches and took a seat beside her.

She nodded. "A few months before we met, I suffered a loss very early in my pregnancy. It was devastating." That explained the sadness I'd seen when we were in Bali.

"Were you...with someone?" *Crew?* I swallowed but didn't reference him by name, hating the mere idea of it.

"No." She dipped her head, her cheeks turning pink. "I was using a sperm donor."

I hadn't realized just how committed she'd been to having children. Using a sperm donor, going it alone as a single mom—that wasn't an easy road. And I remembered the way she'd evaded the topic of children when we'd touched on it briefly in Bali. Now it all made sense.

"And then..." She swallowed. "Once I found out, well, I didn't have any way to get in touch with you."

Whether she realized it or not, she rested her hand on her stomach. She was such a natural, so maternal, and something in me roared to life. Some primal urge to protect her and our baby. And I knew there was no way I was letting her or the baby go.

"Look, Enzo," she sighed. "Or should I call you Lorenzo?"

"Enzo," I insisted. Even though no one else in my life had ever called me Enzo, I couldn't stand the thought of Harper calling me anything else.

"You should think carefully about what you want before deciding."

"What I want is you."

CHAPTER THIRTEEN

Harper

I couldn't help myself; I laughed. *He wanted me?*

I'd come here for closure—to rip off the Band-Aid, as Juliana had suggested. Partially for myself, but more for the child I was carrying. I needed to satisfy my conscience that I'd done everything I could to foster a relationship with their father—for his or her sake.

"*Uccellina,*" Enzo said in a stern tone. "Do you think I'm joking?"

What he *was* was deluded. I was still upset about the things he'd said, about the way he'd made me feel both last night and that last morning in Bali. He might want me, but he damn sure couldn't have me. I didn't care how famous or rich or sexy he was.

And god, was he sexy. I snapped my gaze to his, trying to ignore the fact that he was shirtless and his hair was deliciously mussed. *I mean—seriously?* How was I supposed to have a rational conversation about parental rights with all those muscles and tattoos staring me in the face?

I'd thought about this conversation a million times, and it had never gone like this. It wasn't as if I'd expected Enzo to be excited about the pregnancy, but to accuse me… My eyes stung as rage churned hot inside my chest, worse than any of the dreadful pregnancy heartburn I'd experienced.

I hated that I'd allowed him to rile me so much—again. I wanted to punch him in his stupidly handsome face.

I took a deep breath. "We—" I gestured between us "—don't have a relationship apart from co-parenting this child. And even that's debatable."

"Harper." His tone was sharp. "I'm the baby's father. Of course I'll be involved."

"Right." I stared at the coffee table, though I didn't relax. How was this even going to work? What if he decided not to transfer to LA? Or what if one of us later wanted to move? Or met someone else? "Of course."

He frowned. "Do you not want me to be involved?"

"No." I shook my head. "I mean, I don't know."

Even from my online research last night, Enzo's life seemed complicated. And I never wanted my child to feel as though their father thought they were an obligation. Or made them question his love.

In truth, I wasn't sure what I wanted from Enzo. I wasn't sure I trusted him.

"You're not doing this alone. I'm here, and I'm going to help."

"But are you? Here, I mean. Have you signed with the Leatherbacks?"

"No, but I'm going to."

"If you're doing this for the baby, don't—"

"I'm doing this for us."

I squeezed my eyes shut briefly, measuring my words. "I'd like to try to be friends for the baby's sake," I said, not wanting to get into another argument. "But there's nothing between us."

"Because of Crew?"

"What?" I jerked my head back. "No. We're just friends."

"Does *he* know that?"

I rolled my eyes and stood. I was done with this conversation. I wasn't talking to Enzo about Crew. Though I did owe Crew an explanation.

"*Uccellina*." That voice. The accent. It curled around me, digging in its hooks and reminding me of our time together in Bali. "I'm sorry for what I said." He reached over and took my hand in his. "Truly. I know you would never do what I accused you of."

"Which time?" I snapped, any remaining composure crumbling. "In Bali or this morning?" Because both were completely ridiculous.

He winced but then met my gaze, his expression contrite. "Both. I realize now that you didn't know who I was. And even if you had, I know you wouldn't have sold me out."

I nodded but still wasn't sure I trusted his words. When he'd tossed my camera over the balcony that morning in Bali, he'd shattered more than my equipment. And while he could buy me a new camera, rebuilding trust would take a lot longer.

Enzo had once told me that people were only nice when they had something to gain. At the time, I'd been saddened by his jaded outlook. But now, I wondered if that was what he was doing to me. Being nice because he had something to gain.

Even now, I was questioning his motives for inviting me to stay at Mizuki House. I found it difficult to believe it was purely out of self-preservation because he'd given me unfettered access to him. If he'd been scared I'd go to the press with the story of his driver nearly running me over, he could've offered me money in exchange for signing a nondisclosure agreement. But he hadn't.

"I appreciate you saying that, but how do I know I can trust anything you say?"

He jerked his head back. "What?"

"Enzo, you *lied* to me—about everything." When he opened his mouth to speak, I held up my hand. "Let me finish."

He nodded. I could feel his eyes on me the entire time, and it was both flattering and unnerving. In the months since I'd seen him, I'd wondered if I'd imagined how hot he was. His intensity. His desire. And seeing him again had made me realize just how powerful our connection still was. Even if I didn't want it to be.

"And I can't ignore the matter of your temper." His expression darkened at my words, but I stood my ground, unwilling to bend. "How do I know you won't snap at me any time something goes wrong? How do I know you won't treat our child like that?"

He seemed so different from the man I'd seen playing soccer with the kids in Bali. Was that the real Enzo, or was this private side I'd seen the true one? Was he Lorenzo Mancini, internationally acclaimed soccer star, or my Enzo— a man who was thoughtful and sexy?

"Look," he sighed. "I know you have no reason to trust me, but I feel like there's something I should tell you. Something that might help you understand why I reacted the way I did."

"*Okay,*" I said, drawing out the word.

He stared at his hands in his lap. "While we were in Bali, my ex threatened to tell our story to the tabloids. Well, her twisted version of our story. It was all lies, but the press wouldn't know that. All they'd see was a salacious story that could reflect badly on me and my image."

I frowned, my gut churning at the idea that she'd sell him out. Manipulate him. No wonder he'd freaked out. No wonder he found it so difficult to trust. "That's awful. Is that why you threw your phone into the pool?"

He nodded. "Yes, and while I didn't want to let her threats get to me, they did. It made me question every relationship in my life. It made me tighten my circle and keep to myself even more than I already had."

That was understandable. Even if they'd gone their separate ways, she shouldn't have betrayed Enzo's trust like that. A relationship—and what happened between the two people in it—was private. Or at least, it should be.

I almost placed my hand over his but then thought better of it. "Thank you for telling me. I'm sorry that happened to you."

"It doesn't excuse my behavior, but I hope it helps you understand it."

I nodded. It did, but I wasn't ready to jump back into bed with him—literally or figuratively. I might be pregnant with his child, but there was no need to rush into any decisions.

"I have to go." I stood. "Take some time to think about how you'd like to proceed. Once you're involved, there's no going back. You're either in, or you aren't. I won't do that to my child."

"*Uccellina.*" He stood and faced me head on. "I'm *in*. All the way. I want another chance."

I swallowed and glanced away. It was too much. Too fast. "Enzo, we barely know each other."

"*Cazzate.*"

"No." I shook my head. "Not bullshit. We've spent, what… a week together?"

"Harper, I know what turns you on, and I know what pisses you off. I *know* you."

"If you know me so well, then you should realize that I've never lied to you. Which is more than you can say." This conversation was pissing me off, as was the fact that he could still have such an effect on me.

"I'm sorry." He hung his head. "I don't know how many times and how many ways I can say it, but I'm *sorry*." This time, his apology was said with more determination. "And I'll keep repeating it until you believe me. I just wish we could go back to the way things were in Bali."

I kept looking over at him, my brain on overdrive. We'd had an amazing vacation fling, but then it had completely imploded. I'd expected never to see him again, then…

"What?" he asked.

"I'm just… My head is still trying to catch up with every-thing that's happened the past twenty-four hours."

"Yes. It has been quite the whirlwind. Though every time our paths cross, you seem to turn my world upside down."

I wrung my hands, wondering if he regretted our time together. Wondering if he would even be here now were it not for the baby. Actually, I didn't have to speculate; the answer was a resounding no. And that scared me—for our future. For my child's future.

I'd never admit this, but I'd spent some time online last night when I couldn't sleep, combing through footage from Enzo's games and interviews. Stories about him from reputable sources. Ordinarily, I would've seen it as an inva-sion of Enzo's privacy, but he'd forfeited that right by lying to me. Besides, I reasoned I was doing it to protect my child. I needed to know what kind of man Enzo was.

There were pictures of him with his parents, many with his father. Of him with kids at charity events and even celebrities from Hollywood. With his teammates—holding various trophies above their head as others sprayed them with champagne. And *then* there was his ex. A gorgeous Italian goddess who was young and voluptuous. Long, dark hair. Big boobs. Just a stunning woman.

And while there was some negative press surrounding the breakup, Enzo—or Lorenzo Mancini—was a beloved figure in Italy and across the world. He was known as an aggressive and tactical midfielder, valued for his deft touch and creativity. I'd seen him play with the kids in Bali, but watching him in a match against Juventus had me riveted to the screen. He was incredible.

Even so, I didn't *know* him. Not like he claimed to know me. And what little I knew about Enzo was gleaned from the internet rather than the man himself.

He might be a good team player when it came to sports, but would we be able to work together to co-parent this child? At the moment, I had my doubts.

"Ooh," Lauren said, admiring the giant bouquet of flowers on my table. "These are gorgeous."

"And hella expensive," Juliana said, gently lifting one of the blooms with her finger. "Daffodils aren't even in season."

"Did Crew send them?" Lauren asked.

I shook my head. "Nope. Enzo."

Lauren stilled. "Enzo as in *the* Enzo? The asshole?"

"Yep." I placed a charcuterie board on the table, and my friends oohed and aahed over it. Enzo's flowers were so bright and cheerful. I didn't want to like them, but I did.

"Ooh. He even sent a card." Lauren plucked the paper from the yellow flowers then frowned. "What the heck does it say? I mean, I can guess at some of it, thanks to my Spanish. Let me show you I'm...better?"

I laughed and took it from her. "Let me show you that I'm

a better man than the one I was yesterday. Let me show you that I can be there for you and you can trust me."

"Ah." Juliana tilted her head back. "That makes sense."

"What's that?" Alexis asked, popping a piece of cheese into her mouth.

"Daffodils symbolize honesty and truth. They can also stand for forgiveness." Juliana gave me a meaningful look.

"Hold up. Did I miss something?" Lauren asked as the four of us took a seat at my table.

I'd been preoccupied with work since the event, and I was still trying to digest everything that had happened. I hadn't told Alexis and Lauren about my run-in with Enzo yet, though I'd been hoping to tonight. Juliana knew that I'd talked with Enzo since the party, but I'd only given her a brief rundown.

"Enzo was at the event last weekend."

Alexis blinked a few times. "He *what*?"

"Interesting. And how was the asshole?" Lauren asked, leaning back in her chair.

Hot. I tucked my hair behind my ear. "His name is Lorenzo Mancini. He—"

"Oh *my* god," Lauren said before I could finish. "Lorenzo Mancini is your Italian fling?" She grabbed her phone and typed something furiously before placing it on the table. "*He's your baby daddy?*"

Enzo's face filled the screen, his expression serious. His blue shirt popped against the green field in the background, but it was his eyes that held me captive. His expression that said he would dominate anyone who stood in his path. Like he had me.

I furrowed my brow. This was getting embarrassing. "Why does everyone know who he is but me? I'm the one who slept with him."

"Harper." Lauren laughed. "Everyone in the world knows

who Lorenzo Mancini is. He's Italian royalty. A *fútbol* god. Holy shit…"

I knew she followed soccer. She and her dad had enjoyed watching games together before he'd died. And her mom's side of the family was into the sport. But still.

"I didn't realize you were such a fan," I said, mostly to hide my embarrassment. My complete lack of knowledge when it came to soccer, and sports generally, was partly to blame for this mortifying predicament.

"Mm. Girl. You need to start watching some *fútbol*. A bunch of hot, sweaty men running around on the field. If their endurance in the bedroom is half as good as it is on the field…"

I laughed, though it was mostly to cover how foolish I felt. I wasn't going to confirm her assumption, though just thinking about Enzo as a lover had my thighs clenching. He'd been determined. Thorough. Passionate. Many of the same qualities I'd seen in the videos of him on the field.

"The man is a legend," Lauren said. "He plays forward for Milan FC and captains the Italian national team. At least, he used to. He just signed with the LA Leatherbacks." She tapped a finger to her lips, raising her eyebrows. "Hmm. Interesting timing."

I didn't take the bait. I didn't respond.

"He's also won three Ballon d'Or awards and countless major trophies," Lauren finally finished.

"So, what you're saying—" Alexis jumped in "—is that he's like the Harrison Hayes of Italy?"

Juliana laughed, but Lauren was deadly serious when she said, "No. He's like a level above." She turned to Juliana. "No offense."

"Oh. None taken." Juliana laughed, holding up her hands. If anything, she seemed amused.

"It has nothing to do with Harrison and everything to do

with the sport," Lauren explained in a matter-of-fact tone. "Soccer has more fans worldwide. And a player like Lorenzo..." She shook her head, her lips curling into a smile. "Wow. I mean, *damn*, Harper. The man is hot."

I barked out a laugh. "Did his hotness blind you to the fact that he's an asshole?"

"You tell me," she teased. "You're the one who fell for him."

"I did not *fall* for him." I rolled my eyes. "We had a fling. And to me, he was always just Enzo. Not—" I waved my hands around "—Lorenzo Mancini." All this time, I'd been trying to figure out who he was, and apparently everyone in the world knew the answer.

"Does knowing who he is change how you feel?" Alexis asked.

"No. And yes," I said. "Not because of his wealth or fame but because I guess it helps me understand why he was so freaked out about the photographs."

"True," Alexis said. "But he could've handled it better."

I scoffed. "He could've handled a lot of things better." I sipped some water and said, "I told him about the baby."

"What?" Alexis's and Lauren's eyes went wide, and I wasn't sure which of them had asked the question. Maybe both of them at once in a sort of collective gasp.

I gave them a recap of the conversation, and by the end of it, we were all frowning. "Yeah...it didn't go so well. But then he apologized and told me he wants another chance."

"What'd you say?"

I barked out a laugh. "I told him no."

"Girl, way to make him work for it." Lauren snapped.

"I'm not making him work for it," I said, though he had been trying all week, even from Milan. He'd returned there briefly to finalize his move to LA.

There'd been the camera, which I hadn't accepted. Nor

the check. He'd sent me an obscene bouquet at work. Then the daffodils at home. He texted me daily to see how I was doing. He'd invited me over for dinner once he returned, but I had yet to accept because…what would be the point?

I wasn't interested in being in a relationship with someone who had serious trust issues. Who accused me of lying multiple times when he himself hadn't told the truth.

"So, you have no desire to sleep with him again?" Lauren asked.

I couldn't say no, not if I wanted to answer honestly. But I wouldn't allow my mind to go there. I was going to be smarter this time.

So I said, "It's going to take more than a few text messages and a camera to fix this."

I didn't care who Enzo was. I wouldn't allow him—or anyone else—to treat me like he had. And I sure as hell wouldn't let him treat my child like that.

I'd meant what I'd said; I didn't need his help. And if his life came with the level of crazy Lauren and everyone seemed to think it did, then perhaps the baby and I were better off without him.

CHAPTER FOURTEEN

Enzo

"Are you sure about this?" Val asked.

"It's a little late to back out now," I said, watching as the movers loaded the last of my stuff onto the truck. My assistant, Nico, was supervising them while Val and I finalized some contracts.

"I'm not talking about the Leatherbacks, and you know it."

I kept my attention on the truck. Nico had gone to talk to the men about something. "There's nothing to discuss. I've made my decision."

"Lorenzo." Val's tone was sharp, and she squared her shoulders. "There are many things to discuss. Paternity. The media. You can't seriously think you'll be able to keep this a secret much longer. You're lucky you've been able to contain the news as long as you have."

It was part of the reason I'd been avoiding Mamma during my visit home. She'd always hoped I'd get married and have children. If she knew she was going to have a grandchild, she'd find it impossible to keep it a secret.

"Yes," I sighed, rubbing the back of my neck. "I know. I plan to talk to Harper about it when I get back to LA."

"You should've done it before now."

"I would've." I gnashed my teeth. "If she would talk to me."

Val frowned. "She's still giving you the silent treatment?"

Harper hadn't shut me out completely, but talking to her was like trying to break through the wall on a free kick. Not impossible, but it definitely made it harder to score.

"She's a little upset about how I've handled things."

"Or she's trying to milk you for more by making you feel guilty. By playing hard to get."

I shook my head. "She's not like that."

"Look, Lorenzo," Val sighed.

I shook my head. I didn't want to get into it again. Val and I had already argued about Harper and the baby several times. She wanted Harper to get a paternity test. And I was convinced the baby was mine.

I understood where Val was coming from, and I appreciated her desire to protect me. The problem was, I *did* believe Harper. Even without a paternity test, I knew the child was mine. Or at least, I realized that I wanted it to be true. And that was almost scarier than finding out I was going to be a dad.

"No. Listen. We've been friends for a long time. We've done business together for a long time."

"Why does it feel like you're breaking up with me?" I teased.

"Because, lately, I wonder if you even want me as your agent. Since you insist on ignoring my advice, I'm not sure there's a point in continuing to offer it."

She couldn't be serious. Could she? Even so, my heart started to race.

"Val, please." I wasn't sure whether I was chiding or pleading. "I need you."

She'd been with me since the beginning, and she'd negotiated some of the best deals of my career. She was a wolf. She was ruthless and cunning, and I'd definitely benefited from having her on my team. I couldn't do what I did without her. Her or Nico. They kept my business—and my life—running smoothly.

She'd been there when I'd lost my dad. And she'd been the one to push me to play at a level worthy of his memory. I couldn't do this without her. The idea was incomprehensible.

"I just wonder if maybe we'd be better off ending the business side of our relationship." She seemed hesitant, which wasn't at all like Val.

"Because of this thing with Harper?"

"That's certainly part of it," she said. I was still trying to figure out where all of this was coming from. Why was she giving up? She never gave up. "I'm worried about you. You've had a lot of big changes in a short span of time."

"Don't add to them by quitting on me now," I said.

"I'm not," she sighed. "I'm not quitting on you. I'm just trying to get through to you."

"We both knew this move was coming from the moment LA announced their intent. This thing with Harper merely sped it along."

"You really like this woman, don't you?"

I nodded. "I do. She's different. I think you'd like her too. If you gave her a chance."

If only Harper would give me another chance.

Val, Nico, and I chatted a while longer until the movers had finished. Nico would be moving to LA and continuing to work with me. He seemed excited about the adventure, and I was grateful.

Later that night, alone in my hotel room, I texted Harper. I'd been texting her daily since I'd left. She wouldn't answer my calls. She didn't mention my gifts. But occasionally, she'd respond to my texts, especially if they were questions about LA or something not related to our relationship. I'd had to get creative just to get her to talk to me.

I also found that she was more likely to respond if I messaged her in Italian. I knew she enjoyed practicing the language, so I used that to my advantage. Just like on the field, I'd use whatever means necessary.

Your friend Alexis is a real estate agent, right?

It didn't take long for her to respond, and I wondered what she was doing. I'd continued to stalk her Instagram feed, and I was pleased that she'd posted a few times more recently. An image of the interior of an historic building with lots of beautiful ironwork. And another of some food—a nice-looking salad. I couldn't stop thinking about the fact that there were only two plates on the table. Had she gone on a date?

Uccellina: She is.

Can you give me her information?

She sent me the contact information for Alexis Black-Hawthorne, and I saved it to my phone.

Thank you. Having a good day?

Uccellina: Can't complain.

Is the baby behaving for you?

Uccellina: So far, so good.

I'm glad.

I'll be back in LA tomorrow, and I'd love to see you.

Three dots danced on the screen, and I gripped my phone tighter, trying to be patient while I waited for her response.

Uccellina: I can't. I have plans.

Seriously? Was she really going to continue to shut me out? I'd sent her gifts, flowers, cards. I texted daily. I was trying to do everything I could think of.

Any other woman would've been thrilled with all the things that I'd done. Hell, I'd never had to work this hard. And yet…Harper wasn't just any other woman. She was the mother of my child.

I needed a new strategy.

Ever since she'd told me about the baby, I'd pulled back. I'd let her call the shots. But I was done with that. I succeeded on the field because I played on the offensive. Why should this be any different? It was time to up my game.

"THANKS FOR SHOWING ME THE HOUSE," I SAID TO ALEXIS AS we stopped to talk on the lawn.

I'd arrived in LA a few days before, and I'd been running nonstop. The move had been seamless thanks to Nico's help, but there were contracts to sign, physicals and training, and just so much to do. Harper had been on my mind, and while we'd texted a few times, I still hadn't gotten to see her. But I had a plan.

"It's a nice property," Alexis said. "Good for entertaining, but also private. Gated community. Great school district."

Alexis had been pretty quiet, apart from extolling the features of the house. Though I'd felt her assessing me.

Debating my merit. Wondering if I was good enough for her friend.

I assumed she knew about the baby, about us, so I asked, "Would Harper like it?"

She laughed and then schooled her face into a neutral expression.

"What?" I asked, frowning. What was there not to like? The property was gorgeous. It had all the features Alexis had mentioned and more. A great backyard with a pool. A generous owner's suite and walk-in closets. Wasn't that every woman's dream?

"Let's just say…I can't imagine Harper living somewhere like this." She clutched her tablet to her chest.

"Too modern?" I asked.

She nodded. "And too big. Too showy."

I glanced back up at the house. "Really?"

She smiled and nodded again, though I sensed there was something more she wanted to say.

"Can you find some houses she *would* like?" I asked.

"Yes. But just to be clear, you want me to continue looking at houses for you, as well as ones I think she'd prefer?"

"What?" I jerked my head back. "No. I want one house that we can both live in."

"Oh, um." She glanced down at her phone. "Okay. Does Harper know about this?"

I shook my head. "It's a surprise, and I'd like to keep it that way. At least until we narrow it down to one or two options. She's already got enough on her plate, and I don't want to stress her."

Alexis chewed on her lip and nodded but said, "Sure."

"I get the feeling you don't approve of me," I said.

She ran a hand through her hair. "It's not that I don't

approve. Harper's one of my best friends, and I want what's best for her."

I stepped closer, jabbing my chest with my finger. "*I am* what's best for her. Her and the baby."

She held up her hands. "I'm not disagreeing, but you haven't done the greatest job of showing that so far."

"I'm trying," I said. "I want to be a good partner. A good father."

Harper wasn't just the mother of my child; she owned me. And I wanted her to be mine.

"Just…" She sighed. "Be there for her. Harper's not the type of woman who wants expensive things or big houses. Don't get me wrong—she'd spend her whole paycheck on travel." She laughed, and I could see the love she had for her friend. "But deep down, her family—and her friends—are more important to her than anything. She values loyalty and honesty above all else."

I nodded, knowing she was right. "Which is why I could really use your help."

She tensed, and I wondered if she'd tell me no. Still, I had to try. Everyone had a price, and I'd find Alexis's, even if it meant buying a house I didn't want just to get the information I needed.

"I want to do something special for Harper—surprise her. But she refuses to see me."

"Maybe you should listen. Give her space until she's ready."

"I have." And I was done.

I'd also been going about this all wrong. I was going to show Harper that I knew her, and that we belonged together. I was going to take her back to the beginning.

I explained what I needed to Alexis, and by the end, she seemed… Well, she'd at least agreed to help me.

"Don't make me regret this." She glared at me.

I crossed my heart. "Promise."

After we said our goodbyes, I made some calls and then headed to Harper's. I pulled my baseball cap low on my head and made sure I hadn't been followed before getting out of the car and heading up the stairs to her apartment. The first thing I noticed was that there was no elevator.

She was climbing two flights of stairs every day? What about her groceries? And what about the fact that I'd gotten in without any type of security code?

I shook my head and pressed on. The sooner I bought a house, the better.

I knocked on the door to her apartment and waited. "Just a second," she called, and relief filled my veins. *Perfetto.* She was home.

A moment later, the door swung open. Harper stood there in a pair of sweat pants and a tank top with thin straps. Her nipples pebbled against the white material, and it reminded me of the night we'd met. Then, as now, I wasn't sure I'd ever seen anyone so sexy.

She glanced up at me and immediately frowned. "You're not the delivery guy."

"No, I'm not." I smirked, taking in everything from the pink hue of her lips to the way a few tendrils of hair fell along her collarbone. "But I do want to take you to dinner."

She frowned. "I already ordered some."

"I'll join you, then." I kissed her cheek as I brushed past her and let myself inside.

Framed images hung on the walls, and I immediately recognized them as Harper's work. There were some floating shelves topped with various knickknacks from her travels, vintage cameras, and photographs. When I stepped closer, I recognized some of her friends from the other night—a shot of Juliana on her wedding day and Harper with her.

"Make yourself at home," she said, though I decided to ignore the sarcastic bite to her words.

She could continue to fight this—and me—all she wanted, but eventually, she'd cave. The fact that she'd kept the daffodils I'd sent her had to mean something. As did their placement in the middle of the table—a spot she'd have to see and walk by every day.

There was another knock at the door, and I answered it. The delivery guy blinked a few times when he saw me standing in the doorway, his mouth opening and closing. *Lorenzo freaking Mancini,* he mouthed. Or at least words along those lines. It wasn't the first time something like this had happened to me; I only hoped he'd keep his mouth shut.

"I believe you have an order for me," I said.

"Oh right." He shook his head and pulled something from his bag. "Here you are."

I thanked him and gave him a generous tip before taking the food to the kitchen. I opened the cupboards and found a bowl before setting to work on the food. It was a pasta dish with a butter and garlic sauce that smelled pretty good. Not as good as my *nonna's*, but promising.

All the while, Harper watched, arms crossed over her chest. "What do you think you're doing?"

"Taking care of you."

"I'm not an invalid," she practically growled, attempting to push me aside. "I'm a grown woman who's pregnant."

"Yes." I continued what I was doing. Laying the meal out for her. Serving her. "But everyone likes to be taken care of sometimes. No?"

"No." She yanked the container from my hand, but it ended up spilling all over her shirt and down her chest. I couldn't help it; I started laughing. Again, I was reminded of Bali and our cooking class which ended with a food fight and sex in the outdoor shower.

"This isn't funny, *Lorenzo*." She plucked some noodles from her chest, and my attention was glued to her skin. Thick, creamy sauce coated her cleavage, and I had a vision of emptying myself on her tits.

Cazzo.

And then my brain rewound the past few seconds, and I frowned. "Don't call me that."

"It's your name, isn't it?"

She yanked a towel from the oven handle and wet it beneath the faucet. She dabbed at her shirt, but it was only making it worse. It was only making it wetter and me harder.

"I told you to call me Enzo." I shifted closer, even knowing it was a bad idea. My hard-on pressed against my jeans, and I couldn't seem to stay away from her.

She glanced up at me, her mouth widening into an "o," as if suddenly realizing how close I was.

I took the towel from her hand and wiped it down her chest. She let out a little gasp of surprise, but she didn't try to stop me. So, I did it again, watching in fascination as her skin pebbled with goose bumps.

The washcloth was covered in sauce and getting cold, so I rinsed it with warm water. Our eyes were locked on each other, and I waited for her to tell me to stop. But she didn't. Not even when I slowly lowered the strap of her tank top, revealing her breast to me. Her nipples were darker than I remembered, her breasts fuller.

I swiped the towel over her nipple, and she moaned. I smirked to myself and rinsed it again before continuing my ministrations. This time on the other nipple.

All the while, she gripped the edge of the counter and kept making these little thrusts with her hips as if trying to fuck the air. I wanted to fuck her. Fuck, I wanted her.

I went back again, this time using my hand, my tongue. She arched her back, her breathing ragged as I lavished her with attention. *This* was how I'd wanted to take care of her. Not with food. Not with gifts. But with my hands, my mouth, my body.

And then I knelt to the floor, moving my attention lower still until I'd reached her stomach. Overcome with emotion, I knelt at the altar of her body and closed my eyes in prayer.

"*Ciao, bimbo. Sono tuo papà e non vedo l'ora di conoscerti.*"

"Enzo," Harper whispered, her voice clogged with emotion.

I peered up at her, and I wanted her to see me. Really see me. I was baring myself to her. I was the baby's father, and I couldn't wait to meet him or her.

Something passed between us, and I stood slowly. I slid my hand up her neck, cupping her cheek. Her skin was so soft, so warm. I wanted to sink into her. I wanted to remind her of how good we were together.

I didn't hesitate to kiss her, claiming her lips with mine. Our breathing ragged as we rediscovered each other. Tongues clashing. Her breasts pressed to my chest, hands exploring. Our skin separated by a layer of fabric that I wanted to rip off, removing any barriers between us.

And then it was over almost as quickly as it had started. She placed her hands on my chest and pressed. "Stop. Enzo, please. I can't."

I rubbed my thumb along her lips. One taste hadn't been enough, and I wanted more. "Why, *uccellina*? Why do you deny yourself what you want?"

"Because the last time I let myself have what I wanted, I got burned." There was a fire in her eyes. She stepped back and crossed her arms, covering her chest. "I told you, there is no *us* apart from the baby."

I didn't know what to do at this point other than lay it all on the line. I'd made it a goal never to leave anything on the field. And I planned to do the same with Harper until I'd won her over. I would not give up.

I stepped closer, my voice gravelly. "Maybe not right now. But we *will* be something, *uccellina*. Deny it all you want, but we already are."

I felt it in the depths of my soul, and I knew she did too. I just had to make her see.

CHAPTER FIFTEEN

Harper

I wanted to laugh at Enzo's confidence, but I couldn't. I was speechless. And I was starting to believe he meant what he said. Even so, I was scared.

Scared to let myself fall.

Scared to let myself rely on someone other than myself.

"I should change," I finally said, my skin prickling with awareness. My tank top was still down around my stomach, and I was getting cold. "And shower." Though Enzo had certainly done a good job of licking me clean.

"Would you like some company?" he asked with a wicked grin.

My core quivered with need. Damn him for being so irresistible. And so good with his tongue.

I rolled my eyes. "I can take care of myself."

He narrowed his eyes, but then they darkened with lust. "Mm. I'd like to see that."

Of course he'd turned it into something sexual. It was flattering, but I wondered how many women he'd been with during our time apart. He said he wasn't a player, but he was a freaking Italian soccer god.

And I'd seen the way women talked about him online. The comments on some of the photos were…graphic. He probably got propositioned all the time. Another reason why I should keep my distance. I knew my limits, and sharing wasn't part of them.

"Goodnight, Enzo," I called.

"What about dinner?" he asked.

"I'll figure it out."

"I've got it covered," he said, glancing at his phone. "Go enjoy your shower."

I arched an eyebrow, but then he shooed me toward the bedroom. "*Vai. Vai.*"

"Okay. Geez."

I went to take a shower, spending extra time shaving even though I told myself nothing would come of it. I absolutely was not going to have sex with Enzo. It didn't matter that he'd been so nice lately. The flowers, the camera, the text messages, the…*thing* in the kitchen.

I closed my eyes and enjoyed the feel of the warm water running over my skin. I still couldn't believe I'd let him do that. I wanted to blame it on my hormones—on the crazy sex dreams I kept having in which Enzo was the star—but I knew that wasn't true.

It all came down to one moment. The moment when he'd kissed my stomach. He'd talked to the baby. His words and the gentle tone in which he said them reverberated in my mind. *Hello, baby. I'm your daddy, and I can't wait to meet you.*

And I'd melted.

His muscular, tattooed arms juxtaposed against the loving way he touched my stomach. The scent of his shampoo in those dark waves. His presence.

Unable to resist, I reached between my legs and started rubbing my clit. I was so freaking horny, but I'd meant what I said—I could take care of myself. With one hand pinching my nipple, I used the other to bring myself to the edge, all the while imagining Enzo's hands and mouth. His filthy words and delicious body.

And then my orgasm barreled down on me, making me convulse. I started laughing, giddy from the high. I couldn't believe I'd just done that with him in the other room.

I rinsed off and towel-dried, standing in front of my closet as I debated what to wear. Loungewear? Something sexy? A dress?

What are you even doing? I asked myself.

My stomach growled, so I hastily grabbed a maxi dress that was both comfortable and sexy. I threw it on, adding some lip gloss before heading back out to the kitchen to join him.

I frowned when I saw another man standing in Enzo's place, my body tensing as if preparing for a fight. "Who are you?"

And how can I take you down without hurting the baby?

"My name is Nico," the man said, his English heavily accented with Italian. He held out a note, and I took it from his outstretched hand. I quickly scoured the contents.

Uccellina,

I leave you in good hands. This is my assistant, Nico. I look forward to seeing you for dinner.

Con amore,

Enzo

When I finished, Nico said, "There's a car waiting outside to take you to the restaurant, where Lorenzo will meet you."

"This all seems a bit elaborate."

Nico was tall and thin, dressed in designer clothes, and his smile was warm. "I take it you don't have experience with the paparazzi?"

I shook my head. "Not personally, no."

"They can be intense. Lorenzo is only trying to protect you." Protect me or keep me hidden?

Stop being ridiculous.

I nodded, appreciating the effort they'd put into arranging this dinner. And I had to admit, I was a little excited by the surprise. The adventure. I hadn't done anything like this in months.

I glanced down at my dress. "Should I change?"

Nico shook his head. "You look great. Shall we?" He gestured toward the door.

I followed him down the stairs to where a town car was waiting. The driver opened the back door for me, while Nico joined him in the front. *Hm. Okay.*

I texted Juliana and ate one of the snacks I always kept in my purse during the drive. But I couldn't figure out where we were headed for the life of me. Finally, we pulled up in front of what looked like a warehouse. But it was LA, so you never knew what you'd discover inside.

The driver opened my door, and Nico escorted me inside the building and through a commercial kitchen. My senses were hit with so many delicious aromas at once—butter, garlic, bread. Oh god, I wanted some bread. Preferably garlic bread, dipped in olive oil. Or maybe slathered in butter.

"Almost there," Nico said over his shoulder.

No one paid us any attention, but I wanted to ask them questions. I wanted to taste the food because it smelled freaking amazing.

I followed him through the kitchen to a door and then behind a velvet curtain. There, I found Enzo waiting for me at a table set for two. He stood and smiled.

"Uccellina." He kissed me on both cheeks. *"Grazie,* Nico."

Nico dipped his head and then withdrew, leaving Enzo and me alone. I was finally able to take in our surroundings. The room was dark, the walls paneled in a sumptuous, deep blue velvet. A chandelier glittered over the table, and the noise of the restaurant seemed far away. Candles glowed from atop the table, a bouquet of rich roses and eucalyptus inviting me to sit down.

"Wow. This is…unexpected. Where are we?" I asked.

"An authentic Italian experience," he said, pulling out the chair for me. "Or as close as we can get in LA."

"Not going to lie," I said, taking a seat. "I'm kind of feeling like I'm in a mafia romance right now."

He chuckled and went over to the other chair, dragging it closer to mine before sitting down. Well, okay then.

"You and the mafia." He shook his head.

"Well, can you blame me? You were always so secretive in Bali. Had a huge house. Italian…"

He shook his head. "You have a very vivid imagination, *uccellina.*"

"You have no idea," I said, my mind racing into overdrive as I contemplated all the ways this could play out. All the fun we could have. Me straddling him, riding my way to orgasm. Or perhaps on my knees, his cock between my lips. Or—better still—my body splayed out on the table for him to devour.

"Mm." His lips were at my ear, our arms brushing. "Tell me."

I swallowed hard, feeling as if I'd been caught. But before I could answer, a waiter joined us. He introduced himself and told us about the specials. Enzo started speaking in Italian to ask questions and give him our order.

"Mi scusi," I interrupted. *"Per cortesia, potresti rimuovere la gorgonzola dall'insalata?"*

The waiter seemed surprised to hear me speaking Italian but quickly recovered himself. *"Sì, naturalmente."*

"Grazie."

Enzo finished ordering, and then we were alone once more.

"I thought you liked gorgonzola," he said.

"I do, but I'm supposed to avoid soft cheeses while I'm pregnant."

He nodded. "Anything else you can't have?"

I sipped my water. "Sushi. Uncooked or raw meats, alcohol. And a few other things."

"Anything you've been craving?"

"Yes." I laughed. "For a few weeks, I was desperate for cinnamon rolls. And not just *any* cinnamon roll, but one I was picturing in my head."

He frowned. "You should avoid sugar. It's not good for the body, and I'm sure it's not good for the baby."

My blood simmered. What did he think gave him the right to tell me what to do? "Since when are you a doctor?"

"Studies on processed sugar have shown the harmful effects on the body."

"Enzo," I said, not caring if it were true. Which, in all likelihood, it was. But that wasn't the point. "This isn't up for discussion. I'm not giving up sugar."

"Okay. Okay." He held up his hands and said nothing more.

The waiter returned with some bread, and I immediately dug in. Yum. It was as delicious as I'd hoped. Buttery and rich and fluffy, and… I slowed down, realizing Enzo was staring at me as if I were a rabid animal.

"I'm sorry if I bit your head off," I said as the waiter returned with our first course. I was feeling less stabby now. "I'm super hungry."

Enzo leaned in, his breath grazing my ear as he said, "At

least it wasn't my other head. Though I do love it when you graze my skin with your teeth."

I nearly choked on my water.

"How does everything look?" the waiter asked.

"Delicious," Enzo replied, but he was still staring at me when he said it. And I felt like he was a wolf eyeing its dinner. It was secretly thrilling.

"Do you know if we're having a boy or a girl?" he asked when we were alone once more.

The way he'd phrased it gave me pause—*we're*. It was something so simple, but he was already showing me that he saw this baby as ours. Not just my child or my responsibility, but *ours*.

I shook my head and cut into my food, my mouth watering at the sight. "I won't find out until my sixteen-week appointment."

"When is that?" he asked.

"In about two weeks."

"I was asking more about the actual date and time of the appointment. I'd like to go with you." He paused. "If that's okay."

"I—yeah." I returned my attention to the meal. "Of course. It's on my calendar, so I'll let you know."

He cut into one of the dishes and took a bite. "This is phenomenal. Here—" He held a piece to my lips. "You have to taste this."

The moment I wrapped my lips around the fork, my taste buds rejoiced in delight. "Oh god. That is amazing."

He grinned, then leaned closer. "I'd hoped to give you another orgasm at dinner."

"I-I—"

"You have a little sauce—" He used his finger to wipe my chin. "There."

He licked his finger, his eyes hooded when they met mine. "Mm. That is orgasmically delicious."

Holy hell. I clenched my thighs together as if to ease the ache building there.

For a moment, it felt as if we were back in Bali. Back at the beginning. When everything was fun and spontaneous, an adventure. But then I thought about the baby, and I knew that wasn't true. Life was so much more complicated now.

We might be living in a bubble at the moment, but just like with Bali, it was a fantasy. It would end. He would return to his life, and I mine. Even if we now lived in the same city, we were still worlds apart.

I could not—would not—fall under Enzo's spell again. This was no longer just about me, but also about my child. And I would do anything to protect him or her.

"Where'd you go just now?" Enzo asked.

I shook my head. "Nowhere."

"*Uccellina,*" he chided.

"Enzo, it's fine. It's nothing."

He placed his hand over mine. "If something is bothering you, it's not nothing. Tell me."

I removed my hand under the pretense of cutting another bite. "I guess I wondered how the move was going. You never mentioned it as a possibility when we were in Bali." Though there were a lot of things he hadn't mentioned.

"*Sì.*" He used the corner of his napkin to wipe his mouth. "It was only after I returned from Bali that I learned of the offer."

"Are you happy about it?" I asked, curious.

He stopped what he was doing, his eyes meeting mine. "At first, I wasn't. But I am now."

"What changed?"

"Everything." That one word felt heavy with meaning, at least based on the way he was looking at me.

We resumed eating, and he seemed very absorbed with his meal all of a sudden. "Actually," he said, "there are a few things we should discuss."

"Okay." I hid my hands beneath the table to hide my nervousness. "Such as?"

"How you wish to announce our relationship and the fact that we're pregnant."

I furrowed my brow. "Um..."

"The longer we wait, the less control I have over the story."

I tilted my head to the side. "Story? What story? Why do we have to announce anything? I haven't even told my parents."

He jerked his head back. "What?"

I cringed. "I was going to, but I wanted to do it in person. I planned to tell my family this weekend."

"Your dad's sixtieth birthday celebration, right?"

I gazed at him in wonder. "You remembered?"

He tucked my hair behind my ear, and I wanted so badly to close my eyes and lean into his touch. *"Ricordo tutto di te."*

I remember everything about you too. Despite how many times I'd tried to push the memories away, the simple fact remained—Enzo was unforgettable.

For a moment, I thought he was going to kiss me, but then he said, "I'll go with you."

"What?"

"Sì. Yes. I should get to know your family since we are family now."

"But...*now?*" This was all happening too fast. I wasn't ready.

"You told me you don't visit often, and soon, it will be impossible for me to go." Perhaps sensing my hesitation, he glanced up at me and said, *"Uccellina, per favore."* Damn him. He knew I had a weakness for when he spoke Italian.

I closed my eyes and swallowed. This was either a great idea or a terrible one. Which, I wasn't quite sure.

I felt his breath; the air in the room shifted as he leaned in, hovering just beside my ear. *"Uccellina."* I shivered at his words, his proximity. *"Sei la mamma di mio figlio, prenderò cura di te."*

You are the mother of my child. And I promise to do right by you.

I wasn't sure what he meant by that because my body was in overdrive from his scent, his almost-touch. It was maddening.

"Meeting the family is a big step," I said, thinking he couldn't possibly be serious.

"We're having a baby together. It doesn't get much bigger than that."

"True." I laughed to myself.

"What is it?"

"It feels as if we've done everything out of order."

"There is no 'right order,'" he said, taking my hand in his. He turned my wrist so that my bracelet was visible and stroked the skin above it with his thumb. "There is only what is right for us."

I wanted to believe that, but my life felt so out of control at the moment, I couldn't think straight. One minute, I was mourning a chemical pregnancy; the next, I was pregnant. Enzo and I were great; then he called me a liar.

It was as if the universe were playing a huge cosmic joke on me—constantly switching things up. It didn't feel as if I could count on anything, and I was afraid to get my hopes up.

CHAPTER SIXTEEN

Enzo

"Hey!" Harper was slightly breathless when I opened the door to the hotel suite.

I'd given her a key so she could come and go as she pleased, but she only came when I specifically invited her. And she continued to insist on knocking, never letting herself in, despite the fact that she'd visited several times the past week. We'd eat dinner, watch movies. And while she seemed to have thawed a little since our Italian dinner date, her walls were still mostly impenetrable.

We hadn't kissed again, though I wanted to. This past week had been torture, and I had a feeling this weekend at her parents' wouldn't be much better.

We'd successfully managed to keep our relationship a secret, and I knew a big part of that was due to Nico's help. He facilitated our meetings and found places we could go without being discovered. I knew it wouldn't last forever, but I was enjoying this blissful window for now.

"*Ciao.*" I kissed Harper on both cheeks. "*Sei bellissima.*"

"*Grazie.* We should probably get going."

"Yes. Show me your secret passageways." I slung my bag

over my shoulder and gestured for her to lead the way since she'd insisted on driving us to the Alondra Valley. I'd offered to hire a car. Hell, I would've hired a helicopter if I thought she would've let me.

She started laughing, and she seemed lighter than she had all week. Happier. "Was that supposed to be a euphemism?" she asked over her shoulder.

"No." I tilted my head to the side. "Though I wouldn't mind seeing those either."

She rolled her eyes and continued on. The closer we got to the exit, the slower she seemed to move. I was beginning to wonder if she was having second thoughts.

She stared up at me after we'd exited the rear of the hotel. "It's not too late to back out."

I frowned. "Is something wrong, *uccellina?*"

An emotion flashed through her eyes, and then she buried it. "I look… God," she huffed and peered down at her stomach. She was barely showing, but it wasn't as flat as it had been either. "I haven't even told them I'm pregnant."

I placed my hands on her hips. "You look beautiful." She did—glowing, radiant, sexy. Damn, I'd never considered how sexy a woman would look carrying my child. Not just any woman—Harper. But she also looked nervous, fidgeting with her dress, struggling to get comfortable. "And I imagine they'll be thrilled about the baby, even if they are a bit surprised."

She sniffled and swiped angrily at a few tears. "I don't know. I just… You're being so nice about this and everything. I expected to do this alone, and—" She waved a hand in front of her face. "Gah. I cry over everything."

"We're in this together," I said, desperate to comfort her.

"Together," she repeated, though I got the feeling she didn't quite believe me. It only made me more determined to prove her wrong. I wasn't going anywhere.

I tucked a strand of her hair behind her ear. "We're going to have a baby."

"A baby." A smile flitted at her lips before it vanished again. I ached to see her smile, hear her laugh. For now, this would have to suffice. "I'm nervous," she admitted, and I softened.

"I know. But the sooner we tell them, the better."

She nodded, and she looked so small that I pulled her into a hug. Surprisingly, she didn't fight me. She stood there and allowed me to comfort her.

"Thank you," she said, the words muffled by my chest. I could feel her relax, and it made me happy.

"You good?" I asked when she pulled back.

"Yeah." She smiled, and I believed her. I followed her down the street until she stopped next to a dated champagne-colored sedan.

"*This* is your car?"

When Harper had insisted on driving to the Alondra Valley, this was not what I'd had in mind.

"Yeah. Why? What's wrong with it?" she asked, opening the driver's side and climbing in.

"It's just not what I pictured." I was trying to keep an open mind as I put my bag in the trunk before joining her.

"I know. I know. It's not the sexiest car," she said, firing up the Toyota Camry that had to be fifteen years old. Maybe twenty. "But it's reliable and cheap to maintain." She patted the dashboard.

I stared at the dash. "I feel like I've traveled back in time."

She laughed and pulled out onto the street. "Yeah, it's kind of nice. It's like shooting with film instead of a digital camera. There's just something comforting and fun about it. Nostalgic."

"That's how I feel when I play soccer with kids. It takes

me back to when I first fell in love with the sport. Before all the expectations and the pressure." Before all the drama.

I shifted around, trying to get comfortable. There had to be a way to get more legroom.

"Here," she said when we came to a red light. She reached beneath my legs and pulled a lever that sent me flying backward. I gripped the handle on the door, ready to launch myself out of this contraption. But she merely laughed at my expression.

"This car is a deathtrap."

"Stop being so dramatic." She sighed. "It's one of the safest cars on the road."

"And one of the oldest. No." I shook my head. "It's not the oldest, but it's in that weird time frame where it's not old enough to be cool again." Though I wasn't sure this car had ever been—or would ever be—cool.

She laughed and pulled onto the freeway. "You're such a snob," she said as she turned up the music.

The white stripe of the freeway disappeared beneath the tires as we drove farther and farther away from LA. I wasn't sure whether it was the situation or the woman, but I felt surprisingly carefree.

Everyone was speculating about my performance with a new team, but that seemed miles away. At least until Val's name flashed on my phone. I shifted in my seat but sent the call to voice mail. She didn't approve of Harper, and she certainly wouldn't approve of this weekend away. And I didn't want to hear her opinion right now.

"Tell me more about home." I'd heard about Harper's girlfriends when we were in Bali, and she'd mentioned her family. Even from our brief conversations about them, I knew she was close to her parents and her brothers.

She smiled. "We have these huge annual events where everyone comes together. And there's a great weekly farmers market. But it's just—the spirit of the place, you know? Everyone looks out for one another."

Every time she spoke of home, it was with a sense of nostalgia and longing. It made me wonder why she didn't visit more, especially since she seemed to have such fond memories.

"Why did you move to LA?"

She laughed, running a hand through her hair. Did she have any idea how sexy she was? I wanted to graze my hand up her legs. I wanted to have them wrapped around my head as I gulped down her orgasm. I fully intended to, but I was getting ahead of myself. It was clear that Harper had serious reservations about us, but I was determined to prove her wrong.

"Probably for the reasons you'd expect. Because I was young, and I thought my hometown was boring. There was a whole wide world out there I wanted to explore."

Harper's phone rang, and she glanced at it quickly. "It's Juliana. I'll call her back." It went to voice mail, and then there was a chime, followed by another call. She checked the screen. "My mom's calling. She probably just wants to know if I got on the road. Just—" Her tongue poked out from between her teeth as she concentrated on hitting the button to connect the call. "Give me a sec."

I shook my head. She should not be fumbling to answer the phone while driving. A newer car with Bluetooth and a touchscreen would allow her to drive with fewer distractions. It wasn't about being a snob; it was about her safety.

"Hey, Mom!" Harper's voice was overly bright, and I wondered if I should say hello or stay silent since the phone was on speaker. I opted for silence.

"Oh my god, Harper. It's been insane here." She was talking a million miles a minute, and I wondered if she was always this high energy. "The phone has been ringing nonstop. Patients can't get through to Dad's office. I've had calls on my business line. There's this ridiculous rumor going around that you're dating a famous football player."

"It's soccer," I interjected without thinking. The rumors better not be about Harper and Crew.

"Hello? Who's that?" Harper's mom asked, sounding alarmed.

I pulled out my phone to search the internet for articles about Harper and me. Sure enough, Val and Nico had already sent me a text with links to one. There was a blurry shot of Harper and me hugging in the garage this morning. Then another of us leaving the hotel.

"What the fuck?" I said under my breath.

"The famous soccer player," Harper said in a wry tone. "Sorry, Mom. You're on speaker with Enzo and me."

"Wait. It's true?"

Harper twisted the wheel in her hands. "I was going to tell you when I got home, but yes. It's true, and he's coming home with me. Surprise!"

"He…" Harper's mom paused, perhaps remembering that I was listening in. "Um, hello…is it Enzo?"

"Yes. Hello, Mrs. Allen. Please call me Enzo. I look forward to meeting you."

Harper cringed.

"What?" I mouthed.

I should've known something like this would happen. I'd just hoped to meet her family without my fame sucking all the air out of the room. People could be…funny when they met a celebrity. Odd. And I wanted the focus to be on Harper. On her dad's birthday. Not on me.

Harper shook her head. "Hey, um, Mom. Do you know where the rumor started?"

"Deborah Beaudin called to tell me this morning, but she

heard it from someone else. And I think they read about it online."

I turned my attention back to my phone and started typing out a message to Val and Nico. I wished we could've kept our relationship a secret a while longer, though I supposed I should've been glad there was no mention of the pregnancy. I wasn't sure how Harper would feel, but I hoped that going public about our relationship would make her see just how serious I was about us.

Harper frowned, but then her mom said, "Anyway, I'll let you focus on driving." It sounded like she was in a rush to get off the phone. "See you both soon! I love you."

"I love you too, Mom," Harper said then disconnected the call.

"No going back now," I teased, trying to gauge Harper's reaction to her mom's call.

"Would you if you could?" she asked, and I sensed that my answer was important to her.

"No." Now that I knew about the baby, the offer to transfer to the LA Leatherbacks felt like a sign. Like the universe had been preparing this path for me to move to LA to be with Harper. "I wouldn't. Would you?"

She peered out at the road, but it seemed as if she was seeing so much further ahead. "I'm not ready for this."

"For what?"

"Dating a celebrity. Being a mom. Telling my family. All of it," she huffed.

I smiled to myself. So, we were dating now, huh?

Maybe this wasn't such a bad thing after all.

I WIPED MY PALMS ON MY PANTS AND TOOK A DEEP BREATH AS I followed Harper down the path beside her parents' house. It was a wooden tree house sort of home that had large planks running on the diagonal and teal windows that popped against the rich wood exterior. The setting sun cast a warm, golden glow on the property and the garden.

And what a garden it was. Lush and abundant. A little surprise around every corner, whether it was a wind chime or a water fountain. It was clear that a lot of love had been put into it.

I placed my hand on Harper's back as we reached the arched gate to the backyard, and she smiled over her shoulder at me. I was about to meet her family, and I wanted to make a good impression. I worried what they'd heard—or thought they knew—about me. For all I knew, they were fans. I doubted it since Harper wasn't much of a sports fan herself, but still... Interactions with crazy fans could be awkward at best and downright scary at times.

I had no idea what I was walking into. Would they be happy about the baby? Upset? Harper's family was important to her. And how this went was important to me.

As if sensing my turbulent thoughts, Harper turned to me and placed her hands on my chest. "Relax. They're going to love you."

Her hair blew around her shoulders, and I was so tempted to kiss her. But then she patted my chest and took a deep breath before opening the gate. The backyard was even more magical than the rest. White lights were strung between the large oak trees, and a long table sat beneath a pergola. Some men were working on a fire pit, and the air was filled with the fragrance of flowers and something delicious.

"James!" a silver-haired woman called as I closed the gate behind us. "Look who's here."

"Harper!" His eyes were alight with happiness.

"Daddy!" She grinned, giving him a big hug. "Happy birthday."

"I'm so glad you're here." He pulled back and seemed to assess her before deciding that all was well. "So, so glad, baby girl."

She smiled then turned to me. "Mom, Dad, I'd like you to meet Enzo."

It was then he finally noticed me. Before that, Harper was his sole focus, his entire world. And I wondered if that was what it was like to be a dad. It made me miss my father, and I wondered if he would've enjoyed being a grandfather.

James blinked a few times, then said, "Nice to meet you."

"Thank you, Mr. Allen. I've heard a lot about you."

"Then you should know that everyone calls me Doc." I couldn't get a read on his tone, but I sensed he was wary of me.

I nodded and reached over to shake Mrs. Allen's hand, and she said, "Call me Linda."

"Auntie Harper!" A little boy ran up to Harper and wrapped his arms around her legs.

"Teddy!" She bent over and hugged him. "I missed you!"

She stood, her hand still on his shoulder. "This is my nephew, Teddy. And my brother Landon," Harper said as a couple joined the group. The woman was young but wore a tired smile as she rocked a baby in her arms. "And his wife, Jo, and their daughter, Stella."

Teddy turned his attention to me and screwed up his face. "Who's the tall guy?"

I laughed and crouched down to his level. "I'm Enzo. Nice to meet you."

He narrowed his eyes at me then asked, "Are you *really* a famous soccer player?"

So much for the elephant in the room. Leave it to the kid to run right over it.

"I am a soccer player, yes."

"Want to play?"

"I'd love to," I said at the same time Jo said, "Oh, that's not necessary."

Stella started fussing, and Doc Allen took the baby. He and Linda cooed over her, walking farther into the garden as they sang to her.

"Are you kidding?" I asked. "I've been cooped up in a car the past five hours. I could do with some fun."

"Oh, and spending time with me wasn't fun?" Harper challenged, a sparkle in her eye.

"*Uccellina, con te mi diverto sempre.*" I took her hand and lifted it to my lips, kissing it while holding her gaze.

"Hot damn," Jo said. "I have no idea what you just said, but that was sexy."

"Jo!" Landon glared at her.

"What? It was."

"He could've called her a pig who likes rolling in the mud."

I laughed at their banter. Jo's reaction was typical of many women—they were easily seduced by the accent.

Teddy tugged on my wrist. "Can we go? Please?"

"Let's do it."

Jo turned her attention to Harper. "Do you want something to drink? I think we have some of that pinot noir you love from the winery just down the road."

Harper shook her head. "I'm, uh, good. A bit tired after the drive. I don't want to fall asleep in the middle of Dad's party."

Jo cocked her head to the side but said nothing more as she led Harper to the drinks table. I followed the guys farther into the yard. We kicked the ball around for a while, until the questions inevitably started. Just not the ones I'd expected. "So, Enzo, how'd you meet my sister?"

"In Bali. We were both there on business."

"Where's Chase?" Harper asked from a tree swing at the edge of our makeshift field. She held up a bottle of water for me and shook it as if in question.

I jogged over to her. "Thank you." I kissed her cheek.

"Enzo," she chided under her breath, but it sounded more like a plea.

I hadn't done it consciously, but I was going to use every opportunity to my advantage. Any chance to touch her, I wouldn't hesitate. I took the water from her and gulped some down before returning to the game.

"Here I am!" A blond man bounded through the yard and nearly tackled Harper. I started to race toward them to check if she was okay, but she was laughing.

I clenched and unclenched my fists, adrenaline surging through me as I warred with the urge to protect her and the baby.

"Chase, this is Enzo. Enzo, Chase," Harper said.

"Well, this is interesting." Chase hung his arm over Harper's shoulder. "Isn't it, Lan?"

"Guys," Harper said through gritted teeth.

"What?" Chase lifted a shoulder, and I tried to understand the subtext of their conversation. This was clearly something between siblings. "You've never brought someone home, so I figure this means you're either engaged or pregnant."

Harper froze and so did Chase.

"Oh shit." He glanced at her left hand, then her stomach when he didn't find an engagement ring. "You're pregnant?"

CHAPTER SEVENTEEN

Harper

"Who's pregnant?" Mom asked, joining us along with Chase's wife, Mackenzie.

My neck was hot. Itchy. *God.* I plucked at my top, uncomfortably warm all of a sudden.

This was it. The moment I confessed everything. And after the story posted online earlier today, I knew I couldn't wait. Ready or not, it was time.

I took a steadying breath before lifting my head and saying, "I am."

"What?" Everyone's eyes seemed to home in on my stomach.

I nodded, and Enzo placed his hand on my lower back. "Yes, we're pregnant."

And then the congratulations were flying. Hugs and well-wishes. Tears and smiles. I hadn't realized it, but I'd needed this moment to validate the pregnancy. To make it feel more real.

"Oh, I'm so happy for you." Mom smiled at me before hugging Enzo. "Both of you."

Dad came to join us, and he pulled me into a hug. "Congratulations, honey. Are you feeling okay?"

I nodded, wondering why I'd ever worried how they'd react. I should've known they'd show excitement and care. "I'm feeling great, thanks."

"How far along are you?"

"About fifteen weeks."

"Taking your vitamins?"

I grinned. "Of course, Dad."

Then it was Landon's turn. "Aw, Harp." He pulled me into a hug. My shoulders relaxed, and I smiled through my tears. "Now our kids can grow up together. Well…" He released me and frowned. "At least, I guess they'll see each other at the holidays."

I forced myself to smile and nod.

That had been part of my plan for single motherhood. I was going to save up as much as I could and use up all my maternity leave while searching for jobs in the Alondra Valley. Then I'd planned to move home. Maybe find a little house near my parents'. Attend Sunday dinners.

But now, there was Enzo to consider. My family genuinely seemed to like him, and I'd been impressed with how seamlessly he'd fit in. But his life was back in LA. He'd only just moved there to play for the Leatherbacks. He'd signed a contract that would keep him in the city through the end of next season. There was no way he could move here with me, even if he wanted to.

I didn't want to think about it. Besides, there was no need to decide anything right now. I had months until the baby would arrive.

"Let's eat," Mom said, wrapping an arm around both Enzo's and my waists. "You can tell us everything over dinner."

As we took our seats around the table, everyone was

abuzz with excitement over our news. I felt more relieved than I'd anticipated, and I was grateful my family was so supportive about the pregnancy, about Enzo. They'd only just met him, and they'd welcomed him with open arms.

"So, when are you two getting married?" Chase asked.

I glared at him, silently willing him to shut up.

"What?" He shrugged, glancing around the table. "Everybody's thinking it."

"Oh please. We were together for how many years before you proposed?" Mackenzie asked from beside him.

The tips of his ears turned pink. "Yeah. Yeah."

"Ignore him," Mackenzie said to Enzo. "Chase can be very protective of Harper."

Enzo gave my thigh a squeeze, but I was relieved when the conversation returned to other matters. Ethan Archer was expanding Freedom Tiny Homes, and Chase had gotten a promotion. Mackenzie was considering buying a motel to renovate with a friend. Asher Hansley had moved to New York to work for a famous pastry chef. And so much more besides. I was tired from the drive, but I didn't want to miss a moment.

When Jo excused herself to use the restroom, Enzo ended up holding baby Stella. He cradled her in his muscular, tattooed arms, peering down at her face as if in wonder. I was struck with a pang of longing—both for the man and the idea of him as a father.

Jo returned with the cake, and everyone started singing "Happy Birthday" to my dad. As I glanced around at their smiling faces, I realized how happy I was. I'd missed my family, and part of my grief over my previous losses was rooted in mourning the idea of the life I'd wanted. Moving home. Raising my children here.

Dad blew out the candles, then turned to me with a smile.

"My wish already came true. I can't believe I'm going to be a grandpa again."

"Aw, *Dad.*" I smiled. "You're going to make me cry."

He hugged me to him as the cake was passed around. Not surprisingly, Enzo declined the dessert, but no one remarked on it. They were too busy talking about soccer and the local wineries.

After I'd finished my cake, I yawned, and Dad placed a hand on my back. "Why don't you go to bed, Harper?"

"I'm not that—" I yawned again and finally said, "Yeah. It's been a big day. I think I'm going to turn in."

Enzo handed Stella to Jo. His eyes seemed to linger on my niece a moment, and I was surprised by what a natural he was with a baby. How easily he held her and how relaxed he seemed.

"You two are just upstairs on the right," Mom said.

"Oh, um—" I glanced at Enzo, but he was grinning. If we were sharing a room, I couldn't avoid him. "I figured you'd have Enzo stay in the guest room."

"Oh please." Mom laughed. "You're a thirty-seven-year-old woman. And it's not like he can get you pregnant again."

"*Mom!*" I glared at her. Had she really just said that?

Enzo chuckled, and I elbowed him in the side. "Well, good night," I said in a cheery voice and went inside before anyone else could say anything else.

Enzo followed me into the house and up the stairs to my room. It was down at the end of the hall, and I resisted the urge to peek back at him. Instead, I kept my attention focused ahead, wondering how I was going to share a bed with Enzo and not end up having sex with him.

A floorboard creaked beneath his feet, and I realized he'd paused to look at something. He studied an image of my parents holding hands on the back porch. "Did you take these?"

I joined him and smiled. "Yeah. That's one of my favorites."

"You're such a talented photographer. Why did you never pursue that as a career?"

I lifted a shoulder. "I considered it—briefly. But then I sort of fell into film location scouting, and it took over my life. I figured it still allowed me to use my photography background while providing more stability. Plus…travel."

He chuckled. "Right. But you could travel as a photographer. That's why I was in Bali, you know."

"Really?" I frowned. "You never told me that. I thought you were there on vacation."

"I was, but I also had a photo shoot."

"Ah." I tilted my head back. "That's where you disappeared to that first morning I was at the house."

He nodded and placed a hand on the small of my back. "Thank you for allowing me to come home with you. Your family is lovely."

"Thank you." We continued down the hall to my room. "I think you made quite the impression on them."

"Oh yeah?" He grinned. "And what about you?" He turned to me, tucking a strand of hair behind my ear. "What's your impression of me now?"

I shook my head and turned away, busying myself with my bag. "It doesn't matter."

"It does to me," he said, coming to stand behind me.

"Honestly? I'm impressed."

I was impressed by how he'd handled my family. By their reaction to him. And I was impressed by the way he'd jumped in to help, whether it was with the cleanup, holding baby Stella, or whatever.

He placed his hands on my hips and pulled me back to him. "Impressed, huh?"

"Don't let it go to your head," I teased.

I could feel his hard-on against my back, and I wanted him to touch me. Kiss me. I was dying here.

I was so close to letting him, and then we heard a door close down the hall, and it broke the spell. Enzo stepped back, and I nearly stumbled forward. I'd been so close to giving in. What was I thinking?

"I'm going to change and brush my teeth." I moved for the door with a small bag and some clothes.

I locked myself in the bathroom and stared at my reflection in the mirror. "What are you doing, Harper?" I asked myself again.

I pressed my palms to the counter and squeezed my eyes shut. *It's just two nights. You can do this. Stay strong.*

Stay strong?

This was Enzo we were talking about. The man who'd given me the hottest sex of my life was just down the hall after months of not seeing him. Months of hating him while my body craved him. And now, we were sharing a bed. In my childhood room at my parents' house.

But it was more than that. Enzo had apologized. He'd really made an effort lately. He was nice to my family. To me. And I didn't know what to think. I'd interacted with celebrities, and I knew the toll publicity could take on them. Even so, it stung that he hadn't felt comfortable enough to trust me with the knowledge of his identity. And it wasn't just the lies either; he'd accused *me* of lying. *Twice.*

I shook my head and finished changing, messing with my nightgown until it looked just right. And then mussing it all up again. I didn't know why I cared. Nothing was going to happen between Enzo and me. And I did mean *nothing.*

When I returned to my room, Enzo's back was to me. I watched him through the opening as he dug through his bag.

As someone who loved to travel and traveled for a living, I believed you could tell a lot about a person from their baggage. Did they roll the contents like me? Use packing cubes like Juliana? Did they bring six pairs of shoes like Lauren? Or were they a psychopath who just shoved it all in there in one big mess?

From what I could see, Enzo's clothes were all well organized, and he had a few pairs of shoes—tennis shoes. Some workout apparel. A small DOPP kit—efficient but stylish.

I was beginning to feel like a stalker, so I opened the door and stepped inside. He strode toward me, his eyes intent on mine. He paused when he stood before me, our bodies inches apart. He stared down at me, tension and heat vibrating between us. I held my breath, waiting for his move as his eyes darkened with lust.

But then, he brushed past me, his skin barely grazing mine. I felt his touch all the same—the flames licking at my skin just as always. "I'll be right back."

I tried to get comfortable on the bed, attempting to ignore thoughts about the last time we'd slept together. There hadn't been much sleeping. I fluffed the pillow and shifted, still uncomfortable. Growing hotter.

Enzo returned and closed the door, promptly reaching behind his head to tug on the neck of his shirt.

"Wh–what—" My mouth went dry at the sight of his glorious abs, and I felt as if I'd walked into a trap. Damn, that V was insane. "Are you doing?"

And why can I not stop staring?

"Getting ready for bed," he said, as if it were the most obvious thing in the world.

Suddenly, the space seemed so much smaller, the walls closing in, pushing us closer together. He was a large, looming presence, and he seemed so at odds with my small-town past.

"Yes. But do you have to sleep shirtless?"

"If you remember, I typically sleep naked."

I huffed and punched down my pillow. I didn't need the reminder. I'd already been imagining him naked. "You're lucky I'm even letting you sleep in this bed."

"Maybe you would feel better if you removed more clothes," he offered. "You know—make us even." His brown eyes glittered with amusement, his jaw set in a line. But it was his chest that drew my attention, the muscles, the ink, on full display.

I rolled my eyes and flopped onto my back. "That's not happening." I stared at the wood beams that lined my ceiling so I wouldn't gawk at him.

"Why? It's not like I can get you pregnant again," he teased, using my mom's words from before.

I cringed and covered my face with my hands. "I cannot believe my mom said that."

"Come on." He chuckled, prying away my hands. "It was funny."

"Honestly, if she knew about the failed IUIs and the condoms, she'd realize how miraculous it is I got pregnant at all."

He shifted beside me, tucking his arm beneath his head. "You don't think it's a sign? This pregnancy?"

I shook my head. "I think it's biology."

"You had three failed procedures before you met me. And while I'd like to claim it's all down to my superior sperm, I believe there's a reason *you and I* are having this baby together."

"Maybe," I said on a yawn.

"Definitely," he said with such conviction that I turned to face him.

I took a deep breath. "Enzo, I told you—"

"Hush, *uccellina.*" He placed his hand on my stomach, the tattoos so striking. "Let's just enjoy being here together—the three of us."

I melted a little at his words. At the way he was already thinking of and referring to our baby while gently touching my stomach. It was everything I'd always wanted.

But it was a lie.

Enzo and I weren't a couple. And when my brother had mentioned our kids growing up together… Well, his comment had reminded me of just how complicated my life had become.

I'd always planned to move home to raise my child, but now there was more than just the baby and me to think about. Enzo was involved. What if he wanted to move back to Italy? What if he met someone else? What if they had kids together? My chest felt tight.

"Why do you look like you're freaking out right now?"

"Because…" I sucked in a jagged breath. "Just forget about it."

"Harper, I'm not going to forget about it. Even if I wanted to, I can feel the energy and anxiety rolling through you. I don't want that for you or the baby."

He pushed himself up on one side, took my hand in his, and started massaging. It felt freaking amazing. Perhaps even better than the daily massages we'd gotten when we were in Bali.

"Have you ever heard the phrase, *Non tutte le ciambelle riescono col buco?*"

"Not all donuts…" I furrowed my brow, but I was so distracted by what he was doing to my hand that I didn't have the brainpower to translate the rest.

"Have a hole," he finished for me. "It means that things don't always turn out as planned."

"Now I'm hungry," I said, half teasing.

He slowly removed his hands from my skin and stood. "What would you like?"

I blinked a few times. Was he serious? I wasn't sure I'd

ever been with anyone who wanted to take care of me. Not like Enzo. And while I could take care of myself, it was nice. I'd thought it was just him trying to impress me in Bali, but I now realized it was part of who he was. Someone who liked to serve others. Who enjoyed being part of something bigger than himself.

"You really don't have to do that," I said.

"I'd like to. Now, tell me what you want."

"I'd kill for a muffin." I batted my eyes at him. "I'm guessing my mom has some on a cake stand in the kitchen. If not, there's likely a stash in the freezer."

He nodded quickly then disappeared into the hallway. When he returned, he bore a proud smile and produced a muffin from behind his back.

"Thank you." I reached for it, my stomach already growling. I removed the wrapper and promptly devoured the treat.

Enzo chuckled and joined me on the bed. "Hungry, huh?"

I nodded.

"You want another one?"

I shook my head. "I'm good. Thanks."

"Now you're making me hungry." His eyes were hooded when he rubbed his thumb over my lips, parting them slightly, slowly.

I closed my eyes and bit back a moan. Being this close to him after months apart only reinforced the memories. The ache I still felt for him despite my efforts to ignore it.

And while I could've stayed mad at him for his accusations, for the lies, I could understand why he'd done what he had. Enzo might be passionate and hotheaded at times, but he seemed genuinely contrite.

I was still trying to reconcile the fact that my Enzo was actually the world-famous soccer player Lorenzo Mancini. He had fame and wealth beyond my wildest dreams, but it all seemed so far removed from here. And the more I got to know him, the more I could understand his desire to separate himself from that life.

"Enzo," I sighed, wanting nothing more than to sink into this moment, into him.

I was so tired. Tired of doing it all on my own, of carrying this big secret. Of being freaking exhausted. And for the first time, I didn't feel so alone.

The past few hours had been a roller coaster of emotions, and it felt like the ride was finally pulling back into the station. My nose burned, and a tear streaked down my cheek.

"Don't cry, *uccellina*," he rasped. "Please don't cry."

His expression, his words, the fact that he was here—it was all too much. My eyes fluttered closed, and I sensed he was going to kiss me before he did. He pressed his lips to my cheek ever so softly, kissing away my tears.

He kissed me again, this time on the lips. It was gentle and sweet, and I opened my eyes to find him staring back at me.

"*Sei così bella.*" He tilted his forehead to mine. He'd told me I was beautiful. And in that moment, when he repeated, "*Così bella, amore mio.*" I believed it.

He cupped my cheeks, running his thumbs back and forth. "I missed you. I missed the way you make me feel."

"How's that?" I asked, curious.

"Like a different man. Like the man I want to be, not the one everyone thinks I am."

I liked that I got a secret part of him, a side that no one else saw. That was just for me.

"I missed you too," I said, finally admitting it to myself. I'd been miserable since leaving Bali, and it wasn't just the hormones.

He peppered kisses down my neck, and everything about his touch was gentle. He didn't stop, and my skin heated everywhere he touched. I hadn't seen him in months, and I was pleased to realize that so far, my memories matched up with reality.

And then…he held me to him and smoothed down my hair. I didn't know how long we lay there, just holding each other. His skin was so warm and his hold comforting. I kept waiting for him to initiate sex, to push for more. But he didn't, finally pressing a gentle kiss to my temple before returning to his side of the bed to switch off the lamp.

I was glad it was dark, so I wouldn't have to hide my disappointment. I couldn't believe he was going to stop. Why now? Why was he pulling back when my body was urging full steam ahead and my mind was finally on board?

I shifted, trying to get comfortable before finally turning so my back was to him. The bed dipped behind me. He rolled so that he was spooning me, his arms draped over mine. This seemed a lot more intimate than sex.

"Um, is this necessary?" I asked, though I didn't want him to let go.

He nuzzled into my neck. "I'm just trying to bond with my child through cuddling."

"Mm. And I suppose it's just convenient that said child happens to be located inside me."

"Exactly. Sleep now. *Sogni d'oro*, Harper."

"Sweet dreams to you too," I whispered.

The longer I lay there, the more I tried to convince myself that he'd done the right thing. We'd had a vacation fling, but now our lives were intertwined in a way that couldn't easily be untangled. Having sex would only complicate the situation further, and I wasn't sure I could keep my feelings out of it this time.

CHAPTER EIGHTEEN

Enzo

I blinked a few times in the darkness, the hoot of an owl punctuating the stillness of the night. Was that what had woken me? A light on the nightstand caught my eye, Mamma's name flashing on the screen.

I assumed it was about Harper and me. I'd put off talking to Mamma, and I knew I needed to tell her about the baby. I honestly wasn't sure how she'd react, but I had a feeling it wouldn't be as positive as the reception we'd gotten from Harper's family.

Mamma had always wanted grandchildren, but I didn't know how she'd feel about Harper. We weren't married. Harper wasn't Italian—or even Catholic, for that matter. But I did love her.

Love her?

I held my breath, trying to sit with that feeling for a moment.

The more I thought about it, the more I realized it was true. Crazy as it sounded, I loved Harper. I was in love with Harper. And we were having a baby together. That was what mattered—the baby and Harper. Everything else would sort itself out. With that thought, I finally relaxed.

I was drifting back to sleep when I heard a moan.

"Enzo," Harper groaned. "Oh god." She blew out a breath, writhing beneath the sheets.

I froze, listening to her in the darkness. Was she... dreaming of me?

I wondered what was going on inside that beautiful head of hers. I'd stopped us from going further once, but I wasn't sure I'd be able to do so again. I pressed down on my cock, the urge to take her stronger than ever. Her scent was surrounding me, and I needed to be inside her.

"Touch me, please," she pleaded, sounding very awake.

Was I the one dreaming now? I was in that state where I was still half asleep, but my body knew exactly what to do.

I rolled so I was facing her, fumbling beneath the covers for bare skin. I was already rock hard, and I needed to touch her. God, how I needed her.

"Yes," she hissed, when I pulled her nightgown down to tease her breasts.

She'd always liked when I played with her nipples, but she seemed even more responsive since the pregnancy. Just thinking of the way she'd reacted in her kitchen had me ready to pounce.

I licked and sucked her nipples until her back was arching. I pressed my hard-on against her thigh, the pressure building. *Fuck*, this woman. What had she done to me?

I peeled her panties aside and teased her clit with my finger. Around and around, I went in a figure eight until she was panting. I brought her to the brink and then slid my fingers down in a V motion through her slit. Then back up again, restarting the whole cycle until she was on the edge once more. Finally, the third time, I let her come.

And fuck if I didn't almost come too.

I continued rubbing her clit until her convulsions stopped, her body relaxing. She let out a satisfied sigh, and I smiled at the sound. I pressed my lips to her temple, and then she rolled over, dragging me with her.

I frowned and settled in behind her, wondering if she just needed a moment to catch her breath. My cock was nestled between her legs, her back pressed to my front. My body was tight with pent-up need, and if I didn't do something soon, I was going to burst.

But then her breathing grew deeper, her body heavier in my arms. And I realized she'd fallen asleep. I shook my head and tried to relax, but my body was drawn tight and my mind was spinning.

The sky was changing from inky black to purple. A glance at the clock told me it was now almost six, and I let out a deep sigh. Knowing sleep would be impossible now, I decided to head out for a run.

The property was magnificent this time of day, the sun rising over the pond, fog clouding the surface as I circled it. It was peaceful, and by the time I returned, I felt more centered. Though my desire for Harper hadn't lessened. If anything, it was even worse after last night. It spurred me on, and I climbed the stairs two at a time.

Harper wasn't in her room, so I showered. I was headed down the hall when a door opened, and I nearly bumped into her.

"Oh, hey." She startled, placing a hand to her chest.

I tried to peer around her, but all I could see was darkness. "Is that a closet?" I frowned. "What were you doing in there?"

"It's actually a makeshift darkroom. For photography," she added, perhaps sensing my confusion.

"Can I see?"

"Um, sure." She stepped inside, and I followed her.

With the door closed, the room was surprisingly dark. Almost pitch black, in fact. And after the sunlit hallway, I couldn't see anything. With the flick of a light switch, a bulb illuminated the small closet, casting everything in a reddish glow. I saw some empty tubs as well as a line with clothespins, but I was more focused on her.

"This is really cool."

"Thanks." She smiled.

I brushed her hair over her shoulder and leaned down to kiss her neck. I sucked on her skin, pulling it gently into my mouth.

"What…" She let out a shaky breath. "What are you doing?"

"Picking up where we left off last night," I said, kissing her shoulder.

"Last night?" I could hear the confusion in her voice. "What are you talking about?"

I met her eyes. "Surely you didn't forget the way I made you come."

Her eyes widened. "Wait." She swallowed. "That was *real*? It wasn't a dream?"

"Do you dream of me often?" I teased, but when her cheeks darkened to an even deeper shade of red that I knew wasn't due to the light bulb, I felt an immense amount of pride. She could fight this—us—all she wanted, but she'd cave eventually. If last night was any indication, it would be sooner rather than later.

"No," she snapped.

"It's okay to admit it. I know you want me." I licked up the side of her neck, and she shuddered in response. "I want you too."

"Ungh." She sagged in my arms.

I sensed she was close to giving in when the door swung open. Bright light poured in, and I squinted against it.

"Oh my goodness. I'm so sorry, you two." Linda promptly shut the door once more. "Carry on," she said from the hall, and Harper covered her face with her hands. "Just, uh, Harper, can you run into town when you're finished in there?"

"Kill me now," Harper groaned. I wanted to laugh, but I knew better.

"What's that, sweetheart?" Linda asked from the other side of the door.

"I'll be right there."

Linda's footsteps faded down the hall, and then I couldn't hold it in anymore. I laughed.

"This is *so* not funny." Harper gave my chest a playful shove.

"No?" I asked.

"Can't blame a guy for trying." I shrugged. "You're carrying my baby, and it's fucking hot."

She laughed. "You have a thing for pregnant women?"

"No. I have *a thing* for you. You're sexy." She laughed, but I was serious. "I mean it, Harper." I placed my hands on her hips. "You're sexy."

"It's the bigger boobs, right?" she joked, and I wondered if she was uncomfortable with the changes in her body.

"It's everything about you."

She glared at me, but it lacked fire. "Now if you'll excuse me, I have an errand to run."

"I'll go with you," I said, opening the door as she switched off the light.

"You will?"

"Of course. But, Harper?"

"Yeah?" She paused at the top of the stairs, and the sight of her stole my breath.

"This conversation isn't over."

She rolled her eyes and shook her head before heading down the stairs.

THE DRIVE TO DOWNTOWN ALONDRA WAS BEAUTIFUL. WE passed by a number of wineries, and I smiled, thinking of my grandparents. I'd told Harper about them, about the winery they'd owned and the summers I'd spent there. Those were some of my favorite memories.

As she drove down Main Street, I recognized a number of places she'd mentioned. The town seemed so cozy and welcoming, and another piece of the puzzle that was Harper Allen fell into place.

It was clear why she enjoyed coming home so much; it was easy to fall in love with the place and the people who lived here. Everyone had been so welcoming and authentic. I'd felt free to be myself without concern for my career. About someone filming me. About anything, really.

I liked Harper's family—I could see a bit of her in each of them, and vice versa. The common expressions. The manner of speaking or gesturing. And flowing through it all was the love and respect they had for one another.

"You can stay in the car if you want," Harper said after she'd parked in front of a row of shops.

"Would you *rather* I stay in the car?" I asked, sensing apprehension.

"I just don't want you to be uncomfortable."

I laughed. "Harper, this is my life. I've been in the spotlight for many years. I'm more concerned about how it's going to impact you."

"I'm fine." She sliced a hand through the air.

Before we could discuss it further, I climbed out of the car and waited for her on the sidewalk. As we walked down the street, she pointed out some of her favorite places—Lick Ice Cream, a florist, and then we came to Bibliolater. A cloth of stars and moons hung behind an elaborate display of books, each of which appeared to be flying.

I held the door open for her, a bell chiming its hello.

"Can I help you?" someone called from within.

I checked out some of the books on display while Harper chatted with the woman at the counter. She made her purchase, and we were headed back to the car when a man's voice called out, "Harper? Is that you?"

She pulled her lips back into a huge smile. "Liam! It's so good to see you."

He hugged her, and I clenched my fists, trying to tamp down the surge of possessiveness currently making it difficult to think.

"Liam, this is Enzo. Enzo, this is Liam. I used to babysit him as a kid." It struck me that Harper had introduced me as Enzo, not Lorenzo. Whether she'd intended to or not, she was giving me freedom in anonymity.

He held out his hand, and we shook, Liam treating me as if I were anyone else. "Nice to meet you."

They caught up for a minute, and then we said our good-byes. We'd almost made it to the car when someone else stopped us. "Wow. Has anyone ever told you that you look *exactly* like the soccer player Lorenzo Mancini?"

"Oh." Harper laughed, giving my shoulder a gentle shove. "He gets that all the time. Don't you, baby?"

I delighted in the clever way she'd handled the situation. I grinned and nodded, playing along. And we were soon on our way once more.

We stopped in Lick, and she got an ice cream before heading toward a bench. I watched a couple from behind my sunglasses as they walked down the sidewalk. They were laughing and kissing as they pushed a baby stroller, and I realized I wanted that. I wanted what they had—family. Love. Connectedness. And I wanted it with Harper.

"Do you know why I liked you so much when we met?" I asked, tempted to kiss her as she licked the cream from her lips.

She shook her head, then proceeded to drive me insane. Watching her enjoy her ice cream cone was making me hard.

"You had no idea who I was. For once, I wasn't defined by soccer or fame or money. You liked me for me."

She peered into my eyes, the emerald shining in the sunlight. "I would've liked you for you, even if you'd told me."

I hung my head, full of remorse. "I know." And I did. "I think I didn't realize how hardened and jaded I've become. How angry I was. Sometimes this life can be exhausting."

"Enzo." Her tone was gentle. "I don't want to hurt you. I don't want to trap you or trick you. I'm just trying to get to know you."

"I know." I took her free hand, needing the comfort of her touch. "I do. It's just you have to understand…Giada may have betrayed my trust, but she's not why I hate the tabloids. She was trying to take advantage of the system, but it's the paparazzi I truly despise."

She frowned, and I felt encouraged to continue. Despite everything that had happened, I wanted to trust Harper. I wanted to build a life—a family—with her. And I knew that required some vulnerability, even if it made me uncomfortable.

I sighed, peering out at the gazebo just down the path, the ducks on the pond. For so long, I'd been like them. Calm on the surface but paddling like hell just beneath.

As much as I hated talking about this, I wanted Harper to

understand. I needed her to understand. Then maybe she'd be able to forgive me.

"When my father died, my whole world was turned upside down."

She'd invited me into her life. Introduced me to her family. I wanted to give her a piece of my past as well.

"My family was grieving, and I felt lost without him. He'd always been a guiding force in my life, and he'd been with me every step of the way. Encouraging my dreams. Making me a better athlete."

She held her ice cream cone in her lap, giving me space to talk again before squeezing my hand. "I can't even imagine how painful that was."

"The paparazzi just saw it as another opportunity for a story. And they made it impossible to function at a time when breathing was already hard enough."

Harper shook her head. "Oh, Enzo."

I let out a deep exhale, trying to tamp down the rage and regret. "That's not the worst part." I stared straight ahead. Even all these years later, I still blamed them for his death. The pain of losing him still felt as fresh as it had the day he'd died.

"Enzo?" Harper finally asked. "What happened?"

"I'd just bought a new car to celebrate being selected for the national team. A Lamborghini. I knew how much he'd always wanted to drive one, so I told him to take it for a spin." I shuddered. "During the drive, he started having chest pains. He was trying to get to the hospital, but the paparazzi had surrounded the car, assuming I was inside. They made it impossible for him to get through."

Harper gasped. "Oh my god, Enzo."

"By the time anyone realized what was happening…" I dropped my head, the wound still fresh. "It was too late. He was gone."

"I can't even imagine how terrible that was for you and your family." She hugged me, and it felt so good. "I'm sorry, Enzo. Thank you for telling me."

"I know I told you in Bali that I didn't want to get married or have children, but I think that's because I was scared. Scared that it would distract me from my goals. From the promises I made my dad. But—" I turned to her "—from the moment you told me about the baby, I realized how badly I *want* to be a father. I want a family." I smiled. "With you, Harper. Because of you."

"I want that too," she said.

"But?" I asked, sensing her hesitation.

"But I need time."

I nodded. "I can understand that." And I could be patient. As someone who'd had their trust broken, I knew how hard it could be to repair. But I wasn't deterred.

As we walked back to the car, I felt more hopeful than I had in a while. In sharing my grief with Harper, it felt as if I'd closed a chapter from my past. For the first time in a while, I was looking forward to the future.

CHAPTER NINETEEN

Harper

We'd just reached LA when Enzo said, "I think you should stay with me—at least until some of the craziness dies down."

I frowned and kept my focus on the road. For the past hour or so, he'd been busy on his phone, and I'd been thinking.

"What? Why?" I asked.

I hadn't been online at all this past weekend. Reception in the Alondra Valley could be spotty, and my family had kept us occupied. Even so, I figured everyone had already moved on from the news of Enzo's and my relationship.

"You underestimate the paparazzi. They may have left us alone in Alondra, but now that we're back in LA and the story's out, they'll be following us. Following you."

"Me?" I laughed. He had to be joking, right?

"Yes." He placed his hand on my thigh. "I don't want to worry about you. My focus has to be on soccer, on winning."

"I didn't ask you to worry about me," I said through gritted teeth. "I'm not your responsibility."

He sighed, and I felt guilty for pushing back when I knew

this was a sensitive issue for him. "I know that, damn it. But I want…I *need* to know you're okay. You and the baby. I'm not trying to worry you, but I want you to be cautious."

"And you don't think you'll be too *distracted* if I'm staying with you?" I asked, mostly in jest.

The idea was tempting. After the dream-not dream last night and then whatever the heck that was in the darkroom, my body was primed to detonate. At this point, I wondered why I was even holding out. Finding reasons *not* to sleep with Enzo was becoming more and more difficult, and I had a feeling the only person I was punishing was myself.

I mean, what more could I want?

He'd been sincere in his apology. And now that he'd told me about his father, I could see why Enzo had reacted the way he had. But it was more than words; it was in his actions. The flowers and gifts were thoughtful, but I was even more touched by how he'd been with my family. How he'd treated me. He was genuinely excited about the baby. He wanted us to be a family.

Besides, everyone already thought we were together. Shouldn't I be benefiting from that?

And as my mom and Enzo liked to point out, it wasn't like he could get me pregnant again. I was already carrying his child. Something he, apparently, found incredibly sexy.

"Fine," I said. "If it's that important to you, I'll stay."

"Thank you." He sounded even more relieved than I would've expected. "I'll ask Nico to get your things."

I rolled my eyes. "I'm perfectly capable of getting them myself."

"Harper," he ground out. "I don't think you understand…"

But the words died on his lips as I rounded the corner to the hotel and a group of photographers came into view. I didn't know how many of them there were. Ten? Fifteen? A lot. And as soon as they spotted us, they swarmed the car.

A pit opened in my stomach. Cameras were flashing, and they shouted their questions like hail being hurled at the windows. It was so loud and overwhelming, I couldn't make out any specifics. Not that I wanted to. We were surrounded, and I gripped the wheel tighter, feeling trapped.

"Don't make eye contact and head for the valet stand," Enzo said in a commanding tone.

I nodded and did as he said. I drove slowly, afraid I'd run over someone's toe, they were that close to us. It was suffocating and terrifying.

The valet opened the door, and I tried not to wobble as Enzo came to help me inside. My heart was racing the entire time, and it wasn't until we were inside the elevator that I sagged against the wall.

"You okay?" he asked.

I blew out a breath. "That was intense."

"Now do you understand?"

"I think I'm beginning to."

ENZO DRAGGED HIS HAND THROUGH HIS HAIR AS WE EXITED the elevator on our floor, making it look perfectly disheveled. The man was hot. So hot I thought I might burst into a ball of flames from the sight of him.

"You okay?" he asked, letting me into the hotel suite.

He was almost hot enough to distract me from what had just happened. *Almost.*

"You already asked me that," I said, mostly to avoid actually responding.

I still couldn't believe that people wanted to photograph us, *me.* Enzo was right; I'd underestimated the paparazzi, at least until we'd pulled into the hotel. My heart was still racing from the incident, and I was glad to be up in his suite. Leaving them far behind—at least for now.

When Enzo took a few steps closer, my heart rate kicked up another notch. His bergamot scent was even more powerful than before, a heady blend of citrus and spice and something else I couldn't quite identify. It had been tantalizing me all weekend.

He slid his hand down my shoulder, and I wasn't sure if he'd intended the motion to be sensual, but it was. When he gazed at me, his eyes were dark, hooded. The air shifted, and he continued to look at me as if a man starved.

He lifted his hand, smoothing his fingers over my forehead and down the line of my jaw. I tried to calm my breathing as he gently explored, his touch sending a shiver racing down my spine. His stare was intense, his molten chocolate eyes fixated on mine.

There was a knock at the door, and my shoulders sagged. Enzo swore under his breath as he went to answer it. I could hear him thanking the bellhop for delivering our bags.

I turned toward the wall of windows, feeling restless. And though some of it had to do with the frenzy downstairs, a bigger part of it was due to this man. This…tension. God, the tension made me feel as if I was going to explode at any minute.

"Harper?" Enzo placed his hand on my shoulder, and I startled.

"I need…" I shifted from one foot to the other. "I need to do something." I glanced around as if searching for inspiration. "Something."

"Like what?"

"Yoga." I nodded. "Yeah. I'm going to do some yoga." It was part of my daily practice, and I'd skipped this morning.

"I'll join you."

"Oh. Um. Sure."

I changed into some yoga pants and a sports bra in the bathroom before returning to the living room. Enzo had changed into athletic shorts and laid two yoga mats in front of the TV. His back was to me as he toggled through the TV options, the muscles of his back making my mouth water. I studied his tattoos but quickly redirected my gaze when he turned to me.

Enzo stared at my feet before slowly lifting his head, his eyes blazing a trail along my body. Most of the clothes I'd worn lately were blousy to hide my expanding stomach, but this was fitted. And my nipples hardened from his attention.

"Where'd these come from?" I asked, taking a seat on one of the yoga mats. It was as if they'd just appeared out of thin air.

"I had the staff deliver them. There's guided yoga on the TV, or we can do our own."

I was impressed. He'd done all that in the time I'd changed?

"Let's do the guided one," I said, trying not to stare at him as he took a seat on his mat. He navigated to one of the videos labeled "Challenging," and I raised an eyebrow. "Challenging, huh? You sure you can handle that?"

He laughed. "I like a good challenge."

"Yes. I'm coming to realize that." I grinned and settled into the first position.

As we moved through the poses, I was impressed by his flexibility and balance. I didn't know what I'd expected, but I found it difficult to stop watching him. The muscles of his abs and forearms, and…

"*Uccellina*," he said, and I turned my gaze back to my mat.

"Yes?"

"You're staring."

I inhaled, moved to the next pose, and exhaled, my chin lifted. "I was merely admiring your form."

He chuckled. "Is that all?"

"Yes," I said on an exhale, pushing off the floor with one hand to lift the other into the air. Only to find that Enzo was facing me, watching me.

He was supposed to turn outward, but he hadn't. Our eyes were level, and his gaze swept over me.

"Your form is very...*remarkable* as well."

Another inhale together. Then an exhale. Who knew exercise could be so erotic?

The next pose was trickier and I did my best to hold it, but my arms were tired. I wobbled and then lost my balance. Before I knew what was happening, Enzo and I were tangled up on the floor, me on top of him.

"Mm. I like this position much better." He smirked.

So did I. My breasts were crushed to his chest, legs straddling his tattooed torso.

"As long as I'm not hurting the baby." His gaze turned questioning, and he held me lightly as if afraid to crush me.

I shook my head. "You—this—it's not going to hurt the baby or me."

He cupped the back of my neck, his eyes intent on my lips as he applied gentle pressure. "*Vieni qui.*"

Come here.

I didn't fight him, allowing him to guide me down to his lips. My breathing was ragged, my nipples brushing against his bare chest with every inhalation. He held my gaze, and I silently begged him to kiss me. To take me.

The words from our first time together were on the tip of my tongue. And I found myself chanting them, as if reciting a mantra. *Ti voglio. Ti voglio. Ti voglio.*

I didn't realize I'd said it aloud until Enzo's lips tilted into a smile. "*Ti voglio anch'io.*"

I want you too.

He brushed his lips against mine, his touch surprisingly gentle. The kiss built slowly as we rediscovered each other, but it quickly turned heated. His hands were on my waist and in my hair. And then he was stripping off my sports bra, flipping us so he was on top.

He peeled off my pants and underwear, his eyes roaming my naked form. The past few months, I'd felt sick and bloated, but in this moment, I felt powerful. Beautiful.

"Perfetta," he said, the word an echo of that first time in Bali. His hand was on my stomach, his eyes on mine. And for a moment, our gazes held, and something unspoken passed between us.

We'd created a life together. A baby. Tears pricked at the corners of my eyes, the enormity of the moment washing over me. I was pregnant. With this man's baby. And he wanted me.

He bent forward so our foreheads were touching. *"Uccellina,"* he whispered. *"Questo è un bellissimo regalo. Grazie."*

I placed my hand over his, our hands covering my stomach. "It is a beautiful gift, isn't it?"

He nodded, and then he kissed me again. This time a little harder, a little more insistent. I got the impression he was trying to be gentle with me, but that wasn't what I wanted. I raked my fingernails down his back, and he bucked his hips.

"I don't want gentle," I said, licking my lips. "I want *you.*"

I writhed against him, and he reached between us to play with my clit. I was already so turned on from the past week that it didn't take much to bring me to climax. The way he continued strumming my bundle of nerves had me alternating between panting and giggling, my orgasm relaxing me more than the yoga ever had.

When he went to grab a condom from his pocket, I said, "I'm clean. Are you?"

Condoms had failed us before, and there was no point using them now—at least not as a method of birth control.

His lips parted, then he said, "Yes. I had a physical when I joined the Leatherbacks. Not that I would've needed to be tested because there's only been you."

I blinked a few times, stunned.

"You really find that so hard to believe?" he asked, tucking my hair behind my ear.

"I'm just surprised, that's all. A man like you…"

"A man like me—what?"

"I don't know. Never mind."

He frowned. "You assumed I was a player, right? Because of my job."

"Well—" I tried to duck my head, but he wouldn't let me, his grip on my chin gentle. "That and because you're hot."

"Mm." He grinned then leaned forward to kiss me. "So are you."

The kiss turned passionate, our hands and lips everywhere. It wasn't enough.

"I promise I'll take my time with you later," he said, standing. "But this first time, I need to fuck you." He removed his shorts before kicking them aside.

"The first time?" I smirked, in awe of his body. It was a work of art. Power and agility. Now that I knew he was a pro athlete—the healthy eating, the physique—it all made sense. "Someone's awfully cocky."

He grabbed my ankles, and I yelped in surprise as he yanked me toward the edge of the mat. "The only words I want to hear from your lips are 'yes' and 'more.'"

My core heated at his command, but I couldn't help but bait him. "What about 'harder'?"

"That's also acceptable." His expression was so stern as he lined himself up at my entrance, I nearly laughed.

But then he pushed inside me, filling me, and I was

speechless. After all this time, it felt so amazing to reconnect. To know that what we'd shared wasn't a fluke or a fantasy, it was real. *We* were real.

He closed his eyes and let out the most satisfied, contented sigh I'd ever heard.

"That was fast," I teased.

His eyes flashed to mine. "What did I tell you?" The words were growled, and my core quivered with delight and anticipation.

He gently pinched my clit, moving his fingers up and down, and I saw stars. "Oh god. Oh fuck." I panted. "Why do I like that so much?"

I swallowed hard, watching his face. Wanting to see him come. But then he flicked my nipples with his tongue, and I was done for. I couldn't see or feel anything beyond where we were connected. And it was the most amazing sensation, like floating or flying or falling. I wasn't quite sure, but I liked it.

He bent forward, resting his forehead to mine. Both of us panting. I cupped his cheek and kissed him and kissed him.

We were still connected, and I could feel him throbbing within me. Our souls and our bodies as connected as two people could be. It was intimate and sexy, but it wasn't nearly enough.

Perhaps sensing my impatience, he pulled out. "On your knees."

I did as he asked, though my legs felt like jelly. And it was only when I was on my knees with my back to him that he gave my ass a hard slap. I winced from the shock of it, and then he smoothed his palm over my skin, the burn giving way to a dull ache as excitement and adrenaline flooded me, pumping through my core despite having just come.

He reached around me, spreading me wide so he could spear me with his cock. And then, as he grunted and thrust, he rubbed my clit until I came so hard I could barely remain upright. It felt so good. So, so good.

And I liked the two sides of Enzo, both as a lover and a man. He could be gentle and reverent, as well as rough and demanding. A moment later, he followed me over the edge, crying out as he pumped into me. And then finally, we collapsed to the floor, sweaty and sated.

"Che bene."

I laughed, still trying to catch my breath. "Just good, huh?"

He gave my ass a playful swat, pulling me to him. And then he surprised me by holding me tight, breathing me in. *"Grazie, uccellina.* That was the most fun 'yoga' I've ever done."

I laughed both at his reference to our "yoga" and at the reminder of our first time together, when I'd thanked him for sex. But it seemed like he was thanking me for a hell of a lot more than just the orgasm. As we lay there, it felt as if I was right where I was meant to be. And while I didn't typically believe in signs, I was beginning to believe in us.

CHAPTER TWENTY

Harper

I was the first to arrive at the restaurant for lunch with the girls, and I glanced at my phone and frowned. The past few days, my social media profiles had blown up. I'd seen a ton of new followers, likes, and positive comments congratulating me on my relationship with Enzo. As well as some negative comments—remarks about me or my appearance. People questioning why we were together. Or, worst of all, threatening me.

I was trying not to let it get to me, but it had undermined my sense of safety, and I wasn't sure what to do about it. For now, I'd made my accounts private, and I tried to downplay the effect it had on me.

I was so absorbed in my task that I didn't hear Lauren enter until she'd placed her hand on my shoulder. I startled.

She frowned. "You okay?"

"Yeah. Yeah. I'm good." I slipped my phone into my purse and tried to push the negative thoughts from my mind.

Juliana and Alexis joined us, and I was grateful we were in a relatively private space in the restaurant.

"Why do you look stressed?" Juliana asked, taking the seat next to me. We opened our menus.

I didn't want to concern my friends, so I said, "There's just a lot going on. If I thought my life was crazy before, it's nothing compared to dating Enzo." I closed my menu.

"So you guys are dating now, huh?" Juliana grinned. "I thought that was just a rumor in the tabloids."

"Yeah. Yeah." I waved her comment away, though I knew she was teasing. I'd talked to her after the weekend at my parents', and she knew everything that had happened since.

"So, when are we going to meet Enzo?" Lauren asked.

Despite her attempt to play it cool, I could see right through her. But if anything, I was amused. She didn't typically get starry-eyed over celebrities, and she was always so unflappable. It made me want to introduce her to Enzo just to see how she'd react.

"I already have," Alexis said then froze, glass of water in midair. Her eyes widened as if she'd realized she'd said something she shouldn't have.

"You *what?*" Lauren asked at the same time I said, "When?"

"He asked me to help him hunt for a house."

Interesting. He hadn't mentioned that, though he had asked for her contact info. But that had been weeks ago. The waiter came to take our order, and then conversation resumed.

"Damn." Lauren shook her head. "I'm so jealous."

"Harrison will be too," Juliana said, though I didn't get the feeling she was joking. It was amusing to me—the way my friends fawned over my boyfriend.

Boyfriend? Baby daddy? Who the hell knew.

People had nicknamed me his "Americano," a popular Italian coffee. I didn't mind that so much, but the negative comments were difficult to ignore. They felt like personal attacks, especially the ones that criticized my body.

I was confident in my own skin, but I imagined even the strongest person would struggle with such hurtful and personal comments. I was both too skinny and too fat. Some people assumed I suffered from disordered eating. Others asked when I was going to get a boob job since mine were so small.

I was already dreading what they'd have to say about the pregnancy. But more than that, it was frustrating to keep such a big secret under wraps. I was finally going to be a mom, but I had to be careful who I told because we needed to time our announcement. *Announcement?*

"Can we talk about the gender reveal?" Juliana asked, and I was grateful for the distraction, even if I knew she wouldn't like my answer.

"I don't know," I hedged. "I'm just so busy lately." And I honestly wasn't a huge fan of the whole idea.

"So busy fucking like rabbits," Lauren interrupted.

"*No.*" Though I couldn't help but smile at the reminder of last night.

"Yes! Yes, you are." She pointed at me. "You've got that good-sex glow."

"It's called a pregnancy glow," I said, but my cheeks heated. "But yeah, the sex is freaking fantastic."

"You should have a gender reveal," Alexis said. "I mean, if you want to. I just—" She sighed. "I know how excited you are about being a mom, and you should celebrate this pregnancy."

We both knew what she wasn't saying—it could be your last. Every time I went to a doctor's appointment, I was reminded that I was considered high-risk just by virtue of my age. Medically speaking, I was "of advanced maternal age." But I felt fortunate to be pregnant at all. And maybe my friends were right.

"Olivia's last gender reveal was super fun," Juliana said. "The guys even said so."

I laughed, thinking of Connor at a gender reveal. He was a former navy SEAL and a beast of a man, but when it came to Olivia and their kids, he turned into a giant teddy bear. It was so sweet.

Lauren frowned. "Shouldn't it technically be called a sex reveal since gender is a social construct?"

"Yeah, but a 'sex reveal,'" Juliana said with air quotes, "doesn't have quite the same ring, does it?"

"No, but it does sound a hell of a lot more fun. I'd go to a sex reveal, especially if it meant sex toys as favors."

I laughed. Leave it to Lauren to turn it into something sexual.

"I'd love to get together and do something fun, but we're still living at the hotel, and Enzo's consumed with soccer." And with both of us traveling soon for work, I wanted to soak up every minute together.

I had a few projects going on, so I was managing those and researching locations for a future film. I had another trip planned, but I was surprised by my lack of enthusiasm. I blamed it on busyness and exhaustion.

"What if I host it for you?" Juliana asked.

"Don't the parents-to-be typically host it? I mean, this is all so last minute."

"Who cares," Lauren said. "It's a party. I say if you want to do it, let's do it!"

I laughed. "You're just saying that so you can fangirl all over Enzo, aren't you?"

"She'll have to get in line behind Harrison," Juliana said. "He's been bugging me about when we'd get to hang out."

I shook my head. "Okay. Let's do this. But I want to keep it small. Intimate."

"Absolutely," Juliana said, and we started working on the plans. I only hoped Enzo wouldn't mind.

That evening, I returned to the hotel suite to find Enzo finishing up some stretching. He stood and gave me a kiss. "I was about to shower. Want to join me?"

I pulled my lower lip into my mouth and nodded, allowing him to lead me to the bathroom. He switched on the faucet, and my mouth went dry as he removed his shorts and kicked them aside. He was gorgeous. An Adonis who checked every box and exceeded all the attributes I could've hoped for on my wish list. Handsome, confident, philanthropic. How had I gotten so lucky?

He helped me out of my clothes, and I sighed with happiness the moment my bra was unhooked. And then we stepped into the shower together. He eyed me hungrily, water sluicing down the hard planes of his chest before trailing over his erection. I licked my lips, and he stepped closer, placing his hands on my hips before pulling me under the warm spray.

"Gorgeous," he husked, and desire pooled in my belly. "Absolutely gorgeous."

He smoothed his hands up my hips, over my back, pulling me closer. And then, to my surprise, he held me. I didn't know how long we stood there. Skin to skin, heart to heart, we exhaled the secrets of our past and embraced the promises of our future.

Eventually, he stepped back and grabbed a washcloth, lathering it with soap. He took great care, washing every inch of me. I'd never felt so treasured or adored. He spent extra time on my breasts, driving me crazy with his touch.

"Spread," he said, when he reached the apex of my thighs. He lifted one of my feet onto the shower seat, then proceeded to lick and suck my clit until I was screaming his name.

My legs were shaking, my limbs loose, and it felt as if all my cares, my worries, my fears had washed down the drain with the soap. Who cared about anything else when this amazing man absolutely adored me?

I smiled what had to be a dopey smile, and he cupped the back of my neck, pulling me in for a searing kiss. I reached for his hard-on, sliding my hand around the shaft, but then stilled when my stomach cramped. I frowned and held a hand there.

"You okay?" he asked.

"Yeah." I forced a smile. "I'm sure it's nothing. I imagine some cramping after sex is normal."

"But you haven't had cramps before, have you?"

I shook my head. "No, but—" He immediately got out of the shower and started toweling off. "What are you doing?"

"Getting dressed to take you to the doctor," he said as if the answer were obvious.

"Enzo." I laughed, though I appreciated his concern. I was concerned too, even if I did think a trip to the doctor was a bit overkill. "It's some light cramping. I'll send her a message through the patient portal and look it up online while I wait for her to respond."

He groaned, covering his face with his hands. "No. Just no."

"What?" I lifted a shoulder, shutting off the water before stepping out of the shower. "Everybody does it. I can see what other moms are going through, and it's really helpful."

He huffed and leaned his hip against the counter. He looked decadent. That was the first word that came to mind. "My girlfriend thinks the internet is better than a medical degree. What would your father say?" He dried his face with a towel. "Actually, why don't you text him with your symptoms and see what he says?"

I barked out a laugh. "Um, no."

"Why not?"

"Because then he'd know we were having sex."

Enzo chuckled, though he didn't dispute it. In fact, he seemed to recoil from the idea as much as I had.

"Wait…" I paused while tying my robe. "Did you just refer to me as your girlfriend?"

"It sounded better than baby mama. But I'll call you whatever you want. Maybe one day, wife."

He didn't wait around for my reaction, instead scooping me up and carrying me back to the bedroom. His words sent a thrill of excitement through me, but I told myself it was too fast. We were having a family together, but we shouldn't let the fact that I was pregnant rush us into such a huge commitment.

"You know, I can walk," I teased, though I didn't want him to put me down.

"Maybe I want you to know that I've got you."

"I know you do," I said as he set me gently on the bed. He removed my robe, tucking me beneath the covers.

The sheets were cool and smooth against my skin, my hair wet on the pillow. And I knew that he really did have me.

He went to the other room and returned with my phone. I thanked him and messaged my doctor and tried to relax. Stressing over this wasn't good for anyone, least of all the baby.

Then I texted Alexis and asked her if she'd ever experienced cramping during her pregnancies. Her response: *totally normal*. Though she did recommend checking in with my doctor to be on the safe side.

"What'd she say?" Enzo asked.

I set my phone on the nightstand. "I'm still waiting to hear back from my doctor, but Alexis said it happened to her too."

He climbed into bed and rested his head on my chest. I massaged his scalp, mesmerized by the feel of his dark curls sliding through my fingers. I laughed, placing my hand on his chest before sliding it lower still.

He placed his hand over mine, halting my progress. "We're not having sex until I know it won't hurt you or the baby."

I was touched by his concern, but my gut told me everything was fine. His dick throbbed in my hand, but still, he shook his head. He placed his hand over mine and then removed it, setting it back on his chest once more.

I pouted. "At least let me make you feel good."

"Watching you come, hearing you scream my name, tasting your orgasm on my lips, makes me feel good."

I climbed on top of him, straddling his erection, but he wouldn't relent. "Nope. If you want to have sex, call your doctor tomorrow."

I wiggled a little, but ultimately sighed and lay down next to him, resigned to the fact that he wouldn't budge. With my head on his chest and his arm around me, I listened to his heartbeat.

"How was your day?" I asked. "Practice go well?"

"Yes. The Americans play a different type of game, and it's a good challenge for me."

"Different how?" I asked, wanting to know about the sport he loved.

"There's a bigger emphasis on fitness and endurance. Plus, the Leatherbacks are a young team. Lots of energy. I think we're going to do well when we face off against Miami."

I lifted my head. "I'm excited to watch you play."

"Yeah?" He smiled, and I could tell he liked the idea of it.

"Yeah." I lay back down.

"What about you?" he asked. "How was lunch with the girls?"

"Good. There's actually something I need to talk to you about."

"Okay." He sounded hesitant.

"I don't know what they do in Italy, but gender reveal parties are kind of a thing here in the US."

"Oh god." He groaned. "Please tell me we don't have to do the colored lasagna thing."

"What?" I cringed. "That sounds terrible."

"I heard about it recently. And I had nightmares for weeks."

I laughed. "No. Definitely no colored lasagna. Just a small gathering with some friends to celebrate the baby—and us."

"And to find out whether we're having a boy or a girl," he said.

I nodded. "That too, though for me it's more about getting together."

"Can't we just find out the baby's gender from the doctor?"

"We could," I said, tracing his tattoos. "But I was hoping you could meet my friends soon, and this would be a good way to do it."

"Of course." He perked up. "If it would make you happy, it would make me happy."

"Thank you." I smiled and pressed my lips to his chest. "We should probably start discussing names."

"What names do you like for a girl?"

"Elizabeth for my grandmother. Lizzy for short. I think London or Sydney are cute. But I know there are traditions in Italian culture, and I want to incorporate them somehow if they're important to you."

"Thank you." He took my hand in his, and warmth spread through my chest. The moment felt so much more intimate than if we'd had sex. "If we're following tradition, and if the baby is a boy, our child would take the name of my father."

"What was your father's name?" Enzo had only ever referred to him as Papà. And while I could've looked it up online, I wouldn't.

"Vittorio."

I nodded.

He was silent for so long, I wondered if he'd fallen asleep. Finally, he said, "I understand that you might have names you would prefer…"

"Sofia is a beautiful name," I said, referring to his mom. "Alexis's eldest daughter is Sophia, but it's spelled with a 'ph.' Pretend for a minute that we weren't following Italian tradition, are there any other names you like?"

"Mariantonia."

"That's a mouthful." I laughed, but then I realized he was serious.

"Mariantonia is my *nonna's* name."

Oh. Oops. "What about for a boy?"

"I haven't given it much thought. Do you have something in mind?"

"Aiden," I said. I'd always dreamed of having a son named Aiden. "It means little fire or little and fiery."

"Aiden," he said, as if testing it out. "Come here, Aiden." He took a breath. "Let's go play soccer, Aiden." I could hear the smile in his voice. "I like it."

"I like you," I said, falling a little harder.

"I'm glad because you're kind of stuck with me now." He lightly elbowed my ribs in jest.

I knew Enzo was joking, but I didn't want either of us to feel like we were trapped in this relationship because of the circumstances. Talk about a recipe for disaster.

He gave my shoulder a shake. "You know I'm teasing, right?"

With my head still resting on his chest, I nodded.

"Harper," he said. "Did I upset you?"

My belly felt like it was full of worms. "I just..." I huffed. "I worry that things happened so fast. I don't want either of us to feel stuck."

"I don't feel stuck at all. In fact, I'm thrilled that this happened. It feels like the start of another adventure." He pulled me on top of him, forcing me to look at him, to face this. "I don't know how to explain it, but us, the baby—it all feels meant to be."

He cupped the back of my neck and pulled me down for a kiss. For a moment, I forgot about the obstacles and the haters. I forgot about my fears. And I allowed myself to indulge in this moment, even if it did feel like a fantasy.

CHAPTER TWENTY-ONE

Enzo

I peered through the peephole and immediately jerked my head back. What was *she* doing here? I hadn't been expecting Val for another few days.

Harper would be home any minute, and I'd been looking forward to another round of mind-blowing sex now that she'd talked to her doctor about the cramping. Instead, I opened the door and kissed Val's cheeks.

"Hey. This is a surprise."

"You wouldn't answer my calls, and we need to talk." I felt a twinge of guilt, but then she gestured toward the end of the hall.

Mamma was walking toward us, pulling a suitcase behind her. My eyes widened. *Merda.*

"What's she doing here?" I hissed.

Val placed her hands on her hips. "I thought maybe she'd have a better chance of talking some sense into you."

"Val," I chided, but then Mamma caught sight of me, and I smiled. "Mamma! What a lovely surprise." I kissed her on both cheeks before giving her a hug.

I glared at Val over my mom's shoulder. What was she

thinking? The season was in full swing, and I had enough going on as it was. Harper and I were finally in a good place again, and I didn't want to blow it.

"Are you in town long?" I asked.

"That remains to be seen," Mamma said, glancing around as if searching for something.

Was she wondering if Harper was here? Mamma didn't typically read the tabloids, but I knew someone would tell her about my "Americano," as they'd dubbed Harper. Which was why I'd called Mamma last week to check in and tell her about Harper myself. I hadn't told her about the baby, but that was news best saved for in person.

"Would you like something to drink?" I asked.

"An Americano, perhaps?" Val offered.

I gnashed my teeth. "Or a water."

"I'd prefer something more *Italian*. A *caffè*, please."

I tried not to react to her dig and called down to the front desk and asked for it to be delivered along with something for Val and me. The coffee had barely arrived when they launched into their intervention or whatever the hell this was. *Bring it on.*

"Lorenzo," Mamma said. "How are you liking your new team?"

I set my cup on the coffee table. "Very much. I'm excited about the season. We have good chemistry."

"Mm." She sipped her espresso and then held it in her lap. "And I suppose the *woman* you're seeing had nothing to do with your decision to transfer."

"I'd be lying if I said she didn't. But ultimately, I did what was best for my career. I always do."

She nodded slowly, and I was surprised by how quiet Val had been so far. Had they discussed this beforehand? Decided on a strategy? It wouldn't have been the first time they'd ganged up on me to persuade me about something since Dad died. But it was the first time I knew with certainty I wouldn't budge.

"Lorenzo," Val said, and it felt as if she was making a point of saying my full name. "Mamma and I came to visit because we are—"

"Concerned," Mamma said. "We are concerned, *figlio mio*. We are afraid you are allowing this…woman to influence you."

I laughed, but the sound was mirthless. "Surely you know me better than that. And besides, you haven't even met Harper."

"No, but…" Val glanced at Mamma. "We know her type. We're just trying to save you from another Giada."

I clenched my fists. "Harper is *nothing* like Giada. And I do mean nothing."

Mamma clicked her tongue just as I heard the lock disengage. I tried to calm myself, hoping to defuse the situation before Harper sensed the tension in the room.

"Enzo, I'm—" Harper froze in the doorway, glancing around at the unfamiliar faces, until she came to mine. "Back. Um, hi."

I stood to greet her, taking her bag and setting it aside before kissing her temple and wrapping my arm around her shoulder. "Harper, this is my mom." I nudged her farther into the room. "Mamma, this is Harper."

"*This* is her?" my mother asked Val in Italian, her displeasure clear. "She's so *skinny*."

I cringed, watching Harper as she struggled to remain expressionless.

"What do you expect?" Val asked, crossing her legs as she continued the conversation in Italian. "She's American."

I glared at them, annoyed by their rude behavior. I opened my mouth to say something, but Harper beat me to it. Instead of responding to their jabs, Harper said, "It's a pleasure to meet you," in crisp, clear Italian.

Mamma raised one eyebrow, clearly having underestimated "the woman." Harper might not be Italian, but she spoke it like a native. I grinned, pride surging through me. Despite the way Mamma and Val had treated her, Harper had been nothing but polite. And she'd quickly put them in their place, speaking their language.

"And this is Val," I said in English.

"Ah." Harper tilted her head back in understanding. "Your manager." She turned to Val and then spoke in perfect Italian. "You were supposed to come to Bali, weren't you?"

"*Sì.*" Val's nostrils flared, and her displeasure was clear. "If only I had. Then we wouldn't be in the situation we're in."

"Careful, Val," I growled.

"No, Lorenzo." Val stood. "I've held my tongue long enough. No more."

Mamma glanced between us, and I knew she felt as if she were watching her children fight. Val might not be my sister, but she'd always been part of the family.

"Um—" Harper glanced between us. "Maybe I should leave. Give you all some time to catch up."

"Not necessary." I slid my arm around her waist. "If Val and Mamma have something to say, they can say it to both of us."

"Fine," Mamma sighed. "I'm concerned that you're moving too fast. There." She threw her hands in the air. "I said it."

I turned my attention to Val, my tone accusatory. "Did you tell her?"

Val shook her head, and I could feel Harper tense beside me. "Tell me what?" Mamma asked.

"Part of the reason I moved to California was because I wanted to be involved in my child's life." Mamma's eyes darted between Harper and me. "Mamma, I'm going to be a father. We—" I held Harper even closer "—are having a baby."

Mamma held her hands to her lips. I wasn't sure I'd ever seen her speechless, but she quickly crossed herself, and I mentally prepared myself for a lecture. Instead, she stepped forward with tears in her eyes and said, *"Dio ci ha benedetti." God has blessed us.* And hugged Harper and me. "Papà would've been so happy."

Val huffed and crossed her arms over her chest. Mamma stepped back to look at Harper, holding her hands as she apologized for her earlier rudeness. Harper took it all in stride, but I hated that my own family had ever treated her that way.

Even so, I couldn't deny my relief. Mamma was excited about the baby, and I knew she'd be supportive.

"Can't you see that she's using him?" Val asked Mamma. "We don't even know that it's his child. And we shouldn't assume anything until a paternity test is done."

Harper straightened. "I have offered to do a paternity test. I also made it clear that Enzo's involvement was neither expected nor required."

"Enzo?" Mamma glanced between us. "Who is Enzo?"

"It's the name she calls me," I said. "The name I asked her to call me," I added quickly. "And I don't need a paternity test to tell me what I already know." I glared at Val.

I appreciated Val's desire to protect me, but she could've handled this better. She *should've* handled this better.

"I am the father," I said, and damn if that didn't feel good. I smiled at the idea, and Mamma smiled too.

She placed her hand on my cheek. "Oh, *figlio mio,* I am so proud of you. And you—" She turned to Harper. "How are you feeling?" She grinned. "This is so exciting. I have always wanted to be a *nonna.*"

I left Mamma and Harper to talk about the baby, while I

went over to where Val was standing beside the window. For the first time, I questioned whether Val had my best interest at heart.

"Can we talk?" I asked, gesturing to the bedroom. "Alone."

She nodded, and I followed her into the room, shutting the door behind me.

I crossed my arms and leaned against the wall. "You were out of line. I know you didn't like Giada, but you never treated her as poorly as you have Harper."

"Maybe because I never saw a future for you with Giada. And with Harper, it feels like I'm losing you. I can't get through to you," she added quickly.

I frowned. "I know I haven't been as available lately, but you're acting as if I've somehow changed."

"You *have*. I see it happening, and I feel helpless." She sighed, and when she met my eyes, hers were watery. "Where's your aggression? Your drive? Everything used to be about soccer, and now it feels like an afterthought."

"Soccer will always be important to me, just as you will always be important to me," I said, grabbing her shoulder and meeting her eyes. "And you're right. Maybe I have changed. But I'd like to think it's for the better."

"I thought you were angry and aggressive because of what happened with your dad and then everything with Giada, but I don't know. It was as if you had all this pent-up energy with nowhere to go except on the field."

"So now you're worried that I won't bring the same level of play to the game?"

"No. I can tell you have a different energy on the field since the move. But you're also on a different team." She was silent a moment then said, "I think you were right to make the change."

I jerked my head back. "Did you just admit that I was right?"

She laughed. "Yeah. Yeah. Don't let it go to your head."

I grinned. "I like the new team. And I didn't realize how unsettled I felt until I met Harper."

She held my gaze a moment. "I'm still not sold on Harper."

"I know you're trying to protect me, and I appreciate it. But I hope you'll come to realize that she's not out to screw me over."

She crossed her arms over her chest. "I hope you're right."

"She makes me happy, Val. Please at least try to be nice." I didn't need Val's approval, but her opinion meant a lot to me.

"I'll try. But can you try to be better about answering my calls? You may have been right about the transfer, but we have a long way to go before the World Cup."

I nodded. "I promise."

When we returned to the living room, Harper and Mamma were chatting animatedly about food. I smiled and joined them on the couch, pleased they were getting along so well.

"Harper tells me the paparazzi have been harassing her. Why have you not done something?" Mamma asked me.

I frowned, my muscles immediately pulling taut. "They *what?*"

Harper rolled her bottom lip into her mouth, ducking her head. "I mean, the word 'harassing' seems a bit strong. And it's not the paparazzi so much as the fans."

"We should arrange security," Val said. "Some of the comments online have been…vicious."

I'd assumed Harper hadn't been online, because she hadn't mentioned it. But then she said, "I tried to ignore them, but I had to make my Instagram account private."

I frowned and turned my attention to Val. It was her job to stay on top of this and develop a plan. "Why haven't you mentioned this before?"

"I would've but—"

"Right," I huffed, waving away her response. I already knew the answer—I hadn't been as attentive in answering her calls.

"I'll have Nico arrange security for her," I said, taking out my phone. I should've thought of it before, but Harper had mostly been spending time at the hotel with me or at work.

"Why do I need security?" Harper asked. *"I'm* not the celebrity."

"You are now," Val said. "I mean, at least as long as you're dating Lorenzo."

I frowned, not appreciating her implication. "We aren't just dating. We're having a baby together."

"Well, if you think this is bad, just wait until they find out about the baby," Val said.

Harper's eyes widened, and I sensed her fear. I knew how she'd struggled to get pregnant. And just how badly she wanted this baby. And after what had happened with my dad, I wasn't taking any chances. I'd do anything to keep Harper and our child safe.

"Uccellina," I said, hoping to calm her. "Most people online are harmless, they're just venting their frustration. It happens every time I miss a shot or my team loses a game."

"Yeah, but unlike you, I didn't ask for this life."

"Unfortunately, it comes with the territory," I said. "Look, I know security might seem like overkill, but—"

She shook her head. "No. It's fine. You're right."

I kissed her temple, surprised but grateful all the same. "I will do anything to protect you." *I love you.*

I just hoped it wouldn't be too much for her—this life that she hadn't wanted.

THE REST OF MAMMA AND VAL'S VISIT WAS UNEVENTFUL, AND they soon returned home. But not without attending one of my games first. I was glad to have that out of the way and pleased that Mamma and Harper had gotten along so well. I knew Val still had her reservations, but she seemed to have come around as well.

Harper wasn't thrilled about her new security, even if she didn't say it. And there were a number of details we had yet to sort out, namely the house. But Alexis and I had been working on that.

"Thank you for coming with me today," Harper said from the exam table in the doctor's office.

Nico had helped us sneak in, arranging everything so we'd go straight to the exam room instead of waiting in the common area.

"Of course." I held her hand in mine, grateful that she allowed it. I was both nervous and excited about this appointment.

There was a knock at the door, and a silver-haired woman in scrubs peeked her head in. "Harper." The nurse smiled, then turned to me. She was speechless a moment before she collected herself and said, "And you must be the father."

I nodded. "I am."

Sylvia introduced herself and then asked Harper some questions. I figured it was fairly routine, but I listened intently.

"You've had some headaches lately," I chimed in.

"I think it's just from stress. I've been tired."

"Still." The nurse smiled. "It's always good to tell the

doctor about any new symptoms. We'll do the exam and then the sonogram. You know the drill. Please disrobe from the waist down and cover yourself with the sheet."

Harper nodded and said, "Thanks, Sylvia," as the nurse closed the door behind her.

"Hey." I tangled my hands in Harper's hair. "I missed you this morning."

She smiled. "I missed you too. I'm glad you were able to get your coach to approve this."

I gripped her chin. "Of course, *uccellina.* I wouldn't miss it for the world." And then I gave her a quick peck. "Shouldn't you get changed?"

She lifted a shoulder. "Yeah. Probably. Though sometimes I have to wait a little while for Dr. Fulton."

"Mm." I placed my hands on the exam table, the paper crinkling as I bracketed her with my arms. "Is that so?"

I didn't wait for her answer, kissing her instead. I'd seen her eight hours ago, but it felt like forever. I caressed her lips with mine, coaxing her to open for me. To let me in. And when she did, I explored her as if it was the first time.

I slid my hand up her ribs to her breasts, squeezing and making her moan. She was rocking into me, so I peeled her jeans down, the elastic waistband making for easy access.

"Enzo." She swallowed, though her eyes were wild with lust and excitement. "What are you doing?"

"Helping you get ready for the doctor," I said, kneeling before her as I removed her jeans. "Though I wouldn't mind doing my own exam first." I inched closer, the scent of her intoxicating.

"What? Enzo," she chided.

But I could tell she was completely turned on by the idea. Fuck, so was I. My dick was pressing against the zipper of my jeans, and I would've killed to be inside her. I spread her legs, and she tangled her fingers in my hair.

I wanted to strip her naked and make her squirm. I wanted to worship every inch of her body until she screamed my name. But a knock at the door interrupted my fantasy.

"You ready?" a woman's voice called.

"Yep!" Harper chirped, quickly covering herself with the sheet before hissing at me to "Stand up!"

I stood quickly and turned away, pressing against my hard-on to try to make it less obvious.

The doctor came in, followed by her nurse. They conducted a brief exam and asked some questions. The doctor lifted Harper's shirt and squirted some gel on her stomach, and I gave her hand a squeeze.

And then my attention was on the screen. I stared at the little black-and-white image, trying to understand what I was seeing. It looked like a little blob inside a bigger blob. Was that really a baby? *My* baby?

"Incredible, isn't it?" Dr. Fulton asked. "There's the head." She indicated to it on the screen. "Two arms. Two legs and feet."

"Strong feet." Harper smiled.

I nodded, still in awe.

"Do you want to know whether you're having a boy or a girl?"

Harper shook her head. "Could you please put the answer in an envelope? We want it to be a surprise until the party."

Sylvia wrote something down and then slipped it into an envelope before handing it to me. "Congratulations." She smiled. "Being a parent is the best job in the world."

I wasn't sure how I was going to juggle my career and my new role as a father, but I pushed those thoughts away. For right now, I was grateful to be part of this family.

CHAPTER TWENTY-TWO

Harper

I stared at the cake again, wondering whether the filling was pink for a girl or blue for a boy. It was the same thing I'd been asking since my appointment two weeks ago.

Two. Weeks.

That was how long I'd had to wait for the gender reveal, and it had made me realize that I absolutely could not wait to find out whether I was having a boy or a girl until the baby was born. I had no idea how Alexis had done it because I was going crazy.

Enzo had been traveling for games, and I'd gone to Vancouver briefly. Now we were both back in LA, and I was excited to celebrate—both his team's latest win and the baby.

"Oh my god, look at you," Lauren squealed. She placed her hands on my belly before pulling me into a hug. "You popped!"

I laughed, peering down at my stomach, which was more noticeably pregnant than even a week or two before. It didn't help that I was wearing an outfit that did nothing to hide my baby bump. The coral dress was an off-the-shoulder style with a ruffled neckline. The ruched sides were flattering but definitely didn't camouflage the bump. "I did."

"You look gorgeous," Juliana said, and Alexis nodded before giving me a hug too.

"Um, speaking of gorgeous…" Lauren stared at something behind me. Her mouth fell open on a whispered "Holy Lorenzo Mancini."

I laughed, glancing over my shoulder to where Enzo was standing with one of his teammates. Enzo's shirtsleeves were rolled up to reveal his corded muscles, and his ink was on display.

"What are we staring at?" Hunter asked in his deep voice, startling us.

"Hey, babe." Lauren turned to him, lifting her head for a kiss. He gave her a peck on the lips before pulling her closer into his side and whispering something in her ear. She grinned and nodded but said nothing.

Hunter excused himself to get a refill, and Enzo joined us a moment later, wrapping his arm around my waist and pressing a kiss to my temple. I smiled, my cheeks heating under my friends' watchful gazes.

"I'd like you to meet my three best friends," I said. "This is Juliana, Alexis, and Lauren."

He shook each of their hands, but I had to cough to cover a laugh when he got to Lauren. She looked as if she might pee herself.

"Um, hi." She tucked her hair behind her ear. "I'm sure you hear this all the time, but I'm a huge fan."

Enzo chuckled. "Thank you. And maybe you can get Harper more excited about soccer. Actually—" He tapped a finger to his lips. "How would you like to attend our next home game with her? Then you could answer any questions about what's happening on the field."

"That would be incredible," Lauren said, barely containing her smile. "Thank you."

I laughed with a shake of my head then turned to Juliana. "Is it time to cut open the cake yet?"

She grinned. "If you're ready."

I nodded. "I'm more than ready."

Enzo and I followed Juliana over to the table where the cake was set up. Behind us, there were pink and blue streamers, and I kept wondering what we'd find inside. *Blue*, I chanted. I really wanted a boy, though I wasn't going to admit it. I'd just always imagined myself as a boy mom.

A photographer came up to take our pictures and capture the moment. Enzo and I had talked about it beforehand and decided to release some of the photos to the press to announce our pregnancy. It seemed odd—to have to publicly announce the fact that we were expecting. I still couldn't wrap my head around this life sometimes.

I held the knife, and Enzo placed his hand over mine. For a minute, it felt more like a wedding than a gender reveal. But I was getting ahead of myself.

"*Sei pronta, amore mio?*" he whispered.

My insides quivered with excitement, and I held my breath as we sank the knife into layer upon layer of cake. When I pulled it out to make another cut, all I saw were blue crumbs and blue icing.

"It's a boy!" I wasn't sure whether I'd shouted it or someone else had because the next thing I knew, Enzo was cupping my face and kissing me.

"A boy," Enzo sighed, his smile radiating love and joy. He kissed me again and then turned to our friends. "Thank you all for coming today. Hopefully, the next time we celebrate, it will be in our new home."

My attention whipped to him, and I tried not to let my smile falter. "Our what?"

"Surprise, *uccellina*." He turned and slipped a key from his pocket before handing it to me. "I bought us a house."

I gnashed my teeth and tried to remain calm as everyone watched on. *What the hell?*

Everyone started clapping, and I didn't know what to do. Did I say thank you? Tell him how I really felt in front of all our friends?

I couldn't take it anymore. While the cake was being served, I dragged him into the bathroom and locked the door behind us. He grinned and stepped closer, placing his hands on my hips.

"Mm. Is this you thanking me for the house?"

"What?" I jerked my head back. How had he so completely misread the situation? "No. Enzo, you can't just buy a house and say we're moving."

"Why not?" He frowned. "You said you were sick of living at a hotel. I thought this was what you wanted."

"I—" I sighed. "I did. Do. But I wanted it to be a decision we made together."

"When? We are both so busy lately, we barely see each other. When would either of us have time to house hunt, eh?"

"I don't know, but…" He was right. But still, that wasn't the point. "You could've sent me listings or something. If it's going to be our house, I would've liked a say in where it was or what it looks like or *something*."

"That's why I consulted Alexis. She's one of your best friends. She knows your taste. And she assured me you'd love this property."

My shoulders deflated. The man I loved had just bought us a house, and he'd done so with my comfort and wishes in mind. And I was complaining.

"You're right. I'm sorry." I brushed some hair away from my face. "Just…next time there's a big decision to be made, I wish you'd talk to me first."

"I thought you liked surprises."

"Yeah." I barked out a laugh. "I do when they're not permanent."

"The house is not permanent. And if you do not like it, we will sell it and buy another." He massaged my shoulders, and I felt them relax. "Okay?"

As outrageous as that idea seemed, I appreciated the sentiment. "Can I at least see a picture? Something?"

"It has five bedrooms." He traced his finger down my neckline. "A pool..."

"Ooh. Really?" It had been so hot out, and taking a dip in the pool sounded decadent.

"Mm." He grinned. "I thought you'd like that, considering how much you loved the pool at Mizuki House."

"It wasn't just the pool I loved..." My core flooded with heat at the memory.

"Now, do you want to return to the party, or..." He swayed my hips side to side, his eyes darkening with lust as he leaned in to kiss my neck.

"Enzo." I pushed against his chest. "We are *not* having sex in the bathroom during our gender reveal."

"Why not?" He continued kissing me. "It sounds pretty good to me."

I shook my head. My mind was still spinning about the house. I hadn't even gotten to process the fact that we were having a boy. My chest tightened, and then a sense of joy washed over me, so powerful I started crying.

"I thought you weren't upset about the house." He rubbed my back.

I grabbed a tissue and wiped my nose. "We're having a boy."

His watery smile reflected mine. *"Ti amo,"* he rasped.

I froze. For a moment, I wasn't sure I'd heard him correctly. "You love me?"

He nodded, cupping my cheek with his other hand on my belly. "I love you, Harper. And you, Aiden."

"Aiden Vittorio," I said, and then I really started crying. I had everything I'd ever wanted. "I love you, Enzo."

His eyes were soulful and loving, and then he kissed me. It was passionate and tender. It was everything I needed and then some.

Was this amazing life actually mine?

"WHO'S THE BEEFCAKE?" LAUREN HOOKED HER THUMB OVER her shoulder. It had been a few days since the gender reveal, and we were meeting to go furniture shopping for the new house.

I rolled my eyes and tried to ignore my bodyguard and all the attention we had garnered. I was still getting used to the idea of dating a celebrity, and sometimes I wondered if I'd be less conspicuous if I didn't have a hulking mountain of muscle following me everywhere.

"He's part of our security team."

And lately, I was grateful to have him around, even if I was annoyed by the fact that I needed a security team in the first place. After the news about our pregnancy came out, Enzo's and my social media accounts were flooded with comments. Nico had been helping me navigate being in the public eye, but it wasn't easy.

"Have you seen Lady Gaga's bodyguard?" Lauren asked. "He's a hottie."

"The one who looks like he could be from the movie *The Transporter?*"

She laughed, and we continued down the line of couches. "Yeah. I guess he kind of does, now that you mention it."

"So, where should we start?" I asked, wanting to get this over with. Enzo had told me to buy whatever I wanted, but the idea of spending his money made my skin feel tight.

"I think I have a good feel for your style, but I know nothing about Enzo's. I mean, apart from what I've seen in some Italian design magazines."

I laughed. "I'm not sure I do either. I've never seen his home—in person or a magazine."

"Really?"

"Yeah. I mean, I met him at Mizuki House, which was a rental. And then he's been staying at the hotel since he came to LA. So, I have no idea what his style is." I frowned.

"What's wrong?"

"I feel like that's something I should know. I mean, we're moving in together. Having a *baby* together."

"Not necessarily," she said. "And people's tastes evolve over time."

"True, but…"

The door opened, and Alexis breezed into the shop, removing her sunglasses and resting them on her head. "Hey." She smiled, approaching us. "Sorry I'm late." Alexis had offered to join us since she had all the blueprints and dimensions from the house.

Enzo had taken me to the house before he'd left for another away game. It was beautiful, if a bit big. After we'd christened the kitchen counter, Enzo had told me to ask Nico for whatever I needed and then suggested hiring Lauren to help with the design. We were on a tight deadline, and despite that, Lauren had been nice enough to squeeze us in between several other projects.

I kept trying to imagine myself living there. Tried to imagine giving up the apartment I'd lived in for the past ten years and the independence and sense of pride that had come along with taking care of myself. Everyone acted like this wasn't a big deal, but it was a huge deal to me.

But what else was I going to do? The apartment was too small—and not secure enough—for our growing family. The hotel was too impersonal. Enzo had bought us a house, and I knew he was excited. So I was trying to be excited too.

"So, I take it the house was a surprise?" Lauren asked.

"What gave it away?" I joked.

"The deer-in-the-headlights look, for one," Lauren said.

"Yeah." I cringed, fingering the tassels on a throw pillow. "I wish I could've hidden my shock better."

"Are you happy about it?"

"I'm not unhappy about it," I said. I mean, the house was gorgeous. And Enzo was so proud. "But I wish he'd consulted me about such a big decision first."

We hadn't talked about what we'd do once the baby was born, but moving home to the Alondra Valley was looking less and less likely.

Alexis nodded. "Trust me, I suggested it. But he was so excited to surprise you."

"I think it's sweet," Lauren said.

I rolled my eyes, but I was smiling as I said, "Of course you do. I mean, he bribed you with tickets to a Leatherbacks game."

"Whatever." Lauren nudged my shoulder with hers. "You know you're more important to me, right?"

I nodded, but I was quiet as we continued to peruse the store. I'd underestimated just how little time together Enzo and I would have while the season was in full swing. Lately, I spent more time with Nico than Enzo, and I was looking forward to the season ending in November. Hopefully, that would give us a few months to get to know each other as a couple before Aiden arrived.

"I get the feeling that something's bothering you, Harp," Lauren finally said. "What's going on?"

"I don't know." I sank down on a couch under the pretense of testing it out. "It's all happening a bit fast, don't you think?"

I glanced at the price tag and nearly swallowed my tongue. *Holy shit.*

"Does it feel fast?" Alexis asked, joining me. "Or are you just afraid that other people will think it is?"

Damn, she was perceptive. "Perhaps a little of both. And now—knowing who he is—I guess I wonder if people will think I did this on purpose. To trap him." He'd even voiced such a concern when I'd first told him, as had Val. And that was a big part of the reason why I'd stayed offline since the gender reveal.

"First of all," Alexis said. "Screw them."

Lauren nodded.

"People will always talk and speculate," Alexis said. "Believe me, I know. But what matters is how you feel about the situation. Because at the end of the day, you're not building a life, a family, with them. You're building one with Enzo."

I knew Alexis spoke from experience. When she and Preston had first started dating, they'd kept it a secret at her insistence. She thought everyone would judge her for sleeping with a man who was not only nine years younger than her, but also her daughter's nanny.

"There is no one timeline," Lauren said, and I traced the curves of my bracelet. "Just like there's no one relationship solution. Some couples get married; some don't. Some have children; some don't. Some consolidate bank accounts; some don't. You have to do what's best for you."

I nodded, considering her words. She and Hunter had been together for several years now and were very happy.

They weren't married, nor did they plan to have children. It worked for them, and I was thrilled for her.

"Does it feel rushed to you?" Lauren asked.

"There are just…so many things happening so quickly. And my hormones are freaking all over the place." It felt good to be honest, because I was scared to trust what was happening with Enzo. It all seemed a little too good to be true.

Alexis wrapped an arm around my shoulder. "It'll get easier. But at some point, you're going to have to slow down and be honest with yourself."

"Slow down?" I scoffed. "Now is not the time for me to slow down. I've got a million work projects going on. I've got stock photo sites asking me when I'll have more images to sell them. I've got the pregnancy—and all the things I need to research about baby gear. I can't possibly do it all."

"That's why you have us." Lauren grinned. "And Enzo. Lean on your friends and family."

I laughed. "I know. I know."

"No." Alexis shook her head. "You think life will slow down once you have the baby, but time only speeds up. And as they grow up…" Her smile was wistful. "You'll be running around to soccer camp and playdates and so many other things. Don't miss out on this time. Don't miss out on your pregnancy—something you've wanted for so long—because you're too focused on the future."

I nodded, taking her words to heart. She was right. I just didn't know what to do about it.

"Have you been doing yoga lately?" Lauren asked.

I shook my head and tried not to laugh at Enzo's and my code word for sex. "I stopped doing pole a few months ago, and my yoga practice has been sporadic. I just don't have time."

"I think you should focus on making time for it. You always seem more centered when you do."

"Yeah…" I hedged. "I know I should."

"Maybe Enzo will do it with you," she suggested.

My cheeks heated at the reminder of Enzo's and my last yoga session. I wouldn't mind another one of those.

"Enzo is crazy about you," Alexis said. "And everyone can see how happy he is about the baby."

I nodded. "You're right. I know you're right. I'm just not used to being with someone like him."

"What? Hot? Athletic?" Lauren teased. Most of the guys I'd dated in the past had been musicians, artists, surfers.

"No." I rolled my eyes. "Someone who wants to take care of me."

"Mm. Yes," Lauren said. "I told you to find yourself a good man, and it sounds like you finally did."

Enzo was a good man. Almost too good to be true. The concern still lurked in the back of my mind that he was only sticking around for the baby. That our relationship was founded on passion and then forged out of obligation. But I pushed it away to focus on the good.

I smiled. "I did, didn't I?"

CHAPTER TWENTY-THREE

Enzo

I woke up with the scent of almonds clinging to my skin and a warm body curled next to mine. *Harper.*

She was cradled in my arms, my hard-on digging into her ass. Sunlight tried to peek through the edges of the curtains, and I closed my eyes and breathed in this moment. She'd been gone again this past week for work; I wanted to soak in every detail.

I pulled her closer to me, letting her feel the effect she had on me. The effect she always had on me. *"Buongiorno, amore mio."*

She turned in my arms so she was facing me and yawned. *"Buongiorno,* tardigrade."

I smirked. "You think you're so cute, don't you?" I teased, thinking back on our first night together in Bali when she'd compared me to that hideous water bear. "You are. But you're also too far away."

These past few months had been an adjustment. Between my games and travel and Harper's hectic work schedule, we barely saw each other. Then you added in a pregnancy and a new house, and life was very busy right now. Busy but so, *so* good. I had a lot to be grateful for.

I'd worried that in our time apart, we'd lose the momentum we'd gained. But instead, the opposite seemed to be true. We made time every day to talk, and I looked forward to hearing her voice. Still, it wasn't enough, but it would have to be for now. Until both the season and the World Cup were over, I had to stay focused on soccer.

I needed to tell her that I'd been selected… I'd been trying to figure out how to break the news.

The Leatherbacks had made it to the play-offs, and as soon as the season ended, I'd be flying out to Italy for some last-minute training before the World Cup. It was everything I'd ever wanted, but…not the best timing, considering how close we were getting to the baby's due date.

"I'm right here." She yawned, but when I pulled her to me, our bodies flush, she gasped. "Oh."

"Yeah. *Oh.*" I grinned.

I trailed my hands along her back, down over her ass, cupping her cheeks to pull her closer. She lifted her leg, draping it over mine and inviting me in. And boy did it feel good, sliding between her wet heat, sinking into home.

"You feel so good. I could stay here forever," I said, kissing her. "I missed you this week."

"Enzo," she sighed. "I missed you too, but we can't stay in bed all weekend."

"Why not?" I nuzzled her neck, holding her tightly as she rocked into me.

"The rug company is coming this morning."

We'd moved in to the new house as soon as we had the keys, even though it wasn't fully decorated at the time. Since then, room by room, it had become more complete. Every time I came home from an away game, our house was closer to done. Closer to becoming a home.

I arched my hips. "Let Nico handle it. It's his job."

"I need clean clothes. I haven't even unpacked from my trip yet."

"So? I prefer you naked." I burrowed beneath the covers and sucked her nipple into my mouth. She let out a gasp, and I took that as my cue to continue. "And we can pay someone to do your laundry or buy you new clothes for all I care."

Her muscles tightened beneath my hands, her body stiffening. "I can wash my own clothes, Enzo."

"I know you can, but why not hire someone else to do it? Especially if it reduces your stress and gives *us* more time together. Time is more important than money."

I rolled us so I was on top, though I was mindful of her growing belly. I hated that I'd had to miss the last appointment because of training. Even though Harper had assured me it was no big deal, it was to me.

I grabbed her wrists, linking them over her head. Her eyes flared with desire, and I grinned. "Don't you want more time for this, *uccellina?*" I bent forward to tease her ear, rocking my hips against her.

"Yes," she sighed. "Yes, Enzo. Just like that."

I knew she couldn't refuse me now. Not when I was making her delirious with pleasure. I silenced any further protest with my lips, mimicking the motion with my hips, until we were both panting and sated.

I was still coming down from the high, when she rolled away from me.

"Hey," I growled when she pushed out of bed. "Where do you think you're going?"

She turned back, leaning over the bed to give me a peck on the lips and the most tantalizing view of her body. "Unpack. Laundry. And I promised Juliana we'd finish the baby registry today. The baby shower is coming up."

She strode across the room, and I watched her body in

awe. I'd always thought she was beautiful—strong yet light. But now that she was pregnant with my child...I shook my head. She was incredible—our baby even more miraculous for what she'd gone through before getting pregnant. And, impractical as it was, I didn't want her to leave my side, not even for a moment.

She tilted her head to the side. "What?"

"You're gorgeous."

She smiled, her skin glowing as if from within. Her hair was mussed, lips swollen, and I couldn't imagine anyone looking more beautiful.

"And you're stalling. The sooner we get this registry done, the sooner we can relax."

"Okay. Okay." I stood, delighting in the way her eyes tracked my every move.

I followed her to the shower, enjoying the large size of our new bathroom. As nice as the hotel was, this home was true luxury with its beautiful tile work and multiple show-erheads.

"I'm glad you're home, *amore mio*."

She smiled, but then yawned again. "Me too. I'm not looking forward to going to South Carolina in a few weeks." Hearing the exhaustion in her voice, I frowned. I didn't care what the doctor said; Harper was working too much. Pushing herself too hard.

At least she'd started limiting her travel to the US, but still. I didn't want her to travel at all.

I smoothed my hands over her hips and down her stom-ach. "You're working too hard."

She huffed and stepped out of my arms, rinsing off before exiting the shower.

"What? You are," I said, switching off the faucet and toweling off. How did she not see it? The constant travel, the long hours, the jet lag. I understood it more than anyone, and I knew what it was like to constantly push the physical limits of your body. But this was a pregnancy we were talking about, and she'd officially entered her third trimester.

"The baby is healthy. And I'm not traveling overseas anymore, even though Dr. Fulton said flying was fine."

"For now. What are you going to do during your third trimester? And what about after the baby's born?" I asked, pulling on some athletic shorts. She'd been in denial about this for weeks, evading the topic any time I brought it up. "You know you don't have to work, right?"

"Yes, Enzo." She glared at me. "I do. I'm not just going to quit my job and live off your money."

"It's *our* money, *uccellina*. Just like this is *our* house." For some reason, I kept having to remind her of that. I was beginning to wonder if she felt like she needed to prove a point or if she was *that* stubborn.

"I just want you to be happy," I said. "And I can't envision you continuing to travel like you are while taking care of an infant."

"What happened to 'we're a team'?"

"Harper." I stepped toward her, softening my tone. "Of course I'll be there every step of the way. But…" I tried to choose my words carefully, knowing this was a delicate subject. "I can't imagine you wanting to be away from our child. Especially not after how long you've wanted to be a mom."

Her shoulders sagged. "You're right. And that was never part of my plan. But neither were you."

"What *was* your plan?" I asked. "I mean, if the artificial insemination had worked?" I'd never thought to ask.

"I'd planned to build as big of a nest egg as I could before the baby came. Then I was going to max out what meager maternity leave I had while searching for jobs back home."

She sighed. "LA is too expensive as it is, let alone with a baby. And I wanted to be near my family."

Her answer both did and didn't surprise me. But still, it seemed like something she would've mentioned.

"You never told me that."

"What would be the point?" She sighed. "It's not really an option now, is it?"

I frowned. We both knew I had another year on my contract. And even then... I shook my head. Professional soccer had been my life for almost twenty years. And while I knew it would end someday, I felt I had more left to give. To the team. To the sport.

"We'll figure something out," I said.

She nodded, though she seemed skeptical. Then she grabbed my hand and placed it on her stomach. "Do you feel that?" She smiled.

There was a faint rhythmic beat beneath my hand, and I smiled. "What is that?"

"The baby has hiccups."

I kissed her. "*Ti amo.*"

"I love you too." Her shoulders slumped, some of the fight going out of her. "And I'm sorry if I bit your head off. I'm tired."

"I bet I know what would help," I said.

"Let me guess," she said in a teasing tone. "More sex?"

"Always." I pulled her closer. "But I was thinking of breakfast."

She laughed. "Yes. Breakfast would be great."

We got ready, and I called Nico to arrange to have a driver to take us to the store so we could finish the registry. Harper and I spent the drive catching up on the past week and enjoying our breakfast sandwiches. We were planning to spend Thanksgiving at Juliana's house, along with Alexis, Lauren, Olivia, and their families. I was looking forward to all the new traditions we'd be starting as a family.

When we arrived at the store, the staff had been kind enough to close so we could shop privately. But there were still a few paparazzi outside waiting to take our picture. I placed my hand on Harper's back, ignoring them until we were inside.

"What the hell is this?" I asked, turning over a package.

"It's a—" Harper ripped the item out of my hand and placed it back on the shelf. She lowered her voice, forcing a smile for the saleswoman watching us from the front. "It's a travel breast pump."

I grunted and pointed the scanner at the price tag on a nearby stroller. It had a leather covering and seemed entirely impractical, but that wasn't the point. It was gorgeous and lightweight—a thing of beauty. Like the Ferrari of baby strollers, and Harper would look damn good pushing it.

"Enzo!" She spun on me with wide eyes. "What the hell? A five-thousand-dollar stroller, that's insane."

Was it? Five thousand dollars was nothing to me. Not like the happiness I knew it would bring Harper.

"Is everything okay?" The employee from earlier approached, batting her eyes as she glanced up at me.

"We were just admiring this stroller. Can you tell us about its features?"

"I'd love to." She smiled like a lion eyeing its dinner, ready to pounce on her prey.

"Thank you." Harper smiled brightly. "But I've researched everything thoroughly, and I know what I'd like." She turned to me, and even though she was dismissing the stroller, it felt as if she were talking about me.

I crossed my arms over my chest, enjoying the way her eyes darted there. The way her skin flushed. God, she was gorgeous. And maddening.

"It's top-of-the-line," the saleswoman said.

"See?" I held up my hands. "Top-of-the-line means it's the best. And my baby deserves the best."

"*My* baby deserves a college fund. I'm not blowing five grand on a stroller he'll outgrow in three years."

"I, um, I think I'll give you two a minute," the saleswoman said, smiling tightly as she backed away.

"I know it's the one you want," I said to Harper after she'd gone.

"Oh yeah?" Harper crossed her arms over her chest. It had the effect of pushing her breasts even higher. Which, in turn, made my mouth water and my cock stir.

"*Uccellina*, what's really bothering you?" I furrowed my brow, guiding her over to a chair nearby.

"I'm used to being thrifty. To watching every penny I spend. I research my purchases. So when you come in and say 'we need xyz,' it feels like you're doubting my opinion."

"I'm not doubting your opinion. I'm sorry if I made you feel as if I am."

When she nodded, I said, "And I know that you stress about money. I wish you wouldn't. I want you to have exactly what you want."

"But that only feeds into what people are saying about me."

I clenched my fists but tried to remain calm. I wasn't aware of what they'd said, but I didn't need to know. It was a distraction, and it didn't matter. But it did to Harper. I kept having to remind myself that she was new to this life. That it was an adjustment and perhaps an unwanted one.

I lifted a shoulder. "It wouldn't matter who you were, they'd try to break you down. You have to ignore it."

"It's just… It's hard sometimes, you know?" She twisted her hands together, her eyes on the floor.

She sniffled, and I pulled her into a hug. Her words were

muffled by my chest. "Sometimes I wish you were a normal guy with a normal job."

I swiped my thumbs to catch her tears. "It won't always be this way, *uccellina.*"

Though, the attention had increased even more after we'd announced the pregnancy, plus the Leatherbacks had qualified for the playoffs. And it was only going to get worse with the World Cup coming up.

She nodded. "I know. And I love how passionate you are about soccer." I smiled. She'd attended nearly all my home games, and I loved knowing she was watching from the stands.

She stood and straightened.

"You good?" I asked.

"I will be."

We shopped a while longer, and she seemed to relax. At least until it was time to leave. A crowd had gathered out front, and as we headed out to the car, they shouted questions that I mostly ignored.

But then one of them called, "Hey! I didn't know your baby mama used to be a stripper."

What the hell?

I stopped and stared at the guy, hoping he could read the threat in my eyes. "What did you say?"

"Enzo, come on. Don't worry about it," Harper said, tugging on my arm.

"No. He is disrespecting you, and I will not stand for it."

"It's fine." She tugged again. "He's just trying to bait you about my pole dancing."

"Yeah. We saw a video." The guy let out a low whistle. "*Damn.*"

That was it. I saw red. I whirled on him and shoved him on the ground. "Don't you dare—" I leaned over and reared back to punch him, even as he covered his face "—talk about her that way. Do you hear me?"

"Enzo!" Harper pulled on my arm. "Enzo, stop! Please."

Rage pumped through my veins. These fuckers got away with murder. They'd killed my dad, and I would not let them hurt Harper.

"Enzo." Harper's voice was calmer. "*Smettila.*"

I stood and straightened. And only then realized how many people were watching us. *Cazzo.*

The security team ushered us into the car and sped away from the shop. I shouldn't have done that. I shouldn't have— I glanced over at Harper, suddenly realizing how quiet she was.

"Are you okay?" I asked. She worried her lip and shook her head, looking as if she were about to cry. "I'm sorry. They shouldn't be allowed to talk to you like that."

"I don't care about that!" She threw her hands in the air. "You should've ignored him. What if he presses charges? What if—" Her skin was flushed with color, and I placed my hand over hers.

"Breathe, Harper." I inhaled slowly and exhaled, trying to push away my concerns. Trying to help her relax. She was too stressed. It was too much. "Breathe."

She regulated her breathing and then massaged her temples. "I hate this."

"So do I, but I can't change it."

She clenched her jaw and stared straight ahead, arms crossed over her chest. I didn't like seeing her stressed. I liked being the cause of it even less. Something had to give.

CHAPTER TWENTY-FOUR

Harper

As soon as I opened the door to the house, my mouth started watering. "Oh my god. What smells so good?" I called out, kicking off my shoes.

"*Ciao, bella.*" Enzo smiled from the kitchen and rounded the counter to give me a kiss. He knelt to the floor and kissed my belly. "*Ciao, bimbo.*"

I smiled and set my bag on the counter. Between the pregnancy and the paparazzi, it was getting more and more difficult to do my job. My ability to travel was limited, and I sensed my boss's impatience, despite how happy she was for me. Then there was the pack of paparazzi who'd tried to follow me around as I'd scoped out local sites. I'd never been more grateful for the security team.

"You're cooking?" I asked, my eyes widening. Why was he cooking?

"*Sì.* Come sit down." He pulled out a chair for me at the table, and I took a seat.

He busied himself in the kitchen, asking me questions about my day.

"Why don't you just quit?" he finally asked, bringing two dishes of *pasticcio* to the table.

"You made your *nonna's pasticcio*?" He'd never cooked his *nonna's pasticcio* for me. This was huge, and it was enough to distract me from his suggestion to quit my job. At least temporarily.

For the moment, I decided to ignore it and focus on the meal he placed before me. I didn't want to fight with Enzo. I was too tired.

It smelled amazing, and my stomach growled in anticipation. I already knew it was going to be an orgasm in my mouth. It almost made me forget about my crappy day.

"What's the special occasion?" I asked, cheese oozing out when I sliced into it. "I thought cooking was a chore."

"I actually found it quite enjoyable. Maybe because I was excited to see what you'd think of it."

"Um. It's freaking delicious," I said around a bite, not caring if I looked like a rabid animal. So, so good.

He chuckled and took a bite before saying, "And it seemed like a fitting dish to celebrate."

"Celebrate?" I asked. "What are we celebrating?"

"I was selected for the Italian national team. I'm going to the World Cup." He grinned.

"Oh my god. That's amazing." I jumped out of my seat and went over to hug him. "Enzo, I'm so proud of you."

He pulled me into his lap, and I could see how happy he was. But there was something else there too… Hesitation? Why? Was it because his dad wouldn't be there to watch him play?

I wrapped my arms around his neck, hugging him close, hating that they couldn't share this moment. "I'm sure this is bittersweet."

"You have no idea." He smoothed his hand up and down my back. "I wish you could be there with me."

My heart clenched in my chest, and I tilted my forehead to his, hoping he'd hear the sincerity in my words. "Me too."

We'd known this might be the case all along, but that didn't make it any easier. The World Cup was in Abu Dhabi and well past the date that I could travel internationally. It was unusual for the World Cup to be held in the winter, but as Lauren had pointed out, Abu Dhabi summers were way too hot for an outdoor tournament. Well that, and allegedly some serious bribery and corruption had been involved.

Enzo shook his head. "Unfortunately, that's not all."

"No?" I asked, wary.

"I have to leave for Italy in a few days for training. And I'll be gone for a month."

I swallowed hard. "Wait. What?" This felt so sudden. My due date was fast approaching. "You're going to miss the baby shower. And…"

"I know it's not ideal, but it's the World Cup. This is my one shot. This was what my dad and I worked so hard for."

I nodded but said nothing as I returned to my seat and picked at my meal. What could I say? Don't go? It was his last chance and his biggest ambition. Of course he should go.

"What did Knox say about the incident the other day?" I asked, ready for a change of topic. There was no point discussing the World Cup. He was going to go, and he should. I just…wished the timing were better.

He cut into a piece. "They gave me a warning. He was upset but understood once I explained what had happened."

I nodded. "That's good. Crew always speaks highly of Knox."

Enzo's fork screeched against the plate. "Crew? When did you talk to Crew?"

"He came to Juliana's last weekend to watch the game." As with all the other away games, we'd had a watch party at

Juliana and Harrison's. It was low-key but fun. And I loved spending so much time with my friends.

"You never mentioned that."

I lifted a shoulder. "We're friends. Our friends are married to each other."

"I don't like it. I don't want you seeing him."

I frowned, anger slithering through me. "You're kidding me, right?"

"No." He leaned his elbows on the table and angled toward me. "I'm not."

I pushed back from the table and stood. I was not okay with Enzo telling me what to do. Who to see or where to go. Since we'd started dating, my choices had been restricted enough, and I was over it. "Do you realize how much I've given up to be with you?"

He jerked his head back and tossed his napkin on the table. "Excuse me?"

That had come out wrong. But now that I'd said the words, there was no taking them back. Besides, in a sense, they were true.

"I just—" I sighed, feeling defeated. Exhausted. Over-whelmed. *Alone.*

"I'm sorry you feel like it's such a *sacrifice* to be with me," he sneered, anger and hurt bleeding through his words.

"I'm not. That's not what I meant." He'd somehow turned this around to where I felt guilty.

He scoffed. "No? What did you mean then? Because I've given you everything, *uccellina.* A beautiful home. A car. Anything you could ever want is yours."

Wow. I blinked a few times, taken aback by his statement. Did he not know me at all?

"That's just it. I don't care about things. I *want* to be able to go to a bakery with my friends without being photographed. I *want* to be able to do my job without being followed. I *want* my freedom."

He clenched his jaw so hard I thought he might crack a molar. "No one's forcing you to stay."

My heart was in my throat. "Tell me the truth, Enzo." I crossed my arms over my chest. "If there was no baby, would we even be together?"

His nostrils flared, and he stood and stalked toward me. "I can't believe you'd ask me that."

"And I can't believe you'd try to tell me who I can and cannot see." I massaged my temples, a headache building. "That isn't love. Love is trust."

This was why I dated the bad boys. Because if I was never emotionally invested, I could never get hurt. But I'd let Enzo in. I'd trusted him. I loved him. And I couldn't imagine my life—or Aiden's—without him.

But he'd never actually answered my question. When he still didn't say anything, I turned and headed for the bedroom. My heart ached. I just wanted to go to sleep and pretend this day had never happened.

***

"Oh, Juliana," I sighed, lifting my hands to my lips. I was overcome with emotion, and I wanted to blame it on my hormones, but I knew it was more than that.

Ever since the fight, things had been tense between Enzo and me. It didn't help that we were both stubborn. Both stressed. I knew he was under a lot of pressure, but I'd wanted something… I don't know. More.

He'd been in Italy the past two weeks, training, and I'd been miserably alone. I was so pregnant it was uncomfortable, and I was counting down the days until Aiden was born. Between the time difference and Enzo's busy schedule, we barely had time to talk. Even so, it felt as if he was avoiding me.

"Aw." Juliana hugged me to her. "I'm so glad you like it."

I nodded and tried to focus on being present in this moment. I fingered the silver design of my bracelet, feeling as if the path of my life had just veered off course again. And I tried to remind myself that that was okay. Normal.

Today was about celebrating Aiden and me. About enjoying what little was left of my pregnancy.

"You've outdone yourself," I said, scanning the room.

How many times had I dreamed of having a baby shower where I was the one expecting? And yet this exceeded my wildest dreams because my best friend had gone above and beyond. I'd always admired the chic style and understated elegance of the events she planned, but to be on the receiving end… I shook my head, swiping away tears.

"I'm sorry you had to rearrange everything at the last minute," I said, knowing how many changes she would've had to make when we'd altered it from a couples shower to girls only.

"Are you kidding? That was no big deal. Honestly," she said when I raised my eyebrow.

"You okay?" Lauren asked, wrapping her arm around my shoulder.

I nodded. "It's all so beautiful." I turned to Juliana. "Thank you."

She hugged me as best she could with my big belly in the way. Thirty-five weeks down, only five to go. Every time I blinked, another month seemed to pass.

My body had been telling me to slow down more, and I was finally listening. Enzo was right. I'd been working too hard, and I wanted to relax a little. Christmas was just around the corner. Not that you'd know it from the weather.

It was nearly seventy degrees, and with my baby bump, I was hot all the time.

"Come on." Juliana threaded her arm through mine, and I waddled along beside her. I couldn't stop staring at everything. The vintage steam trunks, the passports, my... I stopped in my tracks. My photographs.

"Jules," I gasped, my heart swelling with gratitude. "You've outdone yourself."

"Really?" She gave me a cheesy smile, excitement bubbling out from every pore.

"Yes. Seriously amazing. Perfect theme. And the decorations." I shook my head, taking it all in. It was so beautiful and thoughtful. So *me*. And seeing "Aiden" everywhere was... surreal.

"Isn't this amazing?" Mom asked, glancing around. "Juliana." She held a hand to her chest, overcome with emotion. "So incredible."

Juliana smiled. "Thank you, Linda."

"If this is what you do for the baby shower, I can't wait to see their wedding."

"Mom." I glared at her. I wasn't sure there would be a wedding. I wasn't sure of anything anymore.

Mackenzie pulled me in for a hug, and then Jo.

My mom, Jo, and Mackenzie had come down to LA for the shower, and I loved spending time with all my favorite women. I felt more supported and loved than I had, maybe ever. And I was excited about the baby, about becoming a mom. Even if I was concerned about what the future held.

Enzo's mamma and *nonna* joined us on a video call while I opened gifts, and I was overwhelmed by everyone's generosity. Finally, Alexis said, "One more surprise!"

When she returned, she was wheeling in the stroller I'd wanted, and she said, "From Enzo."

Everyone oohed and aahed, and I felt a little lighter. He'd listened to me.

"Time for a game!" Juliana said.

I went to grab my phone and realized it was missing. Though I found that pregnancy often made me forgetful, I could've sworn I'd left it in my purse.

I frowned. "Juliana, have you seen my phone?"

She shook her head and continued passing out the supplies for the game. *Where is it?* I rummaged through my purse. Checked the counter nearby. *What the heck?*

"Mom?" I asked. "Have you seen my phone? I know I brought it with me."

"Oh, um—" She swallowed a bite of her street taco. The menu had featured some of my favorite street food from around the world. It was delicious. "I'm sure it'll turn up."

When I turned to ask Jo if she'd seen it, she quickly busied herself, fussing with all the gifts. I furrowed my brow. Why did I get the feeling they were hiding something?

"Guys." I frowned. "What's going on?"

"Nothing," Jo chirped, but her forced smile made me push. When she didn't crack, I turned to my friends.

"I'll take the pictures." Lauren's tone was bright, and Alexis was too quick to nod. "Then you can enjoy the party."

Another headache threatened, and I rubbed my temples as if to keep it at bay along with the worry. "Will someone please tell me what's going on?"

Juliana smiled at the guests and ushered me out of the room and into Harrison's office. Trophies lined the wall along with a display of championship rings that sparkled in the sunlight. I tried to focus on them instead of the tightness in my chest.

"Breathe, Harper," Juliana said, and it sounded as if her voice was coming to me from a tunnel. "Breathe. Think about Aiden."

"Why do I feel like you're about to give me bad news?" I asked.

She gnawed on her bottom lip. "There was a story that came out."

"Story?" My body felt shaky. "What story?"

"I'm sure there's nothing to it. You know how pictures can tell a different story than the truth." Despite her calm tone, her features were etched with concern.

Videos from my pole dancing classes had already been leaked. What now?

"About me?" I asked.

She grimaced. "Sort of."

"I need to know."

"I don't think it's a good idea. If Enzo or Harrison were here, they'd tell us to stay off the internet."

Fuck that. "Give me my phone." I held out my hand, my mind racing with possible scenarios. Despite her reservations, she caved.

I typed Enzo's name in the internet search window, and a story immediately popped up. The title was "Italy's Favorite Couple Reunited." And then there was an image of Enzo and his ex, Giada, leaving a hotel together.

His ex? I gnashed my teeth. Why was he even with her? He was supposed to be training. He'd barely had time to talk to me, and now I supposed I knew the reason why. I didn't need to read the story because the picture said it all.

I shook my head. *Unbelievable.*

"I'm sure it's been altered or something," Juliana said. "And even if it wasn't, Enzo loves you."

I wanted to believe that. But our argument bubbled to the surface, and I wondered if he'd sought refuge in the arms of Giada. It seemed unlikely, given what I knew of their past. But what was I supposed to think? Enzo had been distant lately, and then there he was, pictured leaving a hotel with her.

My phone started buzzing in my hand, Enzo's name flashing on the screen. I answered without hesitation, ready to demand answers.

Even if it wasn't true—and I sure as hell hoped it wasn't—he'd made a fool of me in front of the entire world. I was pregnant with *his* baby. Hounded by the paparazzi because of Enzo. And *he* was off gallivanting with his ex and pursuing his dreams.

What about my dreams? What about what I wanted?

I'd been doing a lot of thinking lately, and I'd realized I definitely didn't want to stay in LA. I loved Enzo, but I didn't want this life.

"Harper," he said, breathless. "Thank god. I need to talk to you."

"It wouldn't have something to do with Giada, would it?" My blood boiled even as my tone remained calm.

I held my breath, hoping he'd tell me it was a lie. That the image had somehow been manipulated or was an old picture, but the next words out of his mouth were, "I can explain," and it felt as if he'd taken gasoline and poured it onto the fire that was my anger.

"Explain?" I scoffed. "You should explain why it's okay for you to spend time *alone* at a *hotel* with your ex while you insist that I can't hang out with Crew in a group of friends."

Yeah, I was still pissed about that.

"It's not—"

"What it looks like," I finished for him. I'd heard that before. I'd just never expected to hear that line from Enzo.

Before I could stop myself, I said, "You know what? It doesn't matter. None of it matters." I sighed, resignation blanketing me along with sadness. "After Aiden's born, I'm moving home. To the Alondra Valley as I'd planned originally." This had merely confirmed what I already knew. "You were right about the stress. It's too much, and I need—" My breath was shaky. "I need to get away."

"You mean run away."

I gnashed my teeth. "I'm not running away. As much as I love—loved—LA, it's time for a change."

"And what about us?" His voice was rising. "What about my relationship with Aiden? He's my son too."

I lifted a shoulder, though his words struck at my heart. Perhaps I wasn't being fair, but I couldn't do this anymore.

"Please—" Enzo's voice cracked, and I glanced toward the ceiling. "I know you're upset, but wait until I come home. Then we can talk about this."

"There's nothing to discuss. I have to protect Aiden."

"From me?" Pain radiated from his every word.

"From this life. The scrutiny. The insanity of it. I don't want this for him."

I'd had enough of the paparazzi. Enough of the drama. Enough of everything. I just wanted to go home. Maybe I was running, but could he really blame me?

The line was silent a moment before he said, "Please, Harper. I'll do *anything* to fix this. Ask anything of me—it's yours."

"Let us go."

His breathing was heavy, his voice choked with emotion. "Anything but that." He swallowed. "*Per favore, uccellina. Sei irrinunciabile.*"

"Irreplaceable?" I laughed, but the sound was mirthless.

I didn't feel irreplaceable. I felt breakable.

"*Ti amo. Ti do il mio cuore.*" I closed my eyes when he spoke, trying not to let his spell penetrate me. "*Sei la mia vita.*"

I love you.

I give you my heart.

You're my life.

He said something else, but the words sounded garbled. Almost...far away. I stared ahead, feeling as if I were floating out of my body. Watching from above.

My last thought was for Aiden, and then there was *nothing.*

CHAPTER TWENTY-FIVE

Enzo

"Harper? Hello?" I said into the phone, but she didn't answer.

I stared at the screen in disbelief. *Did she just hang up on me?*

I'd poured my heart out to her, and she was leaving? Without giving me a chance to explain? She'd lectured me about love and trust, and yet she wasn't willing to do the same for me.

I hung up and called back again, but it went straight to voice mail. I left a message, anger vibrating through my words. Even so, concern twisted my insides. It wasn't like Harper to back down from a fight. If she'd hung up on me, she was really pissed.

Before I could try Harper again, there was a knock at the door, and then Val let herself in. She took one look at me and frowned. "What's wrong?"

I furrowed my brow. "Harper won't answer my calls. She says she's moving home."

"She saw the story about Giada, I take it?" When I nodded, she rolled her eyes and took a seat on the couch in the hotel suite. "Harper should know better than to believe the tabloids. But I can't say I blame her. You and Giada looked very cozy."

"It wasn't—" I huffed.

"Yeah, I know. But for now, you need to focus on the tournament. The team leaves for Abu Dhabi in a few hours, and you're so close to achieving everything you've ever wanted. You just need to get your head in the game."

Easier said than done. I'd been a mess since leaving LA. I felt bad about my fight with Harper, and I hated that I had to miss the baby shower. I didn't like the way we'd left things, and now I felt even worse. Did she truly intend to leave LA?

I'd always known there'd be sacrifices with my career. You didn't get to this level and stay there without giving up something. But lately, I'd wondered if it was worth it. Was this what I really wanted?

My phone rang. I scrambled to answer it. "Harper?"

"No, um, this is Dr. Fulton. Is this Lorenzo Mancini?"

"Yes." I frowned. Why was Dr. Fulton calling me? "Is everything okay?"

"Are you on your way to the hospital?"

"No." I jerked my head back. "Why? Should I be?"

"Harper's had a seizure, and we have to operate immediately." Panic gripped me so tightly I thought I might burst. The baby wasn't due for… Well, the baby was very early. I couldn't think straight, and the math really didn't matter at this point.

"We'll do our best to help both Harper and the baby," Dr. Fulton said. "But if we can only save one of them, who should we…"

The rest of her words blurred, as did my vision. It was an impossible choice. The woman I loved or our child?

Harper would be devastated if anything happened to

Aiden, but I couldn't live without her. The pain of losing him might kill her, but losing Harper would wreck me.

It was as if my entire universe shrank down to that one moment. Everything hung in the balance. Everything that mattered to me.

"Please don't make me choose," I pleaded to Dr. Fulton, the universe, whoever would listen. I was struck with fear, spearing my fingers through my hair. I'd never felt so helpless.

I was a world away from Harper at a time when she needed me most. And I needed her.

"What's wrong?" Val asked. "What's going on?"

I shook her question away, focusing on Dr. Fulton. "Both of them."

"I'll do everything I can, but that may not…"

"Harper," I finally said, my shoulders slumping. *"Harper."*

"I'll call as soon as I have an update."

I dropped my head into my hands, the enormity of the situation bearing down on me. Even if we won the World Cup, it might cost me the love of my life. There was no question in my mind that I needed to go home to Harper, but that would mean giving up a dream I'd worked a lifetime to accomplish. I didn't want to think about how disappointed my papà would be.

"Lorenzo?" Val placed her hand on my back. "What's going on?"

I shook my head, tears streaming down my face. I almost wished Harper had hung up on me because this was so much worse.

"Harper…seizure." I could barely form a coherent sentence, I was so gripped with fear. "The baby." I stood. "I need to—" I couldn't breathe, my heart was pounding so hard. "I have to—"

"Breathe, Lorenzo." Val took my hands and lifted them above my head. "Breathe."

"I can't—" Spots danced before my eyes. "I—"

"You can," she said, forcing me to look at her. "You must."

When I'd finally calmed down enough to speak, I hung my head and said, "I have to go. I have to be with Harper."

Val's voice was steady when she asked, "Are you sure?"

I nodded, certainty sweeping through me with the resolution. There was no doubt in my mind. Harper and Aiden needed me, and I would put them above all else. Even my dream to play in the World Cup.

"Yes. I need to talk to Coach. Can you tell Nico what's going on and ask him to book me a flight? I don't care how much it costs. I want to leave as soon as possible."

"Of course."

The next hour passed in a blur. Fortunately, I'd already packed, but I had to sign some documents. And then Nico and I were off to the airport. I still hadn't heard from Dr. Fulton, and I tried not to read too much into her silence. I'd texted with Harper's mom. And I was anxious for news.

And then, I finally called Mamma. It rang twice before she answered. I explained the situation, and then she said, "Oh Lorenzo. I will pray for you. All of you. Of course you must go to Harper."

"But Papà..."

"Would be so proud of you. You know that, surely?"

I lifted a shoulder. I didn't know anything right now apart from the fact that I needed to be there for Harper.

"The only thing more important to your dad than soccer was family," Mamma said.

I nodded. "I know, but the World Cup..." I sighed. "It was his dream."

"Yes, *his* dream. And you've honored his memory in so

many incredible ways. But he's no longer here. Harper is, and she needs you."

I nodded, knowing she was right. And while I'd already made my decision, I appreciated her support. "Thank you, Mamma. I love you."

"I love you too."

A new text message came in from Val. It was a picture of a piece of paper. On it was the symbol Papà had often drawn. The symbol like Harper's bracelet. *Papà. Harper.*

"Non tutte le ciambelle riescono col buco." I smiled, though it was tinged with sadness, memories of my dad mixing with those of Harper.

Sometimes it was difficult to think that two of the most important people in my life would never meet. And my father would never meet my son. Would I even get to meet Aiden?

But Papà was right. Things didn't always turn out as planned. And I knew Val approved of my decision, despite whatever happened with my career because of it.

While Nico and I waited to board, I couldn't stop thinking about my argument with Harper. About what she must have been thinking and feeling. What if she died, and her last thoughts about me were that I was a liar and a cheater? What if she didn't realize how much I loved her?

Giada, Crew, all of it, seemed so trivial. And I hoped, I prayed, that Harper and Aiden would be all right. It didn't matter if she wanted to move to the Alondra Valley; we'd find a way to make it work. But that was the least of my worries now.

The door to the car opened, and Nico peeked his head in. "Ready, boss?"

I took a deep breath and slid my sunglasses into place, steeling myself for the greeting I'd receive. The paparazzi shouted questions at me as we walked through the airport, and I ducked my head and kept moving. I needed to get home. I needed to see my *uccellina* and make sure she and Aiden were okay.

I closed my eyes and pinched the bridge of my nose. Fuck. Fourteen hours seemed like an eternity.

We were about to board when my phone rang again. I tried to answer, but my hands were shaking so much, Nico had to do it for me.

"Lorenzo?"

"Yes." I could barely force the word out.

"This is Dr. Fulton. Harper's out of surgery," she said, and while I wanted to be relieved, her tone told me the worst wasn't over. I braced myself, though I didn't know how I'd bear it if anything had happened to her or Aiden. "She's not out of the woods yet."

"And Aiden?" I was almost too scared to ask. I placed my hand over my heart, afraid it had stopped beating for a moment.

There was an announcement over the airport PA system, making it impossible to hear. I hadn't been able to make out anything she'd said.

"I'm sorry. Can you please repeat that?"

"Aiden was delivered by C-section, and they've taken him to the NICU."

"Thank god," I exhaled. "Thank you. Thank you." I didn't know whether I was saying it to Dr. Fulton or God, but I didn't care. I was just so very grateful they were both alive.

"Juliana, hey," I said, jogging down the corridor to where she was standing outside Harper's hospital room.

I'd intended to stop to pick up flowers on the way, but I'd already waited long enough to see Harper and meet my son. I could've used a shower too, but all I cared about was getting to them. Holding them—my family.

Something in Juliana's expression shifted when she saw me, and it gave my heart a painfully long pause.

"What's wrong? Is it Harper? Is Aiden okay?" I wasn't sure how much more I could handle at this point. The past eighteen hours had been the most stressful in my life.

"They're both recovering." Her voice was flat, as was her expression.

My entire body slumped. "Good. Good. Where is everybody?"

"Doc is sitting with Aiden, and I just came out from Harper's room to get some coffee. Everyone else went home to rest."

"Thank you for being here for her," I said, giving Juliana's shoulder a squeeze. "Now, if you'll excuse me—" I headed for Harper's room.

"Enzo." Juliana placed her hand over mine. "Wait."

"What?" I furrowed my brow, dropping my hand.

She worried her lip then said, "I was with her when she had the seizure. I saw how upset she was. I think you should give her some more time to recover first."

I jerked my head back. "What?"

There was no way I could stay away from the woman I loved when she needed me most.

"She's still so fragile right now, you know?" Juliana looked as if she might cry. "And I'm afraid that she'll find seeing you distressing."

I didn't know what to say to that. I just wanted to explain and make things better.

The door to Harper's room opened, and Dr. Fulton

stepped into the hallway. "Enzo," she said, glancing between Juliana and me. "Congratulations."

"Thank you." I forced myself to smile. To act normal.

"I'm glad you're here. I was hoping to give you an update on your partner's condition."

Juliana went into Harper's room, leaving Dr. Fulton and me alone.

"How's she doing?" I asked.

"All things considered, she's doing well." Dr. Fulton sighed, and I could see the exhaustion in her features. "She has a condition called eclampsia. Her blood pressure skyrocketed, and it resulted in a seizure."

The room spun, and I tried to focus on her words. "But she's okay now?"

"Hopefully," Dr. Fulton said. "She's still at a critical point, and we're going to need to do everything we can to manage her blood pressure. We had to give her medicine during the C-section to prevent additional seizures. And we will continue to give her medicine and monitor her blood pressure closely."

"How long has she had this?" I asked, thinking of the appointments I'd had to miss. Had Harper known?

"It came on suddenly, as is often the case."

Suddenly, as a result of our argument over Giada. *Cazzo.*

This was all my fault.

"For now, we need to keep Harper calm. Help reduce her stress as much as possible."

I nodded, remembering Juliana's words. "Thank you, Dr. Fulton. I really appreciate you and all the staff taking such good care of them."

"Of course." She tucked her tablet beneath her arm, and I turned to leave.

Juliana was right. She'd been with Harper when she'd had the seizure. I'd upset her. And now I needed to put Harper first. I didn't want to jeopardize her recovery by pushing for something that would distress her. Even if that something was me. For the moment, there was nothing I could do for Harper.

"Where are you going?" Dr. Fulton asked.

"To meet my son."

CHAPTER TWENTY-SIX

Harper

I stared up at the ceiling as if in a daze. My baby had been ripped from my womb. My stomach had been stapled shut. But it was my heart that was the most battered and bruised.

I was broken and sad, and my son—my baby—was hooked up to a respirator in the NICU. I'd seen him briefly before being wheeled to my room, and he was beautiful. Beautiful and miraculous but struggling.

And he wasn't the only one. God, I felt as if I'd been to hell and back. My body—I was on so many drugs, it was difficult to keep track of them all. A cocktail of painkillers, antibiotics, and who else knew what. I was dirty and exhausted. Defeated and broken.

I knew I should be grateful to be alive. That my child was alive. But I was… I let out a deep sigh, my bones weary and my heart heavy. I didn't know how I was going to get through this. Especially not when it felt as if my body had been plowed over by a Mack truck—repeatedly. Worst of all, the one person I wanted to comfort me had caused me immense pain.

There was a knock at the door, but I continued to stare at the ceiling. The nurses and doctors came in and out as they pleased. I so appreciated them and their efforts, but I just wanted to be left alone. I was so tired. So very tired.

"Hey, Harp," Dad said, taking the seat next to my bed. "You're awake. How are you feeling?"

I lifted a shoulder as the door closed, grateful for the privacy. "Okay, I guess." I tried not to cry when Dad took my hand and held it in his.

"You've been through quite the ordeal," he said. "You scared the shit out of me."

I laughed and wiped away a tear. "I'm not sure I've ever heard you curse."

"I felt the situation warranted it. We were all scared, and I know Enzo was too."

I scoffed and turned away. Enzo was in Abu Dhabi, and I hadn't heard from him since our fight. Did he know I was in the hospital? Did he even care?

Dad rubbed my hand, and it was so comforting. His warm, gentle touch. "Enzo's a good man. He loves you and Aiden. He's been here nonstop, doing everything he can for the two of you."

I frowned. "What are you talking about? Enzo's in Abu Dhabi."

Dad shook his head. "He's here. He came as soon as he found out you were rushed to the hospital."

"What?" I shrieked. Why had no one told me this?

"He and Nico bring your team and the NICU team snacks and coffee every shift change. He checks in on you every night. Enzo's been sitting with you while you're sleeping. Then he goes to the NICU and stays with Aiden all night. He's been learning how to care for him."

None of this made any sense. There was no way Enzo would give up on his dream to win the World Cup. None.

Dad nodded. "I think you should talk to him." He paused. "Only when you're up for it. I will not have you jeopardizing your recovery, but I fear for your heart."

He was right. And knowing that Enzo was here—that he'd sacrificed his dream for me?

"I want to see him." I needed to see him. Needed to know what had happened.

"Of course." Dad stood and headed for the exit.

A few minutes later, Enzo stood in the doorway, a large bouquet of blue flowers in hand. He opened his mouth to speak, but I shook my head, tears forming in my eyes.

"Oh my god. You're really here." I lifted my hand to my lips, scanning his form. Apart from the dark circles beneath his eyes and the worry creasing his brow, he looked as handsome as ever. He also seemed nervous, gripping the bouquet tightly, his lips in a line, almost buried beneath a thick layer of scruff.

"*Uccellina,*" he croaked, looking as if he might cry.

I blinked a few times, certain I must be hallucinating despite what Dad had told me. It wouldn't be surprising, considering all the drugs I was on. Enzo stepped forward and placed the flowers on a shelf near the door, directly in my line of sight. I wondered what these blooms symbolized.

"I'm sorry." He came to my side.

"What are you doing here?" I glanced at my phone to check the date. I'd been so out of it, and time had seemed to pass in weird increments since I'd come to the hospital. "Why aren't you in Abu Dhabi?"

"I told you—" he took my hand in his and kissed it "—you are my life, and I cannot live without you."

"But the World Cup, the..."

He leaned forward, pressing his forehead to mine. "You and Aiden are more important to me than anything."

My jaw dropped. "What? But you can't just—"

"I can, and I did." He smoothed my hair away from my face. And when he looked at me, I didn't feel despair; I felt hope. "And I do not regret it one bit."

He fell to his knees before me. "I'm begging you. *Ti prego* —" His voice cracked on the the last word, and I nearly relented. "I'm so fucking grateful the universe gave me a chance to be with you. And I will spend the rest of my life trying to be worthy of you. Please don't leave me."

The sight of this strong, tattooed man humbling himself before me was almost more than I could bear. But then I remembered the images of him with Giada.

"What happened with Giada? Why were you with her?"

"I don't think now's the—" He stood.

I crossed my arms over my chest. "You said you could explain, and I want an answer." We needed to clear the cobwebs of the past before we could move forward.

He sighed. "She threatened to go to the tabloids again."

I gnashed my teeth. Would she ever stop? And what was Enzo so scared of?

"I figured she wanted more money," he said, and I could feel my blood pressure rising the longer he explained. "And I was right. But it was worse than that."

My stomach churned with unease. "Worse how?"

"She had pictures…" He shook his head. "She threatened to tell everyone that I'd hit her."

"What?" I jerked my head back. As passionate and as rough as Enzo could be in bed at times, I could never imagine him hurting me or anyone. "You mean, like spanking during sex?"

He nodded. "At first, I'd thought she was into it. But when I realized she wasn't, I pulled back. I made myself be gentler to give her what she needed."

As much as I hated the thought of Enzo with another

woman, I appreciated him telling me what had happened. Trusting me.

"I hadn't…done anything like that with her in years. But she said she'd taken pictures of her skin with red marks from my hand. I'm not even sure if that's true, but she threatened to show them to the press and tell her story. She figured after the incident with me shoving the paparazzi and then being in the spotlight so much for the World Cup, now was the time to cash in."

"Wow."

"Yeah. Supposedly she'd been holding on to them, waiting for a chance to screw me over."

I wished I could've been at that meeting to give her a piece of my mind. How dare she…

Enzo placed his hand over mine. "*Uccellina,* you have to stay calm."

Our eyes met and held, and despite my anger, I forced myself to calm down. "That is *so* wrong."

"And that's why I was meeting with her. Val couldn't reason with Giada. She refused to talk to anyone but me."

"Why didn't you tell me?"

"Because I knew it would upset you, and I hoped to just deal with it and move on. But that backfired. I'm so sorry for…everything. You went through something so traumatic. And I'm sorry I was responsible for that."

"What?" I gasped. "No." I grabbed his hand. "No. You are not responsible for what happened."

"But the stress. And your blood pressure. And…" He cleared his throat and said nothing more. It hit me that his concern might be the reason he'd waited to see me. He hadn't wanted to risk upsetting me.

"Enzo," I said, waiting until he'd looked at me. "What happened was not your fault. It was no one's fault."

I hoped he was listening to me, because I meant it. About this and his dad's death.

Enzo glanced to the ceiling. "I was so afraid I was going to lose both of you."

I hadn't considered it from Enzo's perspective. I'd been too busy fighting for my life. And then fighting for Aiden's. But now that I'd taken a step back, I realized how scary it must have been for him.

"When Dr. Fulton called me, I was…" He swallowed hard. "I've never been more terrified."

"I'm sorry too. I'm sorry for doubting you. And I'm sorry you had to come home and miss something so incredibly important."

"I didn't *have* to. I *wanted* to." He cupped my cheek. "*Ti amo con tutto il cuore*. You know that, right?"

I nodded. It had taken me longer to realize it than it should've, but I knew—baby or not—Enzo loved me with all his heart. "I love you too." A tear snaked its way down my cheek before he caught it with his thumb. "And I meant what I said about moving home, but only when the time is right for our family."

"Shh." He smoothed my hair away. "Don't worry about that now. We will figure it out."

"I don't want you to retire until you're ready. All I know is that I want to be together. I want us to be a family."

He wrapped his arm around me and kissed my temple. "That's all I want, *uccellina*. All I've ever wanted."

EIGHT WEEKS LATER, AIDEN AND I WERE SITTING ON THE swing out front of our rental house when Enzo pulled into the driveway. I waved to Enzo and smiled, giddy at the sight of him after a week apart. He climbed out of the car and carried his bag up to the front porch.

"*Ciao, Papà!*" I called, waving Aiden's little hand.

He smiled down at our son. "*Mi sei mancato, angelo mio.*" He kissed the top of Aiden's head, and I melted at his greeting. Then he gave me a peck on the lips and said, "*E tu, uccellina.*"

He'd nicknamed Aiden his angel, and I loved the way he doted on our son. We both did. He truly was our angel baby—such a sweet little boy who brought everyone around him so much joy.

He certainly brought me a lot of joy. Being a mom was... everything I'd hoped for and more. It had its messy moments. Long nights. And I was definitely tired. But every day, I felt a little stronger. Every day, I felt a little more like my old self. And my body and mind began to heal.

I'd started working again, slowly. I'd been sad to leave my job as a film location scout, but I was excited about the future. I'd slowly started taking on photography assignments and relished the flexibility. I loved being behind the camera again, and I was grateful that Enzo had encouraged me to pursue it.

I didn't go online. I didn't read the news. I spent time with my family, and I ignored the rest of the world.

And every day, I fell a little more in love with both of them. Enzo treated Aiden with such care and patience, and it seemed as if fatherhood had transformed him. He'd had to go to LA the past few days for some events, and we'd missed him.

I still couldn't believe Aiden was eight weeks old. Because he'd been born early, the expectations for his development milestones were different from a full-term baby. At least for the first two years. Even so, he was doing so well. All the doctors and nurses had remarked on that fact when he'd been discharged from the NICU. As well as how fortunate he was to have such devoted, loving parents.

Aiden made a grunting sound, and I smiled down at him. Olive skin, dark curls, slate-gray eyes that were slowly turning hazel. Enzo's genes were strong, and he'd given me the most beautiful gift of our son.

"Do you want to go for a walk?" I asked, grateful to be away from the hospital, away from LA. We'd moved to the Alondra Valley as soon as Aiden was released.

We were still hunting for the perfect house, but in the meantime, we'd rented a nice place not far from my parents. We never missed Sunday dinner, and I loved being near my family.

We'd head back to LA when the season started. But for now, I was enjoying the peace of being back in my hometown.

"Let me just put this inside." Enzo soon returned with the baby sling.

As we walked around the property, we talked about everything and nothing at all. There had been a bit of back-lash after Enzo had left the World Cup. Of course, they'd been disappointed that he couldn't play. But there had also been such an outpouring of love and support, that I could see why he loved the fans so much.

Eventually we stopped at a bench by the pond under an old oak tree. Enzo had Aiden strapped to his chest, and Aiden's eyelids were growing heavy as Enzo sang an Italian lullaby he was fond of.

"I hope you know how much I love Aiden." His voice was gruff but his expression tender as he looked down at our son.

"I do." I nodded, admiring the way he rested his large hand protectively on our son's back. "I see it in the way you care for him. In everything you do for him."

"It isn't just for him." When he looked at me, his brown eyes shimmered with emotion in the afternoon sunlight. "It's for both of you. *Ti amo, uccellina.* More and more every day."

The corners of my lips tilted, and I leaned into his side. "*Ti amo.*"

We sat there a while longer before returning to the house. Enzo went to put Aiden down for a nap, and I cleaned up the kitchen. Though Dr. Fulton had cleared me for sex two weeks ago, I hadn't felt strong enough. And Enzo hadn't pushed. But I was ready now. More than ready.

I craved that connection with him. I needed to feel like myself again. I needed to feel unstoppable. And Enzo always knew how to make me feel powerful. Invincible.

"He was tired," Enzo said, returning to the kitchen. He came up behind me, wrapping his arms around me and dropping his chin to my shoulder. "I missed you."

I leaned my head back, setting the towel on the counter. "I missed you too."

"I may have found us a house."

"Did you buy it?" I teased.

The movement was barely perceptible, but he flinched. "Enzo?" I chided, turning to face him. "What did you do?"

"I did *not* buy it. I know better than to make such a big decision without you."

I smiled and smoothed my hands over his shoulders. When he winced, I frowned. "What's wrong? Are you hurt?"

"I have a surprise for you."

I furrowed my brow as he took a step back. What the heck was he talking about?

"I know you don't like surprises that are permanent—" He reached back and pulled his shirt over his head before dropping it on the counter. "But I hoped you'd make an exception."

I was speechless at the sight of his naked skin, then he

turned, and I saw it. I stilled, my fingers trembling over his body as I took in all the new ink. The skin was still red around the edges

The most beautiful wings cascaded over his shoulders and down the backs of his arms. They were so detailed and delicate, yet also somehow masculine. I coasted my fingertips over the design, feeling as if they'd always been there. Or were meant to be.

"When did you get these?"

"Last week, but I've wanted to get them since Aiden was born. Since he's my angel, and you're my *uccellina*, wings seemed appropriate."

I smiled, pressing my lips to his shoulders. His back. I couldn't believe he'd branded his skin with a reminder of us.

He shivered from my touch, and my body ached for him. I slid my hands around to his front, gliding them down the muscles of his abdomen. Lower still, until I was fumbling with his belt and pants. Releasing his cock. Pressing my front to his back as I teased him.

"Do you want to do some yoga?" I asked, using our code word for sex.

"Really? Are you sure you're up for it?" he asked.

"Yes. I need you." I continued touching him.

"Fuck yes. That feels amazing," he rasped. "I want to touch you. I *need* to touch you."

"What are you waiting for?" I asked, smiling when he spun so that I was in his arms. Trapped against the counter.

He cupped my face with his hands, his eyes intent on mine before he smashed his mouth against mine. It was a claiming and a homecoming, and I'd never felt so much passion from one kiss.

And then his lips were on my neck, his breath warm against the delicate skin. He palmed my breasts, and I arched my back, seeking more. "God, you're sexy. You're going to have to tell me what you feel up to. I don't want to hurt you."

I gripped the edge of the counter, tilting my head back as he slid a hand up my thigh. Goose bumps rose along my skin, my sex dripping with desire. He'd filled the hole in my heart with his words, and now I needed him to fill me. To complete me.

"I want you. I need you. All of you." I grappled with his pants, eager to remove them.

"You have me." He pulled my underwear aside, teasing my clit with his finger. And when he tugged my dress down, laving my nipple with his tongue, I nearly fell over. I would've, if he hadn't been there to catch me. "Always."

And I knew it was true. Regardless of what anyone else said about us or what challenges were thrown our way, nothing would ever come between Enzo and me again. Because we were a family.

CHAPTER TWENTY-SEVEN

Enzo

Cameras shuttered as I entered the room. The empty Leatherbacks stadium served as the backdrop. Knox was sitting at the table at the front, and I joined him, unbuttoning my suit jacket.

"Good afternoon," Knox said, standing to shake my hand.

I smiled and shook his hand with very mixed emotions. Harrison and I had talked about this moment, about how difficult it would be. And I appreciated his support. He'd become a good friend over the past year, and I respected him as both an athlete and a man.

I bobbed my head in greeting. I could barely say hello, yet I was supposed to give a speech about my retirement. I had no idea how I was going to make it through. Twenty years. I'd devoted twenty years of my life to the sport. And while I knew it was time for a change, this transition didn't come without some sadness.

"Lorenzo has a statement he'd like to make," Knox said, giving me the floor.

I took a seat next to him and took a deep breath. I'd memorized my speech but brought note cards. I set them on the table and tugged on my sleeve, smiling when I caught sight of my tattoo there. It was the same design as Harper's bracelet, similar to the symbol Papà would draw to remind me that the path of life wasn't always straight or perfect. I couldn't have asked for a better mentor or career.

I glanced up and searched for her in the audience, smiling when I spotted Harper sitting next to Val and Mamma. She smiled back, and I straightened in my chair. It was time.

"Thank you for coming today," I said. "I'd like to thank Knox Crawford and the Los Angeles Leatherbacks for giving me this opportunity. Playing with the Leatherbacks was an honor, and I can think of nowhere else I'd rather end my career."

Cameras clicked, and I took a sip of water from the glass on the table then cleared my throat. "I am grateful for the support that the fans, the teams, the coaching staff, and my family have always shown me."

It was getting harder to talk, my throat clogged with emotion. I rubbed a hand over my face as the reality of what I was doing sank in. There would be no more games to prepare for. No more drills. I'd walked onto the field for the last time. I'd played my last game as a professional athlete.

"I consider myself fortunate to have had such a long career. Playing soccer has been the greatest privilege of my life, surpassed only by becoming a father." I smiled through my tears, a surge of pride giving me renewed determination to carry on.

Aiden Vittorio, *mio figlio, mio angelo*. My son. My angel.

He was almost one year old now, and I couldn't believe how much he'd grown. Every day, it seemed as if he was doing something new. He filled me with so much joy. So much purpose. And I was proud to be his father.

I was also looking forward to spending more time with him and Harper now that I was retiring. It was a bittersweet moment, a time to reflect on all I'd accomplished, while looking forward to what was to come.

Apart from my family, I was excited to take a more active role in Success through Soccer. Harper and I had purchased a home in Alondra Valley—a house and a winery, actually. We were closing on it soon, and Nico was going to handle the move while we went to Italy for Christmas.

"I aspire to be the type of father my papà was. He was always supportive. Always encouraging me to be a better athlete, a better man." I glanced toward the ceiling. Wherever he was, I hoped he was watching down on me with pride.

I might not have won a World Cup, but I'd achieved so much more. I'd won countless awards throughout my career, but I would've traded all the money, the fame, the trophies, to be with Harper. To have our son.

"I want to thank my partner, Harper, for her love and support. *Uccellina*—" I met her eyes again, unafraid to hide my emotions, my love. "You ground me. *Ti amo.*"

She mouthed the words back to me through a watery smile. *Ti amo.*

I held a hand to my heart and took a deep breath before resuming. "I'm very proud of the career that I've had. It is a dream come true, and I look forward to using the skills and knowledge I've acquired to help the next generation of players through my foundation, Success through Soccer."

I rubbed my nose, trying to hold it together. "I am one in a line of many players who have dedicated themselves to this sport. And regardless of where I trained, first with Inter Roma, then Milan FC, the Italian National Team, and now with the LA Leatherbacks, it's been an incredible experience."

I glanced down at my notes, not wanting to forget anything. "Thank you to my agent, Val. And my teammates. I have learned so much from each of you, and you helped me grow both on and off the field."

I shuffled the notes. "Thank you to the fans for all your support. I know many of you were disappointed when I left the World Cup unexpectedly last year, and I appreciate the outpouring of love and support you showed my family and me when my son was in the hospital. Just like when my papà died, you—the fans—were what got me through. What kept me going. From the bottom of my heart, thank you." I held my hands together in prayer and bowed my head. "*Grazie di cuore. Grazie per tutto.*"

The audience burst into applause, and I sat there, trying to soak it all in. The entire time, my eyes were on Harper as she smiled and wiped away her tears. I felt like the luckiest man on the planet with the way she was looking at me. I was ready to move on.

WE STOOD AT THE HEADSTONE, AIDEN IN MY ARMS. HIS DARK curls smelled sweet, his skin providing warmth on the cold winter day. I knelt to position the flowers on my father's grave, and when I stood, Harper placed her hand on my back.

"*Ciao, Papà,*" I said. "There is someone I'd like you to meet. Well, two people, actually," I continued speaking in Italian.

Harper and I spoke in Italian when we were at home with Aiden. He babbled all the time but had yet to say his first word. He'd been crawling for a while, and he was fast! I had a good feeling he'd start walking soon.

I bounced Aiden in my arms, and he giggled, his hazel eyes lighting up with joy. I gave him a big kiss on the neck, exaggerating the smacking noise like I knew he loved. He laughed so hard, it made Harper and me laugh too.

Harper thought he resembled me, and he did. Similar skin

color and hair, but he had her smile. Her sweetness and curiosity.

"Papà, this is Harper. My love. The mother of my child." I pulled her close to me and kissed her head, the frigid air swirling around us. "And this is our son, Aiden Vittorio." I smiled and wiped away a tear. If only he were here. If only he were still alive.

"Papà." Aiden frowned, and I stilled.

I turned to Harper, sadness replaced by astonishment. "Did he—"

She grinned and covered her mouth. She nodded. "I think so."

"Did you just say my name?" I nuzzled Aiden with my nose. "Did you?" I grinned and tossed him into the air, loving the sound of his squeal.

"Papà!" Aiden said again when I caught him. "Papà. Papà." He kept repeating it, and it sounded like popcorn popping.

My chest was bursting with pride, and my cheeks ached from my smile. "*Ti amo, angelo mio.*"

When Aiden started getting restless, Harper offered to walk around with him. I was grateful for the moment alone with my thoughts and with my dad.

I waited until she was out of earshot then said, "I'm going to ask her to marry me." I dug in my pocket for the ring and pulled it out to show him. "I wish you could meet her. I wish you could meet both of them." I swallowed. "I miss you so much. I was so lost without you, until I met her."

I laughed, remembering my introduction to Harper. It seemed like an eternity had passed and no time at all. "You'd like her. She keeps me in line. Keeps me grounded."

The wind whipped through the cemetery, and I pulled my jacket closer and shoved my hands into my pockets. The hairs on the back of my neck stood on end, and I closed my eyes, leaning into the sensation. I didn't know if my dad was watching, but I wanted to believe he was. I wanted to believe he was here.

"You're always with me." I placed my hand over my heart and the tattoo on my chest. "I carry your lessons and your love with me through life. And I will pass them on to my son." I kissed my fingers and pressed them to the top of the headstone. "I love you."

Aiden's laughter rang out through the air, and I smiled. For the first time since my dad's accident, I felt happy. Weightless. The grief would always be there, but it wasn't as crushing.

When we returned to Mamma's, I went to put Aiden down for a nap. I sat in the chair for a long time, just holding him and soaking in his baby smell. I wouldn't trade this for anything in the world. Who would've guessed I'd love being a dad?

When I returned downstairs, Harper was in the kitchen with Val, learning how to cook from my *nonna*. I leaned against the doorframe and watched them work side by side, speaking in Italian, flour dusting their skin.

Over the past year, Val and Harper had become good friends. They'd bonded over their love of good food and wine. As well as their mutual dislike of Giada, though she was no longer an issue. Thanks to my influence and Val's ingenuity, Giada had landed herself a spot on the Italian version of *The Bachelorette*. She relinquished all photos and signed an agreement not to speak to the tabloids about our relationship. She was too busy looking for her Prince Charming anyway. I shook my head. Whoever the unsuspecting fool was, I felt bad for him. Though, if he was willing to go on reality TV…

Harper glanced up at me and smiled. Her hair was in a bun on top of her head, wispy tendrils framing her face. Her cheeks were pink from the warmth of the kitchen, her lips kissable.

"I guess you were wrong," she said.

"Was I?" I arched an eyebrow. "About what?"

"Your *nonna's* teaching me how to make her secret *pasticcio* recipe, even though we're not married." She used the back of her arm to brush some hair away from her face.

Nonna lifted a finger. *"Non ancora."*

Not yet.

"*Nonna*!" I glared at her.

"Cosa? Il tempo passa e io invecchio."

Harper laughed, and I shook my head. My *nonna* was right; she wasn't getting any younger. Neither was I.

"*Uccellina*," I said. "My *nonna* makes a good point."

She laughed, clearly not realizing what was about to happen. I'd had the ring for months, and I'd been waiting for the right moment. Doc had given me his blessing. Surrounded by my family, I couldn't imagine anything better.

I stepped closer, rounding the island to stand next to Harper. I took her hand in mine, not caring if I got messy. That was part of the fun.

"Life with you has certainly been an adventure." I chuckled and took a deep breath. "And I can't wait to spend the rest of it together." I knelt before her and opened the box with the ring. "Marry me, Harper."

She glanced around the room then back at me. Everyone was watching—Val, *Nonna*, Mamma. But I only had eyes for Harper.

She cleared her throat, mirth dancing in her eyes. "Are you *asking* me?"

I rolled my eyes but smiled all the same. The only place Harper liked giving up control was in the bedroom. "Harper Allen, *ti prego,* will you marry me?" I batted my eyes, though this was no joking matter.

"Since you asked so nicely." I could tell she was doing her best not to laugh. "*Sì*." Oh, she was going to pay for this later. "Of course I'll marry you, Enzo."

I slid the ring onto her finger, the two diamonds sparkling in the light. A salt and pepper pear was set next to an Old Mine cut diamond. Dark contrasting with light. Shadow and sparkle. Just like us. One of a kind. Just like my *uccellina*.

Harper tugged on my hand, and I stood, smiling as everyone offered their congratulations.

She cupped my cheeks and pulled my mouth to hers. "*Ti amo*, tardigrade."

I laughed, not even bothering to protest her nickname. "*Ti amo, uccellina*." I kissed her back, putting my whole heart into it. She was my life. My world. And soon, she'd be my wife.

CHAPTER TWENTY-EIGHT

Harper

"I can't believe you're leaving LA for good!" Juliana said.

"Me either." I laughed. We'd returned from Italy and were spending a few days in LA before officially moving to the Alondra Valley. "But I'm excited. Even if I will miss you guys."

I glanced over to the couch where Harrison and Preston were making silly faces for Aiden, along with Alexis's daughters, Sophia and Blair. Hunter and Enzo stood nearby, watching. Enzo was always watching—a protective and proud father.

I was going to miss my girlfriends. Los Angeles had been my home for the past twenty years, and my friends—Juliana, Alexis, and Lauren—were more like sisters. But I had to do what was best for Aiden, and that wasn't LA.

Juliana sighed, wrapping her arm around me. "I know you need to do this, but I'm going to miss you so much."

"I'll miss you too." I bit my lip, fighting back tears. I knew they'd all come for the wedding, but that was still six months from now. It seemed like a long time away.

"This is going to be a good thing," Alexis said, joining us

with a bottle of prosecco and two glasses. Lauren followed behind with two more glasses.

Just as Alexis was about to pop the cork, I said, "I don't know. This feels too bittersweet to be a celebration."

"Harper," Juliana said. "Do you remember the night I was moving out of my old house—the one I'd shared with Ryan?"

My lips automatically curved into a smile at the memory, and I nodded. The four of us had sat on the back patio for hours, drinking and talking. At the time, I'd wanted to be a mom so badly, I ached. For many years, it had seemed like a dream that would never be realized. A dream that I'd sacrificed to travel the world and have my career. And now, the opposite seemed true.

"That was definitely a bittersweet moment," Juliana said. "But you know what? We still drank prosecco and ate charcuterie and talked and laughed."

That felt like so long ago. Juliana had sold her house and was moving in with Harrison. As much as she loved him, the move was tinged with sadness. She was saying goodbye to her past and moving on with her future. Just as I was now closing this door on an amazing chapter in my life.

"You have always been there for me," Juliana said, a tear winding its way down her cheek before she quickly wiped it away. "And I will *always* be there for you. No matter whether you live in Fall River or Timbuktu."

"Me too," said Lauren. And Alexis echoed her sentiment.

I sniffed and glanced to the ceiling. "Hey! I'm really trying not to cry here."

Alexis opened the bottle and poured us each a glass. We lifted our glasses into the air, and Juliana said, "To friendship."

"To friendship," we all repeated. And then I swallowed down the sparkling beverage.

I stared into my glass, the bubbles so happy and light. I

tried to hold it together. "I'm going to miss you guys so much."

"It's not forever," Juliana said with a smile that I was sure she meant to be reassuring. "It's just for now."

I rolled my eyes and groaned. "Is that another one of your Zen guru's sayings?" I teased, using the nickname she'd given Harrison when they'd first started dating.

"You know..." She scrunched up her nose. "I think it might be. Or maybe Deepak Chopra. Or did I hear that on Marie Forleo's podcast?"

The four of us laughed, but then the mood turned more somber. Juliana was right—this wasn't forever, but it was the beginning of something new and different. As much as we all wanted to say that our friendship wouldn't change, I knew it wouldn't be the same. But I had faith that it would continue to evolve and grow as it had always done.

"It's the big day," Juliana said, fluffing out the bottom of my gown.

The lace gown was strapless and fitted to my body before flaring out around my legs. The intricate pattern had been woven just for me, and I'd never felt more beautiful. My hair was down in long, loose waves that hung past my shoulders, and a simple veil completed the look.

"Are you ready?" Lauren asked, while the makeup artist touched up my lipstick.

I laughed. "Ready for what? Enzo and I already have a house, a life, a kid, together."

"True, but it's your wedding day. This is a big deal!" Alexis said.

Six months had passed in the blink of an eye. I'd seen my friends more than I'd dared hope for. And Aiden was now walking and talking up a storm.

"Mama!" Aiden called out for me on the monitor. "Mama!"

I smiled and headed toward his room, Juliana on my heels. "Let me get you a robe or something to protect your dress."

"It'll be fine," I said, opening the door to Aiden's room. Alexis, Juliana, Lauren, and I had taken over the house, along with my mom, Jo, and Mackenzie. The guys were getting ready in the barn we'd just finished converting into a space for events. And the tasting room would be ready to open to the public in a few weeks.

Enzo might have retired, but he was still active in the sport through his foundation. And now he had the winery to run. I'd continued to take freelance photography assignments, and I loved the freedom and flexibility.

"This place looks great," Alexis said, joining us.

I smiled. "Thanks."

She'd only seen pictures of the property but had yet to visit. Alexis had connected us with a local agent—Vanessa Nguyen—to help us secure the winery and house. Lauren had visited a few times to help with the interior design, and I loved seeing her touches throughout the space. She'd done a great job of making it feel both beautiful and livable.

"Aiden." I smiled, opening the door to his room. Apart from the amazing darkroom that Enzo had surprised me with, Aiden's room was my favorite place in the house.

Aiden smiled and squealed as I picked him up from the crib. He was getting so big. Sometimes it was easy to forget he'd been born five weeks early and spent so much time in the NICU. He was healthy and well and such a happy little boy. A chubby one, too.

"Oh, it looks great in here," Lauren said, admiring all the details. The built-in bookshelves with all the children's books I'd collected during my travels. Even without reading my note inside, I could remember where I'd purchased each and every one. And I was so happy they finally had a home.

Sunlight filtered through the window, rows of grapes glistening in the sun. It would be vintage soon, and then the grapes would be harvested and the wine made. Enzo was excited about it, and I was glad he had something to occupy him during retirement.

"It looks great, thanks to you." I grinned, elbowing Lauren.

Aiden reached out for Lauren and said, "Lor-lor," his name for her. She smiled and took him in her arms, talking to him as she bounced him up and down. I smiled at them and then joined Juliana where she stood next to the crib, her hand lingering on the edge.

"Having second thoughts about children?" I asked, though I was pretty sure I already knew the answer.

"No." She smiled wistfully. "I was actually admiring the artwork."

I glanced up at the wall where the batiks Enzo and I had painted hung on either side of Aiden's crib. I smiled. "Enzo and I painted those in Bali."

"They're beautiful."

I nodded. "They are."

I couldn't believe that was two years ago—almost to the day. So much had changed since then. We'd had a baby. He'd retired. We'd moved to the Alondra Valley and bought a winery. And now we were getting married.

As always, it was out of order. But as Enzo liked to remind me, there was no "right order." There was only what was right for us. And this town, this new adventure, were definitely right for us. I could feel it deep in my gut, and I could envision many happy memories here.

There was a knock at the door, and Landon said, "Almost showtime."

"Awesome. Thanks," Juliana said.

Juliana had helped plan our wedding, but Landon was executing the vision so that she could enjoy the event with us.

"Should I tell Doc we're ready for him?" Landon asked.

I nodded. "I'm ready."

I gave Aiden a kiss, and Lauren carried him out with Alexis. Juliana remained behind with me while we waited for my dad. I assumed he'd gotten caught up in some conversation, and the idea made me laugh.

"You look absolutely stunning," Juliana said, handing me my bouquet. It was a mix of sunflowers and wild flowers that had come from a local farm and bed-and-breakfast, Alpaca Acres.

I glanced at my reflection and smoothed my hand down my stomach. The stones on my engagement ring caught the light, and I smiled. Enzo had picked the ring because he said it reminded him of us, but I often caught myself thinking of the day we met. The design was dark and light, a study in contrasts. Just like he'd been a man of hard lines and shadows, standing in the sunshine.

I liked to tease him that it looked like the colors of a soccer ball. But I loved that he'd selected something so unique, so me. It was one of a kind, just like our relationship.

"Thank you for making this day special," I said to Juliana. "I'm so glad you're here with me."

"I wouldn't be anywhere else." She gave me a watery smile then pulled me into a hug. "You're my best friend, Harper. And I'm so, *so* happy for you."

"Jules," I chided, pulling away and swiping beneath my eye to catch my tears. "You promised not to make me cry."

She laughed and dabbed at her cheeks with a tissue. "I know. I know. I'm sorry. I just— Gah! I can't think of anyone more deserving of happiness."

"Now you know how I felt when you married Harrison." I smiled, and so did she.

Sometimes it was mind-blowing to think of how far we'd all come. The past few years had seen so many changes for all of us. Alexis had remarried and had Blair, with a third baby on the way. Lauren and Hunter had a fur baby they adored and a second house in Paris. Juliana had found a second chance at love with Harrison, and she doted on her bonus daughter, Olivia. And I had fallen in love with Enzo and given birth to Aiden. And through it all, our friendship had been the one constant.

"Harrison and I finally found a vacation home," Juliana said.

"That's great. Did you decide on Vail or Big Sky?"

She looked as if she might burst from excitement. "Neither. We bought one here—in the Alondra Valley."

"What?" I jerked my head back. "Seriously?"

"Yep. We're thinking of spending the summer and Christmas here. And when we're not using the house, we'll rent it out."

"Oh, that's the best news!" I gave her arm a squeeze. I was so happy that she loved my hometown as much as I did. And that we'd get to see each other more often now that Enzo and I had left LA permanently.

There was a knock at the door, and Dad cleared his throat. "You ready?"

Juliana gave me a hug. "I'll see you out there." Then she said to Dad, "She's all yours, Doc."

He smiled. "Not for much longer." He stepped into the room and kissed my cheek. "Oh, Harper. You look beautiful."

"Thanks, Dad. You look rather handsome yourself."

"This old thing." He brushed his knuckles against his lapels, but I could tell he was proud of his new suit. Enzo had insisted on buying it for him as a gift. They'd become close, especially since the move, and I loved that my dad treated Enzo like another son.

I laughed and looped my arm through Dad's. "Let's do this."

"Yes, let's. Otherwise, I fear your groom is going to break down the door and toss you over his shoulder."

It wouldn't be the first time.

I laughed to myself as Dad led me outside, where everyone was waiting. Our gardens were lush and blooming thanks to Mom's landscaping expertise. Two rows of chairs lined the aisle, and they were filled with friends and family. Enzo's mamma, his *nonna*, Val. A number of his teammates from throughout his career. Friends and family from my past and present—everyone was there to celebrate us.

Enzo stood at the front beneath a pergola draped in flowering vines. The music shifted, and everyone turned to face me, but I only had eyes for my groom. I saw him before he saw me, and I felt the same way I had the first time I'd laid eyes on him in the market in Bali.

He was devastatingly handsome in his gray suit and white button-down shirt. His olive skin glistened in the sun, his smile bright as he focused on Aiden. His dark brown hair was tousled as always, and just like that first time—like every time—something about him made it difficult to look away.

He lifted his head, and I knew the moment he saw me because his mouth formed the sexiest "o." And then he scanned me from head to toe, his gaze a smolder. Everyone else ceased to exist. It was just the two of us, and my skin heated from his intensity.

He placed a hand over his heart and mouthed, *"Mio dio."*

"Mama!" Aiden cheered, and everyone laughed, even me. Enzo and I smiled at our son as I took my place at the altar, whispering, *"Ti amo,"* before he did the same.

We recited our vows—a mix of Italian and English. Traditional and modern. The ceremony was something uniquely our own, just like our love story.

And then the officiant pronounced us husband and wife. Enzo took me in his arms, claiming me with a kiss that set my skin ablaze with desire. Everyone clapped, and I couldn't wait for our wedding night. We'd both been so busy lately with the move and the wedding and raising a toddler, that I was craving some alone time with my husband.

"I have a surprise for you," he said a while later, kissing my temple as the photographer took our photo.

"I think you've given me enough surprises for one lifetime," I teased.

"I don't think I could ever give you enough."

"Well, don't leave me in suspense." I wrapped my arms around his neck, and he smiled down at me.

"My beautiful bride. My wife. My life…"

"Yes, husband." I smiled, loving the sound of the word "wife" on his lips and "husband" on mine.

He kissed me. "We're going on a honeymoon."

"We are?" I grinned, but then my face fell. "What about Aiden?" I'd rarely been away from him.

"Your parents agreed to watch him."

"For how long?"

"Just a few days."

I narrowed my eyes at him. "How many is a few?"

"Sette." He coughed into his hand.

"Seven?" I stared at him. "That's not a few. That's a *week*."

"Yes, but just imagine how much *yoga* we'll get to do," he said with a wink.

"Mm." I sighed dreamily. "I'm imagining how much sleep we'll get to have."

He chuckled, sliding his hand down to cup my ass. "That too. We can do anything you want."

"You still haven't told me where we're going."

"*La luna.*"

"You're taking me to the moon?" I joked. "Well, that *is* exotic."

Enzo said nothing more and gathered Aiden in his arms, throwing him in the air before holding him close again. Aiden giggled and laughed, his little cheeks puffing out even more. I loved watching the two of them together.

"What's that smile for?" Enzo asked, holding Aiden to his chest.

I shook my head. "I like watching you with him."

"Do you have a thing for dads?" he teased, reminding me of our conversation where I'd accused him of having a thing for pregnant women.

"No. I have a thing for you. You and only you."

"I have a *thing* for you too." He waggled his eyebrows, and I elbowed him.

"That was bad, Enzo."

"What?" He lifted a shoulder. "I'm a dad. I made a dad joke."

I laughed. "Um, no. *That* was not a dad joke."

He leaned in, his lips hovering beside my ear. "*Sei la donna più bella che abbia mai visto. Non vedo l'ora di toglierti quel vestito.*"

Enzo's words rang in my ear. *You're the most beautiful woman I've ever seen, but I can't wait to get you out of that dress.* I couldn't wait either.

We joined our friends and family for an Italian feast that

was to die for. But it was the sense of belonging, that meant more to me than anything. That was why we'd moved here after all. To be closer to family. To build a community. To spend time together.

"Dance with me," Enzo said, holding out his hand for me.

I smiled and slid my hand in his, allowing him to lead me to the dance floor. A slow, sensual song was playing, a breeze wafting through the vineyards along with the Italian lyrics.

Juliana and Harrison swayed on the dance floor, their cheeks pressed together. Lauren and Hunter danced and laughed with Aiden. And Preston twirled Sophia, while Alexis watched on with a smile, Blair sleeping in her arms.

"Are you happy, *uccellina*?" he asked, holding me close.

"Very." I leaned back to peer up at him. "Are you?"

He nodded, his expression solemn. "Apart from Aiden's birth, today was the most important day of my life."

"What about the Leatherbacks championship?" I asked, knowing how thrilled he'd been about the win. Not to mention another Ballon d'Or. I was still in awe of all his accomplishments, and yet he was proudest of us—his family.

He shook his head. "I would trade all my awards and all the highlights of my career for you and Aiden. The two of you are irreplaceable." He tilted his forehead to mine. "*Ti amo.*"

I smiled as he kissed me and said, "*Ti amo.*"

As I peered out over the vineyard, surveying the land we'd purchased and the life we'd made, I realized I had everything I'd ever wanted and more. Friendship. Love. Family. Home.

There'd always be a part of me that craved adventure and travel, but I was no longer using it as an excuse to run from my feelings or myself. Aiden had taught me the power of unconditional love. And Enzo… Well, through his love, Enzo had taught me how to love myself.

That night, after everyone had left and we'd put Aiden to bed, we made love as husband and wife. And as I lay in his arms afterward, sated and happy, the soundtrack of my childhood and Enzo's heartbeat lulled me to sleep. I was home.

CHAPTER TWENTY-NINE

Harper

We rushed across the sand, hands linked. With Enzo's longer strides, it felt as if he were dragging me along, trying to hurry me up. I laughed into the night air, my hair whipping across my cheeks as the moon bathed the sand in pale light.

The short walk to the staircase on the cliff felt more like miles, the stolen glances and whispered words not nearly enough to satisfy my craving for him. I fumbled to remove my shoes as we rushed down the hall toward our bedroom. Enzo was behind me, his hands on my hips, his lips at my ear. If we didn't get inside, if he didn't get inside *me* soon, I was going to explode.

As soon as the door was closed, he backed me against it. I unbuttoned his shirt, eager to see his inked skin and chiseled muscles again. Eager to have nothing between us. I pushed the material aside, fanning my hands over his warm, smooth skin.

His eyes were dark, and I shivered from that look, from the promise in his gaze. A breeze blew through the open curtain. My nipples hardened and not from the sudden shift in temperature. As if sensing that, his eyes darted there, and he removed my dress with a flick of his fingers. One strap, then the other, and it pooled on the floor at my feet. He growled with satisfaction as he appraised me.

"*Quanto sei bella.*"

I smiled at his words, knowing he'd tell me I was beautiful regardless of whether I was dressed in a designer gown or nothing at all. But I wanted to see more of his breathtaking body too, explore it.

He trailed a finger over my shoulders, across my collarbone, down my sternum, leaving a trail of fire in its wake. I giggled, trying to shield myself as he moved along my panty line, the sensitive skin incredibly ticklish. The corner of his mouth tipped into a grin, and he traced the line again.

"Enzo." I laughed, trying to cover myself. "You're torturing me."

"This?" He arched an eyebrow, looking devilishly handsome as he dipped his finger lower. "This is nothing."

He knelt before me, and my hand automatically went to his head. My wedding ring sparkled from between his curls, and I held my other hand to my mouth, tears forming at the corners of my eyes. Was I dreaming? Because it certainly felt like it. I had a man who loved me—a man who was so incredibly sexy and caring. And we had a beautiful son together. It was everything I'd ever wanted.

"Those are happy tears, right?" he asked when he met my gaze.

"Yes." I swiped them away. "Yes, Enzo."

He slanted his mouth over mine, and the world settled back into place. Nothing had ever felt more right.

"Need to be inside you," he rasped, my breasts brushing against him as he cupped me over my panties. They were wet, and I was aching for more.

"Yes. Please." I fumbled with his belt, unbuckling it before pushing his pants aside. I needed him. "Now."

He pushed my underwear aside, rubbing his head against my slick heat. He made a few passes, and when I didn't think I could take it anymore, he pushed inside me, filling me, stretching me wide.

"Yes." I dug my heels into his back, adjusting to the sensation, the connection. I gasped when he applied his thumb to my clit and started circling. "I mean, holy shit."

He covered my mouth with his, swallowing my moans as he supported himself on the bed. We were wild and savage and needy and panting. Between his corded, tattooed forearms and the dark look in his eyes, I was done for. And when he whispered words of love and devotion in Italian, I detonated.

He leaned forward and picked me up, carrying me over to the outdoor lounge chair. All the while, he was still inside me —throbbing, pulsing, his body providing delicious friction for my clit. And then he started pounding into me once more, his muscles tense, jaw taut.

"*Ti amo,*" he grunted and slapped my butt, setting me off. "*Ti amo.*"

I cupped his cheek, scarcely able to speak as pleasure overwhelmed me. "*Ti amo.*"

He rested his forehead to mine, our eyes locked as I unraveled. And then he was coming, pumping fast and furious as he exploded inside me. Our bodies as connected as two people could be, our voices crying out to the universe.

He held me to him, his lips on my neck. His breath warm on my skin. "*Grazie.*"

I smiled. "*Grazie.*"

We sat there a moment, the cool breeze wafting over us, though it did nothing to cool my passion for this man. I didn't think anything would.

I sighed. "I can't believe we've already been here three days."

"I know." My muscles were loose, my smile lazy as the moon shined down on us.

"Thank you for this. I should've known when you said *la luna* that you meant Mizuki House." I grinned.

I'd wanted to revisit Mizuki House, and our honeymoon was the perfect occasion to do so. Maybe one day we'd bring Aiden back with us, or our friends. But for now, I was happy it was just the two of us.

He smoothed his hand up and down my back before grabbing my ass. "I promised you the moon, and I deliver."

"That you do." I kissed the tip of his chin, and he smiled, pulling me closer.

"Harper," he said in such a serious tone that it gave me pause.

"Lorenzo."

He swatted my butt. "You know better than to call me that."

"Mm." I wriggled against him, the ocean crashing from across the pool and the yard beyond. "What are you going to do about it?"

"Whatever I want." He cupped the back of my neck and pulled my face down to his in a movement that was somehow both rough and gentle. He always knew just what I needed, but part of that was because I told him what I wanted. "You're mine now." The words were spoken with a dark promise that made my toes curl.

"I always was."

I no longer felt the need to run, unless it was into Enzo's arms. And as we sealed the vow in the place where it had all begun, it felt as if the universe was smiling upon us.

"Wherever you go," he said, then kissed me, "I will follow you."

"Is that a threat?" I teased.

"No, *uccellina*." His expression was solemn. "It's a promise."

LOVE NOTES

Need the English version? Keep reading. ;)

Uccellina cara

Auguri per un buon San Valentino, mio amore.
Sono sicuro che Aiden si divertirà con i tuoi
genitori permettendomi di averti tutta per me,
perché in questo periodo, mi sei mancata.

Quando sono andato in pensione, la mia paura
era di avere troppo tempo libero. Fin troppo
tempo. Invece no. Come noi sappiamo non tutte le
ciambelle hanno un buco!

Riflettendo sulla mia vita, giocare per il Milan
FC sembra quasi facile ora. Tra il trasloco,
l'apertura della cantina, la fondazione Success

through Soccer, Aiden e te, sono sempre impegnato. Non cambierei una virgola.

Amo la vita che abbiamo creato insieme. Amo il nostro angelo, Aiden e amo te. Mi hai fatto capire che nella vita c'è più del calcio. Sei il mio cuore, la mia vita, e in pochi mesi... mia moglie.

Non vedo l'ora di sposarti. Non ho bisogno di un anello per dirmi ciò che so già: sono tuo, solo tuo. Sempre e per sempre.

Tutto il mio amore
Enzo

For those of us who aren't fluent in Italian like Harper and Enzo, here's the love letter translated into English.

Dear little bird,

Happy Valentine's Day, my love. I'm sure Aiden is going to love spending the day with your parents, and I'm going to love having you all to myself for a change.

I've missed you lately.

When I retired from professional soccer, I thought I'd have so much time. Too much time. At least, that was my fear.

What a joke! Though, as we both know, not all donuts have a hole.*

Looking back on my life, playing for Milan FC almost seems easy now. Between the move, getting the winery ready to open, my Success through Soccer foundation, Aiden, and you, I'm always busy.

And I wouldn't have it any other way.

I love the life we've created together. I love our angel, Aiden. And I love you because you helped me see that there's more to life than soccer. You are my love, my life, and in a few months…my wife.

I cannot wait to marry you. Though, I do not need a ring to tell me what we already know —I am yours. Only yours, always and forever.

All my love,
Enzo

* *Non tutte le ciambelle hanno un buco* is an Italian saying that roughly translates to "Not all donuts have a hole." It means that things don't always turn out as planned.

Acknowledgements

Whew. Harper and Enzo. They took me on quite the journey.

This story was definitely a labor of love, and I couldn't have done it without the support of so many wonderful people.

If you read the note at the beginning, you'll know that I struggled with this story for personal reasons. But that's a big reason why I write—to explore people's emotions, even my own. It can be painful at times but also cathartic. Therapeutic.

Once I finally stopped fighting it and surrendered, this book was so much fun to write.

My daughter was actually a driving force behind this book. She was always asking me what was going on with Harper and Enzo, and I think she could tell how passionate and excited I was about their story. She got the very, very tame version, of course. ;)

But the fact that she kept asking, kept caring, meant so much to me. As did my nana's support. She passed away while I was writing this book, but I can still hear her voice in my head during her weekly calls when she'd ask me "Are you still writing?"

Finishing Harper and Enzo's story, and the Love in LA Series along with it, has been bittersweet. This series has been such a blessing to me, helping me through a global pandemic. My own health issues. It has brought me so much joy and enabled me to connect with so many wonderful people. People like you.

Thank you for reading *Irreplaceable.* I love writing for the pleasure of it, but seeing reader's reactions is definitely a highlight. To all the bloggers, bookstagrammers, booktokers, and readers who get excited, who post about my books, and who have shown me a sense of genuine community and support—thank you!

To all the authors who have been so kind and generous. Who have welcomed me into this community and been so supportive. Not to mention all the authors who have joined me for Writer Wednesdays. Talking to each and every one of you has been both fun and inspiring!

A big thank you to the Hartley's Hustlers and my Girl Gang (not just for girls!). You rock! I cannot possibly tell you how much your support means to me! I appreciate everything you do to promote my books and to encourage me throughout my writing journey.

Special thank you to Korey for coming up with the name for the LA soccer team Enzo transfers to. I loved how unique the Leatherbacks was and appreciate the opportunity (even small) to bring awareness to such a precious and endangered species—the pacific leatherback sea turtle.

Thank you to Jos for reading this book with an eye for the soccer details. I researched a ton in preparation for this book and wanted to make it as accurate as possible. Thank you for offering your invaluable insight and passion for sports.

Thank you JudyAnnLovesBooks for helping with the Italian translations as well as providing an understanding of Italian culture. It was fascinating and so helpful. I cannot tell you how much I appreciate your assistance not only with that aspect but also several other details. You really helped bring the final piece of the puzzle together, and I'm so grateful for your insight. And for suggesting the Italian songs for the playlist!

To Angela. Sometimes it's like you're in my brain. I appreciate your attention to detail. Your encouragement and support. And your willingness to dive in on this adventure with me. Thank you.

To my editor, Lisa with Silently Correcting Your Grammar. I so appreciate your attention to detail, and your patience with my questions. You always go above and beyond and this time was no exception. I value your insight and your friendship.

And with this book more than any other, I appreciate your honesty. Thank you for helping me make it a stronger story.

Thank you Kirsten Kiki for being honest about, well, everything. You have helped me so much, and I'm so grateful for your advice and friendship.

Thank you to Ellen, as always. Thank you for being so supportive and positive, for being a friend. And thank you for sharing your incredible eye for detail. Your comments are always priceless, and this book was no exception! I couldn't do it without you.

A huge thank you to Kristen for being such an amazing friend. I value your judgment and honesty, and I so appreciate your support. We've been through so much together, and I treasure your friendship and advice. Seriously, I cannot thank you enough for all that you do. You're always willing to read "just one more time," and I so appreciate it.

Thank you for reading this story over and over and *over* again countless times until it finally felt right. I wanted to do Harper and Enzo's story justice, and I couldn't have done it without you.

Thank you, Jade. You make me a stronger writer, and you challenge me on pacing. You are so clever and always provide great insight. I'm so grateful for your friendship, and our long chats!

Thank you to Brit! I love writing strong, badass female

main characters, and you help ensure that they live up to their potential. And that the men who dare to love them do too.

A huge thank you to all my beta readers. Thank you for making me a stronger writer, for offering your unique insight and advice. You each bring something different to the table, and I'm always amazed and impressed by your suggestions. I'm so incredibly honored to have you on my team!

Thank you to my husband for always encouraging me. For always supporting my dreams. You are better than any book boyfriend I could ever imagine. You constantly build me up, and I couldn't ask for a better partner.

Sometimes I can see the solution but not how to get there. Thank you for your insight and your encouragement. For always believing in me.

And to my daughter, for always putting a smile on my face. You are spirited and independent, and I wouldn't have it any other way. Dream big, my darling.

Thank you to my parents for always being so encouraging. For reading my books. For being my biggest fans!

Dear reader, if this list of people shows you anything, it's that dreams are often the effort of many. I'm grateful to have such an awesome team. And I'm honored that you've taken the time to read my words.

About the Author

Jenna Hartley is USA Today bestselling author who writes feel-good forbidden romance, much like her own real-life love story. She's known for writing strong women and swoon-worthy men, as well as blending panty-melting and heart-warming moments.

When she's not reading or writing romance, Jenna can be found tending to her growing indoor plant collection (pun intended), organizing, and hiking. She lives in Texas with her family and loves nothing more than a good book and good chocolate, except a dance party with her daughter.

www.authorjennahartley.com

Also by Jenna Hartley

<u>Love in LA Series</u>
Inevitable
Unexpected
Irresistible
Undeniable
Unpredictable
Irreplaceable

<u>Alondra Valley Series</u>
Feels Like Love
Love Like No Other
A Love Like That

<u>Tempt Series</u>
Temptation
Reputation

For the most current list of Jenna's titles, please visit her website www.authorjennahartley.com.

Or scan the QR code on the following page to be taken to her author page on Amazon.com

SCAN ME

9 7 9 8 9 8 8 2 7 2 2 8 1